10677426

IDEA

FACTORY

Michael Ikevos

Copyright © 2014 by Michael Ikevos

All rights reserved.

It is illegal to reproduce any portion of this material except by special arrangement by the publisher (or author). Reproduction of this material without authorization, by any duplication process whatsoever, is a violation of copyright.

ISBN 978-0-9936182-2-2

Published by Mihail Kosev

Contact info: michaelikevos@gmail.com

First edition

Table of Contents

"No problem can be solved from the same level of consciousness that created it?"

Albert Einstein

Rebecca

The cold never stopped them. They would come at dawn and stay last, until the icy sunset settled in. The next day – it was all over again. Shivering, wrapped up in their warmest clothes and fitted with their best boots, they could not wait for their turn to come. Deceivingly, it never seemed they had to wait that long. The distance to the gate appeared to get shorter very quickly, although in effect, this was merely an illusion. People were staring at the main gate of the Idea Factory and this created a false impression of increasing proximity and thus, adeptly tricking one's normal perceptions. Folks were standing and waiting.

The staff at the Idea Factory was working at their full capacity and spared no effort. They simply met each of the diverse visitors one after another, without complaining, showing no preference or dislike towards any of them. They were impartial and displayed no emotions on the surface. The most important of all was that the person, who had entered the warm interrogation room, left content and happy with the idea, which they had just paid for. It was irrelevant, whether the customer was crazy or mentally ill, nor did it matter if their general view of the world was fundamentally messed up and wrong. No. None of this made any difference. Luckily for the idea-consultants, most of the clients were sane. They simply had different problems in their lives, to which they could not figure out a solution without help, so they came along and queued. The Factory offered an answer to any dilemma.

In the first few minutes of arriving, the visitors studied their surroundings. In fact, this process did not last that long because there was nothing to attract their attention. The tall pine trees stood on both sides of the straight-line path and behind them, there was nothing but more pine trees. The icy branches, covered in millions of needles, blocked the view above, due to the tons of wet snow on them. Hence, one quickly moved their eyes away straight towards the Factory, or where they were supposed to look.

A lot of the potential clients, who were a little nervous, and they looked as if they were getting "cold feet", wished to establish close contact with their fellows in waiting, hoping that this would dull the feeling of loneliness, exacerbated by the negative temperatures. Those, less shy, talked, seeking in most cases simply the act of conversation, rather than its meaning. They explained why they were waiting at the foot of the snow-white hill. Some of them had rehearsed those words repeatedly in front of the mirror at home, just so they presented themselves at their best. They feared that if they did not express fully and clearly the problem that had made them walk all the way up here, then their expensive purchase of idea might prove to be not worth a penny. The curmudgeons, who had vowed to never say a word, were very few. The listeners listened and nodded affirmatively. They tried to be polite and did not want to interrupt and be rude to people, who might happen to be waiting all day, just an inch behind or in front of them. Then, their turn to speak would come, though, sometimes, they did not take this opportunity. Anyhow, it was not important what one would say outside there, but what one would hear when inside. At some point, people would get fed up spending several hours listening to others and there would be a moment, when they just stood around bored, waiting. How long this would take was relative to say. "Will I be lucky to get in today?" was a question that bothered everyone's chilled brain, hidden under the thick hat. Bodies shivered uncontrollably, but felt warmer with every inch, with every step, made forward in the right direction. The thickened blood thinned out, resuming its normal liquid form. Folks also magically regained sensation in their numb extremities. The time had come. It was your turn at last.

The interrogation room welcomed warmly the frozen visitor. They described the room in this typically police term for some obvious, but at the same time, totally obscure reasons. The large one-way mirror, behind, which were, seated several detectives, while their colleague conducted the interrogation on the other side, was an image that anyone, who had seen at least one detective movie in their lives, had in mind. The "voyeurs" carefully observed the behavior of the person and the way they answered the questions. The good and the bad cop often swapped, thus offering a way out of the situation, entirely to the benefit of the arrested person, or they accused him/her directly in being the perpetrator. This would inevitably amplify the panic effect, leading often to self-confession.

The premises, where the idea-consultants worked, were the same size as the rooms in Police stations. There were the same identical one-way mirror screens, too. The only difference was that there was no one on the other side of the glass window. Absolutely no one! The conversations with the client were never watched or tapped. There were two metal chairs and a table in the center of the room, which were permanently fixed to the concrete floor. The light bulb, hanging from the ceiling on a piece of thin cable, was the final detail that no respectable interrogation room could go without. The main thing that made the way these rooms were called questionable, was the nature of what was taking place in there. Everyone came voluntarily and paid to get in. There was not a hint of pressure, applied towards the client. Andir did not bother too much thinking about this, but was preparing to meet his first visitor for the day and hopefully, offer the best possible idea. The problem had to be solved. Unfortunately, it was not always that easy.

"Welcome, take a seat, please! My name is Andir, idea-consultant, Second rank." said politely the host, sitting straight on his anchored chair. He had no intention of standing up to meet his client, because it was not part of the internal regulations guide. Standing up and shaking hands was, of course, an internationally recognized etiquette, but not here, not in the Idea Factory.

"I am Rebecca." anxiously introduced herself the unusually tall young woman, who had just entered the room. She carefully closed the door, as if there was an imminent danger of damaging it in some way. She hesitantly glanced at the empty chair.

"Rebecca. Pretty name! Right, then, Rebecca, please, take a seat, opposite me. I'd like you to relax and not to worry about anything. Feel free to take off your jacket. It is quite warm in here."

"OK." she replied and removed her warm ski jacket with a kind of learned movement, then slowly hanged it over the back of the chair. A pink polo-neck top was revealed, which suited her very much, as if it was made and fitted especially for her and no other woman would look so effortlessly perfect in it. She took off her hat, displaying the full volume of her curly blond hair. Her long thighs were very long indeed. Her white gloves matched her winter jacket and when she took them off, she exposed her fingers – each of them finishing with a differently colored nail. Andir had not had such an amazingly stunning woman as a client for a very long time, if ever. 'Beautiful' would have been an understatement, in terms of the way this woman looked. And what was she doing here?

"Are you ready to begin?" Andir asked, staring at her voluptuous forms for longer than he should, and imagining how any suckling infant would happily appreciate them.

"I'm… ready." hesitantly replied the client.

"Rebecca, our conversation will go through three stages. Each one of them will start and finish, when I think it's appropriate. At the end of the third stage, I shall deliver to you the idea that I consider it is most suitable in your case. You may not believe so, however, it will be final. Do you understand?"

"I do, Mr. Andir."

"Good! Let's begin with the first main step. Why are you here? I want a thorough and honest answer. If you are not completely sincere with me, firstly, you'd be lying to yourself and secondly, the idea you've just paid for, and you're about to receive, won't correspond to your real problem. Is that clear?"

"Yes, it is." Rebecca snapped in an attempt to sound slightly more confident.

"Please, answer the question "why are you here?" You will begin to speak in exactly one minute. It is up to you to decide when that is."

"But I don't wear a watch. How am I going to…"

"It doesn't matter, when you believe that sixty seconds have passed, you can start."

Rebecca nodded to show that she had understood the rules of the game.

Andir began with the essential non-verbal scrutiny that every customer, who happened to come and sit between the four walls of his interrogation room, had to undergo. The purpose of this was for him to make a full analysis of the person opposite him, all in the space of one minute, and before receiving any actual information from the clients themselves. This process rigidly followed the established model, he had been taught of at the Academy, and any type of improvisation was not permitted. This approach was crucial for the idea-consultants and often the good job done depended entirely on it.

4

If standing straight, she was approximately 6ft 1inches tall, if not taller. She looked about 30 years old, but Andir could not bet on it. She could easily pass as being 25. Her clothes were going to contribute the most to making a good judgment of her. On the back of her show white jacket, and on the right side on the front, there was a large red print of a bear – a clear sign that the clothing was a product of a ski apparel manufacturer. Strange! The Idea Factory was situated on the top of a nice small hill, which resembled a mound rather than a mount. This hill was the highest point in a radius of several thousand square kilometers. There were not any conditions for skiing in the vast plain, surrounding the Factory location. Sports like biathlon or ski running were disciplines that were unheard of in the area. The regular and plentiful snowfall in the region, however, did not entice folks to attach the long boards to their boots as a means to go from one place to another. Any exception to this would have been looked upon as being a rather eccentric choice, to say the least. "Most probably the jacket is imported… Who knows?" Andir put the coat to one side and moved onto examining her bright pink polo-neck top. The typically lady's color flashed with brightness and lit the room in a pink light. Over the polo-neck collar, Rebecca had displayed a gold necklace, with a pendant in the shape of coin in the middle, also gold. The experienced idea-consultant immediately noticed the four 18-carrat gold rings, distributed evenly between both hands. One of them had a medium sized transparent precious stone. Andir was not that big on minerals and gems, but guessed that it was either a zircon, or a diamond. The latter seemed more likely. She did not wear a wedding ring. A bracelet, made from the same precious metal, could be seen on the right wrist of pretty Rebecca. All this expensive jewelry spoke clearly about the material status of the tall unmarried visitor. "Why didn't she opt for a consultant of First rank, then? The old dogs always offered some phenomenal ideas to everyone, who dared to part with a substantial sum of money. Most probably, the money was not hers and no one knew that she had come here?"

Her black leggings, her fluffy white boots and the white hat with a playful pompon were not worth too much of an attention, that was why Andir retracted his thoughts to his first impression of Rebecca, from the second she entered the room. She was timid. The woman looked like a new employee, who had just got lost in a multilevel office building on her first day at work, trying to get to the right floor. She hesitated, when invited to take a seat. She was not in a rush to take off her jacket like almost every other visitor of the Factory. Folks could not wait to get rid off their big winter clothes, because inside, it was very hot indeed. They realized quickly that they would be boiling within seconds if they did not remove their coats soon enough. The droplets of sweat, running down their foreheads, prompted them to do so almost straight away. Rebecca's smooth white face had also reacted to the changes in the temperature, turning red like in a person, who was plainly nervous and incorrigibly shy. She did not take much notice of the room, when she came in, nor did she see the scarce cold furniture and the rectangular mirror behind her. She was sitting with her legs crossed, very lady-like, her hands were resting on her lap, and her whole attention was focused on Andir. Nothing else mattered to her.

"I'm not... I'm not sure if a minute's passed, but I think it has..." she reluctantly interrupted Andir's deep-in-thought analysis, which was almost near completion, anyway.

"I am all ears, Rebecca."

"Well, I'm here, because I have a problem. I'm trying to find a job and so far, I haven't discovered what I'm looking for. I hope you can suggest something to me or even tell me directly what job I should get. I've come for a piece of advice." Rebecca stopped, convinced that a few stiffly delivered sentences were more than enough to explain the reasons behind her visit.

"I understand." Andir uttered, not because he understood anything, but simply out of habit. "Continue, please."

"That's it."

"Are you certain that there's nothing else you could add?"

"There's nothing I could think of. I'm looking for a job."

"Right, then, if that's the case, we can move on to the second stage of our meeting. Rebecca, I will start asking you different questions and I expect completely honest answers from you. You need to know that the slightest divergence from the truth could reflect negatively the end result of my work. Is that clear?"

"Yes, it is, Mr. Andir."

"Please, tell me a little bit about your family."

6

"No way! My quest for a job does not concern my family." She scolded him in a tone of voice that she would certainly deploy, when swearing at her worst ill wishers. Her backlash rebutted her timorous image.

"Fine, but it concerns my job. Please, answer the question!"

"And what about if I don't want to?" the overly attractive client snapped and clenched her teeth, throwing sparks of animosity.

"You are probably familiar with the admission rules of the Idea Factory? Anyone, who does not follow strictly the instructions of the idea-consultants, while on the premises, must leave prematurely and…"

"You can't do this to me!" Rebecca became red like a fully ripe tomato, and this was not down to the temperature in the room.

"It is entirely in your interest to answer all my questions, and if you don't, at the end of our…"

"Ask me anything you like, but I don't want to talk about my family. This is too personal."

"I am sure it is, but it is not up to you what we do here. The rules…"

"I'm not answering this. Next question?" Rebecca crossed tight her arms, locking the access to anything, connected to her closest relatives. Then she turned her head and demonstratively raised her chin up. Clearly, the mule in her was not going to give in. Andir could have just sent her away there and then, but he was way too much intrigued.

"Rebecca, every idea-consultant has the right to do one restart. I believe that now is the time to take advantage of this opportunity."

"What do you mean by this?" she asked, glancing back at the idea-consultant.

"It means that we forget about everything being said so far and start again. May I ask you to ignore all, I've just said and in return, I'll forget every word you have shared with me."

"And you think I could be fooled…? You will probably ask me about my family again!"

"It won't be again, Rebecca! I never asked you in the first place! Remember, we've already forgotten all about it!" Andir was good at restarts, although, he rarely resorted to them, unless the case was an

7

exception like this one. "My name is Andir, idea-consultant, Second rank. And you are?"

"Rebecca. My name is Rebecca, and there is no way you could know my name, because it's the first time you hear it!" she replied sarcastically. Her restlessness was getting even more apparent. It was hard to conjure up a good idea for someone, who lacked a decent level of self-control.

"Nice to meet you, Rebecca! What brings you here?"

"Should I wait for one minute?" the touchy visitor asked sulkily.

"This won't be necessary."

"I'd like to find a job and I'm not sure what kind it should be. Full stop."

"I understand. Now, I'm going to ask you a few questions. Please, answer me honestly, so I can be most useful to you in delivering the right idea that you have paid for, otherwise, the result will…"

"I'm not telling you anything about my family." Rebecca uttered just to be on the safe side, sensing that the actor, opposite her, was going to swerve the interview into the same direction like before, during their 'well forgotten' conversation.

"I've never asked you about your family and I have no intentions to. However, I would like to make some conclusions about your parents. I think that…"

"Why do you need to do this? I've told you, I'm here, so you can tell me what job I should get. Stop veering towards my mother and father, you…" She was about to finish her sentence with an insult, but she came to her senses at the last second.

"Rebecca, I'm trying to help you. The information about your family may hold the key to what could be the most suitable occupation for you! Many people follow into the steps of their parents professionally and there's nothing wrong with this. Often, the parents like to keep the tradition alive and yearn the family trade or vocation to be passed from generation to generation…"

"Cut it out!" the sweet tall beauty shouted and slammed the metal table with her hands, producing quite an unpleasant startling noise. She looked as if she was about to jump and claw all over Andir's face with her fashionably painted nails.

8

"Calm down, Rebecca." Andir appealed in a cool and composed tone of voice. "If that's what you want, I will not raise this issue again, but remember, the end result, after our meeting, may not satisfy you fully, namely because of your unwillingness to talk."

"Even if that's the case, this is my problem, isn't it, Mr. Andir?"

"Yes, this is true." the idea-consultant confirmed. He only agreed with her, because he feared that, otherwise, she was going to grab her stuff and leave, depriving him from her presence. "Please, tell me everything about your education and qualifications. As you know, in order to find employment, you need to meet certain criteria and the requirements that potential employers have set out. What could you offer them, Rebecca?"

"Well, I am an engineer, but I don't feel like working in this field." she replied wearily, but still with some anger left.

"I understand. And why?"

"Because this is not my thing. I don't like it."

"Don't you find this profession even slightly interesting? After all, you have spent years studying, in order to obtain qualifications in engineering."

"No, I don't. I realized that it's not for me even during my time at university. I could never imagine myself as someone, who designs different machinery and equipment. This job is not for me."

"Why, then, did you choose to become an engineer? You could have left and started something else, a subject that you liked."

"I don't know. It was too late, when I realized. I don't know." she shrugged – a clear sign that she really had no idea why.

"Rebecca, do you have any other qualifications, which could help you find the right job for you? Any additional skills you may have?"

"Well, I don't..."

"So, apart from your qualifications in engineering, you don't have an affinity to any other professional field, if I understand correctly?"

"I don't, I guess..." she hesitated, thrown off slightly by the roundabout way that she was questioned.

"Rebecca, please, correct me if I got this wrong! You are an engineer, who does not want a career in engineering, and you don't have any other qualifications?"

"Eh-r-r, yes. You could say this, yes."

"Could you, then, tell me a bit more about your hobbies? What do you do in your free time? Often, people make their living by doing what they like doing in their spare time."

"Not much. I haven't got any hobbies. I'm just looking for a job that I'd enjoy doing."

"Do you practice any sports? Do you like cooking, or going to the movies?"

"No, I don't." the visitor replied, without much thought about what she had been actually asked.

Rebecca was a hard nut to crack. Andir had encountered this sort of clients before, who confused him and made his work a real drag. He realized that his previous experience was not of any use in this case, however.

"So, you never played on the volleyball team, for instance? Your height would have been a plus in sports such as this, like basketball, also! With regards to your possible culinary skills – there are numerous examples of women, who have not thought of how capable they are in this field and how easy they could get a job as chefs, if only they dared leave the safety of their own kitchens. I also mentioned movies, because there are plenty of survey companies, which would pay the keen movie enthusiast to take part in their sociological polls. These are only examples, by the way, and that is why I'm asking you these questions." Rebecca listened to his detailed explanation, but she did not show much interest. Her short answer 'screamed' with total indifference.

"I don't like jumping around. I don't cook and I don't go to the cinema."

"I understand. Let's change the nature of our conversation a little, then. Rebecca, tell me about your last job, even if you did not like it."

"I've never worked before."

"So, after you left university, you did not get a job?"

"No, I didn't. I wasn't sure what I want and started looking for opportunities."

"Right, so you've been looking for a job for 3-4 years, without actually having anything particular in mind and…?"

"Well, for five years." Rebecca interjected so she could put the facts straight.

"I understand. You are looking for the perfect job, which would suit you best, so you never have to change it."

"The perfect job doesn't exist, Mr. Andir! Do you consider yours perfect?"

"You're right! Every job, as good as it can be, has its negative sides, too, sometimes. But we are not talking about me now. Did you have a summer job, while at university?"

"No, I didn't."

"Why?"

"I don't know. I guess, I didn't need to, or didn't feel like it. Who knows?" the gorgeous woman smiled, as if pleased with her own lack of knowledge.

"Rebecca, from all that's been said so far, I can conclude that you cannot establish what the most suitable career choice would be for you. What stops you from finding out are your own inner contradictions. Let's do an experiment! I think this could help."

"What kind of experiment?" the client responded with suspicion. She associated the word "experiment" with laboratory tests, involving dead creatures or little white mice.

"We'll change places. Please, come and sit on my chair and I'll sit on yours."

"Why?"

"Just do it, Rebecca, and remember that everything that takes place in this room is designed entirely to benefit you and it is done in your interest." Andir stood up first and thus provoking the same action from her, although, she still looked a little hesitant. They swapped places and both sat down in the opposite warmed-up seat. "Please, make yourself comfortable and look around you to get accustomed to your new position. You have one minute again. When you decide it has passed, let me know in some way."

Andir was not sure what to do. The minute of silence seemed to be what he needed to make his mind up about what direction their unproductive conversation should take. The methods, he had employed so far, followed closely what was written in the textbooks for idea-consultants, however, they led to no results. Rebecca was not sharing anything that was essential and she was simply too secretive for someone, who wanted to take advantage of the services, offered by the Idea Factory. Her fit body did not let on any helpful information, neither. Her perfectly smooth long legs were crossed and her slender and elegant arms had gently embraced her body. This was a clear sign that she was not in a mood to share anything about herself. Her face did not give out any emotions, unless the topic about her family was mentioned, when she really showed her annoyance. She did not look stupid and she gave the impression that she was fully aware why she was there, but at the same time, she answered some of the questions, as if she was not very well informed, or that she plainly did not want to be in this environment. She was a complete mystery. Andir expected that the change of sitting positions might lift the curtain up a bit. In his chair now, she glanced at the large mirror for a moment and then, looked back in the left eye of the idea-consultant, then, into his right one, just for fun.

"The minute's up." she uttered with certainty. Although, she did not move her lips, she had counted to herself up to sixty.

"Alright. Then, we're ready to begin. Rebecca, we've swapped places, because we're going to look into your case from a slightly different angle. I'd like you to listen to me very carefully and say the first thing that comes into your head. Do you understand?"

"Yes, I do."

"Do you know, Rebecca, I want to change my job." Andir said with almost friendly voice, trying to make the false statement sound as true as possible. "I don't feel like working as an idea-consultant anymore, despite the prestige and good salary that this profession brings. I want something new, something different and you have to advise me on my prospects."

"Well, I don't know, you could..."

"Not yet, I haven't finished. Before you share with me your valuable piece of advice, I'm going to tell you a little bit about myself. My mother worked in a textile factory and my father was employed in a farm, just outside the city of..."

"Why are you telling me all this?" Rebecca sounded jumpy, fearing that if the idea-consultant opened up about his own parents, this would inevitably lead to some questions about her mammy and daddy. "Cheeky sod!"

"Because, you will benefit from this. Please, don't interrupt me! When I finish, you will have the opportunity to speak. Is that clear?"

"Yes, Mr. Andir." she replied anxiously, ready on full alert to receive an 'attack', connected to the same old, but well forgotten subject.

"At college, I specialized in Economics." he continued, still keeping the nature of their chat safe and neutral. "I was at the top of the class. In my last year, I took an additional specialty in the field of Psychology, which brought me the award: "The best student" in my year. After college, I enrolled in a fast-track training program for sea captains, 2nd class. The enthusiasm was there, but I quickly realized that it wasn't my place there. Two months later, I left the ocean behind and enrolled in the Academy for idea-consultants. I was chosen to work in the Idea Factory. Now, however, I feel that the time is right for me to have a change in career. I want something new. What do you think, Rebecca, I should do? Please, could you share your opinion, having heard a little bit about my history." Andir considered giving even more details about himself, but he noticed, in her deep black eyes, that she was getting obviously bored with his uneventful life story. So he stopped midway to what he had intended to tell her.

"I don't know. I'm not sure…"

"Rebecca, tell me honestly what you think? There isn't a right or wrong answer."

"I don't know, maybe…maybe…"

"Relax, just tell me." Andir encouraged her. He disliked very much when people tended not to finish their sentences.

"A prison guard – you'll be good at it." she shot out the answer, which was probably the last suggestion, the idea-consultant would expect to hear.

"How did you come up with this? Wouldn't it be more logical if you recommended I go back to my sea crew experience, or try a career in business, or even have a go at farming…?"

"I don't know. You asked and this was the first thing that came to mind. I knew you wouldn't like it, but as you insisted…" she apologetically replied, however, without too much of a regret about her words.

"Rebecca, could you explain yourself? Why do you see me as someone, who would be good at supervising convicted people?"

"Well, the way you behave is like…, eh-r-r, like…, like … a prison guard."

"And how does a prison guard behave? Describe, please!"

"I don't know! I answered your question. How am I supposed to know how one behaves?" she appeared nervous again and the vein across her left temple was visibly growing larger.

Andir felt he could not keep this up. Clearly, Rebecca was one of those people that if they played a game of associations, she would always blurt out something unusual, in comparison to what was going on in the predictable heads of the other 99% of the population. If <ball> was the word, she would come up with something like <lasagna> or <lizard>. So no one could imagine what the answer to her job search query could be possibly in her own head. Andir had the intention to ask her about what her advice would be to an engineer, who did not want a job in engineering, but he realized that this approach was pointless.

"Actually, there is some validity to your suggestion. I'll be honest like you've been with me. As a child, I thought I could become a policeman, who chased the baddies and put them straight in prison. This is not exactly a prison guard, but it's not that dissimilar. Rebecca, may I ask you to swap places again? I have a few more questions to ask and then, we'll move on to the final stage of our meeting." the "castling" took less than a few seconds and before her nicely shaped derrière touched her good old chair, she hastily asked:

"So, you've come up with something, then?"

"Be patient just a little longer, Rebecca! How important location is for you, with regards to your future work?

"I don't know. How do you mean location?"

"I mean, what city or town you would consider moving to if you find work there? What country? Do you understand?"

"Yes, I do now. Location is irrelevant to me."

"This is quite useful information. Now we come to the money issue, your monthly salary. How much would you be happy with?"

"I don't know." she shrugged her shoulders again.

14

"Everyone has some expectations for the minimum they'd like to be paid, before entering into some sort of employment, don't they?"

"I guess so. I've told you, I have never worked before, so I haven't given much thought to this question."

"Now I'm giving you the opportunity to think about it and answer. To help you, I suggest you consider your monthly expenditure during the last year. Don't worry if your calculations are not quite accurate. I need to hear an approximate figure."

"O-o-oh! Then, I'll never find a job!" Rebecca laughed out loud – a state of emotion she had not exhibited so far. She placed her hand over her mouth like a lady and tried to stop her laughter to no avail.

"Could you tell me why?"

"Ha-ha-ha, well, because I doubt that any employer would agree paying me that much. But, Mr. Andir, I'm not looking for work for the money!"

"Please, explain, how come? People work for money, unless you're interested in voluntary work for some charity?"

"No, no, no. I'm not keen to do any voluntary work, but at the same time, I don't need money, either."

"I understand." Andir said automatically, but he could not figure out the clear contradiction in her words. "If your wages are irrelevant to you, this makes my job much easier. Rebecca, I believe we can now move on to the third and final stage of our interview."

"So you, now, know what I should do for a living?"

"The idea has crystallized, however, as I've told you before, you may not like it and…"

"It doesn't matter! Tell me, tell me!" Rebecca could not wait anymore. Despite being someone, who disliked begging favors, she was prepared to plead with the idea-consultant, should he continued to procrastinate the answer.

"Just one last question: If you've been looking for a job for the last five years to no avail, if you're single and have no particular hobbies, then what do you do with your time, all day, Rebecca?" Andir asked, fully aware that the person, opposite him, might interpret the question as an insult that could result in a very possible smack in his face.

"Not much! I just wonder what job I should look for and simply keep on searching…"

"Is this constantly on your mind?"

"Well, not constantly. I do go out with friends in the evenings and in the daytime, I like going to the shops. I love shopping. I like it a lot, actually. You could say this is my hobby, having asked me about it before."

"I understand. Rebecca, we've reached the final point. Are you ready?"

"Yes, I am." she leaned forward, in order to soak every word, which was about to come out of his mouth. She did not want to miss a syllable. The perfect soft spheres pressed onto the table, attracting a very wet look from, otherwise, the unruffled idea-consultant, who stopped thinking about his job for less than a second.

"The idea is: You should not work."

"Is that it?" Rebecca frowned, thinking she might have not heard well.

"I haven't finished. You should not work anything else, but keep doing what you've been already doing."

"But I'm not doing anything at the moment!" the attractive guest said in total belief she was right.

"That's correct. Your job, in the last five years, was to look for a job. Just keep on doing it! Considering your personal history, you shared with me, and the information I managed to gather about you during our interesting chat, this is the best idea I can offer to you."

"You must tell me something different! This is stupid!"

"Yes, it is. To an extent, it is stupid." the idea-consultant agreed confidently.

"You lied to me! I'm not leaving until you tell me the real idea that's going around in your head. Come on, I know there is one. You're kidding me, aren't you?"

"No, Rebecca, I'm not. I did not lie to you and I'm not joking. This is my conclusion. I'm giving you a minute again and then, I shall let you know about the reasons behind my decision."

"Enough with this minute palaver. Tell me immediately." she shouted, again with an angry mask on her face. Despite all, she looked staggeringly stunning.

"Be patient!" Andir requested rather calmly. Although, he was not in the slightest. He was burning on the inside. He wanted her. Here, now, on the table or even on the floor – it did not matter. He imagined everything, from start to finish. This impious and lewd thought pierced his mind at light speed, like a bullet that left no wound. He got rid of it quickly, though. He should not think like this, it was against the Factory rules and it was unprofessional. It never happened, the thought. It had never existed in his head, and even if it had, it could never be proven. His consciousness was clear again.

Rebecca began to count to sixty once more, but this time, she did it through her angrily clenched teeth. She counted up faster and thus, she almost halved the astronomical minute. The woman was so livid after she heard the absurd idea that she did not even try to grasp what she had been told. Andir, however, was happy. He did not show it, though, and he did not intend to until the customer left the room. But yes, he was over the moon. He had done a very good job, yet again. The idea was perfect.

"Done! The minute's up. Tell me, now, the actual occupation I should look into." Rebecca was beyond doubt impatient at this point, certain that Andir was joking with her. She could not know that the idea-consultants never, truly never joked with their clients.

"Listen to me carefully, please! Rebecca, the best job for you is to continue searching for a job, as you've been doing for the last five years. I understand you may not like the..."

"Let's restart the process again and then, you'll be able to tell me a better idea. Let's do it right now." the client anxiously suggested.

"That's not possible. We've taken advantage of this opportunity and you're not permitted to take a second restart."

"But how? I... I... there's no way this to be... but... I don't get it..."

"Rebecca, I'm asking you for one last time to let me explain the reasons behind my idea. If you don't stop interjecting, you won't get an explanation and our meeting will end. Do you understand?"

"Well, go on, then!" she submitted but she did not want to listen anymore. She wanted another idea. Different, not that one. Different.

"It's quite simple, Rebecca! Sometimes, the simple and obvious solutions are the right ones. From what you've told me, I understand that you are financially secure and you do not have the usual financial motives for finding a job, like most people. You have never worked before, but this doesn't stop you, it seems, from having a lifestyle, which fully satisfies you. Your only thrill in life is exactly

17

this – the actual process of looking for a job. Have you ever thought what would happen if you find work tomorrow? Imagine, you're employed and what next? The excitement that kept you going in the last five years would be gone. You'll be earning money that you don't really need. And the work, even if it seems perfect at the beginning, sooner or later, you'll get fed up with it and find it rather boring. That's always the case! Your search for a job has brought you as far as here. You've been waiting outside in the cold to pay a huge sum of money for an idea. This money is the equivalent to the potential annual salary you could have made if you were employed. The enormous motivation that springs out from the search process is a very useful driving force. You should not terminate this unless, one day, you come to a decision yourself that it is time to stop looking and you actually start working. This should depend entirely on you. Do you understand, Rebecca?"

"A-ah?" came out of her wide-open mouth. She was staring at Andir, but she could still not comprehend anything. What does he mean by that she should keep looking? And what exactly should she be looking for? And where? Though, isn't he...? But of course! That's it!

Rebecca looked down. She fixed her dizzy gaze at the metal table. She breathed out noisily a couple of times and stroked the table with her right hand, as if it was her own child. She smiled. One could say that in this moment she experienced an enlightenment of some sort. She uttered after half a minute:

"I guess, you're right, Mr. Andir!"

"I'm glad you understand, Rebecca." he replied, without hiding for the first time that he was quite pleased with himself.

"And now what? I should continue searching, then?"

"Yes, that's right!"

"But for how long? I don't know when I should stop?"

"You do know, Rebecca! Only you could decide for how long and there isn't any idea-consultant, who could help you in this. It's all down to you."

"Is it that simple?"

"Actually, yes, it is. It's simple."

"What about if I never find work and I keep looking my entire life? How can I stop searching?"

"Rebecca, I believe the time will come when it's right. Today, it's not the day, however. My impression is that you won't have to wait that long. I'm certain of it."

"Really?"

"Yes, I am, Rebecca. It's inevitable! There'll be a time, when you will want the searching to stop. You'll realize that you are not able to go on like this and you'll decide that it's time to start work."

"But I guess, I want to... now. Well, I'm not sure what I want..."

"Shall I tell you how I know that the time has not come for you, yet? The fact that you're here and not at a job interview with a potential employer proves that you're not ready!"

"I guess so. It seems you're right, Mr. Andir. Thank you." her anger had transformed into sincere gratitude, which she would have happily expressed through a big bear hug if she could. Of course, the idea-consultant could not allow any physical contact between them, no matter how pleasant he would have found that.

"I should thank you, too, Rebecca! It was quite challenging for me, in professional terms, to come up with an idea for someone like you."

"Mr. Andir, please, take my apologies for my outburst at the beginning. My parents are very affluent and I just don't like speaking about them. Often, people see me as the daughter of such and such, and not for who I am. And by the way, you may have told me a different idea if you knew who they are."

"Actually, I know, Rebecca." Andir called her bluff only to make her see him as someone, who was powerful within his own interrogation room. Well, in theory, this was exactly the case.

"But how? I've not mentioned anything to you, and..." The astonishment only enriched the palette of emotions on her face.

"I just guessed. The final stage has come to an end and with this – our meeting, too. Please, you can leave the room now. Have a nice day, Rebecca!" the idea-consultant nodded, pointing at the exit.

"Have a nice day, too, Mr. Andir, and thank you once again for the idea. It was worth the money I paid."

A minute later, necessary to make herself winter proof by putting on her white jacket, her white hat and white gloves, Rebecca left the idea-consultant alone. Andir did not stand up to see her off, nor did he shake her hand. He was not permitted to do so, despite having the urging desire to touch his attractive visitor.

The next "misguided" soul, in desperate search for a solution, headed towards the vacant room. He was made to wait for a little while because all idea-consultants needed some time of readjustment after each client. They had the right to relax for ten minutes before meeting the next one, if they did not want to be influenced by their previous impressions, when delivering the new idea. Andir and his colleagues would commonly resort to the following technique for clearing their minds. They tried to focus their thoughts on something from their personal lives, outside the workplace. Often they would go back and try to remember the morning, for example, from the moment of getting up to their arrival at work that day. Additionally, they would try to name randomly countries and cities. Counting backwards also had a similar effect.

The memory of how Andir's morning started flooded into his head. Then he uttered out loud the name of a country. He shaved, in his thoughts, and just about pictured himself brushing his teeth, when he saw Rebecca's reflection in the bathroom mirror. He focused on the tiny details about where exactly his clothes were, how he picked them and put them on. He remembered making his breakfast and in what order he did everything, but when he named a country for the fourth time, he noticed it began with the letter "R". The funny thing was that he was not even sure if such country existed. Andir realized that he was experiencing strange symptoms. He stood up and went near the door. Beside the door handle, there was a red button. He pressed it and went back in his chair. Red buttons like this were often associated with some sort of an emergency, like fire. Although, a sound of an alarm could not be heard, the full on fire in his head meant that he was about to be left alone for a good half an hour.

The idea-consultants sometimes did not cope well with the task of clearing their minds from their experience with all sorts of crazy visitors. So when the standard methods, they had been taught at the Academy, did not work, they simply pressed the button. By doing this, they were given more time and in essence – the opportunity to relive their last encounter, reminiscing about every detail, and a chance to focus on the image of the last customer, as if he or she was still there, in the interrogation room. The logic behind this approach was clear and simple, based on the standard bipolar model. Good and Evil. Hot and cold. In this instance, if one could not get rid of the memory of an event and force their mind to forget it, then they should be let relive it all over again. Andir was considered as being one of the most confident and professional amongst his colleagues. He was simply nonchalant and usually unaffected by his work; however, even he, sometimes, resorted to the button-option.

Rebecca was an interesting case, although, he could easily use this label to describe many other clients he had worked with over the years. Each of them had come with their reasonable or irrational storyline, with their difficult or simple problem. They all had come to hear the right solution, the right idea. The attractive rich daughter, who had no idea what to do with her life and whose needs were fully satisfied to the extent that she had no appreciation of money, was definitely a client, who was one of a kind and unlike any other that had set foot in Andir's interrogation room. Well, this was not really the reason for needing to meet her again, or to be precise, picture her image in his head once more. How many people around the world were in Rebecca's shoes? Thousands, or hundreds of thousands? Possibly even more! People, who had everything they needed to live a normal life, but instead, they went on looking for something else. They might have felt they wanted the perfect job, despite that they did not really need to work, or they had not realized that their current job was as good as it got. They might have felt that somewhere, there was a better place to live, not being able to see the benefits of living where they were. They might have been looking for the perfect partner, fully aware that he or she did not exist and no one was ever perfect. The question was why? Andir had never thought that deeply about these issues. He realized, however, that the answer was not simple and that he could not really figure it out. Not that day anyway. He could not indulge in thinking about this at that moment, because it would have cluttered his mind unnecessarily and it would have forced him to press the red button again. Any professional idea-consultant, no matter of what rank they were, would have acted like this. Nevertheless, most importantly, Rebecca was happy on her way out of the Idea Factory and she was going to keep searching. What kind of job and when she was going to find it remained unknown. Probably never! Andir managed to put a stop on thinking about their chat that ended so unexpectedly for her, within the time frame, allocated by the button. "Finished! Next, please!" he uttered to himself, ready to meet the new client.

Sam

The slightly humped middle-aged man, who displayed a bearded face, made a couple of steps into the room and stopped. He carefully looked around, despite that what was worth seeing was situated in the center, in front of him. He looked as if he had just been imprisoned and now he was studying his cell, where he was going to spend the next ten years, at least. The "prison guard", or his temporary "cell-mate" was already in, waiting for him. However, the visitor did not even notice Andir. He had not looked at him, not even once, since the metal door slammed behind him with its characteristic mechanical click. The mirror. He became aware of it and went quietly towards the glass. Why was he trying to be quiet when there was not anyone asleep in the room, after all, Andir could not figure out. The man's face was inches from the glass mirror. He stroked the surface with his dirty fingers, which were on display through the mutilated half finger gloves. Did he just sniff it? Yes. He sniffed the glass. Andir remained silent, observing the man's behavior. He did not rule out that in this way he would obtain valuable information, which could help him come up with an idea for the hobo in front of him. Well, the man looked like one, anyway. The idea-consultant decided to wait and let the visitor speak first. Soon he got tired of studying the mirror and simply settled in the immovable metal chair. He carefully placed his thick grey coat on the back of it. His clothing was so dirty, as if it had been rubbed with a piece of briquette. His dark-blue woolen jumper had black marks, too. The overly suspicious visitor was not only filthy, but he could have smelled better. The stench quickly soaked the air in the small interrogation room, making the idea-consultant switch from breathing in through his nose to use his mouth more for that purpose. He promptly realized that the disgusting odor tasted bitter and that it would take at least ten minutes for the ventilation system to

22

neutralize it and disperse it in another portion of sufficient quantity of freshness.

"Hey!" the stinker said and for the first time, he looked at his elegant host. He leaned over and in a low voice continued. "Get closer! Who's there at the back? How many of them?"

"What do you mean, Sir? I don't understand. Could you…"

"Hey, don't make out you don't get it. Come over 'ere!" The clear waving gesture with his right hand did not get the expected result. Andir only settled back even more comfortably in his chair.

"Please, explain what you mean!"

"Tell me who's behind the mirror? They are watching us, aren't they?"

"No one is watching. I understand your worry, Mr.…."

"Sam." the paranoid grubby client blurted out his name straight away.

"Sam, there's nothing you should worry about. I am here in front of you and I am the only person you're going to speak to. My name is Andir, idea consultant, Second rank, and today, I shall offer you the best idea that…"

"Yes, but they are behind me, not in front of me. Can't you see that the mirror is behind me? Hey, don't play up with me!" the guest hissed venomously, raising his index finger in reproach.

"I can see your point, but there's no one at the back. There's no one behind you!" the idea-consultant calmly reassured him.

"Don't give me this sh*t! Can you prove it?"

"This is not necessary, because there isn't anything to prove."

Come on, then, let's go and check the back room." the guest was prepared to inspect the premises in person, certain that he would find at least two unwanted viewers, snooping on them. The rules, however, did not tolerate such liberties.

"I am sorry, Sam, but I cannot provide access to this room for you. There isn't really anyone there!"

"But one could see through the glass from the other side, couldn't they?"

"You're right. If there was someone on the other side, they could watch us and we would not know about it." Andir did not mind to provoke occasionally his clients, not so much to annoy them, but purely for his own pleasure.

"Hey, smart ass! I don't want anyone to watch or listen to us. I've not come here to talk to everyone about what I've come for…"

"I understand. Sam, this is exactly how it is going to be. And now, may I ask you if you are ready to proceed to the main reason of your visit, here, in the Idea Factory?"

"Not yet. Wait a minute." the visitor said in whisper, leaving his uncomfortable metal chair, and walked towards the mirror. He stared at it, as if to try piercing the reflective surface with his eyes and see THEM, behind it. He didn't see anybody. A few seconds later he stopped with the crazy gawk and knocked a couple of times with his knuckles. He did not like the sound of the solid glass, which was around 2 sq. m in area. It was much thicker than he thought. He knocked again, but this time with his fist and much harder. The sound that followed did not offer a satisfactory answer to whatever question he had in his head. Clearly disappointed, suspicious and discontented, the guest went back to his chair. He rested his elbows on the metal table and said quietly:

"Go on!"

"Do you mean that you ready to begin?"

"Go on!" the invite was uttered slightly louder.

"As I've just mentioned, my name is Andir, idea-consultant, Second rank. Sam, you have paid for my services and I will do my best to meet your expectations. Our conversation will go through three stages and each of them will start and finish at my discretion. Is that clear?"

"But can they hear us?"

"Who?" Andir asked. Sam's question was really out of sync with what it had been just said.

"Those, behind the glass. Say, there was somebody there, could they see and hear us, or just see us?"

"The glass pane is very thick, so the sound of someone speaking normally cannot go through, to the other side. Your whisper definitely won't be heard." the idea-consultant reassured him, although he had not got the slightest idea, whether this was true.

"Super! Carry on, then!" his overgrown face broke into a catty smile. If his beard was not so black and matted, but white, he could have, then, very successfully taken on the role of the guy, who brought presents at the end of every year.

24

"The first part of our conversation involves you describing in greatest detail the reason behind your visit today. Please, answer the question "why are you here? You will start speaking after one minute. Is that clear?"

"Hey, you're not playing some sort of trick on me, are you?"

"These are the rules, Sam. It is not a trick. After one minute you can speak."

"You're not kidding me or something? 'Cause I'm not up to any jokes."

"Not at all, Sam. The pause before the first stage is mandatory and it always lasts sixty seconds."

"Sixty, then, you say?" he repeated anxiously and lifted his left sleeve to clock the time.

What an exquisite watch, and quite expensive, too – was the first thought that passed through Andir's mind, when he began analyzing the client. Despite looking at it for about a second, the idea-consultant was certain that the body of the elegant time-tracking artifact had been given a golden bath for an indefinite period and the precious metal had sufficiently covered the whole surface. The matt brown leather band suggested that some exotic animal had parted with its life. This was obvious even to an amateur. The dial was impressive, as well – the Roman numerals were easy to read. They were positioned on the hour, giving some extra class to the watch itself and its proud owner, no doubt. And what does it all mean? Sam is not as poor as he looks? His coat, jumper, the old jeans, which seemed to belong to a bygone fashion era, half a century ago, in all, the signs point at the fact that he has no money. But then, how did he manage to pay for the services of an idea-consultant, Second rank? Well, there could be several explanations of how he got the cash, including a property sale, a lottery windfall, a loan from a rich relative or a friend, and of course, he could have stolen it. Homeless people were infamous for their difficulty to resist snatching someone's handbag, especially if the deed was likely to get unnoticed.

The idea-consultant had to stop pondering over the possible origin of the huge sum of money or the cost of the golden watch. This was not of primary importance and besides; he would waste precious seconds of the allocated minute.

Andir's experienced eyes had noted Sam's apparel, but he had not observed his client's shoes, yet. He could have looked at them in detail at the beginning, when Sam was striding up and down, across the room; however, the idea-consultant decided to do it, just now. He leaned back, as if inadvertently, so he could get a good look from under the table. They were expensive, no doubt, and had a special metal toecap that one could not see on cheap winter models. The leather was very fine and classy. Why was he pretending he was someone that he was not? The customer's face, then, went under Andir's scrutiny. It was completely consistent with his filthy clothes. His dark wavy shoulder-length hair had not been treated with the standard hygienic products for a long time. Together with his two-month overgrown beard, it looked greasy and matted. His moustache could not win a competition in a category for length and volume, but it would definitely come first for its awarding asymmetry. It was double in size on the right, in comparison to his other side.

The idea-consultants had been trained to always analyze the features and external characteristics of the client; to export any kind of available information, but they were advised to never absolutely take it as face value. They were advised to have the benefit of the doubt that not all was what it seemed. Andir followed closely this rule. It was very possible that Sam was rich, but some sort of problem, he had, made him disguise in such a pitiful way before his planned visit to the Idea Factory. One way or another, it was going to be revealed before the end of today's visit, whether Sam was truly poor or everything was a farce and a staged performance.

The behavior of the guest was strange, but at the same time, quite normal, indeed. People generally noticed and asked about what was behind the big mirror, when they found themselves in the interrogation room for the first time. They might have not been that suspicious about it and none of them really went on to sniff it, but by all means, the curiosity was there. Sam looked very confident and he knew what he wanted. He took the lead immediately at the backdrop of Andir's passive attitude. The man definitely stood his ground.

The minute had passed and the poor-rich customer spoke in a voice that made the idea-consultant strain his ears significantly. Andir had to rely on reading his lips, a skill that he could not say he had mastered.

26

"Hey, I'll start?"

"Please, answer the question "why are you here?""

"My case is quite unusual. I'll speak, but it will be hypothetically."

"How do you mean?" Andir asked not because he was not aware of the meaning of the word, but just to make sure that there was no misunderstanding.

"Hey, stop playing up! You know what I mean!"

"I think I understand, Sam. You mean…"

"Yes, you get it, of course. But you choose to play the fool. I know all your manipulative games here. You can't fool me, not me! That's why I'm speaking only hypothetically."

"This is your right. So now, are you going to answer my question?"

"Alright, alright, just stop pushing me. I'll tell you. I'm here to ask you something. Hypothetically!"

"And what's that?"

"You're not going to tell anyone what I've told you?"

"I won't. We are under restrictions of sharing any information that has been disclosed to us during the interviews."

"That's good. I'm beginning to like you. Now tell me, as you are such a smart ass! Hypothetically, what would you do if you had to get rid of a corpse? What's the best place to do this? Hypothetically!" his last word remained hanging in the air until Andir uttered his answer.

"Sam, is this your problem, which has brought you here?"

"Aha! That's it and it's not a small deal…"

"Have you got anything to add? And if you don't, we could proceed to the next stage of our meeting?"

"Got nothing to add! Go ahead!"

"I'm going to ask you to answer the following questions. You must not lie to me; otherwise this could affect badly the idea you are about to get in the final part of our conversation. Is that clear?"

"Hypothetically, there's no reason for me to lie." Sam replied hypothetically and winked playfully at the consultant.

"Are you ready for the next stage?"

"Go on! I'm ready!"

"Going over, again, the reason that has prompted you to visit us, I come to the conclusion that hypothetically, as you've put it, there is a human body, which you would like to hide somewhere that no one could ever find it. Is that correct?"

"You got it! Well done, you!" Sam's praise sounded like that of a primary teacher, commending a pupil for writing a perfect sentence.

"Let's make this clear, Sam. You wish the corpse to be never found by anyone?"

"That's it, never, not after a week, not in hundred years."

"I understand. Tell me where is it now... the body? This sounds somehow better than a corpse."

"Hey, this is none of your business." the fake hobo told him off in whisper. He was more hostile than before.

"Actually, if you don't wish to be disappointed by my idea that you've paid for, this information is important to me, so I can give you a precise..."

"Forget about it! Just tell me what to do with it, 'cause I've been scratching my head for ages and I only come up with nasty ideas." Sam made a sour face in disgust.

"Fine. If you are not going to tell me the body's whereabouts, then, at least answer me this. How heavy is it?"

"Hmm, what does this have to do with it?"

"It will be useful to know the object's weight."

"Hypothetically, it's about 70kg, or there about. But I'm not very certain."

"Sam, I guess you've got a car?"

"Yes, I've got an old banger. She is very keen to desert me, but I won't let her." A pauper with a car? Was this not a mutually impossible combination? Or maybe, it was over twenty years old? These old cars cost nothing!

"Do you think you could manage to put the body in the car by yourself, without assistance?"

"Of course! No problem with this! What are you on about, anyway? Do you mean I should drive off somewhere and dump it? Dude, where, where is the question? I thought of a few places but I'm not sure it won't be found. Also, it can't be too far in case the cops stop me on the way. And I'd like to think of some humane way, that's what they call it! Isn't it? I'm not a beast or anything after all!" the client asked rhetorically, despite the fact that his appearance did not do him any favors – he hardly looked like a member of the human race.

"I understand. Sam, why don't you bury it somewhere, where no one could find it?"

"Listen, this is exactly what I've been saying, but where, I don't know. Every time I think of a place I get scared someone will see me. They, people, always snoop around, f**king all the time…, and always poke their noses in someone else's business…" only the thought of somebody finding out about the corpse gave the tramp a near panic attack. His breathing changed and he started to look around as if to check whether anyone had come in the room in the meantime and was standing behind him. He turned his head around sharply and stared at the mirror again. He almost raised the subject about the invisible spies behind it once more: how many of them were there and why for God sake were they watching and listening to him? Andir sensed where his anxiety was leading him, so he quickly tried to bring him back onto the main problem, namely – finding a solution on what to do with the human remains.

"Don't distract yourself with the imaginary persons, Sam! You're here to receive an idea and I shall give it to you. No one will ever know what's been said between you and I. Are you ready to continue?"

"Yes, yes, go on…" the visitor hesitated, looking back at the idea-consultant.

"Sam, I'd like to know why you are the one, who has to get rid of the body? Can't someone else do it for you? I imagine you couldn't really opt for an official burial in this instance?

"Are you crazy?" the client raised his voice significantly and then, carried on in his normal annoying whisper. "No way I'm going for a burial or any other nonsense. Grab a spade and I'll dig it myself. But where, this is what I'm asking you? Where?"

"I understand your concern, Sam. I do, indeed, and very much so. The second part of our meeting has come to an end. Finally, I can share with you my idea. There is a chance that you may not like it; however, taking into account everything you've told me, I believe that it is truly the best available in your case."

"Hey, hang on a minute! Aren't you rushing me a bit, here? Go on, ask me more questions!"

"There's no need for that, Sam. Your situation is interesting, but far from complicated. Any idea-consultant would have managed to solve this very quickly and those, of the First rank, would have been much quicker than me, believe me!"

"You're kidding me! Really?"

"That is correct. A particular feature of our work is the swiftness we apply, when we conjure up the ideas for our clients."

"Shoot it out, then, 'cause I haven't slept for days. Where should I throw this corpse?"

"Throw is not the best of actions I would prompt you to choose. Last question, Sam: did you kill this person?"

"No way, are you crazy?" firmly and positively the suspect replied. His wide pupils did not move – a sure sign he was saying the truth.

"I had to ask. Thank you for your honest answer. Now my idea is ready. We shall proceed towards the final stage, when we will..."

"Hey, man, cut it out, 'cause my patience... Just, spit it out!"

"I understand your impatience. It is reasonable in the context of your motives that have brought you here today..."

"Come on, you're killing me now!" Sam uttered and one could not be sure if he was joking or being serious.

"This has not been my intention by all means, Sam! So right then, here is the idea – The body must be interred in the nearest cemetery. In this way, no one would ever discover it and at the same time, the demised will be treated with all due respect."

"Man, didn't I tell you that there's no way I could bury it there. No way!"

"Sam, let me explain myself and you will see that..."

"No point explaining anything to me, when I'm telling you that this can't happen. No way!" quietly stressed on the visitor.

"Actually, there is a way. Please, hear me out, so you can understand exactly what you should do, so..."

"Hey, you are not gonna give me some impossible nonsense, are you, now?"

"Not at all. Allow me to defend my idea and you will see that in reality, it is feasible and totally pragmatic."

"Go on, then! We've got so far, so let's see!" the member of the stinky homeless community reluctantly agreed. He was determined to get an answer from the sleek smart ass in front of him.

"Sam, tell me, do you know where the cemetery in you place of permanent residence is located?"

"The cemetery? I know where it is, yes, I do. And?"

"But do you know that in every cemetery, there are always a few empty graves, dug beforehand and ready, where later, as you can guess, the coffins are placed. And until that moment comes, the holes get covered, in case of rain or snowfall." Andir paused, waiting for the affirmative answer.

"Yes, right, I've seen them, but if I put it in one of those and on the next day, when they see the fresh soil on top – everyone will guess, you know?" the guest asked, openly questioning Andir's intelligence.

"I never said that you will have to cover it with soil, Sam. There's..."

"So, what – throw it down there and just leave it for everyone to see it? No way, I'm doing this! They'll do me for it straight away. I'm not so stupid!"

"No, you are not, Sam, so I am positive that you will comprehend everything that needs to be done for the plan to work in practice. The details are very important, indeed, and if you do not follow my instructions precisely, you may fail. Is that clear?"

"Yes, yes. Come on, dude, go ahead! I'm listening." the client was now quite enthusiastic. He could not wait to hear the end of the story.

"Firstly, you have to load the body into your car. To avoid being seen by the neighbors, you should do this in the middle of the night. I believe, you're smart enough to pick the best time for this action yourself. The next step involves driving to the cemetery. Despite the 24-hour security there, you won't have any trouble getting in, as by law, everyone's allowed to visit their deceased loved ones at all times. When on the inside, you need to find the exact location of these holes. So you don't do this in the dark, my advice is to go there the previous day and do a research first."

"Hang on a minute! What if there aren't any empty graves?"

31

"Most averagely big cemeteries will have at least ten such holes, so in reality, it is impossible to not see any. Also, as you're aware, the preparation of a burial takes a few days, as everything needs to be pre-planned."

"Yes, that's true, but if someone sees me snooping around or in the moment I actually ditch the body in the hole... what am I gonna do then?"

"That is possible. But if you've done your homework well, it is more likely that you will succeed unnoticed. Remember, Sam, the idea could be put into practice and become reality only if you follow closely my instructions. Any detour will result in a potential failure, which only you will have to take responsibility for and..."

"Alright, alright, I'll be careful. And then what? What's next?" Sam's voice trembled, as if everything was happening that moment. Despite him speaking very low during the entire meeting, the irregular vibration, felt in his vocal cords, only gave out his true anxiety and concern.

"Next, you lay the body in the hole and cover it with soil. Just a few inches should be enough. The hole will be still ready to embrace whatever it was dug for and you will feel at ease that no one will ever find out what you've done."

"But the gravediggers will see the difference in the depth of the hole and I'll get caught..." Sam uttered worriedly, as if in expectance of being handcuffed there and then.

"No, you won't." Andir opposed immediately and continued. "They will see the difference, you can be sure of that, but don't forget, Sam, the gravediggers do this all day long and their rule is to never dig in the same spot, ever! They will not bother with it as long as the body is well concealed. When the time comes for the grave to get used, they will simply lower the coffin carefully and after the ceremony, as usual, they will fill the hole once and for all."

"Hey, are you sure that this is how it's going to happen?"

"I'm positive. Sam, do everything as I've told you and your problem will be solved."

"Eh-r-r, I'll try. What else have I got?"

"With this, our conversation has come to an end. I'll have to ask you to leave now, to allow the next client enter the room."

"No one's watching us, are they? There isn't anyone there?" Sam asked, pointing with his head at the mirror.

"No, there isn't."

"And you're not going to tell anyone about why I've come here?"

"I'm not. Please, leave the room."

"You're cool, man. OK, bye!" yet another happy customer said in quite a regular voice for the first time.

Sam put on his thick dirty coat over the dirty knitted jumper. Then, he made an attempt to shake hands with Andir to show his gratitude for the good idea, in which his trust grew by the second. When his hand remained hanging in the air, Sam winked and quickly left the room.

Left by himself again, Andir prepared for the next client with a problem, still pondering over the idea he gave the poor hobo. Yes, he was not rich, the consultant was certain about this. The watch was probably a fake; the boots were not that expensive, as he had first thought. The cash - he had just got hold of it somehow. So what was the conclusion? A mistake. Andir had made a small error of judgment. Even the idea-consultants sometimes made mistakes, but the important thing was that the idea was the right one.

How easy it was to conjure up a solution to Sam's "dead" problem! Actually, Andir took advantage of his experience with a similar case he had three years ago. At the time, there was this smartly dressed middle-aged man, who needed his advice. He was a lawyer and looking very proud with the fact. His visit to the Idea Factory was connected with a client of his, who had a substantial amount of cash that needed to disappear suddenly for the time he was going to spend in prison. The bank robbery was a success; the bags were full of cash – each, weighing more than the seventy-kilo millstone around Sam's neck. The barrister did not like the idea he got at first. Not that it was not original, but he considered it as being way too bold, even for an unscrupulous man like him. Andir gave him the following advice: to ask a fellow lawyer to deposit the huge sum of money in the same bank that it was robbed from. The authorities would have simply not thought of looking there. There were plenty of solicitors, who could secure the legality of this operation on paper. Simple. The customer's fear that an involvement of a colleague of his would fail the operation was unjustified. It was widespread that lawyers, well, most of them, were prepared to sell their own mother for the right price.

Both ideas were identical, although the difference between dealing with money or a corpse was not so negligible. Andir was taking a full advantage of everything he had learnt in the Academy. Their tutor, an idea-consultant, First rank, taught them about what was the easiest way to hide something, so no one could ever find it. "You place it amongst its own kind!", was what he had told them. Not everyone in the audience managed to decipher his wisdom correctly at the time. Practice had proved, however, that this was the best solution. Hide cash where money was and a dead body – in the graveyard. Andir was going to offer the same solution every time he encountered a similar problem in the future. It always worked.

The next customer entered to meet the idea-consultant, Second rank, whose mind was clear and uncluttered. After that one came another one, and then, another one until the sunset put a close on the working day. When the sun disappeared completely behind the horizon, the gate would be demonstratively locked up in front of the people, queuing in the freezing cold. The next day – it would start all over again. The interesting start of the working day ended with some boring and totally predictable customers, who came for trivial solutions for their trivial problems. In the early afternoon, a visibly retired woman came along, who was dressed in a rather provocative way. Andir expected an intriguing turn to their conversation, but within minutes he realized that she was yet another woman, who could not accept the qualitative changes in her appearance, caused by the quantitative changes in her age. She wanted youth. The idea-consultant did not need that much time to convince her that there was not much she could do about this. His advice to her was that she should simply think that she was as young as she felt, demonstrate her youthful spirit as much as she could, ignoring anyone, who dared ridicule her for it. What the hell if people saw her as some crazy old dear, who behaved like a tipsy teenager. It would not be the first case, and besides, she really liked the idea she paid for. End of story!

The minute the suspended light bulb went out, the interrogation room ceased to exist until the next day. The idea-consultants would sneak out incognito along the icy narrow road, heading back to their homes. Depending on how well the road was cleared from the snow, Andir would get to his place just in time for his supper. The perfect supper was the one he was going to order over the phone from some good restaurant, or he would settle for the average result of cooking something himself. The lack of lunch break at work forced the consultants to have just two meals a day, which had an adverse effect on their stomachs. Andir found it very hard to get used to this downside of the job. In the first few months he experienced horrendous pains in his stomach that he had to conceal from his clients. To compensate for this food injustice, he included an extra mealtime just before he went to bed, usually at midnight.

The three-storey building that he lived was occupied by six idea-consultants. They knew each other, but never got together at any occasion. It was actually prohibited, in case they started to talk about their job. Their communication, at most, comprised of exchanged greetings at the start or at the end of the day. Should one run out of salt or sugar; they were better of popping out to the shops, instead of bothering their kind neighbors and colleagues. Half of the curriculum at the Academy was related to learning the best ways to come up with the right ideas and the other half was greatly devoted to teaching the consultants about the strict rules to follow and the way of conduct outside the Factory. What they could not do and why was drilled into their heads every day. The same rules applied to everyone. When Andir started his career in this rare field, he followed the regulations from day one. He never thought to break a rule, knowing he would be caught at once. It was easy. It was common for employees to do the opposite of what they were supposed to, on the sly, when no one saw them. That was not the case with the idea-consultants. They always got caught. More or less. This would happen during the annual tests, conducted by their seniors, when junior staff would pose as customers. If the consultants got exposed by the committee in doing something outside the rules, they simply had to say good bye to their working life at the Idea Factory. The newcomers, of the Third rank, who were inexperienced in hiding their mistakes, lost their job first. Those, of the Second rank, like Andir, were more skilled and had better self-control, so they usually passed the test if they made a minor error. Who would supervise the old dogs - the best consultants on the job? The regulation book stated that they applied control amongst themselves. Inevitably, this meant that the discipline, in their case, was much more liberal, in comparison to the lower ranks.

Of course, Andir was free to have social life outside the Idea Factory, as long as it did not involve any of his colleagues and he kept all work-related information confidential. This proved to be very difficult, because people recognized the idea-consultants from a mile and never missed the chance "accidentally" to present them with their problems, hoping to get a second opinion. Basically, people wanted from Andir to work extra hours for free and usually saw him as someone, who only dished out paid advice. This was quite a pity, but nothing much could be done to change it.

Aware of this open or not so evident attitude towards him, Andir was not under any illusions that he would ever get the chance to meet interesting people, who he could go out for a beer with after work, chat about sport, movies or music. People generally did this all the time, but never when a consultant was at their table. Very rarely some folks would treat THEM as regular guys and did not take advantage of their job position. Strangely enough, people, who did not need the services of the idea-consultants, formed an extremely tiny minority. Everyone had problems. They all complained and moaned about their lives. They always had the worst experience, the biggest problem, the most awful luck. But, oh, it was a miracle! In this tiresome crowd, there were people, who were actually content with what they had, or who were prepared to solve their own problems by relying on their own resourcefulness. Those were the ones that Andir was searching for, in the hope to put an end to his lonely existence and find friends, not users. So far, all his efforts to make friends had failed. Well, the situation was quite different for him a year ago, when he was one very happy idea-consultant. During this period he had a girlfriend, but she predictably left him not long after. Predictably it was, because it was really a great challenge for anyone to be in a relationship, if they had to watch every word, every move they made. This applied even when the topic of the conversation was something trivial like the weather or the price of food products. The code of conduct, imposed on the consultants in relation to their personal lives, proved to be a difficult test even for the most passionate love. The main and most important rule was to avoid sharing of any confidential information with loved ones. Hard to apply control over this, but still it was inevitably discovered if a consultant had been "singing" work-related stuff to his girlfriend, i.e. how his day had gone, etc. Few words, compliments, small talk and mainly listening, those were the things that the idea-consultants had to be satisfied with in their verbal communication with relatives and loved ones. They were prohibited of saying anything, when back at home, which would jeopardize their job. Life was not easy for those consultants, who had decided to tie the knot. At least they could compensate their hard family life with the huge salary they received. The amount they were rewarded was unrealistic, considering the hours work they put into. "Actually, the price of a good idea is inestimable", as proudly one of the most charismatic tutors at the Academy liked to say at every opportunity he got.

The warm meal was delivered a few minutes later, which caused Andir's stomach to anxiously rebel in a rumble that was louder than the Sam's whisper today. The delicious and nutritious food was divided into two uneven portions. The larger got consumed immediately, whereas the remaining part was to be eaten a few hours later. Andir had a big TV set, which he very rarely watched, however, because he had tons of literature to read, first, in order to improve his job skills. Well, he had read everything, at least, ten times, while he was still back at the Academy. Certain paragraphs he even knew by heart. Following, nonetheless, the principle that one could always learn something new, Andir just kept reading and reading the same old books and it was unlikely that he would have ever stopped. That evening, he was concentrating on reading about the different manipulative techniques, applied to the customers in the interrogation room. This activity only increased his desire to go to sleep that he almost forgot to eat the remaining part of his dinner. He quickly engulfed the food and fell asleep.

Andir was so used to his morning routine, which never caused him any mental stress. His preparation for work was so automated that he always managed to get to the Factory on time. Well, almost. The idea-consultants of all ranks happened to be late for work occasionally, due to bad weather. Often, the unique winter conditions made it impossible for any type of vehicle to move. People had to sit and wait at home or in their cars until the mesmerizing snowy tornados did not voluntarily ceased their endless one-way swirl. That day, there was not any such natural phenomenon on the cards; however, the road was very icy and slippery. Andir felt anxious on the soft leather seat behind the wheel, anticipating an out-of-control head-on with an oncoming car or hitting the road guardrail. The narrow road, he diverted to, led to the back entrance of the Idea Factory. Thus, the consultants arrived unnoticed by the clients, who were just beginning to get in line on the opposite side of the building. The staff was not to see the queue. The idea-consultants were not supposed to see the long string of folks, shivering with the cold, as the scene could have disturbed their ability to offer wise and helpful ideas. Ten minutes after Andir's arrival, he would be introduced to his first client. The lucky one. The one, who had managed to get there so early that he, did not have to wait for hours in the cold. It was bearable, when it did not snow and there was not a wind, but this happened quite rarely. The bitterly strong wintry wind would literarily penetrate through the clothes and body. People felt a sense of inevitability, as if the white death was around the corner.

The idea-consultants were regarded as smart, intelligent people, who were not deprived by a pinch of humanity. Despite that they were prohibited from showing their emotions, some of them did feel compassion towards the visitors, who were truly subjected to some weather extremes. Those, who were arriving last, of course waited the longest. The clients would be kindly invited to take a seat, but they did not always respond at once. People needed time to warm up and to realize that they were indoors, where they felt hot. Andir had a female client more than a year ago, who had underestimated the icy wind and had kept one of her hands unprotected from the cold. Indeed, she had got a truly sound idea for her serious problem, but in exchange she ended up with two of her fingers damaged for life. Well, everyone knew that people subjected themselves to all this of their own accord. From the very beginning, it was clear that the Idea Factory had its limited capacity. Some clients were given more time, as they required a thorough analysis of their problem, in order to receive the well-deserved and costly idea. Others got it after only a few minutes, but its quality was never jeopardized. The daily estimate of the approximate number of people, who would get in, was determined by three consultants, First rank.

The pine tree, which was thirty-meters high, was not any different from the rest of the trees around. It was distinct only with its dividing role - the person, standing next to it, was the last one that had a realistic chance to get in. The rest, queuing behind, were unlikely to succeed. The tree's special function was marked by several 5cm-wide lines. The pictogram resembled a zebra, according to some, where others thought of it as being an unfinished Native Indian totem. Everyone was aware of the tree, including the locals. Everyone knew about it. Every time the queue was formed in the morning, it was clear that it stretched way beyond the boundary tree. The optimists, who were standing just a few meters behind it hoped that they might get lucky, if the consultants speeded up the pace, but those in the line behind them – What could they possibly be waiting for? Hundred, two hundred - the number constantly increased. The next person would come and join the queue, fully aware that it was pointless, but somehow not grasping this fact. Their position in the line meant that they would manage to get in not any earlier than the following week, should the Factory was open for business continuously. The idea-consultants did not bother to oppose to people's stupidity outside the Factory. They had no power to do so. The pine tree showed the truth. Behind the tree, all that followed was a matter of good will, and plenty of it. Hope froze last.

The pathway, leading to the Idea Factory, was clear of people at the close of the working day. No person was expected to be around the pine tree. The new formation of the queue began every morning at 8 o'clock sharp. No one was supposed to be near the tree at this time. Physical force, applied in order to jump the queue, was prohibited. A young guy, an idea-consultant, Third rank, had to watch the people in the line from his watch room, which was situated a meter below the Factory roof. Whenever he noticed inappropriate conduct and infringement of the rules, he would make a detailed note of the culprit's description and then sent it on to the guards at the gate. The baddy never got admission into the premises. Sometimes, the security guards did not even wait for the person to reach the entrance. They simply removed the perpetrator from the queue. Well, very rarely someone would try to be clever and jump the queue – there would be two cases per year, if that! People fearfully waited and behaved themselves if they did not want to jeopardize their chance to get in. Pushing, kicking, swearing or nudging people's ribs with elbows was definitely not on. Candidates, who were born fortunate enough to be taller, proceeded faster with their bigger strides. Everyone, generally, took utmost care of keeping things cool, so nothing went wrong at the last minute, just outside the gate. The consequences of unseemly behavior were clear to everyone - there was simply no second chance for the blacklisted.

Elisabeth

The idea-consultant, Second rank, confidently waited in his seat. The expressionless face was a mandatory feature for those, working in the Factory. Andir's pokerfaced mask not only suited him immensely, but it looked as if he had acquired it at birth. He did not make unnecessary movements or gestures unless he really needed to. He rarely even blinked in case he missed something important, while examining clients' behavior. His breathing was controlled and noiseless. He never showed any emotions, just a hint of them, and he was always focused, removing all anxieties. The official dress code, adopted by the Factory staff, included a white shirt and black suit. The tie was considered a distracting accessory. Andir had to keep his appearance and look as subtle and unostentatious as possible. His shiny black shoes did not attract attention, either. Nevertheless, no matter how self-composed and professional he tried to appear, sometimes, his clients proved to be a real challenge for him. A challenge that he would find really hard to overcome. In the late afternoon, a very interesting customer entered the interrogation room. At first glance, the visitor seemed like an easy to read, even a little helpless opponent, but in effect, the person was the biggest nightmare for any idea-consultant – a child.

"Hello. What's your name?" Andir asked in the friendliest and the warmest way possible. The rules were clear and such familiarity was not encouraged, but the little girl was a special client, who deserved a personalized treatment.

"E-li-sa-beth." she spelled out her name, stressing on each syllable.

"Pretty name you have, Elisabeth. And, now, would you like to come and have a seat? Go on, don't be scared!"

"No!" the visitor made a sulky face and refused firmly. To emphasize her words, she stamped with her little foot and crossed her arms in front of her.

"Alright, Elisabeth. We can talk as we are, if you like, but when your little legs get tired, you'll come and sit down, won't you?"

"Hmm, yes."

"Elisabeth, you know why you've come here, don't you?" the little princess nodded a couple of times in agreement. "Good. You know where you are? This is the Idea Factory, where people come and I help them by giving them ideas. Do you want me to help you, too?"

"Hmm, yes."

"Very well, Elisabeth, because this is exactly what I think I'm going to do. Are you ready to sit down now? Come here! You can take off your jacket, because it is quite warm in the room, and when you leave you will put it on again, so you don't catch cold, yes?"

"Hmm, yes." the little girl slowly and hesitantly got closer and did exactly what the strange nice man had told her. She dropped her pink jacket on the floor and then, she put in quite an effort, in order to climb up on the big chair. She leaned forward, rested her small arms on the table and looked up at an angle that was bigger than 45 degrees. She stared at Andir. Her wide-open black eyes had no intention to move away from his face even for a second.

"Are you comfortable like this?"

"Hmm, yes."

"Betty, I imagine this is how your friends call you?"

"My name is Elisabeth." the young visitor felt rather upset, when her pretty name was shortened and she sulked again.

"Alright, Elisabeth. I'm sorry! I promise I won't make the same mistake again. Elisabeth, you will tell me why you're here, won't you? This is the first question I ask everyone, who's come to see me." the child nodded affirmatively. "Alright, Elisabeth. Let's have a little rest for a minute and then you're going to tell me why you've come here today, yes?" a silent agreement was again what the small child managed to express.

"How terrifying!" was the first thing that came to Andir's mind. This sentence began frantically knocking around in his skull. How could one analyze a child? This was a little person, who legally had very few rights. Across the world, minors depended entirely on their parents. However, everyone was equal once they set foot in the Idea Factory. Once the clients paid the required sum and waited patiently in line, they had the right to be served, when it was their turn. The consultants could not discriminate people for their age, etc.

Andir was not very keen on kids, especially teenagers, for obvious reasons. He was not any different, when young. Yes, he was the same hormonally confused person at that age. He was meeting the wrong people, went to inappropriate places. He thought he knew everything and frequently changed his views about the future. In his long working experience, he had encountered several young people in need of paid advice. More often than not, those clients were simply the spoiled brats of rich parents. There would be some, who had gone downhill and picked a life of crime. They truly wanted to change directions before it became too late. Totally regular and predictable customers they were. Never until that day, however, a five-six year old child had entered the interrogation room. So young! Her legs did not reach the floor and her head could be just about seen a few inches above the table. The little girl probably did not weigh more than a well-fed cat. What a day!

Andir tried to take no notice of her tender age and went ahead with his standard analysis, following the procedure by the book. Clothing. The little one was well dressed. Under her jacket, she had just taken off; she wore a woolly red jumper with a picture of purple smiley dinosaur on it. Her black leggings also suited the weather. The consultant noted that she had not waited too long out in the cold, because she had managed to get in well before lunchtime. She did not have a scarf and gloves. Neither she got a hat. Did she lose those on the way? And where did she come from? The town was quite far away to walk. This kid had either got lost or she had come with her parents, who had left her for a minute unsupervised. Then she probably picked the money accidentally from her mum's purse and then got in here. She might have thought that her parents were already inside. However, Elisabeth did not look distraught in the slightest and kids usually got very upset if they lost their loved ones

42

from sight even for a minute. Andir was on the wrong track, clearly. He did not finish his evaluation but instead, went back to the way she was dressed. The fact that she did not wear gloves and a scarf was obvious, whereas the reasons for this – not so much. If he checked her left pocket, he would have found that the winter accessories were right there, neatly put away before the little one was let in to see Andir. Most probably her fluffy warm hood replaced the need for a hat.

The next step of the observation involved Andir trying to make some decent conclusions about Elisabeth's character. Although, this seemed rather pointless. With adults, it was an easy task due to the fact that they had an established personality, whereas children, especially very young ones, were very hard to read. Or at least, their character was not fully developed. She was timid, but all kids were timid. She did react rather emphatically to the modification of her name, but most likely this was the way she felt about it. She was cute, but all children were cute. Her auburn straight hair playfully curved around her ears, but this observation hardly gave away any useful information. Neither did the charming freckles on her forehead and around the nose. She was well looked after, clearly, and did not come from a poor background. Nonetheless, this did not make any difference, either. She did not take notice of the mirror behind her, or of anything else in the interrogation room. She did not find all this interesting to her. There was no reason to find it interesting. What a dread, again!

The minute had passed long time. It was obvious that Elisabeth was not going to speak first. She was sitting quietly. She did not fidget on the chair. A few seconds before the minute had gone, she moved her little finger towards one of her nostrils. Probably, her parents had taught her that this was an unseemly behavior, especially when there were others to see, because she quickly stopped picking her little nose and looked down ashamed. The minute was up, but she was still staring at the floor under the table. Andir had to get her attention back, despite the rules stating that the client was supposed to answer the question without being reminded to do so. Actually, all this might be some sort of misunderstanding?

"Elisabeth, who did you come with here today?"

"With mummy." the little girl happily replied and then she fixed her eyes on the strange adult again.

"And where is she now? She is maybe outside, looking for you, yes?"

"Hmm, no."

"So she is not looking for you? Does mummy know that you're here?"

"Hmm, yes."

"And you're not lost, are you?"

"I'm not that small." she snapped at him ardently. She did not like Andir's suggestion at all.

"I understand, Elisabeth. Your mum's brought you here. And the money, did she give it to you? The money you paid the man at the entrance, to the right, behind the glass?" the idea-consultant simplified every word, but not because he doubted the girl's intelligence. She was just so small that she probably needed to stand on her toes to reach the counter-desk, where all clients paid for the consultants' services.

"Hmm, yes."

"Elisabeth, why are you here? Why did your mum bring you here, give you money and send you to see me? There must be a very good reason for this, yes?"

"Hmm, yes."

"Are you going to share it with me?"

"I want Tommy back. He's go-o-one…" in less than a second, her eyes filled with tears and she started crying. Her weeping was surprisingly soundless, but inconsolable and her waterworks could have easily filled a teacup within a minute.

"Alright, Elisabeth. I will help you find Tommy, but please, don't cry. Please, stop! Please!" the idea-consultant was fully aware that he was begging her and that, in other circumstances, this was an absolutely unacceptable conduct in the interrogation room. He had no choice, however, and had to resort to these extreme and desperate measures of counteraction in order to make her stop crying, as his unease about the situation was spiraling out of control and turning into panic.

"If I have to finish my job well, you should not cry. Besides, big girls don't cry, do they? How old are you?"

44

"Six and a half." she answered, snorting back as she felt her nose running again. The 'half' seemed to be important to her and Andir decided to use this to his advantage.

"Oh, you are big! And a half? That makes it almost seven. Come on now, stop crying and tell me all about Tommy! I'll help you find him. We are not going to cry anymore, are we?" she nodded and tried hard to cut down the waterworks. It looked like the tears were going to stop as quickly as they had started. After all, she wanted to find Tommy and this was a very strong motive. "Who is Tommy? Is he a friend of yours?"

"Hmm, yes." she confirmed, while wiping the last traces of her crocodile tears that were running down her cheeks.

"Elisabeth, if we want to find him, you need to tell me everything about him, yes?"

"Hmm, yes."

"Do you love him?"

"Hmm, yes, but he's go-one!" this question was a bad idea, considering that the kid burst into tears again.

"Elisabeth, don't cry! We can find Tommy only if you calm down, yes? Promise me that you're not going to cry anymore!" another nod in agreement followed. Andir thoughtfully waited about a minute for her to regain her composure and asked his next question, in the hope he would not cause the dam barriers, located in the corners of her watery eyes, to "break" again. "Your friend Tommy clearly is very close to your heart, isn't he?"

"Hmm, yes."

"Did he get lost?"

"Hmm, yes."

"And your mum and dad don't know where he is?"

"No." she replied in certainty that this was the truth.

"Elisabeth, when did you see Tommy last? Was it a few days ago, a week, a month, a few months?" the little girl nodded hesitantly on the third suggestion, unsure of the actual real answer, as she could not be aware of how long one month was. "So this means that you haven't seen Tommy for a while, doesn't it?"

"Hmm, yes." Andir hurried up with the next question, when he saw that she was about to start crying again.

"Elisabeth, maybe, Tommy has gone away for some time and he's just forgotten to let you know, yes?"

"I want Tommy back!" the child whined. Her eyes immediately filled up again, bursting with liquid, which, unfortunately, could only run downwards. The idea-consultant noticed what was about to happen and with a hasty voice, tried to persuade her in the happy end of the story with the dear lost friend.

"Elisabeth, we'll find him. We will find him! Everything will be alright and very soon, you and Tommy will play together again. We'll find him!"

It was evident that the approach had to be changed, as well as the type of questions, he asked. Andir decided that if he learned a little more about her and the place she came from, he would manage to get some helpful information about Tommy, too. The consultant believed that Tommy must be some neighbor kid she had been playing with and that he was not living there anymore. Why did her parents not succeed in thinking of some white lie about the whole thing? All parents were guilty of this. It happened all the time! They could have easily made up a story about how her little friend Tommy had to leave town with his mummy and daddy, because they were moving places. Then, they could have left her to come to terms with it for a few days and then find her new friends. Kids forget easily, especially, when there was a replacement at hand. Why, then, did her mother personally bring her to the Factory? Moreover, she did not mind spending the huge sum of money on her child. Couldn't the mother conjure up something about Tommy even if she was not aware of what really happened to him? It was all very strange, but the client was always right.

"Elisabeth, where do you live? You do know what town you live in, don't you?" she once again responded with delay, due to yet another 'portion' of tears. When the last trace was wiped out, her red eyes looked at the man, in despair, and she gave her answer, which was identical to almost all previous ones.

"Hmm, yes."

"Will you tell me its name?"

"Hmm, yes."

"What is it?"

"I don't remember." the child confessed without any qualms about her lack of knowledge.

"You don't remember the name of your town? Alright, it's not so important. Do you remember, then, if your mum drove for a long time before you got to the hill? Was it like an hour, two hours or longer?" she nodded at the last suggestion, the one that it revealed nothing.

"Elisabeth, Tommy lived in the same town, didn't he?"

"Hmm, yes."

"Did he live on your street or it was a different one?"

"Hmm, yes."

"Good. Then he was a neighbor of yours, yes?" his assumption about the neighbor-kid seemed to be the most likely one. Alas, the little stubborn devil did not agree.

"Hmm, no."

"But didn't you say you both lived on the same street?"

"Hmm, yes."

"Where did Tommy live, then?"

"At my home."

"At your home? So he was staying with you as a guest?"

"Hmm, no."

"What do you mean by 'no'? Is Tommy your little brother or cousin?"

"Hmm, no."

"Why did he live at your house, then?"

"I don't know." the child replied and shrugged. Poor her, she really had no idea.

Andir felt as if he was reaching a dead end. This was such a rare occasion for him. He was asking the right and most logical questions, but to no avail. She and Tommy lived in the same town, on the same street, but they were no neighbors. Fine, the boy lived at her home. That was possible. But he was not visiting, neither was he a relative of hers. So how? It looked like that the idea-consultant, Second rank, had been confronted with little Elisabeth's wild imagination. Tommy, her imaginary friend, the best friend she had... But how could an imaginary thing disappear? Why did her mother bring her here? What a nightmare! Andir felt like being left alone. It would have been great if the staring kid left for a minute or two. The rules did not permit this, however. Hang on, who was Tommy actually?

"Elisabeth, can you describe Tommy to me? What does he look like? Is he big?"

"Hmm, yes."

"Is he tall? How tall? Taller than you?"

"Hmm, no."

"Right, how tall, then? Can you show me?" Elisabeth stretched out her right hand to show Tommy's real height. This was exactly how tall was an average dog. At last, the identity of Tommy was revealed! Or maybe not?

"Elisabeth, Tommy is a dog, isn't he? Your best friend?"

"Hmm, no." she frowned, discarding Andir's theory at once.

"He is not? He is not a dog, nor is he a child, is he?"

"Hmm, no."

"And what creature is Tommy?"

"I don't know." the girl replied not because she did not know what Tommy was, but because she did not understand fully the meaning of the question.

"Elisabeth, I need to know everything about Tommy! Only then I can help you. You're going to tell me, aren't you?" despite him keeping his cool, Andir felt that he was just a step away from dropping his customer. This would have been the first ever instance of failure in his long working experience. They were called 'zero' clients and included every customer, who could not be helped by consultants of Second and Third rank. The payment was refunded and the clients were sent on to meet a consultant of First rank. There, for free, they got their idea, which could vary in quality and range from being a decent solution to some idiotic suggestion. The top ranks never failed. They knew everything and could do anything. Always!

"Hmm, yes."

"Who is Tommy?"

"My teddy bear."

"Your teddy bear? Tommy is a teddy bear? A soft toy?" Andir concealed swiftly his thrill from managing to discover the true identity of her missing friend. His face remained a mask and his voice did not quiver a smidge. In reality, however, he felt so moved as never before in his long career.

"Hmm, yes."

"Your teddy bear Tommy is missing and you don't know where he is, yes? Your mummy doesn't know, either, does she?"

"Hmm, no. I want To-o-mmy!" oops, it looked like she was about to start crying again.

"Elisabeth, don't start crying, please! You promised me, didn't you?" Andir reminded her, when he realized where everything was heading to. Then, he simply offered her the idea she had come for that day. "Elisabeth, I don't know where Tommy is, but what I know is where his little brother is. He wants to meet you and become your new best friend. Tommy's asked him to do this."

"Where is he?" her eyes lit.

"Your mummy knows where you can find him. When you go to her, ask her straight away about where Tommy's brother is. She'll remember." the subliminal message in the consultant's idea would be clear to anyone that was half intelligent. Hopefully, the mother was not an exception and she could decode the meaning of Andir's advice. When Elisabeth shares her marvelous news, the mum should simply go to the nearest toyshop and buy a teddy bear that looked like Tommy. Then, the parent had to apply some ingenuity and her very good acting skills to convince the child that the new toy was definitely Tommy's true brother, who had come especially for her to become her best friend and play together from then on, day and night. Simple or what? Well, it was all in the hands of the mother.

"Where is he?" the little girl was so excited that leaned out of her seat towards the only person that could help her.

"Your mummy will tell you. I can't. Elisabeth, our meeting has come to an end. I have to ask you to leave the room and go to your mum. You remember what you need to tell her, don't you? You just say: "Mummy, the man told me that Tommy's got a brother and you know where he is." Will you remember this?" Andir hoped the child would learn the line by heart. Even if she could not, the important thing was to remember the gist of his advice.

"Hmm, yes."

"You remembered everything, yes?"

"Hmm, yes." she nodded so excitedly the last two times she replied that Andir worried she might get vertigo. At least, he was convinced that she would manage to relay his advice correctly to her mother.

"Come on now, get yourself dressed and off you go, straight to your mummy, yes?

Her "Hmm, yes" followed as usual and then, Elisabeth happily did everything the nice man had told her to do. Then, she shot out like a bullet. She did not have time to shake hands with Andir on departure. She did not say 'good bye', either. This was not important. The best thing was that the job was done. Her a little bit toothless, for obvious reasons, smile lit her face and this was the last image Andir saw – a happy ending of the "crying saga" with a title "Elisabeth". Her excited grin managed to subdue the early feeling of discomfort and unease, the idea-consultant had at the start of their meeting. Yes. It was true that working with kids was the hardest job ever.

The biggest error, Andir made in his last case, were the too many suggestions he gave to his client. To be fair, the kid's answers were very brief, but this was no excuse for a consultant, Second rank. Not after so many years of experience, anyhow. He missed to divide the conversation into three stages – a mistake, for which he would have been shown the door at the Academy. He did speak to her like a child and although she was exactly that, it was considered as a discriminative practice. Moreover, the closed format of his questions prompted Elisabeth to reply automatically with 'yes' or 'no' – another big mistake. This approach prevented Andir from finding out who the real Tommy was. He was actually a panda. The story went as follows. The panda was given to her as a present for her second birthday. The toy, then, was slightly bigger than Elisabeth herself. It was a well-known fact that little children could become easily attached to things like toys or clothes. But with little Elisabeth, things went out of control, in that sense. She never let go of her little friend and carried him everywhere with her. Her parents decided that this severe dependency was becoming a problem. They found it abnormal for a child to be that obsessed with a simple black and white toy-panda. The mother was especially worried that Elisabeth would be dragging her pal with her, when she started school.

50

Teachers and other children's parents would undoubtedly consider her daughter as being a bit weird. She could not live with such a verdict, the public shame had to be avoided at all costs. The parents tried to prepare Elisabeth and explained that other children would not take their toys to school, but instead they were going to wait for them at home. The obstinate kid did not even want to hear about a scenario of separation. She cried hysterically, making her parents crazy. They had no choice but submit to her whims and let the toy be. The fight was unequal and bitter. They made every effort to persuade her, but Elisabeth never gave in. Her mate was forcefully taken off her hands for a few hours once, but the situation turned for the worse, as Elisabeth stopped eating. They gave her the toy back along with her favorite pancakes. She adored pancakes. Poor kid, she became enslaved by a toy. We are all prepared to do anything for our friends, right! The grownups were also amazed at her determination to guard her friendship with the toy-panda. Her father, too, tried to solve the problem. He did not want his child to be seen as having problems that needed the attention of a psychiatrist. Unlike his strong-headed wife, he resorted to reasoning with his little girl, but to no avail, however. He did not get even closer.

The trick, involving distracting her attention with alternative toys did not work either, because Tommy was still in sight. He was the center of her universe and this could not be changed. She held him so tight in her little arms that if he was a person, he would have been long hurt by then. Her parents wanted the best for their daughter, so they were on the verge of taking things into their hands. They had no other choice but to take her to a specialist. In this way, unfortunately, they had to admit that there was something wrong with her. What the hell! They had to do this. They attended a couple of appointments, however, she refused to talk about the problem. She never liked the man with the glasses, either. She told him nothing. She did not say a word, clutching to her toy.

Tommy was still having an adverse effect on Elisabeth. There was no light in the tunnel. Her mum and dad could not just sit and wait until she was fifteen and realize that the panda was nothing more than a toy. Finally, they resorted to the only radical solution that was left. The man in the house sneaked one night, while his child was asleep, and took away the panda into undisclosed direction. It was burnt. The following morning, there was the expected monstrous crying. Everyone thought that the grief would pass within a few days. They were right, but Elisabeth's determination to stop eating, soon made her end up in hospital. While there, hooked on a drip, someone mentioned the Idea Factory to her devastated mother. "A wonderful place, where one gets a solution to their problems. Without exception." One day after her release, Elisabeth, who was still refusing to put anything in her mouth, except for water, headed up North, together with her parents. They traveled through the night, so they get there first in the queue. Mummy and daddy took the time to explain to her, in the car, that the nice man in the big metal house would tell her where Tommy was and that he was going to answer all her questions. Before they "passed the ball" to the unsuspecting idea-consultant, they, too, had tried to flog to her the real tale about Tommy's fate of burning, as well as some ten made up stories. Elisabeth did not believe any of it. She had lost all faith and trust in her parents, because they were the ones, who had picked on her best friend. No one, but only they were to blame for all this. That was why Elisabeth accepted so eagerly Andir's idea, him – the stranger, whereas she ignored everything suggested by her family, who were supposed to stand by her from birth.

They arrived at dawn. Her father had an impressive physique, so without much effort, he managed to get into a favorable position, near the gate. Mother and daughter waited in the car, away from the cold. Although the rules stated that no one could step in and wait on behalf of the true candidate, when little Elisabeth came to replace her dad, gripped with the cold, neither the staff at the entrance, nor the people in the queue objected. He gave her the envelope with the cash and kissed her good bye, as if they were about to part for a very long time. He had also suffered in all this, though he did not show it.

Andir did not even suspect the true scale of the drama in this family, caused entirely by one toy-panda. Well, it was better this way. His main concern was that the client left pleased with her idea and that the crying had stopped. Despite that he did not follow the rules, he was determined that his actions were 100 per cent reasonable, in a professional sense. And at the end of the day, Andir also managed to learn something from the little girl. The mistakes he made during the interview with her taught him a valuable lesson that he could have never learned at the Academy. In a little while, the next customer was about to come in the interrogation room. Hopefully, he or she was not going to be a child. Hopefully!

John

Incidents rarely happened on the premises of the Factory. The despair, which was the driving force behind the decision to queue in minus temperatures, sometimes changed its nature all of sudden. From one extreme, like sobbing uncontrollably, people quickly took to the other extreme, in a space of a second they were bursting into hysterical laughter. Some of the desperate clients, however, crossed the line sometimes. If they were not happy with the expensive advice they had received, they resorted to mob law and tried to extort the right solution from the unhelpful and ignorant idea-consultant with their fists. Less than ten seconds after the screams of the poor consultant were heard, the security guards would barge in to prevent the budding of a fight in time. So far, all brawls came to a mere exchange of blows and the odd slap in the face. The regulations allowed for self-defense actions in these instances, so the attacked did not simply turn into a punching bag. The idea-consultants took full advantage of the possibility to strike back and despite that they did not aim at breaking the nose of the aggressor, this did happen several times.

Andir avoided violence and hoped to keep it that way in the future. He was capable of calming his customers down, so they felt secure and safe in his interrogation room. He never opposed to them in a direct way, but always acted tactfully and applied his diplomacy as much as he could. These exact skills had made him a very good idea-consultant, Second rank, but unfortunately, they did not save him from the hard smack on the cheek, a very unhappy fat female client of his gave him once. Even though, he was a young rookie at the time, the smack and her fingers imprint on his face were never to be forgotten. From that day onwards, he closely watched the movements of his customers' hands. He also observed very carefully the safe distance between him and them. The metal table was not that wide, so Andir always made sure he leaned back as far as he could. In that way, he remained out of reach. The consultant never allowed the visitor to walk behind him, even if this was meant to be done in a friendly manner.

Well, no matter how careful and alert one was, surprises were always possible. Even the most peaceful and open client could be as much of a potential threat as someone, who was the explosive type that was ready to jump on you at the first wrong look towards him. Aggression could be seen, first, in the eyes. Then, it would run down towards the hands and feet and turn them into a powerful weapon of destruction. Andir knew this very well, but that type of awareness did not help him much in his meeting with the next visitor. This person could have cut the marker pine tree down faster than anyone else in the queue.

The morning was not any different from the rest. It was all the same, only the date and the day of the week were inevitably new. It had snowed again – more than twenty centimeters. The snowplows had cleaned the roads in the night, but the job was done rather insufficiently. Andir was running late for work about half an hour. Finally he arrived at the Factory. Warmed up and ready, he had taken his usual position on the metal chair to wait for the customer to come in, like he did every other working day.

"Hello! Please have a seat!"

"Good Morning!" the visitor said and quickly did what he was asked.

"What is your name?"

"My name is John."

"Nice to meet you, John. My name is Andir, idea-consultant, Second rank, and today, I shall come up with an idea for you. Our conversation will go through three stages and each of them will start and finish, when I say so. In the final stage, you will receive the idea you have come for, no matter if you like it or not. Is that clear?"

"Yes, it is, Mr. Andir." fearfully replied the guest.

"Alright, then, we can start with the first stage. John, you need to explain, in detail, the reason that has brought you here today. But first, we shall pause for a minute and then you will begin with your answer about why you are here. Is that clear?"

"Yes, Mr. Andir, it is clear!"

"One minute!" the host said, indicating the countdown.

The big middle-aged man, who was weighing at least a hundred kilos, looked sad and troubled. The experienced idea-consultant noticed this first, however, he was aware that he should start his analysis with the way the client was dressed. A lumberjack. Andir was certain about the client's occupation, judging by the green working jacket, he was wearing. The logo of one of the biggest wood companies could be seen on his back and sleeves. Moreover, the company's nearest manufactory was only half an hour away from town. The smell of wood, coming from the guest, also confirmed Andir's assumption. The working trousers were green, too. They were made from hardware material, which protected the woodcutter from bloody incidents with machinery or sharp branches. As he was wearing his working gear, John must have just come from work, or he was taking a second shift, straight after his visit to the Idea Factory? Both considerations were equally possible because the operation of the wood processing facility was 24/7 during this time of the year. His brown hat was not designed for the winter conditions, but still, plenty of people wore those in minus twenty. The hat was not part of the guy's uniform, because the logo on the front was that of a popular car brand. Andir was not concerned about the gloves, as he noticed them, well-tuck in the man's right pocket. He wore steel-capped working boots, designed to protect his toes.

The idea-consultants carefully observed the client's clothes, in order to determine their social status. In this case, it looked like John was an ordinary worker with a fair wage, who probably did shift work. His weathered face hinted that he was predominantly working outdoors. His deep wrinkles around the eyes aged him by ten years. In reality, he was no older than 39. Andir was not trying to guess John's age. He simply knew that no one above forty worked outdoors in the wood industry. Once the woodcutters reached this age, they were replaced by their younger and physically stronger colleagues. The health and safety regulations in the field were strictly observed. John was clean-shaved, which was not typical for people, doing his job. Most loggers grew their beards not only because the facial hair protected them against the elements, but also for superstitious reasons. At the start of every season, they stopped shaving in belief that this would bring them luck and keep any incidents at bay. Those, however, happened regularly, and ranged from the odd bruise to leaving someone disabled for life. Fatalities also occurred, but fortunately, not in recent months.

The appearance of the customer was well analyzed, and all necessary information – successfully obtained. Next came his attitude and the way he behaved in the interrogation room. He looked like a good person, who had a grave problem. This was what Andir thought, based on John's nervousness and his open anxiety. He went near the metal chair, a little bit too slowly. He did not take off his coat, which was a sign of his unease. His hat remained in place, as well. He did not move, nor did he attempt to look around his new environment. The mirror that almost everyone else believed was hiding some anonymous spies, did not provoke his interest, either. He was looking down, somewhere under the table, avoiding any direct eye contact. Andir hoped, John would relax a little, because the more apprehensive he appeared to be, the harder it was going to be for the consultant to come up with his idea. John was aware that the minute was up. He knew he had to answer the question, but was too afraid to begin to speak.

"John, the minute has passed. Please, tell me why you are here! You must be honest with me, because if you don't speak the truth, you're simply lying to yourself. Is that clear?"

"It's clear, Mr. Andir." the client confirmed even more timidly.

"Please, answer the question!"

"Mr. Andir, my wife's left me. That's why I'm here. I want her back. I want us to be together again. Like before." John was still looking at the floor. He spoke in a very weak voice with somewhat dramatic connotation. It was unlikely that a big and strong man like him would start crying, but one could never know for sure.

"John, have you got anything to add before we proceed to the next stage?"

"No, that's it. I just want her back! Badly!"

"Alright, then. I think we can now get to the second stage of our conversation. John, tell me a bit about your relationship with your wife, from the time before you got married to the day of your split. First, how did you two meet?"

"She was my neighbor, Mr. Andir. We were childhood friends." the woodcutter stopped speaking and closed his eyes in attempt to go back in time and relive the happy memories of them being kids, who loved playing together from dawn till dusk.

"Please, continue!" Andir prompted him. He wanted to avoid unnecessary delays.

"After high school, she left to study in a different town. In a few years, she came back and we got together. I've always loved her. And I still do." the revelation was honored by another twenty seconds pause, when the man, very moved indeed, lifted his crestfallen head and put a sincere, but scarce smile on his face. "Then, she left me, Mr. Andir. She simply went. She didn't say why. She was just gone. She left me all alone." dark clouds laid on the troubled visitor's face, bringing indescribable sorrow in his eyes.

"I understand, John." Andir said with a tiny bout of sympathy, this time. He was not allowed to show any emotions in front of anyone in the interrogation room, but John deserved it, really. "Tell me, what was your relationship, while living together? Did you argue often? Have you ever parted, say, for a few months, for instance?"

"No, Mr. Andir. We were always together, every day. She was always with me. We got on beautifully. We were the perfect couple." the big strong man drifted again back to the past, so Andir quickly asked the next essential question.

"Where did you live?"

"First, we stayed at my parents' house, but later, we moved to a rented place of our own, just the two of us, together with my little dove…"

"What was your life like, when it was just the two of you? Did anything change in your relationship?"

"No, Mr. Andir. I was working, she was working, too. All day, we just worked. But I love her so much…" his eyes filled with tears unexpectedly quickly, like it happened with cute little Elisabeth. The difference was that he managed to apply control over breaking the "dam wall". Well, a couple of salty and watery deserters appeared on his face, but John swiftly wiped them off with his not so clean sleeve.

"I understand, John. And do you have any children together?"

"We don't have children. She didn't want any. I begged her many times and at the end, I gave up. She didn't want any!"

Interesting! His last words were uttered with open discontent, as if he was still very angry about her refusal to have an offspring together.

"How vital was it for you to have kids with her? It is possible that your differences on this exceptionally important matter made her leave! John, you never mentioned her name to me?"

"Mary. Her name is Mary, Mr. Andir. She did not go because of the issue with the children. I stopped raising the subject from the very beginning, when we were still living at my parents. My mum kept going on about it, as we were one big family. She was pushing me to try and convince Mary."

"I understand, John. I'd like to ask you a very important question and I expect a true answer from you. Have you ever hit her during an argument?"

"I've never laid a finger on her! Never!" the visitor cried out loud, as if he wanted to be heard by everyone in the building, so they believed him that this was the truth. When the vibrations of his voice echoed and quieted down, John looked up and fixed his eyes directly on the idea-consultant. Full of rage, he felt like tearing Andir into pieces, aware that this would not prove to be very hard. His nostrils flared. He was breathing rapidly. His tomato-red face was as much a sign of his inner fury as it indicated the effect of him being still in his coat.

"I understand, John. I did not mean to be provocative with my question, but I had to ask. Thank you for your honest answer." Andir's calm response concealed his fear. He shivered with terror. If he was a kid, he was definitely going to wet his pants in that moment. He could not remember when was the last time he felt so scared of a customer. In fact, he had never experienced such a terrible fear, caused by a client, before. "Let's continue, John. Why do you think Mary's left, since you have not had any major relationship crises? Why did she leave you? Do you have some reasonable explanation?"

"I don't know, Mr. Andir. I've been asking myself the same question. One day, I got back from work and she was gone. She did not leave a note. She did not phone. I went to talk with her sister, but she did not want to see me. I asked her mother, too. They just don't tell me where she is. The only thing I was told was that she was finally free from me." the client, who was ready to explode and splash the walls of the interrogation room with the consultant's blood a minute ago, now, shrank in the chair like a kitten. Poor man, he fell again into despair. He closed his eyes. He looked quite suicidal.

"I understand, John." Andir uttered, without compassion this time. The fright the lumberjack gave him a moment ago, killed any previous feelings of pity towards him. "Is there a chance that Mary's left you for another person? Maybe, she has been seeing someone secretly and has waited for the right time to go?"

"She is not a whore! You bastard...! My Mary is a good woman. She is not a whore!" the client stood up furious all of a sudden. He leaned over and slammed the table with both his heavy fists. This resulted in creating a dent in the metal flat surface. A timid sheep, a minute earlier, now he was a beast. The kitty turned into a lion! Or maybe, he showed the average cheetah in him and the 'King of the jungle' was yet to appear on the scene? The sound of the slams made Andir stop breathing, as if John had pressed the button, which controlled the heartbeat. The idea-consultant grew very pale. He felt that he could not move a single part of his body. He froze, trying to lean as far back as he could. Well, this could not possibly help him, because John's calloused hands were able to reach him. At the Academy he was taught that he had two options in cases like this. He could try to calm John down and carry on with the task or he had the choice to call as loud as he could for the security guards and put an end to the meeting prematurely before it was too late. His professionalism won.

"I didn't say this, John. Please, calm down. Please, sit down! You need to understand that my questions are free of any personal suggestions. Their purpose is to help me come up with the best idea for you. If you really want to find your wife and get back together with her, I have to know the reason for your split. Do you understand that?"

"I am sorry, Mr. Andir, I... I just... She's not a whore. Not her!" the scary customer, who was obviously capable of changing his moods from one extreme to the other within a second, was now on the verge of tears. He was sincerely repentant, because of his burst out. John looked down again.

"I believe you, John. I never said she was! I don't know Mary in person and I wouldn't dare say anything derogatory about her. Now, are you ready to continue?"

"Yes, I am, Mr. Andir. But tell me what should I do, how can I get her back, where should I look for her? My Mary!"

"This will come in the final stage of our conversation. We are not there, yet. John, I'd like you to understand me correctly: even if you receive the best idea, which helps you get back together with your wife, you might lose her again should you repeat whatever made her leave you in the first place! Do you understand?"

"Yes, I do, Mr. Andir. But I never did anything. She just left. I got home, the door was unlocked and there was no one at home. She just wasn't there. She was gone. She was gone..." he repeated in whisper.

"You mentioned that you tried to find her through asking her relatives. Your attempts failed at the beginning. Have you contacted them again recently? They may be more responsive this time and share some information with you."

"I ask them every time I see them, Mr. Andir. They say nothing. To get rid of me, they just say that they don't know anything, but they do. They know where she is. I know that they know."

"John, have you thought about asking someone else to do this on your behalf, finding Mary?"

"Mr. Andir, I asked all her friends, but they told me nothing. All her female friends, I called them numerous times, but they knew nothing, either. They said they didn't know where she was..."

"John, what I meant was if you tried to hire a professional to find Mary. Wherever she is now, she must have left some tracks behind. Experienced detectives could discover those tracks."

"She's too far away, Mr. Andir." the client said with certainty.

"How do you know that she is far away?"

"I just feel it. She has run far away from me, Mr. Andir. If she was nearby, I would have felt it. We had a very strong connection and I always sensed her, but now, she's very far from me."

"I understand." Andir agreed, because he realized for sure that his client was not right in the head. However, the payment had been made and he was obliged to come up with an idea. "John, my next question is a bit sensitive, so please, be aware that I don't mean to make you uncomfortable by it. May I ask you about your personal life after Mary's left you?"

"Yes, Mr. Andir, you may ask. I don' mind. I'm sorry about before, but I just haven't seen her for so long…"

"Don't worry about it, John. Tell me, after Mary, have you ever met a woman that you like and that you've felt you could have a relationship with? Have you thought about moving on?"

"What relationship? I love Mary, my Mary, and when I find her, she'll be with me again. We'll be together forever!" His rage was growing again, like tsunami waves, which were inevitably heading towards the 'low shores' of the consultant's position.

"Of course, John, I don't doubt your love for her, but still, have you seen a woman recently that you like? The way she looks, I mean!"

"I have, Mr. Andir, but I haven't seen anyone better looking than my Mary."

"I understand, John."

"Mr. Andir, when are you going to tell me where to find my Mary? You do know where I should look for her, don't you?"

"John, be patient! We are coming to the end of the second stage and then during the third one, I shall tell you the idea you have come for, here, at the Idea Factory. Just a few more additional and clarifying questions, please! When did Mary leave you? According to your words, it sounds like it wasn't that long ago?"

"It happened four years ago, but for me, the time has passed in a flash. I still call her name every day I get home from work. I expect her to appear and meet me, then, tell me that dinner is ready and that she's been thinking all day of me like I have of her. Hope is what I've got left, Mr. Andir."

"Four years is not a short period, after all, John."

"As you know, Mr. Andir, time is relative. For me, it's been just like four seconds."

"I understand." Andir agreed, although he did not, in reality. Deep down in himself, he believed that all this was simply nonsense. "Let's say you find Mary, what will be the first thing you're going to do? Your first reaction?"

61

"I'll give her a hug, kiss her and I'll take her home, Mr. Andir, where she belongs. With me. My Mary should be with me, at my home."

"That's right, John. Excuse me, but I need to go out for a minute. When I come back, we'll continue our conversation. I won't be long." Andir stood up and calmly left his interrogation room. This action indicated that he had completely capitulated, due to his very unstable client, considering that leaving the room was absolutely prohibited. Exceptions were allowed only when consultants had serious grounds and they feared that their physical health was under threat. Actually, there were several scary moments during the interview, but a real danger to Andir's life was about to arise, when John heard his idea. The idea, which had cost him a few monthly salaries and that he, relied on getting Mary back. Andir went back to his client, after he had warned the guards to stay alert. They were only waiting to hear the code word before barging in to take the crazy man out and prevent anything bad happening to the idea-consultant. The code word was trivial – he had to call out <HELP> as loud as he could.

"John, I think it's time for the final part of our interesting meeting. Before I deliver my idea, I'd like you to know that I'll try my best to explain in detail my reasons behind it. Is that clear?"

"Yes, it is, Mr. Andir. Tell me how to get her back, please! My Mary!" his eyes were full of tears. They were tears of despair, which were waiting to become tears of triumph and victory. He was about to discover the 'how' and the 'where' of finding her. Mary was going to be with him again. Every day, every night. At least, this was John's dream.

"The idea is that you, John, need to move on and carry on with your life. You should find another woman. Now, I shall explain to the best of my ability why I believe that this is what you should do and I will…"

"You, bastard! I knew it! You don't want me to find her! You're against me, too. My Mary!" the raging customer jumped on his feet and there was a knife in his hand all of a sudden. It was a short-blade knife, but this was not going to stop him from cutting Andir into tiny pieces.

"John, calm down! Let's be reasonable! Please, calm down!" the idea-consultant sat still in his chair. The coward in him produced the panic appeal for the common sense to override his emotions. He did not shield himself with hands, as they were going to be the first thing to meet the sharp blade. He had to call out the code word. He needed to do this at once. But why was he not calling the guards? The woodcutter leaned over like a shot to reach for his victim, who cringed with his eyes closed. The consultant was afraid to watch his own slaughtering. Well, who would want to, in his shoes? The security guards were eavesdropping behind the door, when they heard John's anxious burst out. They put two and two together and barged in, without waiting for the code word. The client turned around to meet them, prepared to defend the occupied room with his life. There was no fight, because the rubber batons were much longer than his flip knife. He was still conscious, when they carried him out.

Andir could not move. He felt his body as stiff as a plank of wood. He felt his neck, as John had aimed at it in his deadly attempt to strike. Blood. His right hand was stained from the vital red liquid, which was coming from a small scratch. That was the aftermath – a tiny graze and an insignificant quantity of blood. Andir recovered slowly and asked the guard, who was still there, to leave the room. He wanted to be alone. The consultant pressed the red button.

Too late. That was the answer to why it all came to this. The meeting with the lonely, desperate and clearly mentally unstable customer had to finish much earlier than it did, well before the knife appeared in his hand and the consultant's life was endangered. It was Andir's fault for the delay. He was still in shock, realizing that his leg muscles felt like stone. Twenty minutes after the incident, when Andir started to feel his body back, he thought that it was time to re-evaluate the situation. He had to think about who John actually was and carefully consider how he should avoid risking his life, when dealing with customers in the future.

Family feuds were often the problematic topic of conversations between idea-consultants and clients. Men and women, although, it was predominantly women, who came with a story about their partner, making life a misery. They all wanted advice about how to change the unbearable status quo and turn the clock back, when love and respect reigned in their relationship. In most cases, Andir saw no light in the tunnel for the concerned, so he simply suggested that they all moved on and went their separate ways.

The woodcutter was very easy to read. His answers revealed his extreme attachment to his wife, to such an extent that he took her for granted. This was actually Mary's reason for leaving him so unexpectedly. Unexpectedly for him, of course, and not for her family and friends, who had been aware of the real picture all along. Andir wondered how long the poor woman had put up with being treated in this humiliating and possessive way by her husband. Most likely, he had banned her from going out without him, or talking to other men… She probably had to do everything he had told her to. John was totally mental. An experienced idea-consultant, Second rank, should have seen the obvious and put an end to the meeting earlier on. Anyone would have done this. John's sad and troubled face had made Andir feel sorry for him to an extent, but this was no excuse. The idea-consultants had to amputate their feelings at work. The only way they could help the customers with their problems was if they looked objectively from a neutral position, unaffected by their emotions. Andir failed. The truth was unpleasant. In his personal ranking list, this was his biggest failure since he had started work at the Idea Factory. The depressing verdict on his performance was the negative side of things. On the other hand, he would become a better idea-consultant in the future, having gained the experience from the situation. From now on, he would make no compromise if he felt his life was even slightly endangered. His sense of self-preservation grew immensely in a very short space of time. He was the most important! He mattered the most, not the client. The client came second. Always!

The minutes, the button had allowed for him, nearly passed and it was time for the next visitor to come and meet Andir – the man who almost turned into a murder victim a little while ago. The idea-consultant hurried to straighten himself up. He had to look perfect. The red stain on his collar, as well as the blood on his hand, were not going to help in any way in finding solution to the client's problem. On the contrary, these signs would have compromised Andir's position. The consultant cleaned the stains, left by John, he changed into a new white shirt, brought to him by one of the guards, and then, he felt ready again to do the job, he was being paid for.

64

Andir managed to go through the day somehow, without paying much attention to the facts. The cases were easy. At last, he finished work and it was time to go home, where he felt safe.

At the Academy, they emphasized on the wall, which every consultant had to put between him and the client on a daily basis. This worked on the same principle as the mirror in the interrogation room. Influence had to "flow" in one direction – from the consultant towards the customer. The wall prevented the reverse action. Thanks to this invisible barrier, Andir and his colleagues went back home after work, impervious to their clients' stories. The consultants had a sound sleep every night, regaining their strength for the following day, when they were going to rely on the wall again, during their meetings with strangers. Regularly one could notice slight cracks in the consultants' imaginary walls, but this was part of the work and not a reason to worry. The client would leave and it was then, when the wall was going under quick repair and become ready to meet the next customer in its full glory a few minutes later. The wall would withstand whatever came at it, until it needed another cosmetic stitching. The cycle repeated itself again and again and thus making the wall stronger and stronger.

John did not succeed in killing anyone, but he caused a substantial damage on Andir's wall. The harm was done and it would take some time before the wall resumed its previous pristine condition and form. The first evening of his second life, Andir spent trying very hard not to think about what happened. Nevertheless, this was exactly what he was thinking about. He was reliving the entire conversation with John, from the very beginning, pondering over every single word that had been said, every gesture or slight movement of his head, his arms, until the end, until the pivotal moment, when he nearly got killed. And then, everything would start all over again. Once more, nervous John entered the room and once more, he would start talking with a heartbreaking voice and a gloomy face about the woman, who left him – his Mary.

Andir could not sleep that night and this was apparent on the following morning. His eyes were red and he was yawning constantly. He arrived at work and as soon as he set foot in the well familiar room, the memories from yesterday flooded his head. He felt John's presence. The smell of wood had not dispersed from the previous day. Or did he imagine it? Waiting for the first lucky customer, who had been queuing the least in the cold, Andir was sick worried if his 'nightmare' was about to suddenly come in. When a woman, pleasant and kind looking, entered the room, he felt relieved. Later, when he was waiting for his second client, once again, he anticipated that it would be the woodcutter. This time he pictured him carrying an axe, and not the tiny flip knife, which he had smuggled, unnoticed, through the security check. It was a lady, who opened the door again. The same fear did not leave him until the end of the working day.

Two long and sleepless nights had passed, during which the symptoms of classic post-traumatic stress deepened progressively. Andir's terror that John was going to appear from nowhere to finish him off, disregarding the number of witnesses, extended beyond the Factory grounds. He was in panic even in public places. The possibility was real. The woodcutter was let to go free. As the incident was not considered that serious, the Police was not involved. The Factory followed a lenient procedure in cases like this. Not very often they resorted to the local law enforcement authorities. John was free to look for Mary, but he might have added Andir, too, on his search list? Who knows? The idea-consultant stopped going out after work. He delegated his shopping task to the porter and generously paid him for the service. Safely back at home, the first thing Andir did was to secure the two locks of his door. For better security, he would put a chair under the door handle. Despite living on the last floor, he would ensure his safety by locking the windows, too, should anyone decide to break an entry from the outside. During the night, when one could slice the silence with a knife and everyone was tucked in their beds, Andir would get up and meticulously check everything. At least three times, he would do his rounds in the apartment, in search for something out of the ordinary like a broken lock or a window, left ajar. Worst of all was that the more he was looking for a breach of his security, the more he was uncontrollably shaking with fear. Andir was intelligent enough to know that even if he discovered the door unlocked, despite the clear memory of him locking it twice before bedtime, it was going to be simply too late. There would not be time for escape, because HE would be already inside the apartment. John would be in, ready to finish him off, in a mercilessly bloody way, what he had only hinted at in the interrogation room.

Although everything, during the checks, was how the consultant had left it, his fears grew by the day. Andir not only doubled his midnight rounds in the flat, but he began to experience painful panic attacks on the motorway, when he happened to be stuck in a traffic jam. The reason was that his car was brought to a still and so he was. If John was driving behind, he could take advantage of the situation and simply get out of his car and go to Andir's vehicle to... The consultant had become addicted to constantly checking his rear-view mirrors, in which he would have only seen the approaching well familiar figure, unable to impede John's deadly intent.

A month later, Andir's mental state was in pieces and he thought it was best if he left. He considered leaving not only his job at the Factory, but the town, too, even the country. To run away was not a bad decision, as it would give him the sense of security he needed so much. If he was thousands of kilometers away from John, only then, he would have the luxury to live a peaceful life, unconcerned about his safety. Andir quickly got rid of the defeatist thought out of his head. This was not like him. He never gave up. He would cope with it all somehow. Unfortunately, the only people he could rely on for help, his colleagues, actually, were not allowed to interfere and assist. The regulations at the Idea Factory were clear: a consultant could not become a client. Never! The only way for this was if the employee left the job and joined the queue. However, once he had used the services of his colleague out of despair, the person could not return to his position and carry on working as an idea-consultant. It was absurd for Andir to hope that the customers could trust his judgment and ideas, if he had been waiting in line alongside them, not so long before.

Andir had to manage somehow by himself and move on. The methods, he could apply to overcome his post-traumatic stress, were quite simple and straightforward. "Don't think about the incident!"; "Focus your mind on positive thoughts, rather than negative!"; "Meditate!" The advices sounded too easy to do, but it took Andir more than six months until he felt reasonably comfortable to go to his local store and stop looking nervously in the rear-view mirrors literally every two seconds. Fortunately, during this long period of paranoia, Andir's customers did not prove to be a challenge, in a professional sense, so they all kept going home, very pleased with the ideas they got. There were not any aggressive and belligerent people amongst them, but Andir kept his level of cautiousness high. For instance, twice he nearly stopped the interviews with some agitated visitors. Nearly, because he realized in time that the customers were just a little nervous and did not intend to show any violence towards him.

John never appeared on the scene. Andir did not see him wandering about near his block of flats. When driving down the streets, none of the people behind or in front of him looked anything like the lumberjack. Now that the image of his ferocious face was no longer stuck in Andir's mind, the process of recovery of the invisible wall had speeded up immensely.

Richardson

Andir had regained his confidence. He managed to erase completely the constant fear and thus, he continued to be one of the best idea-consultants, Second rank, that had ever worked in the Idea Factory. Well, this was not going to last long. Richardson, a consultant from the highest echelon, wanted to meet him after sunset. There were two possible reasons for one to get invited by one of the best colleagues, First rank. The unpleasant option was Andir to get the news that he had failed the annual tests and the Factory no longer needed his services and it was time to part with the job. Actually, it was clear at the day of the exam, whether one had to pack his bags, but sometimes, the final decision of the committee was unnecessarily delayed. The second option was getting a promotion. As moving on the career ladder could be only upwards, at last, Andir might get the well-deserved chance to join the God's chosen club. There were no serious reasons to believe that he would be dismissed from work. The tests were hard as usual, but he passed them without any problems. Andir had not breached the rules, either, unless… unless, the incident with John had anything to do with it? However, nothing serious really happened then, and the rebuilt wall between them had remained intact, even after the actual life-threatening episode. Andir lied with an enviable grace about the way he felt after the attack, but did he really manage to fool the old dogs? The committee of three idea-consultants, First rank, had accepted his word with an open indifference. Richardson was present at the interrogation. He just watched everything. He was best at this. He was famous for his piercing look, which did not let anyone to deceive him. He detected the slightest twitch in someone's pupils and the tiniest treacherous change. The only option for those, who could not bear his penetrating eyes, was to look away. This was exactly what they did, although, in that way, people got entrapped in their own unconscious non-verbal behavior. They stared at the ceiling, fidgeted on the chair, scrutinized their own hands or other parts of their bodies. Those were all symptoms, which made it easier for them to get caught of lying.

Andir was walking fast towards his promotion, but he slowed down just a few meters from the door. A wave of fear went through his entire body. Richardson might have caught up with him at the test and realized that Andir's wall had been made into pieces. But why, then, would he want to meet the consultant now?

Andir was in two minds, when he entered the common interrogation room. This was how the consultants of the lower ranks called the large conference hall, where the torturous tests were held every year. Otherwise, after sunset, the room was used by the seniors for their discussions about the future of the Idea Factory. At their last working meeting, it was decided that Andir needed to be summoned. The time had come.

"Andir, sit down!" testily ordered Richardson, as soon as he saw his subordinate, waiting at the door.

"Do you mean here, Sir?" the visitor pointed at the wooden chair, which was clearly positioned for him to take. Andir was supposed to sit at the large oval table, a few inches away from the non-existent corner, should one imagined that the piece of furniture had been rectangular. Opposite the guest was the chair, placed for the host.

"Yes, there. Give me a minute to put these documents away and we'll start with you."

This meeting, too, was starting with the mandatory minute of silence that preceded the first stage with every client. Well, Andir was not confronted with a customer. It could be considered that it was the other way round. However, he could take advantage of the delay in their conversation and submit the host to his analysis. The idea-consultant was very well aware that his endeavor would prove impossible, but he felt he should utilize the free minute somehow.

The smart super expensive suit was of much higher quality than the one, Andir was wearing. There was a slight luster to the dark colored material that made the garment uniquely fashionable, but at the same time, it carried the air of some classical models. The shirt cost the same as ten of Andir's shirts, at least. The black shoes were also terribly expensive, despite their plain look. The short and reasonable conclusion that one could make was that Richardson was an old snob. Was this a big deal? Not really, as there were many others like him. It was not a secret that the rest of his colleagues in rank also liked pricey gear and regularly threw piles of cash away, which often exceeded the money that top models would spend on their several hours long shopping tours. Someone petty would ask if all the consultants had to wear the same black suits, black shoes and a white shirt with no tie, why then, did the best of them need to spend a fortune, when the end result was pretty much the same? The suit might be unique to touch, but the consultants did not touch each other. The material might have been imported from the other end of the world, where, in some small nondescript factory, young women slaved away for twelve hours a day, in order to produce the hand-made fabric... But did this matter to anyone? The leather shoes, made from the skin of some almost extinct animal, would have impressed only people, who were interested in the story behind the origin of their unique raw material. If you were unfamiliar with that story, even if you tread on the toes of the person, who wore them, without saying sorry to him, your conscience would still remain clear. You had treaded on some black shoes, so what? The shirts – they were not even worth talking about! Who would notice the difference, if you had one hundred clean white shirts, which you changed daily, even if they were a famous brand and made from expensive material? "No one!" would be the answer, of course! Black was black and white was white. The poor small-minded person, who dared asking pointless questions would be shut up at once with the following answer: "Because they did not care and they could simply afford it!"

70

Andir moved onto the physical characteristics of his subject of study. Richardson was tall and lean. His weight did not match his height and this made him look even taller than he was. His face was very gaunt, as if he suffered from some incurable disease that was about to finish him off. The hollowed cheeks made him look severely undernourished. Of course, these suggestions were far from the truth. Richardson was as strong as a horse, surprisingly tough and ate plenty of healthy and wholesome food. The consultant looked up at the guy's snow-white short hair. It was very thick, so the senior man probably had to trim it every two weeks. The eyes. The essence of the idea-consultant, First rank, was hidden in those eyes. That person was capable of beating his toughest and most experienced colleagues and could conjure up an idea for the hardest and most unsolvable problem. As the eyes are the window to one's soul, it meant that Richardson's eyes, being blue, permeated plenty of light. Yes, they were unrealistically blue. One could easily compare them to precious stones or crystals.

Andir left Richardson's main weapon alone and carried on hesitantly with analyzing his personality traits. How could he see through his character, though? Where should he start from? Should he begin with the only fact he had heard about him? Yes, he was an authoritative man, with an enormous ego, who did not put up with being criticized. But this was a well-known piece of information. It made up the shell, but what was underneath, in the center? The problem, here, was that Andir tried to determine what Richardson was like, but he had never come across that type of personality in his long experience. People like him did not queue in line, nor would they ever do it in the future. Obviously, the task, he undertook, was unfeasible to solve. Andir was about to put a stop on his unfinished analysis, when the host, who had just completed his administrative chores, addressed him with an open hostility:

"Andir, you're not trying to analyze me, are you?" Richardson asked, sounding very offended, when he just settled down on his seat. His eyes immediately scanned Andir's body and soul. "I asked you to give me a minute and I did not expect from you that you will start analyzing me, as if you're at work. How dare you?"

"I didn't, Sir! I did not try to analyze you..." caught red-handed, Andir tried to lie, but he quickly had to correct his mistake, covering shoddily the fib. "Well, yes, I…I did put you to my analysis a little… When you said "a minute" and I thought I could make use of it as if I was with a customer. It's just a reflex, Sir. I'm sorry if I have…"

"I know, I know. Don't worry! Everyone does this." the idea-consultant, First rank, put Andir at ease, pleased with himself that his little provocation worked in the way, he wanted. "Andir, our job is full of clichés that often we cannot escape from. For instance, if I tell you that our meeting, today, will go through three stages, you will inevitably associate each part with those you have, when you are with a client, won't you?

"I think so, Sir!"

"Can you see how predictable you are, let along this mob, waiting outside? I'm telling you, Andir, people are far too easy to read!"

"Yes, that's right, Sir, but I don't think that there are no exceptions. Maybe, it is easier for you, but if we take into an account that you're an idea-consultant of First rank… Well, then, it is to be expected…"

"Nonsense!" Richardson snapped at him. "There's no difference between you and I, here. It is a piece of cake if only one finds the right approach towards the client. Anyway, I did not invite you here to talk about work."

"I suppose, you didn't, Sir."

"Andir, how long have you been working with us?"

"Almost twenty years, Sir."

"Twenty, in four months. I've checked the records about when you were sent to us from the Academy."

"And four days, Sir, to be precise! Four months and four days."

"Whatever!" Richardson uttered, leaving Andir's time specification totally unheeded. "Twenty years is a long time, Andir. How do you feel after such a long period of offering ideas?"

The consultant, Second rank, doubted that his host was even remotely interested in the way he felt, but he was obliged to give him an honest answer.

"Good, Sir! I like my job and I want to keep doing it!"

"You are scared that I'm going to fire you today, aren't you?" his shifty smile indicated that the question was purely rhetorical.

"Actually, the thought crossed my mind before I came in, Sir, but, then, I don't believe I deserve to be dismissed. I'm conscientious at work and I always observe the rules." Andir said totally unfazed. He did not even tremble. If he did, he would have been caught straight away.

"That's correct. You're a good idea-consultant and you've been passing all the tests without a hitch. Talking about exams, what happened at the last one?"

"Not much to report, I passed it, Sir. You were present in the room, then, but you didn't ask me any additional questions, only the other two examiners asked me..."

"I remember, Andir, don't play up with me now!" the God amongst the idea-consultants raised his voice.

"I'm not playing up, Sir. I'm sorry if you took it this way, I just..."

"Why did you lie at the test? My colleagues missed to notice, but I got you! Why?" Richardson's lean and long body leaned over threateningly towards his victim. He did not intent to squeeze his neck with his scrawny hands. No, no, he did not mean to harm him in any way. Nevertheless, Andir felt an enormous pressure, as if a very heavy printing press, hanging over his head, was about to squash his body and fragile bones. He wanted to run away, but this would have been the end. He wanted to look away, but this would have been the same as admitting his total defeat. He felt like taking a deep breath and calm himself down, but this would have been taken the wrong way, too. At the end, he picked up his courage and collected his composure, as much as he could, and said calmly:

"I don't know what you mean, Sir! I was honest all the time."

"No, you were not, and you know it." the pressure grew. The smug look on the torturer's face did not give any scope for opposition.

"No, Sir, I don't. I really don't know what you mean!"

"Hmm, you're good. You're good now! But then, you slipped and I saw it!"

"Sir, I honestly don't understand what you're talking about..."

"Of course, you don't understand. This is the best strategy. Not to understand, and you know I can't catch you on this! Certainly, if my colleagues and I decide to put you under the grill, we'll succeed at the end, but this is not what I've called you here for!" Andir's self-control was enviable at this moment. He knew that he was being provoked and Richardson was calling his bluff – a trick that the examiners often deployed.

"I don't know what you're talking about, Sir. Please, let me know of your concerns…"

"Andir, I'm telling you again, don't play your little games with me! We both know what I'm talking about." Richardson was clearly getting vexed. In reality, he was intentionally overreacting for the sake of it, so the meeting with his colleague was more entertaining, and he was not actually angry with Andir.

"What about, Sir, I don't know?"

"Wow, you are brave! Ha-ha-ha! I like that! You will fit in well in your new position. Andir, before I tell you why I've asked you to come here, I want you to promise me something!"

"Promise what, Sir?"

"Don't you ever fail again!"

"But I haven't failed, Sir." the consultant made sure his wall looked intact and strong, but Richardson had obviously gone around it somehow. He knew?

"Promise me, Andir, otherwise you're not getting promoted!"

"Sir, I don't know how to promise something that…"

"I've not finished yet!" again, the severe tone of the order, together with the piercing and uncompromising look, cut short Andir's sentence. "Andir, the thing is that you're really the most suitable candidate. Your colleagues are well below your class. However, I want to be sure that if you're joining us, there won't be any more blunders in the future."

"I'll do my best not to…"

"No, no, no!" Richardson shook his head, strongly disagreeing with the choice of words. "It won't work this way! If you're allowing for the slightest possibility of failure from the start, then, sooner or later it will happen exactly that. Idea-consultants, First rank, do not make mistakes, EVER, simply because they are idea-consultants, First rank! Now, just promise me that you'll keep away from any blunders, so I can carry on with whatever's next. I don't want to waste any more time!"

"Thank you for my promotion, Sir, and I promise that I shall never breach the Factory's rules and that I'll do my job as best as before!" the newly promoted idea-consultant, First rank, recited like a school boy, as if he was stood in front of the classroom black board.

"Well done, Andir! You did not admit it! That is impressive! But if I pushed it a bit, sooner or later, you would've done it!"

"I doubt it, Sir. An innocent man could not admit something he has not done. And I refuse to be held responsible for someone else's sins."

"Well said! I like this. Do you have any other witty proverbs up your sleeve? A wise adage that I could ponder about while driving on my way home? Something that my hollow head could benefit from?" the idea-consultant First rank did not try to hide his irony and disdain. Richardson's conspicuous message was: "Don't patronize me! I am smarter and better than you and I will always be better! You're well below my league, you lying bastard!"

"No, I don't, Sir."

"Oh, well! If you're done with showering me with your wisdom, then, let me congratulate you properly with you joining the First ranks! Congratulations, Andir!" now was the time, according to the protocol, that the grinning newly promoted employee stood up and energetically shook hands with his benefactor. There could have been some warm hugs, should they have been good friends. However, nothing of the sort happened, because this was the Idea Factory, after all. This was a place, where any display of strong emotions was prohibited and where people did not shake hands under any circumstances. Never!

"Thank you very much, Sir." Andir said unmoved, trying to conceal any signs of contentment on his face.

"You know what follows now? You are now a Mentor. You remember yours, don't you?"

"Yes, Sir. Of course, I do."

"Did you hate him?"

"No, Sir, I did not have any bad feelings towards him. Because of him, I am what I am now! He helped me a lot and I'll be always grateful to him for what he did for me!"

"O-o-oh, how diplomatic of you! I'll throw up! You're good, Andir, but don't overdo it! If I see my Mentor on the street, I'd smash his face! Good job he's dead. I can't deny that he taught me this and that, but he was a bastard. Was yours nasty?"

"I wouldn't say this about mine, but he was sometimes too harsh with me. Well, I'm still thankful to him, because…"

"Silly nonsense! Stop with this slobbery!" Richardson snapped at Andir, as if he was a kid, who was about to eat his third ice cream without his parent's permission. "You know what's expected from you, when you go back to teach at the Academy, don't you?"

"Yes, Sir. I'm familiar with the procedure."

"Good. There is a slight change this time. The little brat, you're going to enlighten about what 'beast' an idea-consultant is, well, he's been already selected."

"But, Sir, I thought this will be left up to me? Don't I have to choose…?" Andir was clearly surprised. After all, this was a breach of the regulations.

"Have to, don't have to… all the same. The choice of a boy is clear. He's the best. We can't risk it if you take on some idiot with no potential or prospects, only so we need to get rid of him at the first tests."

"I understand, Sir! I shall work with whoever you've decided on."

"Are you going to make him suffer? Be honest!"

"I'll give my best shot to prepare the candidate in the best possible way!"

"Right on, you will make him suffer, then!" Richardson stressed on the last word in a kind of sadistic sounding way.

"You could say that, Sir, but it would be all done by the book. I consider to be quite strict should I detect any gaps in knowledge, regarding the rules. For me, observing them is of utmost priority."

"Andir, don't try to be better than you actually are. Especially, with me. As you'll soon find out, when you become a fully qualified idea-consultant, First rank, we are painfully honest, here! We don't have time for your evasive and cagey nonsense!"

"I'll do my best to fit in, Sir!"

"Ha-ha-ha! You do have a sense of humor. We say if you'll fit in or not. It's not up to you!"

76

"Yes, Sir, you're right…"

"Andir, the next step of your journey to the Promised Land, I came up with this myself, involves you taking part in the annual tests, sat by the consultants of Third rank. If you catch your guy did something stupid, no matter how small it was, then you'll get the job. They are young, so it will be easy for you!"

"I hope so, Sir. I, too, believe that I can do it!"

"In your first year, what were your mistakes like?"

"There weren't any, Sir. Nothing came up at the tests."

"Wow, what an achievement! Well, this was a long time ago. Now almost everyone's cheating. And so openly, too, that they look ridiculous! The youngsters, these days, are so overly confident. They think that they are cool know-it-alls."

"I guess so, Sir."

"Any questions?"

"No, Sir. I don't think so. I just want to thank you again for the honor of becoming one of you! For me, this is…"

"Stop with this licking my… Get out of here! And make the youngster suffer like your Mentor did to you. I guarantee you that the feeling is great. Go on, get out!" the host uttered again curtly, as he now felt like being freed by his new colleague's company no later than at once.

"Yes, Sir. See you soon, Sir."

Andir left the room as fast as he could. He wanted to avoid being prompted rudely to leave for the third time. Still under the influence of the meeting, he headed home, thinking about him. The charismatic and intelligent semi-God, who was not shy from showing his dictatorial and slightly sadistic tendencies. Richardson was great. One could not deny the obvious, even if they wanted to. Andir was so impressed by meeting the top consultant, First rank, that he could not yet fully appreciate his own promotion. The event had been overshadowed by the man, who delivered the good news. Andir preferred to think about him rather than start enjoying his deserved ascent on the career ladder. Richardson's persona had filled the consultant's mind. The crude language and the constant display of supremacy and power had made Andir feel insignificant, stupid and worthless – a type of emotions that he had long forgotten, he could experience again. His boss was direct, caustic and blunt. He knew when to ask a provocative question and when to make a joke. And his eyes! They had almost engulfed the idea-consultant, Second rank. Andir had looked straight into those eyes, aware that only in this way, he could conceal his shattered wall. Unfortunately, the tremendous efforts had cost him a bit. The terrible headache, he had, was not going away soon. Moreover, somehow he was feeling strangely restless, despite today's happy ending. Andir could not get any sleep that night. Different emotions like happiness, fear, worthlessness and loneliness took turns in his heart in alternating sequences.

One little thing remained ambiguous after this memorable heavyweight meeting. Was Richardson calling Andir's bluff? Or when at the tests, he did see through and found out about his nervous breakdown, caused by the psychotic client John?

The Academy

The evening before the newly promoted idea-consultant took on his role as a Mentor, he fell into a deep thought about his responsible position. He had not been there for a long time. He doubted that anything had changed that much. The Academy for idea-consultants had left a huge imprint on Andir's mind. He owed everything that he had achieved in life to the Academy and the people, who worked hard to prepare him for his vocation. He remembered clearly the turning point, when he left the school and started work at the Idea Factory, as if it was yesterday. He was missing his time at the Academy, but the rules were rules! As soon as his education there was completed, he was prohibited from ever going near the building, let along gaining an entry. The only exception was if he became a tutor to the newly enrolled students or a Mentor. Well, the second condition had become, now, a reality.

Andir was going, where he had not set foot for two decades. Emotions flooded, so he could not relax and fall asleep. While waiting for the natural recovery process to set into motion, the image of his own Mentor appeared in his head. He was a total nasty piece of work, who never stopped shouting at him during the entire period he was assigned to the job. Despite this, he had taught him a lot. The most important lesson, which Andir had to pass on to his apprentice, too, was that nothing was what it seemed. The prototypes, described in the thick textbooks, were too generalized, whereas the real clients were far too different. None resembled each other. They might have been similar in their personality, behavior. Their problems might have also had traits alike, but still, every costumer had their own idiosyncrasies. The Mentor taught him something else, too. Discipline. The good idea-consultant is disciplined towards his clients, as well as towards himself. Jumping from thought to thought, finally Andir drifted into the land of dreams.

The following morning, the Mentor, woke up fresh as a cucumber. It was unbearably cold outside. Something between wet snow and icy rain was falling from the sky. Andir hastily got prepared for work. He had a few minutes, so he waited until it was time to go in the right, but very different from the usual, direction. The Academy that he had to present himself before 10 o'clock, was located on the outskirts of town, just half an hour drive away. Andir truly hoped that his trainee would be receptive and open-minded, and not some brainless fellow. He was slightly worried that the candidate for a consultant, Third rank, was selected without his approval. He felt like going on a blind date. Being in the dark would either bring him a good surprise, or the experience would turn out to be a complete disaster. If they had not changed the procedure at the last minute, Andir would have very carefully selected the student himself, through conducting at least two interviews with each candidate before he made his final choice. Looking twenty years back, his Mentor did exactly this. He had invited Andir and three of his fellow students for some ten-minute preliminary meetings, where they were quizzed, so the tutor got to know them. Then, the son of a bitch treated them alright and asked fair questions. Just two of them passed and attended the second interview, where the questions were harder and far more provocative. At the end, it was Andir, who won over his colleague, who was as suitable for the job as him.

Saved from the same selection process, the young and ambitious Markot could not wait to meet his Mentor. The rumors about the harsh methods, the Mentors applied in the teaching process, were true, but they also possibly existed only to intimidate people in his shoes. Half an hour earlier, Markot was anxiously anticipating

Andir's arrival in the interrogation room. The place was identical to those in the Idea Factory, including the large mirror.

Andir arrived on time. He did not have any spare minutes to look around for memories' sake. The Academy had not changed in the slightest and the consultant headed directly towards the specialized wing of the building. He found the right room and went in. The Mentor had the good intentions not to subject his trainee to the grilling, he had experienced himself in the past, but when he saw the way the grinning youngster behaved from the very start, Andir rightfully reprimanded him.

"What are you doing, you idiot?" he shouted, when he noticed that the student had breached several basic rules. Firstly, he stood up to meet the Mentor. Secondly, he offered his handshake. Thirdly, he was wearing shoes that did not match his suit.

"Eh-r-r, I just…"

"You're a complete cretin!"

"I, I… don't know, I… am sorry, Mr.… Sir…" the youngster stuttered and his face turned totally red. It was much worse than if he saw his mother naked.

"Go back to your seat. I'll enter the room again. What are you staring at me for?"

"Yes, Sir!" the boy hurried back to his chair like a frightened rabbit. He was shaking. His mind was blurred with fear – a sure prerequisite that he was about to repeat one of the abovementioned mistakes.

"You can't be that stupid!" the Mentor, who had come in the room for a second time, shouted even louder. The little bastard had stood up again. What a nightmare!

"But, Sir! What now? I don't know…"

"You do know, of course! You very much well know! The idea-consultants always know. How are we going to do our job, if we tell the customers that we don't know? Sit down! Pull yourself together! You're not a baby, are you? Look at you, ready to start crying! Are you going to cry in front of a client?"

"No, Sir, I… I don't know, Sir…" the consultant-candidate was in shock. He sat down very slowly, as if he feared that his chair was covered in nails. Then, he rested his elbows despondently on the table and embraced his face with his hands. He longed for all this to have been just a bad dream. He wished to make everything to disappear with one move of his hand. He did so, but Andir was still sitting in front of him and carried on yelling.

"You, idiot, look at what you're doing! Sit back straight! Don't touch the table! Don't touch the table, I said! Put your hands, where they should be! Yes, there! Sit straight! Look at you, slouching like a jellyfish. Let's get your face, now, into some bearable shape! Go on, we need a happy face! More cheerful, but don't grin! You must look energetic, calm and cool!" the student tried hard to fulfill the whole list of instructions, but despite his tremendous efforts to change the beaten look on his face, he failed to achieve the desired result.

"Like this, Sir?"

"No! You look hideous, but we'll deal with it later. I'm not wasting my time with basic stuff that you should have learned at the Academy by now! You should have practiced all this there a thousand times at least, if not more. Take off your shoes!"

"Eh? To take off my shoes, Sir?"

"Not really, I'm just here for fun!" Andir sounded serious.

"Aaa-ah! Right, Sir, because for a moment, I thought that you really want me to..."

"Of course, I want you to take off your shoes!" the Mentor raised his voice again. For a second, Andir remembered the voice of his teacher, the way it echoed in his ears, and maybe that was why, he was yelling himself. As if he wanted to get his own back, it seemed. "Tomorrow, I want to see you in black shoes, plain black! Get rid of these... What's this dark-grey thing? I can't even pinpoint their color! You can throw them away!"

"Alright, Sir! Yes, Sir!" the obedient boy deprived his feet from the stability and warmth of his shoe ware. He threw them demonstratively in one of the corners behind him. Andir, however, still looked unhappy. He pulled a face like someone, whose son was supposed to pass his Math test with at least a 'B', but had actually failed. Here we go again! It was not good enough! Despite that the youngster had followed the order, he should not have left his shoes behind him, where the client could see them. If the customer was distracted in that way, this could jeopardize the entire process of creating a good idea for them. The Mentor decided to ignore this blunder, too, which he was certain, would not be the last. It was time to find out how everyone, who knew this ludicrous misunderstanding of a human being, called him, if they wanted to initiate a conversation.

"Name?"

"Markot, Sir! My name is Markot." the student fearfully introduced himself.

"My name is Andir, idea-consultant, Second, eh-r-r... actually... First rank. I shall be your Mentor this week. I will prepare you to the best of my ability for your future job in the Idea Factory. When you complete your training with me, you will, then, start building your career as an idea-consultant. All newcomers are employed in the Third ranks. I guess you are aware of this at least?"

"Yes, Sir, I am. I can't wait, Sir, to start work. It's a dream come true for me, to become your colleague and help all these people in need..."

"Cut this nonsense!" the Mentor snapped, subduing Markot's altruistic enthusiasm. Then, he carried on to the point. "Are you familiar with what's on the agenda? What have we got for today?"

"Yes, Sir, of course, I am. Today, we need to discuss the way the consultant should look and also, stage one, up to the minute, allocated for the analysis. Tomorrow, we'll have..."

"Tomorrow is for tomorrow. We're starting with your appearance and to add, with your idiotic behavior, as well. Why do you think I made you take off your shoes? It's not because I wonder if your feet smell, is it now?" Andir asked, ready to stand up and smack Markot in the face, should he had answered "Yes".

"No, Sir, that's not the reason, but when I think about it, I believe that you wanted me to take my shoes off, so..." While looking for the right words, the young tomfool obstinately began to examine the surface of the metal table – a sure sign that he did not have the slightest idea how to answer the question.

"Have you studied at the Academy at all? This is one of the first things they teach you!"

"Yes, Sir, I never missed a lecture, except for when I was ill, I had a high temperature and I didn't go twice, and..."

"I don't care whether you went to school or not. What I care about is why you don't know the basics! Your shoes don't match the rest of you clothes, which may result in distracting the customer.

82

Look around! Where are we? Is there anything in here that could distract someone's attention? Is there anything here that makes you wonder about its purpose, its origin, or why it's placed here and not over there? Is there?" While Andir was pointing randomly around the room, he felt that his adrenaline was rising badly and that this time, he really wanted to hit the half-baked youngster, sitting opposite him.

"No, Sir, there isn't anything, just the mirror behind you, but maybe…"

"We're not going to talk about the mirror now! The room is minimally plain and the consultant has to merge with its environment. If you wear a bright colorful shirt, instead of the mandatory white, half of the clients will start asking you about where you got it from and this won't help you in your quest of giving them a quality idea. You will just waste time. Valuable time, that is! Do you understand?"

"Yes, Sir, I think I do. I know all this, but I just got a little taken aback by you and switched off, and…"

"What else did you mess up? Why did I yell at you? Think about it. Come on, try a bit harder!" Andir calmed down a little. He wanted his trainee to realize his own mistakes and find the answers to his questions. He did not want to offer everything chewed and ready to him.

"Eh-r-r, I think, when you opened the door to come in and I didn't say… or actually, it wasn't that, eh-r-r… ah, yes, I forgot to greet you…"

"Hmm, and you think that was the problem, not saying "Good morning" to me? You are an idiot, indeed! You're an absolute idiot, a total nit!" the Mentor was furious again. He was screaming from the top of his voice. The unseemly words almost pierced the walls and could be heard by anyone the next door. His face grew red and he moved closer to his student. Andir really felt lake slapping him one with the back of his hand.

"I'm sorry, Sir, I… don't know, I don't know." Markot's eyes filled with tears. Any minute, the little girl in him was about to start crying. His emotional reaction only proved how unprepared he was and how much work Andir had, in order to polish his skills.

"Hey, calm down! One minute break! No talking!"

The Mentor needed a break not so he could subject the lazy student to his analysis, but to readjust himself. This was not him – shouting aggressively and dishing out insults. It was strange that Andir felt like hurting the boy physically. He wanted him to suffer and cause him pain. The idea-consultant had not hit anyone since when he was in 9th Grade. Then, a classmate smacked him in the face and he just gave one back. Andir was simply not a violent person. Worst of all was that he was kind of beginning to like it. He knew he could do whatever he wanted with Markot and yell at him throughout the entire meeting. He could shout at him on the next day, and on the day after next, until the end of the week's training, when the student would either commit suicide, or else – he would throttle his Mentor with his bare hands. He had to put a stop to the futile teaching methods and begin with the real constructive education. Andir was trying to reevaluate his behavior, not letting the disturbed young man out of sight. Markot had not made a single movement, since Andir told him to sit straight and get his hands off the table. His head was tilted slightly to the right, as if he had a stiff neck or something. His face was as downcast as before, despite his Mentor calling for an upbeat expression. The student reminded of a client in the greatest of despair, instead of having the idea-consultant's composed look. This had to be changed. The time was up.

"Look, relax a little. Don't sit so stiff!" the new good-hearted Mentor spoke this time.

"Right, Sir!" timidly answered Markot, still sitting like a statue. He was scared that if he moved, the bad Andir would return and yell again at him. And too right he was.

"I want you to listen to me very carefully. I'm going to tell you all the mistakes you made from the start. You should have known better, but since you made them, I better tell you exactly what you did. Most importantly, don't ever repeat them again! Is that clear?"

"Yes, Sir! It is, Mr. Andir."

"Don't Mr. Andir me! We always address the higher ranks by 'Sir'. You can only call them by their names, when you're off work, outside the Idea Factory. Do you understand?"

"Yes, Sir! I am sorry, Sir!"

"And stop apologizing for the hundredth time. You're here to learn, not to apologize!"

"Yes, Sir!"

"Markot, when I came in the room, you stood up to welcome me. Never, absolutely never, a consultant leaves his seat to take on the role of a friendly host. Do not remove your ass from the chair even if the Queen offers you the honors and comes for a visit. Is that clear?"

"Yes, Sir! It is, Sir!" the "soldier" said in a military style.

"Your next blunder involves your attempt for a handshake. The idea-consultant does not do this. We don't need any physical contact with the client, in order to do a good job. We do not offer our handshake at the beginning of the meeting, nor do we, at the end of it, when he or she is leaving. Do you understand?"

"Yes, Sir! To be honest, I know all this, but, Sir, you're not a client and I just thought, otherwise, if I knew that you're also like…"

"I'm not a client?" Andir asked, feeling quite offended. "Hey, boy, I'm here, because I could be any of the thousands very different clients, who have been through my interrogation room. Anyone, who comes to see you, has to be treated according to the rules. Your Mentor is no exception. The rules are for all. They do not differentiate between people."

"Yes, Sir, it is clear to me, now, but, if I knew that I should look on you as if you're a client, then I wouldn't have stood up and…"

"Cut the excuses now. It's too late. Just keep listening and don't repeat these sort of foolish mistakes ever again!"

"Right on, Sir. I shall try and I'll never…"

"Trying is not good enough. When you have a client, are you going to give him a good idea or you'll be trying to do this? Are you going to solve his problem or, again, you'll try? We do real work and we always complete it. We don't just try. Is that clear?"

"Yes, Sir! Absolutely clear, Sir!"

"Your next gaffe was that you displayed your emotions. Well, I'm partly responsible for this. First of all, you jumped from joy, when you saw me, as if I was Father Christmas, who brought you a full bag of presents. Then, I told you off and you turned into a little kid, lost in the big Zoo and asking every stranger: "Where's mummy?" You looked disgracefully pitiful, Markot! How is the client going to trust you, if you look that pathetic? How will you earn his trust? Where's the respect for the idea-consultant, in this situation? Does a whimpering and feeble consultant deserve any respect at all? Not really! And that is why no client, who's paid a huge some of money, will ever take your idea seriously. They will laugh at you in disdain. They will want to humiliate you. Some may feel sorry for you, when they see that before them is sitting someone even more pathetic than them." Markot began to feel the same way, as described by Andir. The Mentor saw through this and quickly tried to uplift the spirit of the "sinking boat" in front of him, before it became too late. "Self-control! That's the key, Markot. You should not allow for any emotions to go on display. Even if you want to cry, or jump from joy, you'll hold it in, until the customer leaves the room happy with his idea. Do you understand?"

"Yes, Sir! I will hide my feelings better from now on." Markot said in higher spirits.

"It's not a question of hiding it. We're not here to play hide-and-seek. You simply need to apply some self-control. Just don't react to the customer's behavior. Do not show them that they have affected you in any way, even if their story provokes some strong emotions. They have taught you about the wall, haven't they?"

"Yes, Sir! I know everything about the wall, but I was wondering, after all… if one day, it happens that I can't control myself and my wall is not strong enough. What should I do, then?"

"What did they tell you at the Academy? You remember, don't you?"

"They've told us, Sir, that the wall could never break, but if there's some damage to it, then, we should press the red button and take some time off to recover it. But still, if something happens and it gets quite damaged, then, what should I do?"

"That's not possible! There's no chance for this to happen. We always control ourselves in the presence of the customer, no matter how sad, tragic, terrible or funny their story is and whatever reason has brought him or her to us. It's their job to live through it, and ours is to offer a solution to their problem. The wall of the idea-consultant is always strong." Andir said with an absolute certainty, picturing, at the same time, the man, who managed to shatter his. What was John doing right now? Probably, he was looking for his Mary.

"But, Sir, this must be very hard, because, sometimes, you know…"

"No one is saying that it will be easy!" Andir interrupted him before hearing the end of yet another silly statement, born somewhere in Markot's confused mind. "If it was easy, then, anybody could become an idea-consultant. What matters is that you don't get afraid of the challenges you come across. There is no place for fear in our profession. You will learn with time, Markot! You'll get used to it!"

"I will learn, Sir!" the trainee repeated, soaking the enthusiasm of his wise Mentor.

"Well, those were your main mistakes. You made some minor ones, too, but we don't have time to discuss them now. I don't want any from tomorrow."

"Yes, Sir! No more mistakes, starting from tomorrow."

"When I come in the room, Markot, you should not move, or grin like a kid. Don't get all soppy, either, and the handshakes are totally out. Also, don't forget about some matching shoes."

"Yes, Sir, I won't be doing anything that I shouldn't, like I did today. If I only knew that you are like the client… I wouldn't have…" Markot stopped, as he remembered the request to cut out the excuses.

"We shall see. And now, I want to hear what you know about stage one, before the short pause of a minute."

"Sir, this is the time, when we need to meet our client. We introduce ourselves, informing the client about our rank and then, we ask him or her about his/her name. Then, we invite the client to have a seat. When we see the person is settled and ready, we ask about why they've come to the Factory. Of course, we note that the answer should be delivered to us after one minute. We must stress on the fact that the minute pause is mandatory and use this time to analyze the client and try to find out what sort of person he is…"

"What sort of person he is?" Andir repeated, as if the sentence made no logical sense to him. "Sometimes, a lifetime will not be enough, if you try to understand people. Get this out of your head, the idea that you will ever get the chance to fully understand anyone of your clients."

"Sir, actually, I didn't mean that we'll be able to understand the customer completely, but as much as we could, so it helps us to come up with an idea for them."

"This sounds a little more realistic. Now, carry on with the analysis."

"But it's not on our agenda for today…"

"It is now on, Markot." insisted Andir, who was very much aware that he could not receive a refusal.

"Alright, Sir! So, about the analysis, during the first stage, the consultant allocates one-minute pause, but beforehand, he finds out about what the reason behind the client's visit is, of course. In this short time of space, the idea-consultant needs to analyze the person's clothes and their distinctive physical characteristics, which could give him some useful information. In addition, the consultant should try to determine the person's personality, based on their consciously and unconsciously made movements and gestures. Well, based on their whole behavior, I mean."

"Good! So far so good! And how does the analysis end?"

"We finish the analysis with the firm belief that nothing is what it seems, with regards to our preliminary assumptions and first conclusions, we've made."

"That's right, Markot. You've been obviously good at cramming the lessons. But do you actually understand what you've just said?"

"Yes, Sir, I do! I can repeat it, if you like, Sir!"

"Don't bother! I don't need to hear the same nonsense twice. The truth, Markot, is that the analysis you make in this one minute may help you come up with a solution to the customer's problem well before you hear the reason that has brought that person to you. Do you understand what I'm talking about?"

"Yes, Sir, I see things the same. It's just that you explained it in a different way…"

"You're lying! You haven't understood a thing!" Andir felt that the rage from earlier, which was now a little subdued, had taken a starting position again and that it would crush the inexperienced little liar any moment now. He could not go back there again.

"But no, Sir, I…" Markot whined and pulled a fearful face, which did not look dissimilar to that people made, while anticipating a heavy whip on their bare back.

"How did I catch you, you wonder?" the Mentor asked and then started explaining calmly, like a teacher to a bewildered child. "It was easy. While talking, you looked down for a second, considering that you haven't stopped staring at me like a painting in a museum, since I set foot in this room. You hesitated and you sounded like making an excuse again. Markot, if you want to become a good idea-consultant, first and utmost, you should not try to lie to me. I will always catch you! This might not be that important now, because there are no consequences. But when you get caught at the annual test for breaching any of the basic rules, well, then, there's no return. All your efforts to get a job at the Idea Factory will go to waste. Don't be more stupid than you actually are! Do you understand now?"

"Yes, Sir! I'm sorry and to be honest, I did not fully get what you said before." Markot uttered with remorse.

"You are getting boring now with your apologies. I don't want to hear any 'sorry' from tomorrow!"

"Yes, Sir! There won't be any, Sir!"

"Let's go back to what I've told you about the analysis. Don't invest everything in it, but at the same time, remember that it is very important. If you ever have any doubts, when you analyze your client, then, trust your instincts. I know that my advice can't be found in the textbooks and that they have not taught you this at school, but my intuition about the person opposite me has helped me come up with hundreds of great ideas. Our work requires that sometimes we act, based on our instincts. Do you understand?"

"I think so, Sir, but how would I know that my instinct is not deceiving me?"

"You've got a head on your shoulders, don't you? Use your brain and find the best possible solution to your client's problem. I never told you to rely only on your instinct, but that it could help during the analysis. Now, do you understand me?"

"A-a-ah! Now, I do, yes, Sir! I absolutely got it!"

"Don't do this again, either! These broad 'a-a-ah'-s, you sound like you've discovered how to turn snow into gold, or something. Pull yourself together!"

"Yes, Sir, I…" Markot was about to say sorry again and make some more excuses. It was like two viruses that would prove very hard to beat out of him. At least he stopped in time, this time and said again briefly: "Yes, Sir!"

"What would you do if the customer does not begin speaking as expected, after the minute has passed?"

"Sir, I will ask the same question again and I'll wait for his answer."

"That's correct. And then, what's next?"

"Then, Sir, I'll ask the client whether I've been told about everything, regarding the reason behind their visit to the Factory and then, I will announce the end of the first stage." Markot made a sharp gesture, cutting through the air with his right hand. He had obviously forgotten about the ban to gesticulate.

"Don't do this!" Andir said in a near hysterical tone of voice, echoing his yelling from before.

"Sir, I'm sorry, I just wanted to show you..."

"Stop apologizing! Can't you remember what I've been saying to you? Tomorrow, when I come, don't you dare start waving your hands about! I shall personally cut them off!" Not that Andir would endeavor such a mutilating measure. Moreover, he was not allowed to harm his subordinates. Still, his authoritative warning had the desired effect.

"I won't, Sir! I won't do this again, Sir! No more blunders from tomorrow, I promise!"

"I'm tired of you now, Markot. We're done for today!"

"Right on, Sir, but can I just...?"

"No, you can't!" Andir did not want to hear a single word from his unprepared trainee. "Tomorrow, we'll start an hour earlier and don't even think to get here late. I don't care if there's a kilometer of snow outside!"

"Yes, Sir! I'll be on time, Sir! I promise..."

"Enough with the promises! It's rather annoying! Tomorrow, we'll emphasize on certain details from the second stage. We may cover it together with the third part. I haven't decided yet. The theoretical side of it is rather dry and has nothing to do with reality. The sooner you start working with my clients, the better! And now, leave the room, Markot!" the order had been uttered, but the person, who was supposed to follow it, clearly had some rock-hard objections against. The lack of confidence delayed the student slightly and then, he hesitantly explained his theory, the core of which was that the Mentor was wrong. Was that really possible?

"Sir, I don't think I should leave my own interrogation room. You said that I should treat you as if you were a real client and the idea-consultant cannot leave the client alone, unless there's a real danger to his physical health."

"Hmm, that's correct. You didn't slip, here. Well done! You did one thing right today!" the Mentor uttered, hiding skillfully his error. In effect, he had told the young man to leave by habit, because Andir felt quite comfortable during the interview, as if he was at home. Markot was right. Andir was supposed to leave, not him.

"Thank you, Sir! I'm trying! I'll be trying real hard from now on." his face lit, but the Mentor did not reprimand him for this, despite the fact that such happy expression was in breach with the rules. Andir felt a bit soft. At the end of the day, the boy was beginning to use his brain. And that was something.

"Tomorrow, 9 o'clock sharp! Don't be late and don't forget about the shoes, or I'll send you to look for new ones on bare feet."

"I won't forget, Sir!"

Andir stood up from his anchored metal chair and left the room rather disappointed. His debut role as a Mentor proved to be a failure, he believed. He had not imagined the day would go like this. Andir had expected much more from Markot or anyone else, who could have been sitting opposite to him. The level and quality of education might have dropped over the years. The theoretical part of the training was possibly offered in a less systematic way, in comparison to past years, but still, one should know the basics at least! The disastrous start of their interview indicated for some big gaps in the trainee's knowledge that would prove hard to make up for and fill eventually. Well, the promising end of the meeting was not much of an achievement, either. The boy still looked extremely inexperienced and naïve. It was very doubtful that any of his future clients would consider him to be a person of the necessary authority, required for the job. It would not work, basically. Andir wondered if he had been looking so not grown up, young and unsure about stuff, when he was Markot's age. His memory about that time was that he was the complete opposite of the young student. He was more mature, well-balanced and definitely better prepared, regarding each stage of the interview with a customer. Well, of course, he had made a couple of insignificant errors, too. Why, then, did Richardson say that the boy was the best, when, in effect, he was rather mediocre? Where did Markot hide his good skills, which were supposed to help him become potentially one of the best and professional idea-consultants? Andir even supposed that Richardson had joked with him, praising the candidate deliberately, so that the Mentor got the wrong picture about him. And when he later met Markot, Andir would realize the joke. However, there was no reason for the top consultant to do this, really. This would have been considered to be totally unprofessionally of him, to say the least. Moreover, the 'Old Dogs' never behaved unprofessionally. They were quite touchy about the subject, so no one of the lower ranks would ever dare doubt their responsible attitude, related to the work with the clients or with regards to their administrative duties in the management of the Idea Factory. The perfect functioning system only proved that they were highly professional. Andir tried to look at Richardson's choice on the student from every angle, but the only conclusion, he could make, was that his boss did not have the slightest idea about Markot's qualities and skills. He had obviously relied on whatever information he was given by the Academy's lecturers. He could trust them, of course.

The tutors were idea-consultants, First rank, who were lucky enough to practice the stress-free teaching profession, instead of dealing all day with people's problems. Once they had chosen their path, they were not allowed to go back and work at the Idea Factory. Of course, they did not want to do this, either. Anyone, who had managed to get a job at the Academy, stayed there for life. Their work was much easier, but the payment was as high as what people got in the Factory. The stern white-haired old men, all of them – over seventy years old, were teaching their students about the responsibilities of the idea-consultant, when talking with a client. They also explained the 'do-s' and 'don't-s' of life, outside the Factory. The lecturers talked about the general rules and simply about everything that the young consultants were required to know. However, they often missed to make it clear that the theory could not be always put into practice. Probably 95% of it could, but the other 5% were not to be underestimated. This was, where the Mentor had to take over. He was coming directly from the 'battle field', a field, littered with clients' problems and whose perfect ideas cleaned them up one by one. The Mentor had one week to finely tune the young fresh 'idea-instrument', so Markot – the bookworm, would turn into a fully qualified idea-consultant. Was this achievable at all?

The morning on the following day did not suggest at being any different from the rest. Andir had got up again earlier than he should, due to his perfect and pedantically working body clock, which had not got used to his new working schedule. It was unbearably cold again outside and it had snowed as much as it did on the previous day. He needed the same amount of time to cover the distance to the Academy – just over half an hour drive. On that note, Andir did not expect a significantly positive change in his student. Despite his promises for an error-free day, his Mentor was in great doubt about what was awaiting him. There would be mistakes, of course! Some new and even more foolish blunders than the day before could be predicted. The hesitant and strange looking trainee could not turn into a perfect and well-read idea-consultant overnight. Andir entered the interrogation room in anticipation of yet another intellectually mediocre encounter. He was rather led by his sense of duty and not so much of his eager wish to teach Markot. After all, he was a professional, who had a great respect for the rules.

"Good morning, Sir!" the young man in black shoes greeted, without moving from his chair. He did not smile, either. So far so good, or maybe not?

The Mentor did not answer straight away. He stopped a meter away from the closed door and nodded in discontent. He sat down, looking very disappointed. He wished he was wrong. He truly hoped that the possibility of Markot making the same basic mistakes was only in his imagination. Andir expected to see a potentially great idea-consultant. Markot wanted to become one, did he not?

"Markot, you're a hopeless case. Look at yourself. Is there anything that it's not quite right?"

"Sir, I'm not sure... I don't think that..."

"Yes, Markot, I agree with you that you don't think!"

"But, Sir, not that I don't..."

"I'll give you a clue. It's a small thing, but very noticeable. It just shows how scruffy you are and that you have not even made the effort with your appearance this morning! Hmm, now I see that there's more… How did I not notice yesterday? Maybe, I missed it, because I made you keep your hands under the table!" Andir spoke with utter indifference.

"But, Sir, I, I… What have I messed up again now, Sir?" Markot looked down and started scrutinizing the top part of his body. Ten seconds seemed to be enough for him to complete the brisk check. The trainee did not notice anything out of the ordinary, so he felt thoroughly bewildered, wondering about what Andir had in mind this time. The small faux pas from the day before had been polished. "He might want me to believe I've done something wrong and in reality, it is all good? I doubt it!"

"Do you know what's great about white shirts, Markot?"

"I'm not sure, Sir."

"Stains. Stains are very obvious and the one, next to your top button, can be seen from the air. How could you come here today, looking like this? What about your right sleeve? Do you see anything there?"

"One shirt cuff is missing, Sir." the student noted, showing that he could differentiate between left and right at least.

"There, you noticed it, too, at last!"

"Sir, I just didn't notice it this morning. I'm sorry, Sir. It won't happen again. Tomorrow, I'll be more careful and I'll be in a clean shirt with all the buttons in place, Sir, I promise…"

"Your promises are not worth much!" Andir raised his voice, interrupting his whining at the start. "You promised, yesterday, that you were not going to apologize constantly, as you look pathetic. Well, this is exactly what you're doing right now! Do you really think that I won't find yet another unforgivable mistake tomorrow? I doubt it, Markot! I also doubt that you will come even close to becoming a good idea-consultant! If I made a snowman, I'd train it easier than you! Do you know why? Do you?"

"No, Sir, I don't." Markot responded in despair.

"Because the snowman won't change its appearance; won't show me any emotions; won't lie to me; won't talk nonsense; won't wave around its arms unnecessarily and basically, it will do a load more stuff better than you! Do you understand?"

"Yes, Sir, you're right. I'm not good enough to become an idea-consultant. It won't work." Markot looked down in defeat, ready to leave the interrogation room and vacate the placement for someone else, who was much better and more suitable than him. This time, he gave up far too quickly and there was no time for tears.

"Don't you even think about giving up!" the idea-consultant, First rank, warned, in a quest to return the defeated student straight back to the battlefield. "If you do, this will be my failure, too, and unlike you, I don't like to lose. Do you like losing, Markot?"

"No, Sir, I don't, but you've said that I'm not good enough and I also think that..."

"It doesn't matter what I've said and what you think! What matters is the clients and the ideas we offer them. Sometimes, they insult us, they may swear at us, they want to hit us, but we don't care, because we know that we've done our job well. That's what matters. Your job is to think about how you're going to solve other people's problems, not yours. You serve your clients! They are the ones, who pay and provide the idea-consultants with the fat check. Do you understand, Markot?"

"Yes, Sir, I believe so."

"Good! Now, are you ready to listen to what I have to say?"

"Yes, Sir, I am!" the student sounded a bit more cheerful, but still in doubt, regarding his suitability for the job.

"We shall change substantially the training methods for you! I want you to do something. You will find it strange. You may not want to do it, but you'll have to. That's your last chance. Will you do it? Will you do it because I've asked you to and in the knowledge that it will help you become a better idea-consultant? You will turn into a new man. You'll be the new Markot, who knows how to deal with every problem. Will you do it? Tell me that you will!"

"Yes, Sir, I will! I will do it!" the young guy said courageously all of a sudden. Despite the fact that Andir said this in a moderately dramatic tone of voice, it still did the job of convincing the student.

"Take off your shoes."

"But, Sir, these are good today, aren't they?"

"Take off your shoes and don't make me repeat it anymore! Now, take off your trousers, your jacket, your shirt, everything but your pants. Don't forget the socks!" Markot fulfilled the order in no time, oblivious to what was to follow. "Do you know what temperature is outside?"

"Not sure, Sir. About minus five, or thereabout…"

"When I tell you, I want you to leave the room and head towards the emergency exit on the same floor. Take the external stairs, leading to the yard. When out, go and lie down in the snow. I want you to roll about for a bit and really feel the snow. Then, you'll stand up and stay still for one minute. Leave your watch here and just count till sixty. Markot, you'll be the snowman. When the time is up, come back here. Did you get all this?"

"Yes, Sir!"

"Go now."

The young man speeded out in a flash, leaving his Mentor by himself. It was not originally Andir's idea behind the method of eliminating extreme states of mind by making someone going through different extreme conditions. The anonymous idea possibly dated from centuries, but this did not diminish its effectiveness. Andir knew that by using this approach, Markot had his last opportunity to stop being Markot and begin to think like a real idea-consultant.

There were numerous rules and regulations at the Academy, which had to be observed by all, no matter if one was just a visitor, a long-term employee or a student. Any breach of conduct resulted in the immediate dismissal of the perpetrator. Some of the rules focused on the relationship between the Mentor and his student. The instructors had no right to jeopardize the trainees' physical health. A smack in the face was the maximum one could resort to, as it had a strong psychological effect and left no physical sign of what had happened. The burning red cheek would regain color within minutes, basically. Andir knew very well the 'do'-s and 'not-to-do'-s and he did not have any intentions to lay a finger on Markot, who was much younger and fitter than him. Besides, every idea-consultant was very much aware that it was ineffective to persuade people to do anything by force. Clients were also save from torture and suffering.

While waiting for his student to return frozen to death, Andir realized the true scale of the challenge he had just given to him. If anyone saw the almost naked young man, rolling about in the snow, the consequences would have been grave, indeed. Markot would end up leaving the Academy and lose the chance to ever get an employment at the Idea Factory. The Mentor that had made him turn into a snowman would get into trouble, too. Most likely his promotion would be cancelled. Andir could get into the First ranks, but until the week of training Markot did not pass and then, he had to spot a gaffe, made by a consultant, Third rank at the annual tests, the Mentor's new position was not secure. Andir suddenly decided he should get the snowman in as soon as possible and get him back to his human form. Well, he did not have to do anything, as the young man was just coming in.

Markot stood next the metal table with a frozen wince on his face, waiting to be praised for the job well done. He was shivering uncontrollably. His skin was quite red. His legs had grazes and cuts, caused by the energetic rolling about in the snow. The wound on his knee actually needed some medical attention. His arms had formed an embrace around his body, but it was unlikely that they could warm him up. Despite being very hot in the interrogation room, the minute Markot spent outside, like a real snowman, was enough for the cold to penetrate through his skin, then the muscles and right to his bones. Andir noticed the "battle" wounds, which proved that Markot was truly devoted to completing his mission. The Mentor did not feel sorry for him in the slightest, but proceeded directly to the most important question:

"Did anyone see you?"

"N-n-no, Sir-r-r!" the chattering of his teeth had almost stopped. Almost!

"Are you sure? You didn't bump into anyone in the corridor?"

"N-n-no, Sir-r-r, there was n-no one out there! We star-r-ted one hour-r earlier t-today."

"Yes, yes, that's true! Markot, what I've just asked you to do, can have an adverse effect on both of us! You know that, don't you?"

"I d-do, Sir-r! We've b-r-reached the rules, but when you said it would help me and I didn't have to think twice... I'll do anything to not disappoint you, Sir-r!"

"I'm glad to hear it, Markot! But this stays between you and I! Don't tell anyone! Deal?"

"Yes, Sir-r, of course! It's a deal. I won't tell a soul! Sir-r, may I ask you something?"

"Go on, what?" Andir uttered, still wondering if anyone could have seen his snowman. What if someone from the maintenance team… All day long, they clear the snow around the Academy. No. They didn't start until an hour later. Andir could not think of any other witnesses.

"Sir-r, would you tell me now, how this outing in the snow of mine will change me?" his eagerness to find out the answer was well concealed by his frozen expression on his face.

"Yes, Markot, it's simple, quite simple. I shall explain after you put your clothes on. Come on, dress and sit down." his half-frozen fingers and toes found the task rather challenging. The blood from the large cut on his leg was going to ruin his trousers, but Markot just followed the Mentor's instructions. Finally, he was ready and still shivering a little, settled in his seat. Andir spoke:

"Changes, Markot, happen every day. Some don't affect us that much, but others may prompt us to really think about stuff, about our lives, basically, about fundamental issues. You are not ready to become an idea-consultant, you are not prepared enough, your demeanor is simply not professional, but all this can be changed. From now on, every time you feel you are about to lose it, you know, get emotional or something, just remember exactly what you felt today outside. Don't hesitate to stop me if I say something wrong."

"Alright, Sir!"

"When you left the room, you were actually running, which together with the raised adrenalin from your anticipation of the unknown ahead, prevented you from feeling the cold at the beginning. The rolling in the snow has made the blood flowing through your veins more intense, too. But afterwards, Markot, you've stood up still pretending you are a snowman. I hope this was what happened and you did what you were told to do?"

"Yes, Sir!" the trainee uttered, prepared to swear to it, if needed.

"I bet the sixty seconds really dragged for you, ah?"

"Oh, they did, Sir, I nearly gave up at the end… But for you, Sir, I lasted the whole minute!"

"Markot, did you manage to have a little think, during this time, about the behavior you displayed in the interrogation room today and yesterday, about the mistakes you made?"

"No, Sir, I could not. I was so cold that my head was empty of any thoughts."

"That's right! You actually behaved more professionally outside, where you did not have to think or do anything, than you did most of the time in here. However, Markot, this does not mean that I want you to stop thinking altogether! Not at all! Apply everything you've learned at the Academy in your future work, so you can give the best possible idea that your client deserves. And when you feel you're losing it and your feelings are about to pour out in front of your client, or you feel like you're about to burst into tears, remember, then, the Markot in the cold today! This Markot, who was in control of his emotions, is the professional Markot! Do you understand?"

"Yes, Sir, I think so." the student replied, rubbing his injured knee. He could not ignore the throbbing pain.

"Every time you feel that you're losing control, remember the snowman. Markot, what has just happened outside will not make you the perfect idea-consultant overnight, but it's a good start. It's up to you, from now on, if you want to grow and evolve! You can only use the frozen snowman as a starting point and continue to improve your skills! Do you understand, Markot?"

"Yes, Sir, I do! I can do this! I know I can! I understand now everything, Sir!" he sounded far too confident, to the extent of self-deceiving himself. If nothing else came out of this, at least, by the end of his week of training, Markot would believe unconditionally that he could become a decent idea-consultant.

"I hope that's the case, Markot!" the Mentor paused, as to put an end to the "Snowman" topic, and then, he continued the conversation, following the agreed agenda. "We concluded stage one yesterday. The next two steps are far more important. Today, we will go through them and examine some of their specific points. Starting with stage two, what do you know about it?"

"Sir, during this phase, the idea-consultant asks the customer an array of questions, in order to collect as much information as possible about the problem, which has prompted the client to visit the Factory. We can divide the questions into three basic groups. Shall I describe them, Sir?"

"Yes, go ahead."

"The first group involves personal questions. We aim at finding out a little bit about the person, like where they live, what they do for a living, their marital status, what their political and religious views are..."

"No, Markot!" Andir interrupted abruptly. "We never talk directly about politics and religion with the client. Political and religious arguments have no place in the Factory. The consultant may ask questions, related to these issues, only if he is certain that they will not provoke a sensitive reaction. Do not forget this!"

"Yes, Sir, I won't!"

"Continue with the next two groups of questions, and be more succinct, please!"

"Yes, Sir, the second type of questions covers the "historical" side of the problem. We try to understand how, when and why the problem appeared. The final group of questions involve finding out the client's point of view with regards to the problem. Here, I mean, the client's direct and indirect part in the problematic situation, we need to find out whether the client has caused the problem or they may have been on the suffering end..."

"Markot, that's quite enough. I can see that you've learned your lesson, although, almost nothing of what you've mentioned is applied in practice. You are taught, in the Academy, some real clichés, like standardized questions, which sometimes are not in consistence with reality. The customers are always so different. The same question has a different meaning to, say; two different people and carries a different answer with a different value, inevitably. Why don't we just fire away a question, which directly aims at the target – the actual problem?"

"Sir, but I thought that the formal standard questions bring out the best answers?"

"Yes and no, Markot. Not always and this is the danger you may find yourself in, when you start working with real clients. You may ask one about their work, family and try to find out how they got into the problem situation, where you may find asking the next visitor the same questions is totally unnecessary! Simply, that client will need

100

to be asked different type of questions, so the first ones don't sound strange and out of place."

"What type do you mean, Sir, because I can't quite think of any?" Markot asked, fighting against his great desire to scratch his head, as this was what he always did, when he could not remember something.

"There isn't any specific type, they are just different, as different as the customer's needs. Everything is very individual and customized! Do you understand, Markot?"

"Yes, I do, Sir, I guess..."

"Let's move on to the third stage. I want to stop discussing the theoretical nonsense, now, and just get on with talking straight about the clients. From tomorrow, Markot, I'll be coming in this room as if I'm a client and not as your Mentor. I will be presenting you with a problem, which you need to solve by giving me your best idea. That is the Mentor's job, actually, to show the student what is all about in reality and how complex and interesting some of the cases can be. But first, tell me what you know about stage three in brief?"

"Sir, the third stage is the most important one, because this is when the idea-consultant delivers his idea and explains the customer his reasoning behind it. While defending our point, we also need to emphasize on the fact that our idea is unique. It will really help the client and that there is no other alternative."

"Markot, the third stage involves a lot more than just delivering the idea. This is the time, when the idea-consultant lays all his cards on the table. There is no place for mistakes. We don't have time for bad ideas, half-ideas or stupid and infeasible ideas! In the case if we really can't offer the client anything meaningful and helpful, then we could count them as so called 'zero' clients and refer them to a highest rank. This, however, will automatically jeopardize your own status, as it will inevitably bring doubts about your own skills and abilities. I have never had a 'zero' customer, although I have come close a few times."

"And how did you manage to get out of this situation, Sir?"

"You have heard about the 'flat' ideas, haven't you? You must have learned this, surely?"

"Yes, Sir, I have. In the theory of ideas, a flat idea is the one that is rigid and inflexible, it cannot be modified! We also have those that can be partially altered and the ones, which could be completely changed as long as the client follows its core principle."

"Well done, Markot! It looks like that you've got something in your head after all!"

"Thank you, Sir!" the wide grin on his face was a breach of the rules, but the Mentor missed to notice, as it was gone as quick as it appeared. Markot wiped the smile off his face by trying to remember his somber experience out in the cold and in this way, proving to himself that the theory of the 'snowman' is working. The old Markot would have fought off the grin much harder.

"So when you feel that things are not going well and you're unable to come up with an idea for the client, then you can offer him a 'flat' idea, which does not provoke any additional questions. At the same time, the idea should be quite standard, like a template that offers a scope for many interpretations, which could all fit the client's needs, because every one of them seems the right one. Do you understand?"

"No, Sir. What do you mean by giving them an idea that has many interpretations? Aren't we going to confuse the customer in this way?"

"The clients come more confused than you think. We do not add to their confusion, but we rather offer them some food for thought. I may present you with a similar client in the next few days, but let me describe you one of the most common examples from my experience. Say, you've reached the final stage and you still have no idea what to say to the customer. His problem is complex and his explanations and answers to your questions do not give you sufficient information. In situations like this, and believe me, they happen more often than you think, you just pause for half a minute. The client waits, keen to hear the idea, expecting, of course, the best possible solution for his problem. The time passes and you simply make your statement that the answer is that the customer needs to change his life. In its essence, this is a typical flat idea, because it's clear and requires no comment. You elaborate a bit further by saying that you are confident about the clients ability to find out for himself what to change about his life and how. This is exactly your point in the argument – the client knows the what, the when and the how. Do you understand, Markot?"

"Yes, Sir, I do now. But why, then, the client has bothered to come to us in the first place, if he is supposed to know all this?"

"Because we are people that can be trusted. We help everyone. The Factory has this special reputation and the clients trust the service it offers. Sometimes, the belief in the idea plays a bigger role than the actual idea itself. Do you understand?"

"Yes, Sir, I think I do." Markot looked as if he did, with his prominent frown – a standard indication of one being in deep thought.

"Markot, the most important thing is the client to be happy. If you are not convincing enough, then, it really doesn't matter if the idea is the best one for the client, or it is actually not that suitable for their problem. It is all down to you and your ability to convince and 'sell' the idea. Do you understand?"

"Yes, Sir, I do!"

"We could go on, discussing each stage of the process, but just talking won't make you a good idea-consultant. In the following days, you will find out in practice what the real job involves. I would like you to show me your confidence and assertiveness! Don't be afraid of anything and when you feel that things are getting slippery, just remember the snowman! He shows no emotions, always acts and thinks in the right way. You do remember what it was like outside, don't you?"

"Yes, Sir, I'll never forget it." Markot shivered again, as if his body was exposed again to temperatures below zero.

"Do you have any questions, as now it is your only chance to ask? Next time I will be a client of yours. Small talk will be inappropriate. Also, if you slip and address me as your Mentor, then we drop everything for the day and you just won't learn anything. I suppose you're aware of this, so watch it you don't slip!"

"Yes, Sir, I am. May I ask you one final question, about the mirror? We were taught at the Academy that if we need to, we could say that behind it, there is someone, close to the customer or related to his problem?"

"That's right, Markot, but this is a two-edged sword. I have to warn you; do not resort to this, unless you have exhausted all other options. Most clients stare at it all the time and wonder about who could be hiding on the other side. They feel anxious about it. I have to point, in that respect: a nervous client is way much harder to work with. I always say to them that there is no one behind the glass and no one is watching. By the way, this is the truth."

"But, Sir, there will be some situations, when we can use the 'mirror' to our advantage?" the trainee asked, certain that he was right. He even remembered that one of the most unpleasant tutors at the Academy had emphasized on the fact that the mirror had to be used from time to time.

"That's nonsense, actually! There's no need! The mirror, Markot, has not been well thought out and I just wonder sometimes why it has even been put in the interrogation room. It's up to you if you decide to use it to your advantage! Still, you need to be very careful. Do you understand?"

"Yes, Sir, I will be!"

"Well, we're done now!" Andir stood up, prepared to leave. "Get some good sleep and try to make less mistakes tomorrow. The new Markot may not be perfect, no one is, but whatever blunders we make, they should not prevent us from delivering our best ideas to the client. Don't you ever forget this!"

"Yes, Sir, I won't forget. You sound a bit like my father."

"Hmm, your father must be a wise man, then. You should listen to him more often."

"Yes, Sir, I do. He wanted me to get into the Academy."

"That is the best thing a young and intelligent man can do, really! You've done the right thing. What does your dad do?" Andir was curious to know. He supposed Markot was the son of a businessman, a doctor or an engineer.

"I can't tell you that, Sir, I'm not allowed." Markot sounded slightly apprehensive.

"Markot, I doubt very much that your father's occupation is classified information, but if you say so... That is your right and it's none of my business. I shall not ask about this anymore." Andir pretended he did not care. In reality, however, he was dying to find out, but managed to conceal his curiosity from Markot's naïve stare. He hoped that his harmless indifference would prompt the young man to tell him voluntarily about his father's paid occupation.

"Sir, if I tell you, please don't say a word to anyone about this!" the inexperienced student had swallowed the bait almost straight away, confirming the saying: "Three can keep a secret, only if two of them are dead."

"I won't, Markot, and I don't have a reason to do so! Don't worry!"

"I trust you, Sir, but my dad warned me that if I tell anyone about what he does for a living, they will be prejudiced about me. Any idea-consultant, he said, will look on me quite condescendingly, or with envy."

"Markot, I think your father's got carried away. Whatever his job is, I doubt very much, this can have such a profound effect on you. Sometimes, parents are so overprotective towards their children that they may have some unrealistic views."

"Sir, my father is the most realistic man I know. He is an idea-consultant, First rank of eighteen years." the Mentor could not be more surprised. This explained everything, namely, how the unsuitable candidate had managed to get to where he was and admitted in the Academy in the first place. But, there was one thing that did not add up?

"Markot, as far as I remember, the Factory cannot harbor relatives, even if they are distant cousins. When did they change the rules?"

"Sir, you are correct about this, but you see, I'm adopted, so he is not my biological father. Even my surname is different."

"Well, this says a lot. So if you had his surname, what would that be?"

"Richardson, Sir. But I've taken my mum's surname – Jennings."

"Richardson? You're Richardson's son?" Andir's jaw dropped with astonishment.

"Yes, Sir, I am. Oh, no! I shouldn't have told you this! Sir, please, this would not change the way you treat me, would it? I wouldn't like an easy ride because of who my father is. I just got the gist of things... Please, Sir!" Markot was swiftly interrupted by Andir.

"Don't worry, Markot! My determination to prepare you for your job in the best possible way is still the same. Your father had a point to prevent you from talking about him, however. Now, I have to go, Markot. I'll see you tomorrow."

"Yes, Sir, see you tomorrow."

Andir left the interrogation room, leaving Richardson's son in there rather than the clumsy young man from that morning.

"Clients"

The idea-consultants had no right to talk about their work. Everyone knew the rules, however, abiding them required some effort. Markot's Mentor had no problem to keep his mouth shut about what went on in the interrogation room. Some of his colleagues found it difficult to keep a secret. They felt like sharing stuff with their wives and close family, as they needed to get things off their chest. The test results of those consultants, who talked about their confidential work socially, forced them out immediately through the back door of the Factory. That would put an end to receiving a huge salary, although, with it, all restrictions would disappear, too. Beyond their Factory career, the former employees would have to observe only the general legislation, related to not disclosing any classified information. Andir did not care that much whether the idea-consultants prattled around about their clients. He felt apprehensive about Markot and his relationship with his father. The questions, which flooded his head, were hypothetical, but at the same time – very possible. "Would the young man call Daddy that night and tell him that his Mentor was aware of who he was? Would he share with him that the Mentor made a humiliating experiment with his student, which was not by the book? Would he also mention that the Mentor was rather rude and cruel during their first meeting and that he made Markot felt like an idiot? If he did say anything, he would breach the rules... But then, Richardson would never grass on his own son and he could easily hide the fact that he had been informed about all that during the tests."

Andir did not know what to do. The idea-consultant was very worried, because he could not think of anything. The rest of the day was devoted to finding the most delicate way out of this difficult situation. On one hand, if he took the role of some easy clients in the following days, so Markot had no problem with finding solutions for them, this would guarantee him his father's goodwill towards him, regarding the so much waited promotion. On the other hand, Andir wanted to show his trainee the vast diversity of clients and their unexpected problems that could have brought them to the Idea Factory. However, if Markot adhered to his "professional" manner as in so far, he would most likely slip, causing his snowman to melt in no time. Unhappy with himself, daddy's boy would immediately call his father and complain about the impossible clients he had to deal with. And of course, Andir simply had to say, "Good buy" to his promotion. Richardson was going to make sure of this. It was complicated situation, no doubt.

The Mentor did not like making any compromises. He was convinced that people, who resorted to them, would inevitably regret they did at a later date. Also the consultant was not one to complete jobs kind of half way. Well, in this instance, Andir intended to do exactly that. He had made his mind up! Some of the forthcoming theatrical performances were going to feel like a piece of cake, but some would definitely prove rather heavy and unbearable to deal with. "What the hell, whatever will be, will be!"

Following the logic that the best method was to gradually increase the level of difficulty of the tasks, on the following morning, Andir entered the interrogation room, dressed in a faded blue tracksuit and a long black coat. He also wore white trainers with stripes. The props were his own and matched the dress code of at least twenty customers that Andir had seen over the years. They started their conversation and Markot was doing very well. He did not show any emotions and observed the rules perfectly. Andir actually liked his working demeanor for a moment. The stages prolonged a bit, but this was a sign of the young guy applying attention to detail. He had clearly not grasped the concept of asking versatile questions. Nevertheless, the customer's problem was going to get wiped out by his idea at the final stage, even if it was not that original. The "client" did not play up, either. He answered the questions in a very straightforward way, meeting fully the consultant's expectations. Andir did not try to withhold any information. Actually he gave out more in his quest to facilitate Markot in coming up with the idea. Of course, there were some minor mistakes. The trainee felt very apprehensive, when he delivered his solution. He worried if it was good enough, as the last thing he wanted was to disappoint Andir. Well, not that the latter would give him any feedback. The good news was that in this moment of time, suddenly the "Snowman" lent a hand. Markot's face froze. He bared his chattering teeth... His arms straightened and thus, a few creases on his jacket smoothed down, too. He stretched his legs under the table. The situation was under control. The student did over elaborate on his idea, which was a slight mistake. He basically overdid it in his attempt to convince the client that this was the best possible solution to his problem. The average customer would have accepted the idea within a few minutes, but Markot thought otherwise. He protracted his rant, including three unnecessary comparisons and a totally out of place example. Andir kept his cool, but he nearly interjected to say that the client was well ready to leave and there was no need for all this. If Markot kept working at his rate – an hour and a half per client – he would have broke the record. Although, the idea-consultants were not imposed with time restrictions, it was standard for them to spend no more than 25-30 minutes with a customer. Exceptions were possible; some really heavy cases might have taken about an hour. Finally, the meeting finished. Andir left the room, pretending he really liked the idea. The consultant saw him off, looking composed and in self-control.

On the following day, the bad acting of the predictable client was going to be a distant memory. It was time for Andir to show his real creative side and performing skills.

Clients were often full of contradictions, which sometimes bordered insanity. The next client had definitely a screw loose. Dressed in exactly the same clothes like the previous day, Andir came in the interrogation room, prepared at all costs to show Markot how crazy one lunatic could be and how this could turn the meeting into his biggest nightmare.

The trainee approached his customer in the same way as the day before. Markot sounded confident, when he invited Andir to sit down and discuss the problem. The client, however, did not take a seat. He mumbled something under his nose and sniffled rather annoyingly. It seemed he definitely did not want to park himself on the metal chair, but kept striding up and down across the room. Markot asked him at least ten times to have a seat. The interviewer kept his cool throughout. Finally, the customer obliged, but he clearly showed no interest in the consultant's persona. He continued to mutter with a wild look in his eyes. Markot asked why the client had decided to come and when the minute for reflection was about to start, the crazy man questioned the purpose of the big glass. Andir's paranoid query intended to emphasize on how destabilizing the mirror could be, when the consultant was trying to do his job. Markot readily delivered his answer, but to no avail. The young guy actually had to explain about a hundred times that there was no one behind the glass. The customer seemingly accepted it, at last. Andir's idea was to really give him a very hard time. It was not over, yet. The minute was up and the client began with his explanation, which was so difficult to decipher. He repeated himself constantly and the words that came out simply did not make any sense. The client carried on muttering and his eyes were all over the place, but looking at Markot. Half an hour later, the problem was vaguely presented, giving a green light to moving on to stage two. The second part of the interview proved to be even more frustrating. The consultant had to ask each question more than once, where the answers came in a form of just one or two words. The muttering in between never ceased. The customer's mad behavior was "spiced up" with him ferociously gnawing at his bottom lip, as if he wanted to bite it off. But then he would think twice and get his tongue out, licking it with similar enthusiasm. At some point, the burbling made it clear to Markot that the customer was talking to someone, called Tommy or Tony, who was obviously there with them, in the room.

Andir's performance of the loony man did not help in the slightest Markot to do his job, as he would have liked to. He kept asking questions and every nonsensical answer only crushed him even more. He felt almost like giving up. Andir had managed to make him feel like giving up. Finally, Markot resorted to some desperate measures, when he realized that he could not reach the client in any way, let along find a solution to the problem. The trainee was ready to improvise. He was aware that the consultants followed a strict methodology and deviating from the rules was simply not recommended. Despite this, Markot decided that he should talk to Tony, if he wanted to help the mad man. The consultant looked in the same direction as the crazy guy and started asking the imaginary third person some questions. He pretended that he could hear some real answers, which he commented on readily. The brief conversation, which excluded Andir, lasted about five minutes. The Mentor could not believe his eyes! He could not imagine a worse and more ineffective approach. He considered the scene as a failure, to say the least, or a professional suicide, although, these words felt like an understatement, too. The son of one of the best idea-consultants was sitting in the interrogation room, behaving in a crazier way than his crazy client. He did not know what do, neither he knew how to solve the visitor's problem. He simply knew nothing. His very first encounter with someone, who was out of the ordinary, had managed to counteract Markot's entire academic education. Watching carefully his student unproductive behavior, Andir came to the same conclusion as he had made the very first day of meeting Markot: the boy was no good. There was no chance that he would change. It was impossible!

The Mentor changed tactics and facilitated Markot to come up with a solution to the client's problem. After all, the meeting of the three freaks had to come to an end at some point. It was only too bad that the student felt the alms offering. He realized that Andir could so easily break him. Although, he was let to "win", he could not hide his huge disappointment. Even the snowman could not help him in this moment. The Mentor noticed everything and this changed immediately his performance strategy in the following days. The remaining days of the week were going to be devoted to some pleasant one-man shows with a predictable happy ending. The scenarios were going to lack any negative exaggerations and unnecessary dramatics, for sure. Andir hoped to reinstate the positive belief in Markot, despite the fact that he would never become a great idea-consultant. Not ever!

The next customer, who was about to test Markot's abilities and skills, looked very much like Andir himself. He was dressed in a black suit and wore black shoes, too. The guy spoke softly in a calm and patronizing voice. When the minute of silence was up, the visitor started to talk about his biggest dilemma in his life. But there was something wrong! The person spoke as if he was a female client. Why was "he" talking about "her" husband? It took Markot a while to get this. Of course, it was the name that confused him! The visitor had introduced himself with a name that was suitable for both men and women. Nothing could stop Andir to take the role of a woman, despite being dressed as a man. It was actually advisable for the mentors to display an array of possibilities, including female customers, because in this way, the student would have the chance to encounter a different type of problems, which were unlikely to be presented by males, really. Markot was definitely going to benefit from his new assignment as long as he managed to define the problem and conjure up a good solution for it. The client, who did not resemble a woman in any way or form, offloaded tons of desperation straight onto the metal table. The case was rather mundane and the solution – alike. The troublesome personal relationships of women often ended up in divorce, due to their cheating husbands. Divorce was the only problem's solution that Markot had to somehow come up with after the three stages of the meeting with this young lady, who had been stuck at a major crossroad in her life. The student got his composure back quite quickly without the help of the "snowman". He was behaving by the book and within the acceptable thirty minutes, he managed to solve the problematic situation. Markot defended his idea brilliantly, which was a sign that he had regained some of his confidence that had been down beaten by the crazy man the previous day. The woman left the room with the idea of separating from her husband for good. She was going to see a lawyer about it straight away in the hope to get back to her status of a single lady.

The theater closed indefinitely after the successfully resolved case. Andir was not going to show up on the following day, even though his student was going to wait for him. In accordance with the rules, the Mentor had the right to miss a day from work without an excuse or an explanation. The real idea-consultant in him considered the final meeting unnecessary. His student would be the same with or without it. The Mentor had completed his job at the Academy and it was time for him to return to his real freezing to death clients, who were queuing all day long in the cold. Very soon the annual tests were going to begin – the final obstacle before Andir on his way to promotion. And meanwhile, Richardson's son would be making his first steps into his mediocre career as a consultant. The watchdog was right behind him.

Andir's return to his consultancy duties, leaving behind his mentorship job, was not a challenge for him whatsoever. He felt more at home in his interrogation room, in comparison to his own apartment. He had become a perfect machine for ideas, due to his 20-years experience. This machine did not need to be maintained, as it always worked without a hitch. Well, machines could get evolved or updated and Andir was no exception of this. Every idea-consultant would consciously strive towards getting promoted. The higher rank equaled more money, respect and power. Actually, money was not that important. The Third ranks were not so well paid, but to get to the Second level, it took only five years. One only had to pass the exam five consecutive times and that was it. The consultants, just a step away from the top ranks, would start dreaming about being invited to join the elite. It was up to the top idea-consultants to decide who should be invited and when into their ranks. Their decision was based entirely on subjective criteria, i.e. their personal impressions of the candidate during the tests. They would also take into consideration the number of 'zero' clients the nominee had ever had. Some years, no one got promoted. This was not down to lack of suitable contenders. The privileged simply wanted to remind their inferiors that it was not that easy for them to become part of the cream of the crop. Andir was the chosen one. He was so close to the top that he did not actually know what to expect. He did not doubt that it would be great, but there would be possibly some negative sides to it all. What if he did not feel comfortable in the company of the smug old dogs and he felt out of his depth? Or what about the administrative tasks, he might get loaded with, so he had to do overtime instead of going home after work and relax? Everything was possible!

◆ ◆ ◆

Similarly to the customers at the long queue, the staff was very much enthusiastic about the annual tests. Those, anticipating the exams the most, were the Third ranks, because even the tiniest error could cost them their job. The consultants' sleep would often get disturbed a few days before the day of the tests. No one was spared, regarding the sleepless nights, including those, who had been good at their job throughout the year. It was irrelevant whether they had breached a minor regulation or if the examiners had actually clocked any of their mistakes, they could still get kicked out. The random dismissal of a Third rank, even if there was not a valid reason for it, aimed to display the mighty position of the First ranks. The unfair retaliation had caused not one or two consultants with a great potential to lose their job at the Factory and become the unfortunate victims of a huge collective ego.

The exams for the Second ranks were slightly more predictable. One could still get the sack for no reason and thus, the career efforts they had made for years, to get stamped all over, but those cases were very rare. Usually, one knew what they were going to be asked, how they would be provoked to admit the sins they never made, etc. The idea-consultant, Second rank was experienced enough to withstand the grilling and could answer the examiners' questions in the most suitable and appropriate way. Andir spent over a decade in the same position. He always passed the tests without a problem, no matter who were the three members of the examining body. He told them what they wanted to hear and never slipped in their sneaky traps. His only blunder was the incident with John, when his throat nearly got cut. Although, Richardson hinted to him that he "knew", Andir passed the exam and everything carried on as before.

The First ranks also had to pass some sort of tests, which were rather easy to be even called exams. Basically, when asked by the three members of the committee if they had breached any of the rules in the past year, the questioned person only had to say "No" and that was it. Additional questions sometimes popped up, but they were very innocent for obvious reasons. The mocking of an exam was maintained by all concerned parties and the explanation for this was simple: One could not give their colleague the grilling, because they might get in their shoes straight after. Of course, in this case, the revenge would be imminent! The silent agreement to avoid making their lives hard suited everyone, so the top consultants simply enjoyed their vast immunity within the territory of the Idea Factory.

Richardson was right. The young idea-consultants from the Third ranks, always did something wrong, which would come up at the tests. Andir did not feel overconfident that he would be able to catch out the infringer. It was quite possible that the person was actually clean and had nothing to hide. It was rare, but even Andir could boast about being such an example. The last "obstacle" to the top for

113

him, entered the room and sat down still – a sure sign, he was hiding something. The man answered the questions in a very unrealistic way, as if the words that came out, were not his own, but produced by someone else. When asked about his social contacts and conversations with friends, the guy presented a perfect story, which, however, was far too lengthy to be true. Well, nothing could be ever perfect and the idea-consultants, First rank, were perfectly aware of this. They were also qualified enough to know that when someone was talking about an experience, which actually was not theirs and they had no memory of it, then, when reproduced, the made up story was never exactly the same. Andir had asked the consultant about something four times and twice he caught him out with some minor inconsistencies. The tell-tell sign that the man was lying was when he scratched his nose unconsciously. The Factory regulations prohibited the consultants from making unnecessary movements, especially making contact with their faces. When one touches their nose, ear, lips, temples or cheeks, something definitely seemed iffy. The young man might have been simply too nervous about his uncertain future at the Factory, hence, the itchy nose. But at the time, he was looking down at the floor and his body language "screamed" for sure: "I'm telling lies here! You got me!" The time was up and the consultant's fate was about to get revealed. The three-man committee, a member of which was Andir, needed time to decide. In less than a minute, there was the unanimous verdict that the boy should stay, as it was very doubtful that he had breached any of the basic rules in the Idea Factory. A punishment was spared. The guy was not going to get reprimanded, either. The worst that could happen was that he should part with his dreams to ever get to the top. He did get a black point after all and his chance to join one day the First ranks automatically plummeted to zero. The situation could change in his favor; only if he was excellent at all the future tests in the next at least twenty years, together with the demise of the three members of the committee. Well, the chance one to get hit by a lightening was far greater.

The fateful day, when Andir became one of Them, had slipped by. That was it! Andir had become an idea-consultant of the highest level. The dream had come true!

New Parents

Markot, whose real parents had abandoned him, had been waiting in the interrogation room for more than an hour. The Mentor, however, was nowhere to be seen. He did not look like someone, who would arrive late for an important meeting, unless he had a very good excuse. To be fair, the wintry conditions outside were as severe as the day before. Markot was imagining all sorts of fatal scenarios. He was certain that only unexpected accident could be the reason for Andir not to show up. Another hour slipped by. Markot, lonely as anything, realized that he was not seeing a new client that day and his training had finished. The student was supposed to start work in just two days and instead of feeling happy at the prospect of a new beginning in the Idea Factory, he felt deserted, yet again, in the same way, when his mother left him in the orphanage years ago. Memories of his new home flooded his head, making Markot stay for a bit longer in the room.

He was five and could not stop crying. He wanted more than anything to see his mother. The experienced staff made every effort, around the clock, to console the traumatized poor child, but to no avail. They kept telling him that she was coming back for him. They lied to him in the most impudent way, only so the incessant salty flow would stop coming out of his beautiful eyes. It was on the third day, when little Markot's tears ceased. He still had no idea where he was, but he knew he did not want to be there. He wanted his mummy back the most. As he had stopped crying, he was good to be moved with the rest of the kids – a communal room, where eight more orphans lived. It was important that he was not kept isolated, so the process of his social adaptation was speeded up. The noisy group of kids consisted of equal number of boys and girls of a similar age. They had been abandoned like him. Seemingly, they had fun, they laughed, but deep down, each of them was feeling very sad and wanted the same thing he wanted – a mother and a father – the most normal wish in the world. Nothing else. Markot did not feel like playing with the other children. He did not hate, nor loved them. He did not need any friends. He felt comfortable and secure in his own company. He hardly spoke or made any sound. He often refused to eat typically out of stubbornness, but like any small kid, sooner or later, he would give up his protest at the filled up bowl.

The months, between the four walls of the orphanage were slipping by unnoticeably. The various activities and games, designed to entertain the youngsters, simply did not do the job for Markot. No game was fun enough for him. The smile had long left his little face, turning him into the gravest looking and abandoned little resident. The staff's efforts to break through his wall and show him that life was full of beauty, which he could try to see, touch and feel, proved futile. They begged him, tried to tempt him with unhealthy chocolate treats, did their best, but nothing changed. Markot had cocooned himself in an unbreakable shell, which could be penetrated only by the person, who he was never going to see again. The irresponsible wannabe-mothers never came back to the facility. Yet, there was something that the little sad 'walnut' loved to do. He loved watching through his window. The snowy scenery outside hardly changed, but this did not stop him from gazing through the glass for hours on end. He stared at the lonely road, leading to the orphanage. His mother walked away from him, along this icy asphalt road, depriving him from his intrinsic right – to grow as a happy child. Well, the same road brought happiness to him again.

Many childless couples were desperate to adopt. They all, however, needed to inspect what was on offer in the orphanage, before making such an important step for them and, of course, for the child. They had to first see and touch what they were getting. They wished to pick the best and the most well behaved kid. But, not all the children, abandoned by their biological parents, were cute and beautiful. Others were bad-tempered and never missed to hint at the fact that it would be very hard to be brought up as well behaved children. Still, when there was a match between the image of a perfect child in the prospective parents' mind and the actual kiddy, the 'good bye' moment arrived. The children had to say 'good bye' to everything that was familiar to them: their friends, the staff that had taken care of them better than a real mummy. The children had to leave their well-known world at the orphanage. The difficult transition period towards the unknown did not last that long. They very quickly realized that it was much better to have their own room and the new mummy and daddy made everything so the youngsters felt good, indulging them and making their dreams come true. New clothes, new toys that one got bored of in a few days, a double ice-cream – all this was given to them at once. The new parents would help in any situation, and the most important thing – they were never going to abandon their child.

Markot also had the chance to be chosen. Every weekend, for about four months, he had special visitors. They brought him toys; they asked how he was and what he wanted to receive next time; they wanted to play with him and to make him smile. The small child approached the candidate parents with reservation. At first, he accepted hesitantly the gifts and never smiled at them. He seemed even rude at the beginning, because he was fearful and shy to say 'thanks'. All children actually passed through this uncertain period of getting to know their soon-to-be parents, which would determine, whether the two parties were suitable for each other. If there was no chemistry between them and the small person said 'No!', that was it. With time, however, Markot got used to them. He could not wait to see them again next weekend. The fragile connection between them grew stronger, until it was time for him to be taken away from the orphanage. The convincing sign that those were the right people to become his parents was the smile. Yes, he was smiling again. He smiled, when he saw them coming towards the facility; when he hugged them. Markot even started playing with the other children. He changed a lot. Finally, the day had come. He was only six years old then, but he could never forget, when the woman that he was going to call 'mum' from then on, embraced him in tears. His approval had brought out strong emotional reaction and she got into a hysterical, but happy state, which frightened her son a bit – her own son, according to the document, she had just signed. The kid also cried in slight distress. His father did not. He held his composure, but for him the day was also memorable. He stroked gently Markot on the head, got his little hand into his and the three of them headed towards a new happy beginning.

To grow in the family of an idea-consultant was a real challenge. Daddy's huge salary could provide a high standard of living, so one got everything they wished, as long as it was reasonable. Markot got everything. Not only the kid was indulged in all material stuff, he could want, but he also received his mother's attention at all times.

The devoted mother was prepared to do anything, so her son excelled in everything. Her over ambition was very quickly dashed by his mediocre grades at school. Young Markot was not a stupid kid and had no problem studying, but he could not always meet his loving mother's incredibly high expectations. His father, who would come back from work in the evening, also wanted his son to be good at school, so he never missed to reprimand him. Richardson was very well aware of the Factory's policy, regarding relatives working there. Still, he knew that if Markot worked hard at school, he could quite easily become an idea-consultant. The job position that tens of thousands of people dreamt about was going to be simply given to him like a birthday cake, where Markot would be required only to blow the candles. At the time, there were a couple of years left before the idea-consultant with the piercing blue eyes was going to join the highest ranks. Once he was working with the best, Richardson would have been able, at all costs, to get Markot in as well and introduce him to the idea manufacturing process. The father, however, could not prepare his son for the job in advance, because he was prohibited from discussing his work at home. Richardson had to rely on the lecturers at the Academy and the Mentor to do the job at their best. Despite nobody consulting Markot, whether he wanted to follow into his father's footsteps, the plan about his future was fulfilled. It was a bumpy ride, nevertheless. During his turbulent teenage years, the confused adolescent tried to defy his controlling parents. It did not look that he would ever succeed in this. His mother followed him everywhere and she did not give him any space or free time. His father was even sterner. If he sensed that Markot might be having a change of heart about enrolling at the Academy, he would take some extreme measures. He would subject his son to a grueling interrogation, until the youngster confessed his reasons for giving up on the idea, followed up by some long manipulative conversations, when Richardson would present the Factory as the only right choice. The consultant was the professional in this game and young Markot could not fight against his father's superior mental strength. The son would accept his father's views and revoke his own. Daddy was always right.

Like most adopted children, Markot appreciated everything Richardson and his wife did for him. He was aware that many abandoned kids did not get so lucky and no one ever came to take them away. Gratitude made him enroll at the Academy, not so much his personal choice. The curriculum was quite heavy, preventing the students from sidetracking or having any spare time. Time literally flew by and the final day at the educational facility for Markot arrived at last.

In previous years, the Mentors selected themselves the candidates. This year the rules had changed. Only two future consultants out of four of the best students were going to be chosen by a special committee, which consisted of three lecturers. After a brief interview, the tutors would point at two guys, who had to spend a week in the interrogation room with their Mentors. Markot, who did not want to disappoint his parents, had managed to achieve some very good grades, which, however, were not high enough to put him amongst the finalists. In reality, this meant that he was absolutely out of the race from the start. Well, not this year! Richardson was quite cunning and he had hinted that the second suitable candidate should be a student with average grades on the theoretical exams. The mediocre student should also be given a chance, because he might be good at dealing with the real clients, despite not having great marks. Of course, the tutors knew very well in whose home Markot had been brought up. They also knew that his father would not move an inch, either. If they did not agree to his proposal, they could risk later dealing with their short-tempered colleague, who, sometimes, did not hesitate to bite. After all, the boy was not his biological son. Also Richardson had a point with the argument that some people might be good at something and not so great at other things. At the end, the tutors accepted unanimously the change of regulations and thus, provided Daddy's boy with one-way ticket to the Idea Factory.

Teristan

The scrutiny that Markot inspected every square centimeter of material with, took him longer than if he was the vainest woman, stood in front of the mirror. He wanted everything to be perfect, because today was his first day at the Idea Factory. Although his father worked there, the young man had never actually seen it.

Relatives could not go there for a visit. The only way to have a look at the Factory from the outside was if one joined the queue as a regular customer. Markot, however, was brought up as if in a fish tank to ever have any problems that would require specialized paid help. Still, he had seen some photos of it. The building was strange looking, but nice. The pictures were not taken by any of the queuing clients, as it was prohibited. The security staff in the Factory observed very carefully the line of people, who knew anyway that using a camera would jeopardize their chance to get in.

The watchtower was going to kick-start Markot's career, well, the career of a rather unpromising idea-consultant. Boredom in the not so boring life of the consultant, Third rank, took a different dimension. Markot had always had something to chase and his dynamic life was never stagnant. But now that he found his right place, he slowly discovered the meaning of this unknown to him word. He was sitting all day long in the room and stared outside through the window, which constantly steamed. He had to wipe it every two-three minutes to get a clearer view. Without blinking, he was studying the people in the unnecessarily long queue. He tried to notice anything they did that was against the rules, no matter how minute it was. If he noticed any misbehavior, Markot had to make a thorough analysis of the perpetrator. The idea-consultant in the watchtower had to analyze the person, according to the rules, describing the apparel and accessories in the greatest detail. The second step involved a brief description of the two people in front and those behind him. The third step of the analysis involved an explanation of the reasons behind the suggestion that the person should be removed from the queue. Then, this information, which should have not taken more than half a page, was sent to the security staff at the gate via a special tube. Slowly, the well described infringer's turn would come up. Right on the doorstep, in expectation to get an entry in the warm Factory and share his troubles, which had brought him so far away from home, the person would simply get turned down. He would be added to the blacklist and told to go back home. Those clients, of course, were not very happy to be denied the right to pay for a solution of their hopeless problem. The reason for turning them away was irrelevant. They all had to go back, sometimes completely unaware of their mistake. This did not seem very fair, but the admission system worked perfectly in this way. Anyone, who dared to misbehave in the queue, was always caught by the energetic young guy, sitting behind the steamed up windows. The violators would turn round and walk down the path.

During the whole week, when the job depended on Markot's good sight and his mediocre analytical skills, nothing happened. The future customers, frozen and cold, did nothing, which could deny them the possibility to get in. They did not breach the rules. No one jumped the queue; there were no arguments, fights, insults, nothing... The rookie consultant could not know that this timid behavior of the clients was actually the norm. Fear was the main reason for them to act like snowmen, which differed from the one, Markot had to take on the role of, only by the fact that they had to make a step or two forward occasionally. Of course, there were exceptions sometimes, but they were insignificantly rare. Occasionally, some visitors would simply lose it. They would start screaming, crying, pushing others... They would accuse everyone and simply attempt to jump the queue. The obvious misdemeanor would prompt the security staff immediately, who had to solve the problematic situation, sometimes by force. The idea-consultant in the watchtower would simultaneously notice the events outside and conscientiously fill the piece of paper with the required information, then, send it down on its way. Well, the truth was that the security were allowed to initiate stern actions against the infringer, before the official letter "fell from the skies", so this made the existence of the watchtower rather pointless. There was no real need for anyone to sit in there. Anyone, who had to go through being on watch duties, was aware of the pointlessness of it all. The special room possibly had another purpose. It gave time. The newbie, in there, needed some time to adapt and adjust himself to the different environment. He needed to prepare very well for when he had to meet his first desperate client, the one that would be remembered for the rest of his life.

Markot was sitting on the metal chair and waited in his very own interrogation room. He could not sleep the previous night, but did not feel tired. He was totally ready for his first customer, determined to solve his problem.

"Hello, welcome, Sir, please, have a seat!" Markot was beaming, when the middle-aged man opened the door. He nearly gave him a hug – a crude mistake, which was not going to be the last.

"Hello, Mr. idea-consultant! I'm here, because I need money. How can I get it, lots of it and have it in my bank account till the end of the month, otherwise…" the client shot out his reasons for coming, before his worn out dark blue jeans had even touched the chair.

"Hang on, wait a little, Sir, you can't just do this, we have rules here!" Markot told the newcomer off, thus, making another emotional blunder. First of all, he grinned at him like an old friend and now, he spoke as if he was an obstinate neighbor, complaining about the noise made in the wrong hours of the day. "So, there, we have to go through three stages before I tell you my idea, which would suit best your problematic case."

"Right on, Mr. idea-consultant. Whatever you say, no problem." the client raised his arms outwards, as if to guarantee that he would do as told from now on. In the meantime, Markot made another gaffe – he forgot to introduce himself.

"So, right then, you'll wait one minute, which we'll spend in silence, and then, you'll tell me why you're here today. You have to tell me why you're here later, not now!"

"Fine, but I've already told you. There's nothing else to tell… I need money, and that it is very soon, because…"

"No, no, no, Sir! Don't tell me now, you shouldn't tell me straight away! You can tell me after one minute, during which neither of us is allowed to speak. These are the rules."

"OK. I'll wait."

The financially strapped customer stopped talking at last. It was too late for Markot, however. The first stage had been totally flawed already and there was no going back now. He hoped that he could do a good job of the analysis at least.

The client was dressed in dark brown jacket and jeans. He had only unzipped his coat, instead of taking it off completely. Underneath, he was wearing a reddish checked shirt, which the consultant did not like at all. Not that criticizing the customers' clothing was part of the job, but Markot could not help himself, but to resent the shirt. He did not feel the need to look at the shoes, certain that he could solve the case without this unnecessary detail. He could not notice any gloves, or a hat. The idea-consultant had completed his superficial analysis within ten seconds and learned nothing about his client from it.

The physical features, which Markot also had to examine, did not impress him in the slightest. The person was of a slim built and of an average height. His face looked his age. There was nothing unusual about the hands, either. His hair looked ordinary, with the odd grey hair here and there. Markot could not judge much about the client's personality from his behavior or the few words they had already exchanged. The guy looked normal, living his normal life and probably had a regular job. He had possibly done a bad deal, however, or something and ran out of money. The Third rank idea-consultant managed to complete his first task within half a minute.

Markot had good enough grades at the Academy and he could do much better analyses. Every time they were given a similar task at school, his descriptions were detailed and very precise. This time, however, he decided to follow his Mentor's advice and not to pay too much attention to the analytical part, but to rely on his own instincts and try to guess what kind of person had come to see him. Well, no matter how much Markot tried to concentrate in the remaining thirty seconds, he could not feel or sense anything about the customer. He would have achieved the same result, if he had tried to guess what was on one of the wall's mind. Nothing. Andir forgot to mention that judging people, by using one's intuition, took years of experience and it was very doubtful that Markot would manage this with his very first client.

"Time is up, Sir. Now you have to tell me why you're here. Eh-r-r..." Markot stopped suddenly, remembering that he had not learned the client's name, yet. "But first, let me ask you about your name!"

"Teristan."

"Hmm, it's an interesting name, Mr. Teristan. I am Markot." the idea-consultant paused for a second. He looked up at the ceiling and as if trying to remember something. He should also have told the client... Well, he forgot the rule that every idea-consultant was supposed to mention their rank, when introducing themselves. What a blunder! No big deal! No one was perfect! The 'sinner' moved on to, yet, another gaffe, no doubt. "Right, then, now tell me why are you here? I know you've already told me, but let's hear it again."

"I need money, Mr. Markot. At least two hundred thousand, but a hundred thousand will be good to start with. I need it by the end of the month max!" the man with the strange name stressed on the last word.

"Mr. Teristan, if you have nothing else to add, we can proceed to the second stage. I'll be asking you further questions and in order to find solution to your problem, you will need to answer them all. Are you sure there's nothing more you could say about the money thing?"

"That's it. But two hundred thousand is a lot of money, you know?"

"Yes, it is a lot of money!" Markot agreed, trying to calculate how long he had to work at the Factory to earn that sort of money. Actually, it was not for that long.

"It's a lot, no doubt about it, but I need it urgently. That's why I'm here. I can get this amount from a few banks, but banks need to see documents. It takes time to check the paper work and I won't be able to get the loan until the middle of the next month. I've asked them, you see!"

"Right, Mr. Teristan, it's true, banks can be slow. I want to ask you a few questions now. You have to tell me everything, so I can come up with the idea. My first question is: What do you do?"

"I run my own business. Transportation and logistics. We work locally, eight years now... You may have seen white trucks with the initials TR - they're mine."

"I haven't, but this is not important." Markot said in a way that he could have offended the customer. "Next, what is your family status?"

"I'm married and have one child. But what does this have to do with the fact that I need money?" the visitor sounded a little vexed.

"These are just general questions, Mr. Teristan, which will help me get a picture of you and the kind of life you have."

"A-ah, alright."

"Next, where do you live?"

"In the north-west part of town. I live in a three-storey house."

"How long have you been living there?"

124

"As long as I remember. I inherited the house from my parents."

"My next question is: when did you realize that you need this amount of money?"

"Three days ago I found out that if I don't get at least one hundred thousand until the end of the month, I'll lose the house. Problems with the mortgage, you see... It is about to expire. If I don't pay in full, they are taking my house. I re-mortgaged the property, you see, but my business was going good, then, and I could afford to pay. But now... I had to... I gave my last money to come here. Mr. Markot, the situation is very serious. I was a greedy pig and look, now, what this has got me into!" the desperate client tapped the relatively round anatomical object, his head, with his fist. He wished he could go back in time and reverse his fatal greedy decision.

"Mr. Teristan, I'll do my best to offer you the most suitable idea and get you out of this difficult financial situation. I'll do everything so I could help you." the idea-consultant uttered, feeling sorry for the guy. He had forgotten that he should not express his feelings. Where was the snowman now?

"Thank you, Mr. Markot! Things got really out of hand!"

"Let's continue with the questions, because I've got some more to ask. Are you able to extend the date of payment for a bit longer?"

"Of course, I'm not! Would I be here if I could? I've checked with the bank and they don't want to hear about extending anything. The bustards can't wait to rob me and make me and my family homeless." oh, how much he hated those sleek bank clerks, who smiled hypocritically at him with the news that if there was no payment soon, very soon – he would lose his home.

"And your wife? What does she think about all this?"

"She doesn't think anything. She can't stand me and simply avoids me. Good job it's not worse, otherwise she would have clawed my face by now. It's not easy for her and she has to think about the kid, too. How are we going to pay for her college with no money? How?" Teristan grabbed his short hair, as if he wanted to pull it and feel the pain. Well, pain was not going to solve his money problem.

"We'll find a solution. Trust me! You'll make it up to your wife." the "experienced relationship expert" said before asking his next rather dumb question. "Mr. Teristan, what do you think is the best answer to a problem like yours?"

"I haven't got the slightest idea. I haven't stopped thinking and I simply can't think of anything. That's why I'm here, as it's also so near to where I live. Although, to be honest," the visitor leaned forward to share his opinion about the idea-consultant from a close distance. "I don't trust people like you. Don't take offense. It's nothing personal. I hope you can help me and if everything is OK and I find the money, then, I'll tell all my mates to come here, when they have problems."

"Thank you, Mr. Teristan. I have a few more questions to ask. How many trucks does your company own?"

"Twelve."

"Do you own any other properties, apart of your house?"

"No, I don't. I told you, we'll be out on the street, once…"

"Yes, you did. And do you have any relatives you could stay with?"

"But look, once you tell me where to find this money from, there won't be any need to go anywhere else. You will tell me where to find it from, won't you?" Teristan sounded quite worried, doubting for the first time, the very young looking consultant's abilities to solve his money situation.

"Yes, Mr. Teristan. This is my job." Markot assured him. He kept his cool, although he did not have the vaguest idea how to find this sort of money. The fact that he still had some questions to ask before the final stage of their meeting, made him temporarily confident. "Have you discussed your situation with anyone of your friends, colleagues, business partners? Have you asked for their help?"

"No, I haven't told a soul. And, besides, I'm the sole owner of my company."

"Why haven't you begged for the financial support of other people? If you ask some of your relatives and friends, I'm sure you'll manage to get at least some of the required sum of money, which will buy you some time. Banks may be strict and rigid, but once they see the money, they loosen up a bit."

"I can't do this. And my friends don't have that sort of money."

"Why can't you do this?"

"I feel embarrassed. I've failed and I can't now just go around and beg. Everyone will think I'm a failure." Teristan looked down, appearing to be exactly this – a complete failure.

"But these people can help you. One should always turn, first, to their loved ones for help, when in a difficult stage in their life. Just ask them! They will understand."

"They may understand, yes, but they have no money. I was the most successful and affluent of them all, and they still believe I am. Mr. Markot, you're my last hope. Last night, I took my daughter's savings to come here. You know, kids like to save little by little... It's not much, but without it, I wouldn't be here today. My daughter, she got so upset that she said she was not going to school for the day. And how could she go without a penny in her pocket? This is the lowest I have come to in my whole life, the worse thing I've done..."

The idea-consultant dropped his guard again. His earlier spell of feeling sorry for the client was followed suddenly by another, but this time, he felt uncontrollably wretched at the sight of the desperate man. Markot felt bad about the daughter, too, as if it was his fault that the child's future was doomed and not her father's and his ill-judged financial operations. In this grave moment, the consultant thought about the roles his Mentor took on during the training week. He realized how different everything was, once he had a real distressed customer in front of him and not a skilled actor. The client's face expressed true emotions, coming from the inside and did not display carefully calculated mimics. Markot had not resorted to the flawless snowman and he should have. He should have remembered what Andir told him to do whenever he felt that he was veering towards showing his sympathy. It was too late now. The wall of the young and inexperienced consultant had not been crushed. It simply did not exist.

"Surely, Mr. Teristan, you're finding it very hard, but I'll do my best to help you. In a minute we'll get to the final stage of our meeting, when I'll tell you the idea, you've come for. I've got a few more questions, though. Do you think you could pay up your mortgage with your company trucks?"

"What? You mean instead of paying off with cash? I haven't asked, but if I do this, that will be the end of my business. How will I make a living and look after my family? I'd rather kill myself..."

"Don't talk like this, Mr. Teristan. After all, even if you have to declare bankruptcy, the long professional experience you've had, will help you start again and…"

"I can't, Mr. Markot! I can't just wipe out eight years of hard work, day and night, and start all over again. I haven't got it in me anymore, please, understand, I just can't." the visitor's eyes filled up with tears.

"Mr. Teristan, I know this is not what you want to hear. I am sorry! But you see, by clearing all these points, this will help me come up with the best idea for you."

"It's alright. Ask me anything you like, as long as you can tell me where to get this money from at the end! Please!"

"I will, Mr. Teristan. I promise! What about if you sell half of your trucks and buy some time? You could still run your business with the rest?"

"Oh, Mr. Markot, this would have been great if only eight of the vehicles were not owned by another bank. I'm still paying for them. It's just that the creditors are not bothering me right now. The four I own are not worth much, as they are quite old, you see. I should really scrap them… They just cost me, you know?"

"So you don't own eight of the trucks?"

"The company owns them, but they are bought on credit, so if I can't afford the payments, the bank will just take them."

"Right, now I got it." the idea-consultant realized in this moment that one thing was definitely clear in this case – there was no way out of the situation. Clear and simple! There was no positive solution for the problem of his first ever client.

"I've thought about all these alternatives, Mr. Markot, but nothing would work. I have to find this money. I simply have to! I have no other choice. I've even thought I could rob the bank I owe, but I'm not a criminal and I don't intent to become one. If I end up in prison, I'll put my family in a worse situation. I'll have food and a roof over my head, but they would still end up out on the street. I can't do this to them and leave them."

"And you shouldn't, Mr. Teristan. I will find a legal way to get over this. I am almost ready with my idea. Just one more question - How much money have you got left?"

"None. I gave everything I had, so I can come here." the man uttered, ready to turn his empty pockets inside out, if necessary.

"No, I'm asking if you have a small amount of cash, ten, twenty... Could you find that sort of money?"

"Of course, this won't be a problem, but I can't see how it would help, unless you can turn twenty into two hundred thousand?" Teristan attempt for a joke was accompanied by a smile. A smile, however, that showed his clear desperation.

"I can't do that, Mr. Teristan. I wish I could, believe me. Now, we've reached the final stage and I shall deliver my idea to you. I will also explain why it is the best solution to your problem."

"I'm only interested in finding the money. So you can spare the explanation. I'm out of here, once you tell me the idea. I can't get a minute of sleep, unless I sort things out with the bank."

"These are the rules! You can't leave the room until you hear the reasons behind the idea. You can't just leave straight away. It's not allowed and it looks as if I haven't done my job properly."

"OK, then, I suppose I could wait for a minute or two." Teristan agreed, showing his respect for the idea-consultant, despite the fact that he looked so young and inexperienced.

The moment of truth had come. One could not say who was more excited of them both. Markot paused for a few seconds and then shared what his consultant's brainy head had come up with. What else, but one Great idea!

"Mr. Teristan, for me, the best you can do is to try to win the money by getting a lottery ticket. You could also go to a casino. Either way, you will have a chance, at least, to win a big sum of money. Now I'll tell you why I've come up with this idea. I'm sure it sounds interesting to you..."

"Interesting? You think it sounds interesting to me? Is that really your idea? So after the fat fee I paid and half an hour of chit-chat, you're fobbing me off to play the lottery?" the client was stunned. He expected to hear a step-by-step guidance on how to get his hands on two hundred thousand; he waited for clear and consistent instructions to follow.

"I am aware that this does not sound very serious and compelling, but if we take into consideration everything you've told me so far... What I mean is... You don't own anything you can sell

129

to pay off your debts, so there is nothing left for you, but to rely on your luck. You do have a chance, no matter how small it is, to win on the lottery. It is possible. You can win something in a casino, too, but it will be less, of course. You can gamble on other things, go to betting shops, involve in horse racing betting or…"

"Oh, I knew I was right! I was right all the time!" Teristan shook his head and stood up slowly from his metal chair. "You, piece of shit! My family will end up homeless, not yours! The lottery! You, moron!" the raging customer spat, aiming at Markot's face. Although, he missed his target and managed to hit his right shoulder, Teristan did not attempt a second try. He left the interrogation room, pushing the door with a bang. He had no business in there anymore. The solution, he paid for with his last money, was not worth a penny. Life for him, his wife and their little daughter had just ended.

Markot could not move. The slimy attack had turned him to stone. He knew that in ten minutes, a new customer was going to enter the interrogation room, bringing with him a new problem, and thus, Markot had to clear his mind of everything that had just happened. The idea-consultant, Third rank, knew all the techniques, applied in this sort of situation, by heart. He knew that he should forget about Teristan and his money shortage issues as soon as possible and get ready to meet his next client.

Well, but how could he overcome the huge disappointment, he experienced with his first visitor? The man had invested everything he had to come here and got nothing at the end. He was conned in the most arrogant way that he was getting something that was worth a lot, but in reality, it was not. Luck? To rely on his luck and play the lottery! The dumbest idea, Markot had come up with, only proved that he was no good for this job. Yes, he was fully aware of the fact that the idea was stupid. But the truth was that he could not think of any alternatives, no matter how much he tried during the meeting. A good consultant would conjure up more than one solution and at the end of the interview; he had to deliver the most suitable one. If it happened that the idea did not prove to be a great success, the idea-consultant would resort to plan B and throw the rest of his witty suggestions in the game, until the perfect solution was formed. This approach guaranteed zero failures. Markot, however, did not get over the first letter of the alphabet in his choice of plans. Completely crushed and feeling much worse than when his Mentor humiliated him, Markot stood up and pressed the red button. He did this every thirty minutes until the end of his working day. These robotized repeated movements helped him remain in his room alone all day. He spent his time thinking very hard about what he was doing in the Idea Factory in the first place. When the time to go home had come, Markot stayed for another half an hour before he headed towards his car. He did not want for anyone to see him. He did not want any of his colleagues to look at him, walking down the corridor. Although, it was unlikely that anyone would have ever known about what happened that day in his room, he simply wanted to hide from their looks and go home alone. What a shame!

Doing a shabby job on your first day was quite common at the Factory. The same could be said about the repeated use of the button. It was hard to be that good, when one did not have a day of experience. Actually, Markot did a satisfactory job, but there was no way he could have known this. There was no one behind the glass that could come up to him, after Teristan left the room, pat him on the back and tell him that he had done well, considering the client's answers. The best solution to the problem of finding two hundred thousand was that the customer could only try to use his luck here and there.

At the Academy, there were several lectures that focused on problems, which did not have a solution and in that way making them non-problems. In addition, students were taught how to make unsolvable problems solvable. Markot had two options and he actually picked the better one. The first one involved saying to his client that even if money grew on trees, there was still no way, he could collect it within two weeks. The second choice was to abstain from killing his client's last hope, which was already on its last legs. Any idea-consultant from the higher ranks would have finalized the meeting in a similar manner. Markot was oblivious to the fact that in reality he did well.

Downfall is never permanent. Hence, so many people try everything to get up and resurface, after reaching the bottom. The determination to never go down again makes them stronger and resilient to future adverse challenges. A bad experience is sometimes more valuable than a good one and that is a fact. Markot had been fast asleep, lying on his stomach on the bottom of his imaginary idea-swamp. When he woke up, he felt reborn. He checked his body for cuts and bruises. After not finding any, he started to get ready for his second day at the Idea Factory. He was still rather sleepy to feel the fit of energy that was supposed to help him stand up. On his way to work, he tried to convince himself that today he was going to be much better. Clutching the steering wheel, Markot felt strong. He was prepared to squeeze any problem that came his way "by the throat", until it spelled out its own solution. He was also thinking about the snowman. Not resorting to it, the previous day was his biggest mistake. Today, however, the idea-consultant was going to become the snowman. No more errors!

Anna

The second client in the idea-consultant's short career hesitantly entered the interrogation room. She had no idea that the young man, who was going to help her, had decided to behave like a harsh dictator.

"Have a seat!" Markot ordered and pointed at the chair with his eyes. The rules allowed for a stern attitude towards the client, as long as there was a reason for this and this helped the consultant solve the problem. What did not make sense in this case was that the idea-consultant, Third rank, spoke harshly before he had even found out anything about the woman or her reasons to visit the Factory. In this way, the customer could possibly feel hesitant towards the consultant and fail to show their trust by hiding important information. In short, Markot was shooting himself in the foot. His only chance was to succeed in solving the client's problem. "You cannot interrupt me and you must answer all my questions. Before we proceed, I need to know your name."

"Anna." the woman replied, astonished by the young guy's behavior. He was young to be her son, but talked to her as if being at daggers drawn with her.

"My name is Markot, idea-consultant, Third rank. This is the start of the first stage. You have to tell me why you are here. You can speak after one minute. You must not start before that. Do you understand?"

"Yes, I do."

It was her first time in a place like this, but from what she had heard from her friends, she expected to be treated in a more welcoming way. After all, she had paid the fee. She did not breach any of the rules, while queuing. Everything was as it should have been. The slight aristocratic hint in Anna's personality made her question her decision to come here in the first place. Why stay any longer, if she was treated in this way before she had even mentioned the reason for her visit? The perfectly looking lady felt like standing up and leaving, despite that she very rarely acted impulsively. She had paid with her own money, but she could easily get over this without being too dramatic about it. Reason prevailed, however. Anna looked at her ultra expensive wristwatch, encrusted with diamonds, and decided to wait for the minute to pass, hoping that she would be treated with the respect, befitting an elegant and beautiful middle-aged lady.

Markot, nevertheless, had no intention to make the icy, numb snowman that had possessed his body melt a little. The most important thing for him was not to show any emotions, nor empathize with the client's ordeal, so he could come up with a working and effective idea at the end. While the reverse counting from sixty-to-one was taking place, the inexperienced consultant focused on analyzing his female customer. This time, he decided to leave aside his Mentor's nonsense about relying on his instincts. Instead, Markot applied everything he had learned at the Academy. He began with the way she was dressed. His attention was drawn to her denim skirt – an interestingly brave choice on her part, considering the minus temperatures outside. He was not big on women's clothes, but the consultant was informed enough to know that a skirt in this weather was a no-no. Well, her warm black leggings possibly protected her a bit against the cold, but still, a regular woman would have abstained from going out like this. Markot moved his eyes up her body. He was pleased to see that Anna had opted for her favorite knitted blouse. It was sparkly light blue with a discrete label on the left side. She wore a warm looking short black jacket, which perfectly matched her leggings. Her dark colored gloves were in contrast with her white designer hat. She was fashionably elegant, grabbing Markot's attention for longer than necessary. He had to hurry up, if he wanted to complete his analysis in time. The idea-consultant looked down under the table towards her black high boots and her long tempting legs. They completed perfectly her look. The snowman was beginning to melt down. Markot forced his lecherous thoughts to go back to the analysis before it was too late. He turned to his client's physical characteristics.

She was as tall as him, slender and had a beautiful sitting posture. The perfect proportions of her body made her look much younger than her age. Her shoulder-length shiny black hair was also typical for someone under thirty years old. Those, over this 'milestone' age, usually preferred shorter hairstyles in lighter hue. At the same time, her face displayed signs of aging, in contrast with her sculpted body. Fine wrinkles around her brown eyes and a couple of deeper ones on her beautiful neck gave out her real age. The single young idea-consultant had to analyze the character of this provocative, but mature beauty. This was the next step. She had not spoken more than four words, since entering the room of the dictatorially behaving young man. They were uttered with a thin and slightly high-pitched female voice, which could not reveal her personality. Her legs were crossed, as any self-respecting woman in a skirt would do. Her face lacked any expression, neither she felt free to gesticulate a lot. Markot had to turn to her clothes again in the hope to see some clue about her character. Fixing his stare onto her voluptuous curves for longer than he should, he reached a feasible conclusion, but, then, he quickly changed his mind again. Only a strong and independent woman, he thought, could put a skirt in this weather and boots that made her look like a stripper. Her short jacket revealed her bottom – another sign for her willfulness, strong-mindedness and emancipation. On the other hand, these peculiarities illustrated a slight sense of vulgarity and triteness, overexposure and demonstrativeness. It was possible that she was married to a rich guy, who made her dress provocatively, because he liked it that way. Or the expensive inappropriate clothes were given to her as a present by her husband and she would have never worn them if she was left to follow her own fashion sense. What was true? Markot felt confused. Was he confronted with a strong feminist, capable of being the leader of the movement against men or Anna was yet another example of a woman, who followed her husband's whims, only due to the simple but compelling fact that he was filthy rich? No matter what the truth was and whether he would ever discover it, the snowman in Markot managed to hide the pleasant feeling that Anna had brought to him. The minute was up and it was time for some serious stuff. The visitor was also aware of this, but she had decided to wait for the clumsy consultant to speak first.

"Anna, why are you here?" Markot snappily repeated his question. He sounded as if he could not stand to be in her presence.

"Some of my friends really praised you!" she 'swallowed' his disrespect with a great effort, trying to sound as friendly as possible. She had already started to hate him. "Their stories truly impressed me and believe me, I very rarely get impressed. When I've realized that I couldn't deal with this problem of mine on my own, I've decided that it is time to benefit from the services the famous Factory offers and…"

"What is your actual problem? Stop being vague, just get to the point!" Markot sounded like a slaveholder, who was ordering rudely his slave.

"If you insist. But I've paid to come here. You're working for me now. Am I right?"

"You are right, but if you're going to tell me what to do, instead of us getting to the point, then, you'll be just wasting my time. I don't know about you, but I don't have time to waste. There are plenty of customers outside, who will be more than happy to be in your place." Markot said in a very hurtful way. His eyes squinted at her dismissingly.

"But why are you behaving like this with me! Show me a little respect, please. Your salary at the end of the month depends on people like me. I shall not put up with such disrespect…" she was really about to leave if it was not for the snowman's fast interference. He decided that it would not hurt if he melted a part or two down, enough to fill a glass of water.

"Anna, I'll do everything that it is in my power to solve your problem. I am sorry if you are not happy with my way of working, but here, at the Idea Factory, we have a lot of rules that we all need

135

to observe. I'm only asking you to follow the rules during our conversation."

"I shall follow your rules if you explain to me what they are and not just scold me and treat me as if I'm guilty of something. Is that a deal?"

"Yes, I guess so. I will explain the rules to you with pleasure, if this is what you want." Markot smiled spitefully, crossing over the limit, yet again. The client hit back. She raised her chin, crossed her arms in her lap blocking any access to her and finally, she put a hypocritical expression on her face, as if saying: hatred is mutual. "You need to tell me your reasons for being here during the first stage. In the second stage, I'll be asking you questions, which you have to answer honestly and truthfully. The final stage involves the actual idea, which I'll deliver to you along with the reasoning behind it."

"Is that it?" Anna sounded surprised. So many rules, explained in just three sentences.

"Yes, that's it. Now tell me why you are here?"

"I will tell you. I see, now, that you are not going to change you outrageous behavior. At least, I can hope to receive a sound piece of advice. If you fail, I shall visit your boss in person and explain to him what a good-for-nothing idea-consultant you are and…"

"I don't want to disappoint you, but this will be impossible." Markot interjected abruptly in the same way his Mentor did with him. "The clients cannot get in contact with any other idea-consultants, apart of those they have an appointment with. We don't have a complaint box. I'm afraid you cannot complain to anybody, should you feel discontent with my service."

"But this is despicable! You're left to do whatever you want, without any control. I can't believe this! How…?"

"There are very good means of control here, I can assure you. Anna, let's stop this never-ending argument and finish what we've both come here for. I'll do my job and you can get the best idea. Do you agree?" Markot laid his cards on the table. He did not worry what hers could be.

"I agree as long as you change your disgraceful attitude towards me. Otherwise, I'll just…"

""It's a deal! But now, tell me, at last, why you've come here?"

"Alright, then, I shall tell you. I suppose you've heard this hundreds of times..."

"Anna, I may have heard it a thousand times, but this is now irrelevant." a brazen liar he was – she was only his second client in his career. "So why are you here?"

"I have a problem with my husband. He's seeing another woman. He's been acting like a stranger for over a year. He is just not the same. I'm not sure what's happening to him, but I know there's a woman involved. I want to find out who she is and also, I'd like to know what to do with my life." the visitor looked down, not because she was mesmerized by her cool leather boots and their original shiny clasps, but because she was feeling shame. To share with a stranger that her marriage was on the rocks, was to say the least, a huge embarrassment for her.

"Is that it?"

"Yes, that's it." Anna replied quietly.

"I will ask you questions about your personal life, now that we enter the second part of our meeting. You may not like some of them, but these are the rules. Anna, if you want a good idea at the end, you must answer me."

"I will answer those I feel that are appropriate. I'm not responding to anything that is crass!" the guest showed her claws again. By the way she wore a very bright red nail varnish, which was a bit on the whore side.

"It's up to you, but the idea, you've come for, may suffer because of it."

"Don't worry about me. I take the consequences, not you!"

"It's fine by me. How long have you been married for? I hope, my first question does not make you that uncomfortable." the idea-consultant sniggered.

"No, it does not. Eighteen years, seventeen of which – quite happily."

"Have you got any children?"

"Yes, of course!" she uttered this in a categorical manner, as if to say that the query was totally out of place. What normal woman of her age does not have children?

"How many, boys or girls?"

"I have two sons, but they don't live with us. When they were young, they were suffering from cold allergy and often got sick. That's why, they are studying at a boarding school for gifted children, which is far away, down south, of course. Why are you asking me about them? They have nothing to do with our problem. This is strictly between my husband and I."

"I did not say that they have anything to do with this. I'm only asking. What do you do for a living, Anna? I imagine you receive a good income?"

"I am a marketing director." she proudly announced her occupation – the professional peak in her career, after years of devotion and hard effort in her work. Good job for the nannies, otherwise she would not have achieved anything without them.

"And what does your husband do?"

"He's a businessman."

"What kind of business?"

"Trading. He is trading with so many different things that I have lost track now what exactly is he trading with. His business is his business... I don't interfere. I've got a lot on my shoulders." interestingly, by only mentioning her husband's occupation, her face showed the same expression of contempt like when she was talking to the little insecure dictator in front of her.

"So, I gather, your family is financially secure?"

"We can't complain. Of course, there are richer people than us, if that's what you mean?"

"Not exactly. But let's not sidetrack from the main point. Tell me, when did you notice for the first time that your husband was behaving unusually?"

"Last winter. I can't remember what day it was or the exact date, but we argued after work. He wanted me to accompany him on some official meeting at the municipality, but I declined, as I was very tired. I just didn't feel like going."

"So was that it, causing the argument?"

"Yes, that was it, but you don't know my husband. He is very mellow and one could not get him into an argument even if they really tried. He's never been the argumentative type."

"So the quarrel was quite a big one, then?"

138

"Not really, but the way he talked to me about this damn meeting… It just felt as if he did not want me there, as if I was not his wife…"

"So he said that he did not want you to go with him?"

"No, he said that he did wanted me to come, this was what the argument was about, wasn't it? But it just felt that he did not mean it, really."

"How did you come to this conclusion if he never actually said that he did not want you to come?" the male logic spoke in him.

"Intuition! Us, women, sense these things. You, men, think that you can get away, but we always catch you out."

"And what happened after this sensitive evening? You mentioned that your husband is behaving strangely. What do you mean by this?"

"He is not showing me any attention like before. He doesn't want us to go out together anymore. He is somewhat distant with me, which is very unusual for him. He is just a different person. I can't be fooled. I'm sure that he's got another woman and I want to find out who she is." a feeling of spite and revenge made her clench her fists and so she painfully dug her long nails in her own skin.

"Anna, have you found a sound evidence that you husband is cheating on you or all this is just based on your intuition?"

"Just on my intuition?" the visitor repeated with discontent. She was outraged that someone doubted her unmistakable woman's instinct. "You cannot understand, because you're not a woman. I'm telling you, women sense these things. I'm sure of it."

"So you don't have any evidence?"

"I haven't found anything in his pockets, if that's what you're asking me. I'm not like some of these nutty jealous women, who fumble and rummage around, every time their husbands go to the bathroom."

"And why not? If you have bothered to look through your husband's stuff, you would have saved yourself the trouble of coming here, as well as the money you've just spent for my salary?" Markot nibbled at her, because he decided that his image of being cold and insensitive should be spurred on from time to time. Not that snowman had started to meltdown or something, but just in case.

"I've told you! I'm not like this! I want to catch him out another way. I did hire a detective, but this idiot told me that everything was alright. I knew he was lying to me."

"A detective? This sounds like a good idea! But why do you keep insisting on the opposite, without any evidence, if he's already told you there's nothing to worry about?"

"Because I know! I just know! The detective, who knows if he did his job properly... I felt he was just after my money. I am sure."

"Anna, you could've hired another detective?"

"Yes, but if I'm supposed to hire ten of them before I find out who my husband is cheating on me with, I'm better of to come here. You will tell me how to catch him. This is your job, isn't it?"

"Yes, it is. I will tell you how. We still have time before we get to the third stage. I've got a few more questions for you. Have you ever tried to follow your husband and spy on him yourself?"

"No, of course not! I'm not like this, I've told you!"

"Yes, you have. But it's my duty to ask you again. Anna, have you asked any of your husband's friends or colleagues for help? You know, someone, who could give you a reliable piece of information about what time he leaves after work and with whom, for example... Someone, who may have seen him with another woman."

"No, I haven't. There are mainly men and a few secretaries working in his office. He wouldn't go so low to start seeing any of them. His male colleagues – I don't even know their names. I can't ask strangers about something so personal. I'm not like this!"

"Maybe, if you were like this, you would have probably solved your problem by now. Anyway, we've already discussed this. You want a ready answer without jeopardizing your principles. Or am I wrong?"

"You're so transparent, Mr. Markot! I will not put up with your arrogant waspishness and imperious tone of voice, as if I am somewhat subordinate to you. You cannot offend me, so just carry on and mind your own business! You do remember who pays for your salary, don't you?" Anna was very good at this game and she could play it forever.

"I do, I remember very well. I am glad that you also want your complicated problem solved as soon as possible. Have you ever had an affair?"

"What?" she asked fuming. "I will not answer this question. How dare you asking me something like this?"

"If you're having an affair and your husband's found out, he may have decided that it's not a problem to start seeing someone else, too."

"I've told you! You don't know him. He loves only me and he knows that I'm not like this."

"So this means "No", then? You don't have a secret boyfriend?"

"No, I don't have. And you? Do you have a girlfriend? Let's talk about your personal life, eh! I want to know if the idea-consultant, who I doubt very much is going to help me, has a woman? Mr. Markot, is she some silly bimbo that puts up with your outrageous nastiness, waiting for you at home? Or maybe you treat her nicely?" she hated him like she had never hated anyone before. For a second, she wanted him to die and disappear from the face of the Earth forever. Of course, the destructive thought soon passed.

"I cannot answer this. We are forbidden to discuss our personal lives with clients. Anna, we can argue all day long, but we won't achieve anything in this way. So, please, answer my questions! It's not that hard, is it?"

"I will do as long as you ask me normal questions. If they offend me in any way, then I will pass. This, we..."

"We've already discussed that, yes, I know." Markot finished the sentence for her. He was getting fed up. Nevertheless, he decided to carry on in the same spirit. He realized that thanks to his provocative questions, he had managed to come up with the right solution for Anna. "We've reached, now, the final stage. I'm going to tell you what you want to hear from me. If you are not happy with it, next time, you can see someone of a higher rank."

"Have you really thought of a way to find out who she is?" Anna sounded rather skeptical. She could not imagine that this clown was even able to think.

"Yes, I have. My idea is ready. But before I tell you, I'm interested to know what you will do, when you catch your husband and his mistress? You'll pull her hair and file for divorce, I imagine?"

141

"I don't care who this wicked woman is! She doesn't interest me! What I actually want is my old life back, my man back and all the happiness we've had together!"

"But you said you wanted to know who she was?"

"Yes, I did! I do want to know who she is, but only so I can make her leave my husband alone. I don't care about her name or where she lives!"

"And what about if he doesn't want to be with you and picks her? Will you leave him then?"

"I'll never leave him! Never! He loves me and he wants to be with me! I'm certain of it! I only need to get rid of the nasty bitch and give him a second chance. Everything will get back to normal at the end." Anna was yet another woman, who had become a victim of her own theories on love and marriage, which, of course, never quite matched reality. She preferred to keep hoping for the return of her blissful past, instead of seeing the truth and stop deluding herself.

"And what if there is nothing that needs to get back to normal?"

"How do you mean?" she had understood the question perfectly, but simply could not accept the possibility that her intuition might have been wrong this time.

"I mean that your husband may not be seeing another woman, but still feels cold and distant towards you. Anna, I feel your problem is not that clear-cut, that's why my idea will be a little bit different."

"No, no! Everything is crystal clear. I'm sure there's another woman. I'm certain. Us, women…"

"…Sense these things. You've already told me. The idea-consultant, that's me, works with facts and does not rely on the client's intuition, even if that is a woman's intuition. I can tell you how to find out whether there's another woman in your husband's life, not how to find out who she is!"

"But this is the same thing! When I find out that she exists, I'll find out who she is!"

"It may be the same thing for you. It's not for me."

"Ins and outs! Go on! Just tell me!" she snapped at him, realizing that the horrendous meeting dragged for longer than she expected.

"The idea, Anna, is to hire detectives, the more, the better, and just wait for them to tell you whether your husband is seeing someone else. When they confirm your suspicions, they can, then, check her out. You'll learn who she is and the rest of it. I'm sure the money side of it won't be a problem for you."

"Is that it? You are a complete idiot, you know that? You can't be that thick! Yes, you are young, but this cannot be an excuse! What are you doing here, really? I told you that I did hire a detective and he found nothing. So I have to do it again now?"

"Yes, and I'll explain why."

"I don't want your explanation!" the visitor snapped at him again and stood up from her chair. She had no more business there with that loser.

"Anna, you may not want it but you need it. Just sit down." Markot ordered. "I may be urging you to repeat what you've already tried before, but this time, you will get convinced, for definite, that there isn't another woman. There is a slight chance that I'm wrong, but I'm almost certain that your husband has simply stopped loving you and has lost interest in you. Basically, I doubt very much that there's someone else involved."

"That's not possible! You talk without knowing him. You don't know me, either. This is all nonsense! He loves me and wants to be with me. He does. I know he does." Anna's red eyes shed a few tears, which quickly rolled down. Markot was too right.

"Or maybe, it's just you, who does, and for both of you?"

"No, that's not true. He wants to be with me, too... Not just me, him as well, I know he does." there was no stopping for her crocodile tears, now.

"So why are you crying, then?"

"I just, I... I don't, but why did this happen, why...? I've done nothing, but he suddenly changed and started to..."

"I don't know, Anna. I have no idea."

"What am I going to do now? I should leave him, but I love him so much, I just can't." her light make-up had smeared to the extent of making her look scary. She sat down heavily, wiping some of the tears with her sleeve.

"As you've said, I don't know you or your husband. I can see you are finding it hard, but my only advice could be to look ahead and carry on with your life. You're an attractive woman, financially

143

independent and with a good job. So how easy you can do this is entirely up to you."

"Then, I suppose, I should leave him. I should leave him before he leaves me!" woman's spite spoke again.

"Anna, this is not a competition – who leaves who first! Just accept this as one natural development of a long-term relationship. It happens to many other families." Markot had no idea what happened to most relationships and simply relied on the general and widely available clichés.

"Yes, I know. But still, I'll leave him first. He doesn't deserve me. I gave him two wonderful children and now, when he gets back from work late in the evening, he behaves as if I don't exist. I don't deserve to be ignored, no matter if he's cheating on me or not. I deserve a lot better…"

"Do what you think is best for you. With this we conclude our conversation and you must leave now. I consider my idea the best possible in your case. You'll decide whether you will make use of it or no."

"Thank you, Mr. Markot! I am really thankful. You're a smart young man. Thank you."

"I'm simply doing my job. You have to go now." he was unnecessarily rude. The consultant did not want to take down the 'skin' of the insensitive snowman until he was alone in the room again.

Anna stood up, still crying, ready to leave the interrogation room. She did not hate the idea-consultant anymore. She wanted to shake hands with him like any grateful and polite person. Markot shook his head negatively, because physical contact was prohibited.

Often, the first attempt of doing something is not that great, because one lacks the experience. Markot's second trial was much better and surely the more experience he had, the more successful he would become at his job. Well, this was only in theory. The idea-consultant, Third rank, remained alone in the room. He had no intention to press the button. Not today. He was waiting for his next client, convinced that he will help him in the same way he had helped Anna. The snowman had succeeded and it was clear that his frosty stance worked. Markot thought about his very first client – Teristan. If he was firmer with him from the beginning, who knows, maybe, the end result would have been different? Possibly, Markot would have come up with far better idea than urging the guy to rely on his luck.

The idea-consultants worked on their own. No one watched them and no one eavesdropped on their conversations with clients. The consultants had no right to discuss between themselves what went on behind doors, in their interrogation rooms. This prevented them, however, from learning from their own mistakes, because there was no one to point out at their errors. Of course, any misgivings showed up at the annual tests, but not always. Sometimes, the bored members of the committee could not be bothered to ask the young consultants provocative questions, specific to their actual job. They just teased them for fun and made a joke of their inferiors. Let's imagine someone did sit behind the glass and this one was not anyone else, but Markot's Mentor. Well, then, the criticism, which would have followed, was going to be devastating. It would have been much worse than after the first meeting, when Markot did deliver a decent idea, despite the huge cracks in his "wall". A good idea was the most important thing in the job, after all.

Markot's attitude was unacceptable from the start. Why did he try to impose his will in this way, when he was dealing with a lady twenty years senior to him? She was not his enemy or opponent. She had come for help. Where was his respect for the elder? It was not an excuse that she looked younger for her age. Where was the gentleman in him, who was supposed to treat women appropriately? Instead, Markot took the role of the invincible snowman. Well, a man, made from real snowballs of different size would have been kinder and friendlier to her. Markot's harsh iciness, which was too much of it, had played a bad joke on him, like anything that is in its extreme form. One of his major mistakes was that he argued with her. The idea-consultants need to be diplomatic. They should avoid exchanging sensitive remarks with the client, as this would be unlikely to help them come up with the right idea at the end. Moreover, Markot kept asking clichéd questions, some of which, totally unnecessary. Why did he ask about her children? She could have had ten children and they would have nothing to do with the problem between her and her husband. Sometimes, it was important to collect some personal information about the client during the second stage, but the more experienced consultants like Andir rarely resorted to this. Markot had failed to apply his ability to keep a track of time, too. The meeting with Anna went on for far too long. A consultant of the First rank would have finished in half that time. Markot sidetracked a few times and this took up precious minutes. A good employee at the Idea Factory was supposed to be efficient. Efficiency was a synonym of expeditiousness.

Another blunder of Markot was the actual idea he came up with. His move was rather stupid, to say the least. He gave her an idea that she had suggested to him in a way. This, of course, happened occasionally, but why did he not think of something much better, something original, instead of resorting to the ready 'product'? To hire more detectives was not only a feeble idea, but it was not even his. It would have been much better if he suggested to her to call her husband's bluff. By doing this, she would have done a perfect job. In the case of adultery, most men take the bait quite easily. Anna could have played the angry wife, who had answered the phone that day and some strange woman spoke on the end of the line. Who was she? On the following day, Anna should only 'find' a lipstick or something ladylike in her husband's car or at home and hurray! Bingo! If this other woman existed, the husband would quickly own up to it.

Andir would have conjured up more than one idea. The torturous constant phoning, which some jealous women subjected their husbands to, could have been the easy answer to Anna's problem. As long as she learned her man's working schedule, she, then could begin to phone him every time he did not show up as supposed to. No matter how hard he tried to cover up his tracks, she would eventually catch him lying. Basically, with a little effort on Anna's part, she could have collected sufficient information about whether she had been cheated on or not.

Markot's idea was fine, but it was not great. The idea-consultants were encouraged to offer original ideas to their clients, otherwise, the unique nature of the Factory suffered. Anyone, who had gone there, had to receive a unique solution. Even if the idea was not exceptional in that sense, it should at least sound as if it was. The young and inexperienced consultant could have pump up a bit his detectives. They could have been some special agents that had long worked in the secret services. Or Markot could have suggested for Anna to hire detectives from a different town, as they were, of course, so much better than those local ones, she had employed previously. Plenty of alternatives, but the young man did not think of any.

If Andir was really standing behind the mirror, he would have got angry with his former student for allowing some of the final exchange of remarks with his beautiful client. "Attractive woman, financially independent, good job" – what did this have anything to do with the idea? Nothing! Compliments were not allowed. The consultant could resort to flattering their customer only if this helped him get important information out of them, thanks to which, he would come up with an idea of a much better quality. Markot, however, admired her beauty, her career position and her supposedly high income after he had already spelled out his idea. Why the hell did the boy behave in such a strange way? Was he not taught the right stuff and what to do back at the Academy?

In effect, Markot did exactly what he had been taught there, but he customized everything to fit his own views and understanding of the job. The lecturers had always nagged that the idea-consultant had to feel strong and confident in his own interrogation room at all times and that he had all the power in his hands, while conducting the interview. The self-assured consultant was calm and came up with good ideas. If he was week, hesitant and nervous, he would fail at his job. In this case, the young idea-consultant, Third rank, tried to impose his will and display power not because he felt that in this way he would think of a better idea, but because he was afraid of failure. Andir had attempted to change him by offering him the snowman trick, which Markot was supposed to use in difficult and tense situations. Instead, he turned into a permanent pile of snow, hoping that being aloof would help him do a better job. His fear from failing was tremendous, indeed.

"No one can lie to you more than when you lie to yourself!"

The worse of all was that Markot intended to continue with his inappropriate and cold behavior in future meetings with his clients. He believed that this was the right approach, which would lead him to success, so why change it! Sooner or later, however, he was going to end up being punished for his tactless, rude and, sometimes, offensive attitude. One day, one of his frozen up clients was going to

147

bring him to the floor and direct a blowlamp towards the snowman, melting his wrong working practice down to the last icy crystal.

Little John

Every time Markot found himself alone in the room, he took the chance to stretch his legs. He would go round the room about ten times before he sat down in his chair. He wanted to keep going for a bit longer, but he knew that if the client entered the room, he could be caught up, striding in the middle of it. And this was forbidden. The reason behind these short strolls was related to the temperature inside and it had nothing to do with his body, needing to remind itself of its basic motor function. The room, where the idea-consultant, Third rank, had to work, was a little colder than the rest of the interrogation rooms in the building. It was basically situated at the end part of the Idea Factory. The fine heating system could not reach out to the edges and operate as efficient as in the central section of the building. That was the reason why Markot's customers rarely took off their coats and only unbuttoned them. Those, who dared to sit in their jumpers, were risking catching a cold, which the consultant got on his second working day. The preventive measures he had taken did not have the desired effect. The two pairs of thick socks, he was wearing, only desensitized his frozen feet and the extra top under his shirt did the job for only about a couple of hours. Soon after, he would feel the cold again. His hands did not suffer as bad, because Markot had discovered an easy way to warm them up, no matter if he was alone in the room or with a client. According to the rules, the consultants could not gesticulate with their hands and had to keep them to the front, rested on their lap. Markot followed closely this rule, but every time he felt that they were getting numb, he would clutch them into fists and then, stretch his fingers out. This movement resembled the pumping of a heart. It was well hidden from the client's eyes and did not interfere with the creation of a good idea.

The idea consultant was indulging in yet another of his brisk strolls, which always finished with him standing on his toes a few times, when he got a surprise visit. Someone opened the door. A client had turned up earlier than he was supposed to. Markot responded in the best possible way by immediately taking his seat. He straightened his position, ready for work. The door was still open, when the consultant felt a bit shocked by the customer's size. The intruder was enormous in width. He had most probably never missed a meal in his life. The visitor was the largest and heaviest creature that had ever set foot in the cold interrogation room. He must have snacked constantly in between meals, which were probably always a double extra large size. Well, Markot still had to provide the client with the best possible solution for his problem, despite what his feeding habits had been over the years. Confident and calm, the idea-consultant did not intent to succumb to or be intimidated by this mammoth of a human being. He was going to treat him in exactly the same way as the rest of his slimmer clients.

"Sir, please take a seat." Markot uttered in a flat, lifeless tone of voice. This was a trivial invitation, but which the fat guy really struggled to oblige to.

"Pffeu, eh-h, oops... now I'm ready, yes, I'm good, yes, that's right, yes." the inflexible space between the table and the chair was way too small for him. The customer had to breathe in and reduce his waistline by ten centimeters, in order to squeeze in the narrow space and sit down. When he eased off the balloon, a few fatty layers sprawled out over the table. It was obvious that he was not very pleased with the resistance, shown by his stomach, but nevertheless, he was prepared to put up with the unfair punishment until the end of the prepaid meeting. Solving an important problem, sometimes, required putting up with significant discomfort.

"My name is Markot, idea-consultant, Third rank. What is your name?"

"Eh-r-r, John, but they call me Little John, yes, Little John." the visitor replied and placed his enormous paws on top of his gut. Why a lot of large people got a nickname, stating exactly the opposite, was a question that the host did not intend to ask.

"John, we have rules in the Idea Factory and you, like everyone else, need to observe them. We'll go through three stages and at the end I shall tell you how to solve your problem. You must answer my questions if we want our meeting to be successful."

149

"Yes, yes, successful, I must, indeed. Ask me, then, yes, fire away!" Little John said enthusiastically. He could not wait to share what had brought him there.

"We will pause, now, for a minute, when both of us need to say no word. Then, you will tell me why you've come here. You will just have to start speaking first, without waiting for me to prompt you."

"Yes, yes, right, I'll be the first to begin." the fatso nodded in agreement and this caused his quadruple chin to wrinkle into a few further repulsive fatty folds.

The analysis of the subject, despite him being double in size, was not going to take twice as long. The job could have been even done in less than the standard sixty seconds. Markot, however, did not want to rush through this part of the first stage, so he carefully began to study the strange clothes John had put on. Little John. Actually, they were only strange, because they were so large. The dark tracksuit bottoms were worn out on the knees and the color there was much lighter. The gigantic padded top was filled up to the full, so that if its owner made a sudden and unexpected movement, there was the risk that it ripped along the seams and his flesh flooded out uncontrollably. There were visible red stains on his sweatshirt, right below his chin, no doubt, from the ketchup, he had piled on top of his last meal. No surprise there - the black jacket was unseemly enormous. It also showed the signs of wear and tear. The sleeves were slightly cracked around the stitches, which were actually a different color on the right elbow – the evidence of some urgent past patching. Markot was so enthralled by the big, Little John that he failed to notice his shoes at first. Finally he glanced at them only to realize that they had had it the hardest. Literally. They were a large size. The soles were almost non-existent and the faded leather was a sign for the many winters they had endured. Logically, Markot concluded that if this poor whale-like customer wore a hat and a pair of gloves, they would have definitely been in a real bad state.

It was pointless to go deep into the physical characteristics of the client. All obese people looked very similar in a kind of fatty, porky way. It was time to try and judge the character of this fatso. Strangely enough, despite the way he looked, John spoke like a teenager in eighth grade, in a rather pubescent voice. He sounded naïve and hasty. Markot could not guess his age, because his plump

150

face with fat cheeks did not display the regular signs of aging that lighter people's face did. In his case, the deep wrinkles on his forehead were down to him being overweight, not because of his age. Still, he was probably in his mid twenties. He did not seem very intelligent. He came across as openly stupid. Despite the obvious, the idea-consultant tried to avoid making such conclusions. At the Academy, they were taught never to underestimate anyone, even if they looked like a complete idiot. It was important to focus carefully on the client's intellectual capacity - yes, but no underestimating! Markot had no option, but to wait for good Little John to tell him everything that was necessary for the consultant to come up with one fat great idea.

During the mandatory analysis, the mega-visitor was sitting calm in his uncomfortable narrow place. At first, he tried to do something obscure and unbeknown to Markot, but then, John quickly gave up on the idea. Despite being quite chilly in the room, he was feeling rather warm. The layers of fat prompted him to get rid of his enormous jacket. Whatever his motives, the intention came to no fruition. He was stuck and could not move an inch. He tried to turn round and escape from the merciless bite, formed by the table and the chair, but he soon changed his mind. Well, it was not that hot. He better stayed with his jacket on.

"The minute has passed, as you said, so I'll tell you why I'm here, yes, I shall tell you, shall I, yes?" the client did not wear a watch, supposedly because the wrist band had to be much larger than the one on Markot's wrist. It was doubtful that one could buy those in the shop. Still, John spoke, as ordered, on the sixty-first second.

"Why are you here?" Markot asked and at the same time, he was wondering how one could balloon to such extreme size. How?

"I've come here, yes, because I want to surprise my mother, it's her birthday and I want to get her a present, to surprise her, for her birthday, you know? You can tell me how I can surprise her, 'cause I really want to surprise her, a lot, 'cause so few things make her happy and I always disappoint her and I want to surprise her for her birthday and…" the emotional tirade was cut short earlier than John wished. He had to stop talking, because the oxygen was not filling efficiently his exhausted lungs, which had grown flabby and fat. Clearly, he could not bear any simple physical exertion, because he was so overweight. He had to pause for a short break, even after a couple of sentences.

"Surprise, then? You want to surprise your mother?" Markot repeated, despite the fact that he had heard perfectly fine what John had said about five times.

"Yes, yes, that's right, I want to surprise her, 'cause it's her birthday and I want to surprise her, instead of disappointing her again. It has to be a huge surprise, right? Yes… yes…"

"A surprise, then? You want to surprise your mother for her birthday?"

"Yes, yes, to surprise her… my mother… for her birthday… Big surprise, it needs to be big, yes…" the client was panting heavily in a near heart attack way, not realizing that he was being mocked. This was a cruel joke, totally inappropriate, with which Markot wanted to show how much better he was than John, despite the fact that they could not compete, when it comes down to going on the scales. Now that he proved his powers within the interrogation room, the idea-consultant had to put a stop to his ridicules and actually do his job.

"John, I got it perfectly clear what you want from me. We'll move on to the second stage now if you don't have anything else to add?"

"Yes, yes, the second stage…"

"I'll be asking you questions and I expect you answer them all very honestly! Only in this way, I'll be able to tell you what the best present for your mother is. How old is she going to be?"

"Yes, yes, she'll be, eh-r-r… I'm not sure, ah, twenty six plus… twenty four, she'll be…"

"Fifty? Your mother has an anniversary? Such an occasion requires a big surprise, indeed." Markot readily offered the result of the equation, when he saw that the insufficient grey matter in the customer's head was beginning to struggle.

"Yes, that's right, yes, a big surprise…"

"Fine, we've made this clear. What do you do for a living, John?"

"You know, there, on the docks, yes, my mother got me this job on the docks and I work there on the docks…"

"Got it. Where do you live? At your mum's, I imagine?"

"Yes, yes, at hers, yes, I live at home with her, yes…"

"How old are you, John?"

"I'm twenty six, yes, twenty six." this time, he sounded totally certain about the right number.

"John, if I'm supposed to help you surprise your mother, I need to know what kind of person she is. Could you briefly describe her to me?"

"She is my mother, how, my mother, I don't know, she is my mother and she loves me and I love her a lot and I want to surprise her for her birthday and…"

"I don't think you understand my question, John." Markot interrupted him quite abruptly. "Alright, we'll do this in a different way. I'll tell you a few things and you will pick those that apply about your mother."

"Yes, yes, yes, I will…"

"Is your mother nice to you? Does she tell you off? Is she strict? Does she let you do most things or she forbids most of the stuff you want to do?"

"Yes, she allows me to do a lot of things, but she also bans me from doing others, I don't know, she lets me eat whatever I want, regularly she makes for me some of her cookies, it's a secret recipe…" John was dreaming on about his mum's cookies and he felt really sorry about not taking at least one in his enormous pocket.

"And what doesn't she let you do? Give me an example."

"She doesn't let me do, ah, she doesn't let me-e-e… stay late outside, she worries, my mother, a lot about me and she doesn't let me stay late outside, yes, outside. She lets me, but not till late…"

"I got that, John. What does your mother like doing in her spare time?"

"My mother, she cooks, yes, so when I get back home I've got something to eat, and then, something for breakfast and to take for lunch a little and she cooks for me…"

"So your mother likes cooking? "Does she have a choice with such a pig at home?" was the thought that filled the idea-consultant's head in the same way, the industrial quantities of food filled the stomach of the fatso, who was his current customer.

"Yes, yes, she loves cooking, yes, and to watch television, she likes that a lot, to watch television in the day time, yes."

"Doesn't she work? Doesn't she go to work?"

"No-o-o, no-o-o, the doctors said she couldn't, no, no." The fatso waved his fleshy sausage of a finger, the index finger, to be precise, enthusiastic to show how wrong the idea-consultant was.

"What doctors? What's wrong with your mother?"

"She's ill and she's got this ah-a-a... I don't know, it's something so complicated, and I don't know, I don't know..."

"Alright, it doesn't matter, John, it's not so important. How long has she been staying at home?"

"Years, yes, several years..."

"Can you tell me roughly how many? More than two or less?"

"Oh, yes, yes, a lot more than two, yes, a lot more. Twelve, twelve, yes, a lot..."

"Yes, this is a lot. And your father, what does he do?"

"No, I don't have a father, no, my mother, she's told me that I don't have a father." Little John firmly stressed. He had never doubted the authenticity of every word his mother had told him.

"Everyone's got a father, but maybe, you just don't know who your father is? Is that right?"

"No, my mother says that I don't have a father and I don't have, no, I don't..."

"You do. Everyone does, otherwise it's impossible... Fine, we'll leave this." Markot was not a biology teacher and he decided to spare him the life lesson about human reproduction. "John, have you thought about how you could surprise your mother for her birthday, before you actually decided to come here and see me? Any ideas? You must have had something in mind?"

"I don't know, I haven't, I don't want to disappoint her again, and I haven't thought about it and you could tell me... to surprise her I want, and she's got a birthday, and I want to surprise her..."

"What did you give her last year?" Markot interjected, now realizing how unnecessary this model of repetition was that the thick boar had been resorting to.

"Nothing, nothing and, I was at work and I forgot, I forgot..." the greasy pig was truly remorseful about his unforgivable oversight. He suddenly shed a couple of tears, which were quickly wiped off before falling on his worn out top.

"It's alright, Little John, it can happen to anyone, to forget their mother's birthday." Markot said rather tactlessly and in the most

154

inappropriate moment. In effect, he was mocking him again. But why?"

"Yes, yes, but I want to surprise her, now, for her birthday, I want this so much and I haven't forgotten this time…"

"Yes, yes, I got this, yes." the idea-consultant imitated him scornfully. Of course, the stupid John did not see through this. "How much money have you got for your mother's present? I imagine, you've been saving for a whole year?"

"Yes, yes, I've been saving, but I don't have any money, I don't have…"

"But you work on the docks, don't you? And you get paid for this? Haven't you saved a little at least? You need money to get a big surprise present, you know that?"

"Yes, yes, I do have money, I do, but I've just given it at the entrance, here, to that guy…" although, John could not see through the eighteen walls, separating that man from them, he managed to point in the right direction.

"Are you telling me that you've given away all your savings to pay the fee to come and see me?" How could he be so stupid? Well, obviously, he could.

"Yes, I gave the money, because they said that I couldn't get in, otherwise. When I came another time and… and got turned away, 'cause I had to have money and I went back to get some money and I was let in, then." Little John had a wide grin on his face. He was very pleased with himself for succeeding to find himself legally in the Idea Factory.

"So you've been here before, but without any money on you? Does your mother know that you've been here?"

"No, no, she doesn't, I want to surprise her for her birthday, she doesn't know… she's got a birthday, and I want to…"

"John, how do you think you can do this, surprise your mother without a penny in your pocket? You are a complete…" Markot stopped in time. "Can you give her something that you've made yourself, for a present, which does not cost any money? Can you? Can you?"

"I don't know, I don't know, but what…?"

"Something that you can create with your own hands, and which she would like very much. John, have you got any talents, apart from being a super retarded moron?" the second part of the sentence remained unsaid.

"Tale-e-e-nts... tale-e-e-nts..." Mr. "Enormous Round Object, which could be seen from Space", repeated, unsure of what this actually meant. What he was certain of was that whatever it was, it was not something one could eat, because if it was, he would have definitely heard of it before.

"You do know what a talent is, don't you? To be good at drawing, singing, playing a musical instrument. Or something like this. Have you played an instrument?"

"Yes, yes, I have, yes..."

"What?"

"The, the, the... I have played the drums, but my mother told me off for playing the drums and..."

"Because you made a lot of noise?"

"No, no, she said I need to be more active and not to sit in one place for long, and to be more active..."

"Have you tried another instrument or just the drums?" Markot asked, wondering how heavier his client could have been, if his mother did not distract him from the drums. Double???

"The drums, yes, just the drums, I haven't played anything else, no..."

"Alright, John, it looks like that you don't have any talents that you could surprise your mother with, so we leave this on one side. How much money you could find before your mother's birthday? What is the maximum?"

"I don't know, how much, I don't know, to find money, but where from? I don't..."

"You can ask your boss to give you an advance payment. When you explain to him your situation, he'll understand and he'll give you the money. If he's a good boss, he'll do this for you."

"No, he won't, he won't give it to me, he won't, money, no..."

"Why are so sure?"

"Because he said that he won't be paying me anymore and he said that I'm supposed to pay him and that he won't give me any money no more, no..." the client shook his head energetically, causing a dozen of unpleasant folds of skin appear on his face.

156

"Why? Have you done anything at work that made him say this? What have you done, John?"

"I, I'm sorry, but…"

"Come on, you can tell me, don't be embarrassed!" Markot could not wait to hear what kind of blunder his fat client had done at work. He was certain that it was something very retarded and beyond his imagination.

"They told me that if I let them back in the water, I'll get a bonus and the boss will praise me for being his best employee and I let them back, but they made me, they made me…"

"Who did tell you and what did you let back in the water?"

"The fish, all the fish went back to the fishes in the water, but they made me, it wasn't my fault…"

"I did not say it was your fault, Little John. Can you tell me in more detail what happened?"

"They made me let the fish, when the trawler arrived and they told me to let it back in the water, instead of loading it on the truck. Them, trawlers, when they come and the fish go onto these huge trucks…"

"I know that, John. So instead of loading it, you let it back in the water. What was the loss? How much fish did go back in the ocean?"

"All of it, I just opened the main hold, where all the fish was and it ran away, the little fishes just ran away…"

"You let a trawler load of fish go back in the water?" Markot was amazed. The scale of the idiotic blunder that naïve John had made, was bigger than his own gigantic proportions.

"Yes, the whole lot, but my mother told me that it was not my fault, but those, who made me do this, they work on the docks, and I work on the docks…"

"Why did you listen to them? Didn't you guess what would happen? How can you be so reckless?" the consultant used a less offensive word in the last possible moment.

"I don't know, I don't know, they told me, and also the boss was going to say 'well done' to me, and I work so hard, I don't know…"

"John, why don't you leave your job if you are not getting paid for it and you won't be paid in the future? Why don't you just leave?"

"My mother told me that I have to stay and work, because, when I let the fish, people lost a lot of money and I have to work until they tell me and..."

"How will you live without money? Maybe, you have a second job?"

"No, no, there's no way, there isn't any time, I only go on the docks, only there, on the docks..."

"John, if you really want to surprise your mother, you need to find another job and make some money. Otherwise, you won't be able to do it. You can't give her a surprise present without money. When is her birthday? How much time have you got?" this was a good question, but it was asked a little late.

"I don't know exactly, but it's in... in... half a year and a bit more, a few days after half a year, yes..."

"Six months? You're telling me that your mother's birthday is after six months?" Markot allowed his frozen body to loosen up a bit and almost jumped at the piece of information, he had just heard. He could not help himself even if he was made from stone.

"A few days after half a year, or there about, about, about... yes, six months, yes..."

"So, you've started preparing for this early enough. Let's hope that when the Big day comes, you won't forget the date and whose birthday it is!" "Moron!" the idea-consultant could have thought of dozens of nasty insults, but none of them was strong enough to describe the infinite lack of rationality, the thick greasy ball, sitting opposite him, displayed.

"No, no, I won't, I remember, I know when it is, I know, my mother has a birthday, I know..." Little John assured him, uncertain of the exact date in that moment. He remembered the month, but not the day.

"This means that you have plenty of time to find another job, make enough money for the present, which I'm going to tell you about, so you can surprise her."

"But I can't get another job, I've got one, on the docks I work, there on the docks..."

"You'll leave. There's nothing to hold you there."

"But my mother won't let me go to a different job, no, she won't, she won't let me..."

"John, you are not little anymore, so if you really want to surprise her, you'll have to do what I tell you. Find a job, make the money, and you could always tell her about it, after you've surprised her."

"No, I can't lie to her, my mother told me that I should not lie to her and I don't lie to her and I've got a job, there on the docks, I work there on the docks…"

"This is not lying. You'll just delay telling her the truth and let her know about it later. What was your job before the docks?"

"Nothing. I have not worked before and there on the docks, I've only worked there, yes, on the docks…"

"What do you mean by 'nothing'? Absolutely nothing? So then, how long have you been working on the docks?"

"For two years, on the docks, there on the docks, for two years, yes…"

"And what have you been doing before, if not working? You didn't go to college!" Markot was not suggesting, he was noting a screamingly obvious fact. "Did you stay at home all this time?"

"Yes, yes, I was at home, she, my mother, I had to take care of her and I was at home all the time, yes…"

"Why did you start working on the docks, then, instead of staying at home and carry on looking after your mother? It seems that she needs constant care!"

"Yes, yes, constant, otherwise, she won't take her pills and the doctors have to come again and she will need to go back in hospital, but it's not nice in there…"

"So she doesn't have a problem with taking her medication regularly now, does she?"

"No, she doesn't. She remembers to take it and she told me to get a job, there on the docks, to find something there and work…"

"I got it now, Little John. What can you find in your town that is different from working on the docks? Is there anything you could start doing as soon as possible? The sooner you get paid the better!"

"I don't know, I've done nothing else before, apart from working there on the docks and I don't know, I don't know…"

"And how could you know?" "You fat idiot" Markot was sure that the sweat, trickling all over his face was much closer, chemically, to oil than water.

"I don't know, I don't know…"

"Whatever you find, it's doubtful that you'll get paid more than the minimum wage. Without previous experience, you can't hope for more. John, can you tell me, when you were getting paid there on the docks, how much you spent and how much you saved, there on the docks?" this was impossible. The repeating of every word proved to be very contagious. Good job that obesity was not airborne, otherwise, Markot's perfect body was going to turn into two-legged fat ball-like misunderstanding of Nature.

"I don't remember how much, but…"

"Were you usually left with about 200-300? Am I close?"

"Yes, yes, but sometimes, it was 354, and other times it was less, sometimes…"

"354?" Markot repeated the odd sum. Only a crazy man could say such a silly number. "That's not bad. It may not be much, but you can save enough to buy a decent present in six months. You make my job much easier with almost two thousand in your pocket."

"But I owe money there for the fish and I have to give them the money, for the fish, when I earn it, I have to take it there and give it to them…"

"No, you don't have to, John. You've worked at the docks for free, so whatever you make at your new job, it will be all for you. If you give your former boss everything, then, you'll be left with nothing for the surprise."

"Yes, but my mother will tell me to give it to him, she will say this and I will…"

"Don't you remember my advice to keep your new job a secret from her? So she wouldn't know that you are earning money!" the idea-consultant was getting rather vexed. Well, there were not any signs of his snowman changing his solid aggregate state into liquid, but it was quite possible that he reached for his carrot and ate it, if this globe, full of cholesterol, continued to irritate him.

"Yes, yes, but I'll tell her, she, my mother told me that I should not lie to her and I'll tell her that I'm working and that I've got money, I'll tell her…"

"John, you are talking complete nonsense. Can't you get it that if you tell her everything goes to pot? Even if you remember her birthday this time, you won't have any money for a present and you'll disappoint her again, as you always did before." the annihilating criticism crushed the big baby and he started crying. He had to be consoled, if the conversation was to be continued, not that this could be called a conversation.

"But... my mother... she said, said... that I shouldn't, shouldn't..."

"Enough with my mother this, my mother that! John, if you want to surprise her, you must listen to me. If you don't, I can just tell you to leave immediately, because you don't comply with the rules." a development like this was very possible, because the client clearly obstructed the consultant's job.

"But... she, my mother told me... said... she will tell me to..."

"It doesn't matter what your damn stupid mother is going to say, she is irrelevant, forget about your mother for a minute at least, don't you want to...?" the raging idea-consultant could not finish his sentence. He leaned to the right and collapsed on the floor. Someone turned the light off. Not the one in the room, but that in his head. Markot lost consciousness.

The idea-consultant, Third rank, had misinterpreted the use of power and this caused the power cut in his scull. The insults, thrown at the client's mother, activated every cell in his body, including the fatty ones, so he hit Markot. The victim blinked in this moment of time and could not see the approaching huge fist. John was fast as a cat and he could make any professional boxer envious of him. His move was the biggest surprise in Markot's short career. He had never been attacked so far, apart from receiving a few insults and being spat on once. There was no way that the consultant could have known about the fact that if anyone insulted his mother, Little John would turn into the Big Scary John, who was prepared to defend the name and honor of the women, who had brought him into this world. He would lose control over his huge body, fearlessly and without hesitation, he would throw a punch straight at the person, who had dared talk nonsense. He was famous for being sensitive about the subject and people, who knew him, could joke about anything with him but never about his mother. When the retarded pig allowed several tons of fish to go back and join their natural habitat, he did not feel revengeful towards his "colleagues", who had made him perform this great idiotic act. John did not even fall out with them,

161

only because the holy image of his mother was not involved in this costly joke.

Markot came round into the living world again. The first thing he saw was the grey floor in the interrogation room. He was so close to it that he could not focus well on the blurred image. He felt a sharp pain in his back, possibly because of the strange position he had fallen into. With great effort, he managed to kneel, by resting on his left hand. The doggie's position seemed to work, but his aim was to stand up on his feet. Markot resorted to his other hand in this difficult exercise and finally, he stood up in his full glory. Actually, the glory was not that full, because of his limited sight, caused by his closed eye. This was the eye that had met up with John's fist, which like anything else was double in size. If anyone wondered, whether the fist was fatty enough to subdue the blow, well, then, the idea-consultant would have been the first to dispute the logic of this suggestion. He carefully touched the area, where his left eye was supposed to be, and got horrendously scared. The enormous ball with a size of an orange was not meant to be there. Worse of all, he could not see anything with this eye. When Markot closed his undamaged eye, he fell into the deepest darkness, much darker and sinister than if he turned the light off in the room. The damage, caused by just one surprise blow was too bad. Unpredictably bad! The headache was going to pass, no doubt about this, but was the eye that had taken the punch, ever going to get back to normal, or Markot had to take the role of the one-eyed pirate from now on? The victim sat down on the metal chair, but stood up almost straight away and went to press the button. It looked like that the fat attacker had left the room not long before, because there was no one new in the interrogation room. The idea-consultant was going to press the lifesaving red button every thirty minutes until the end of the working day, as he did not want to be seen in this condition. He went nearer the glass and looked at himself. What a troll! The swelling was much bigger that he imagined and the dark purple-blue color was a sign of possibly a very serious damage and deep lacerations. His cheekbone was probably broken, but Markot did not want to check. He did not want to touch it. He was afraid of the pain. Slowly he sat down on the chair, which was designated for his clients and fell into deep thought. He was analyzing himself.

There were plenty of questions he should answer, but one was throbbing in his head the most. Why? Markot was not asking himself why John had hit him, but why he behaved as he did? Why was the snowman so arrogant, unprofessional, crass and rude with someone, who deserved such treatment the least? One was supposed to help people, who were week, had been unfairly treated, had been suffering, were simply overweight or retarded. This was the reason for everyone to want to work in the Idea Factory, was it not? Did they not teach them, at the Academy, how to help people? No one had ever mentioned there anything about making inappropriate jokes with the client, resorting to open ridicule or crushing people's dignity. Markot had actually a very mellow personality. The little orphan had never displayed such low human qualities. Never. He could not see an example of such behavior, growing up in a family, where the father was an idea-consultant, First rank, and the mother hovered around, like a hen, and made sure everything was provided for her only son. He did not pick up this attitude from the street, either, because there was not such a lowlife amongst the kids, he used to play with as a child. Why, then? Why did he treat his customer like this, especially when he was aware that Little John could not even sense the fact that he had been mocked? What was the point to waste a joke on someone, who was not going to appreciate it or get offended by it? Markot realized that he was enjoying the nasty game with John. The consultant felt great at the possibility to do whatever he wanted with his customer, without caring about the graveness of his utterance. Why? Markot was not provoked, insulted or threatened. Well, John might have shared information with difficulty and he might have mumbled a bit, but this could not be a motive for Markot's behavior, for the idea-consultant, who was supposed to help folks.

Late in the afternoon, after he pressed the button yet again, Markot finally discovered the real reason. He realized whose fault it was. It was not his, for definite! Markot was not himself in the interrogation room and he did not regard himself as being Markot. It was the snowman, who called John's mother stupid, and Markot was simply hiding behind him. The snowman felt sincere joy, when he heard the idiotic story about the fish. The snowman found it truly invigorating to make fun out of the client. Markot would never dare do this. The nice warm-blooded Markot would have felt sorry for the customer, who had become a victim of some idiots, he worked with, there on the docks. The consultant would have empathized with John's hardship and unjust fate, which had deprived him from the ability to reason like an adult. John was going to remain a child forever, who worked for free on the docks and lived with his lonely sick mother. He had probably suffered horrendously at school, where cruel kids had never missed the opportunity to laugh at him every day. Then, John had to go home after the lessons, which he could not understand much, and take care of his ill mum. Markot began to cry. He felt like placing his head on the metal table and simply wait for the hangman to finish him off. He did not want to live anymore. Not after what he had done. He did not deserve to live.

Crushed to the ground, the idea-consultant resumed some of his sanity a little before the end of the working day, which closed, as usual, with the indescribably beautiful winter sunset. Now that he had discovered the culprit of his evil attitude, Markot decided to get rid of him for once and for all. The snowman, who was there to help him in any tricky situation, was now going straight in the furnace. Within seconds, it was only the real Markot, who remained in the interrogation room. The end! From now on, the idea-consultant was going to do what he had been recruited for at the Idea Factory - help people. He was going to show his emotions, empathize with the clients' problems; he would shed tears and be sympathetic, despite the fact that all this breached the rules of the game. It was all forbidden, but the young idea-consultant wanted to be himself. He was going to follow his own rules and do his best to come up with the greatest ideas that actually worked. He was never going to insult and ridicule his clients. Of course, Markot would keep observing the basic model of the three-staged conversation. He did not intend to apply his own personal methods to his work, but just allow some of the emotions that made him human. An error. What a big error! Yet again!

Markot did not feel great on his way out of the Idea Factory, because he had an orange instead of an eye. Completely reborn and with a transformed working philosophy, the idea consultant did not want to be seen in this injured condition. He was ashamed from what he did to Little John and despite the fact that no one would ever know what happened in his interrogation room that day; Markot did not feel like meeting anyone. He sneaked towards his car two hours after sunset. The new idea-consultant, who thought of himself as better than the Good Samaritan, could work after hours, for sure. If he could only find the fat client, who had purified his mind out of all nastiness, and just help him. He could give him enough money. This would not be a problem in the slightest. He could help him choose the most suitable birthday present for his mother, a present that would surprise her as never before. The big occasion was quite ahead in the future, so Markot had time to redeem his guilt. He could mend his mistake. He could do a lot more than this. He could help John lose weight. He could find the best diet and the healthiest food for him. He could hire a tutor, who would teach him the basics that John had missed to grasp at school. In this way, he would become smarter, more rational, perceptive and shrewd. He could find him a better job, which was well paid and where workers were better colleagues to him. He could do anything, as long as he managed to find him. Although Markot had half a year to play with, before the anniversary event, impatient to look for John, the idea-consultant headed towards the nearest town with a port. It was not hard to make that choice, because there was only one place that fitted the picture, with regards to where Little John could have lived.

The idea-consultant, Third rank was not stupid at all, but halfway, driving towards the city, he realized that this venture was not a very smart move. How would he find Little John if he did not know his address? Fishing boats did not operate after dark. Moreover, the harbor was huge and this was not an insignificant problem. Even in the daylight, it would prove hard for one to find the retard in one day, despite him being visible from as high as the stratosphere. Markot decided that if he put John's biggest fault to his advantage, he might be a step ahead in the quest of finding him. He was going to ask about. John might be working dayshifts, but there must be someone after sunset, who had heard about the extremely fat and very round human being - the fatso that once had let a trawler load of fishes free. The altruistic act could have not remained a secret for long from most dockworkers. Let's hope John had become renowned enough in the meantime.

The idea-consultant was good at geography and knew the location of all the big towns in the country. He knew about the size of the population, approximately how far they stood from the Idea Factory and what they were famous for. The city, where Markot believed Little John and his sick mother lived, was well known for having the biggest port in the Northern parts of the country. Apart from the hundred of ships that came and went all the time, there were also the three nautical museums, which attracted the tourists to these unfriendly shores. Well, Markot did not go there to enrich his history knowledge but to find his savior and thank him for the healing miracle he had done with him.

He left his car a few meters away from the barrier, which controlled the admission of vehicles into the harbor area and continued on foot. The security guard did not have the slightest idea and could not tell the smartly dressed, bruised visitor, where the fat Little John could be. At least, the guy managed to help a little by explaining to Markot that there were another seven security checkpoints at the harbor, so it was possible that his colleagues might have heard something about the retarded rotund boy. The idea-consultant entered the vast area of the port to pursue his unusual for him detective task and headed towards the nearest people, he noticed. There was a group of some foreign sailors, laughing about only hundred meters away from him. They were clearly enjoying the fact that they had reached dry land for the first time in twenty-four days. How little one needs, sometimes, to experience truly spontaneous happiness! Eager to just get drunk, the mariners could not understand what Markot was trying to ask them. Naturally, they were well brought up 'citizens' of every sea and ocean and sincerely wanted to help him. Struggling with his lack of knowledge of the foreign lingo, it took the idea-consultant half an hour to realize that those were not the guys, he could expect some useful information from. If Markot tried to reason with the situation, he would have comprehended that most people, he would see at this time, were either part of a crew of a passing ship, or they were night workers, hence their inability to enlighten him about John, who worked only in the daytime. Markot, however, did not think about these things and carried on, eager to ask anyone that he came cross. He eventually stood in front of two trucks, risking his life, and prepared to ask their drivers about Little John. Instead of a reply, he got back deservedly plenty of cursing. The drivers had to catch up with schedules and did not have the time to talk about some unknown extremely obese creature. Still confident and full of belief, the idea-consultant walked around for another hour, but to no avail. No one had heard about the fat dockworker, who was capable of releasing tons of fish back in the water. "Was this the right town? Maybe, John worked for free on different docks? No, no, it must be here, I just need to look for him a bit harder!" said to himself Markot, while leaning on the frozen metal railing, which was supposed to protect people from falling into the deadly ocean. He felt like crying again. He thought once again about the sin, he had committed earlier in the day and the feeling about deserving to die came on even stronger. He was at the perfect place, if he wanted to commit suicide and put an end to his pitiful life. If he jumped, within minutes, his body would turn into yet another piece of junk, which would sink towards the already polluted bottom of the sea. There was a little chance he would ever be discovered. As if he was reading his mind, the driver of the truck, parked right behind him, pressed the horn. The powerful jumpy sound was a signal for the crane operator that the back of the lorry was ready to take on the next container, full of stock. The random sign of fate got Markot out of his stupor and returned him to the world of living. His suicidal thoughts vanished.

The uninvited late visitor, now, allowed himself to notice the intensive working process that went on around him. The nearest ship was being frantically unloaded, because several hundred of colorful containers had to be brought down before dawn. It was interesting to see how many meters the waterline would go up, when the last metal box was removed and freed the ship from its weight. The identical white trucks parked in their designated places to receive what they had come for. Then, they would leave in undisclosed direction, only to be replaced by the next heavy-duty brothers of theirs. Although, the whole process seemed perfectly organized and automated, there were always hidden risks during the operations. The crane-operators and the drivers had to be extremely concentrated. Well, the danger of any of the four workers in the sky to drop their load was minimal. But still, there were sometimes precedents. Just over a week ago, one of the most experienced crane-operator managed to put the container a few inches out of place. The uneven distribution of weight, along with the gravity still in action, made the container drop on the floor with a bang. The truck nearly turned over. Fortunately, no one was injured, but the two guys, who were directly to blame, got temporarily suspended. The crane-operator and the driver were not coming back to work until the situation got clear about whose fault it was. One blamed the feckless driver for moving in the last moment and thus making the incident imminent, where the other insisted that the flitter-brain high up there had not placed the goods where he should have. The situation showed the management of the port again that human error was the biggest threat to machine-operated processes. Say, if everything was controlled by a decent computer, it was doubtful that things would have gone out of hand in this unfavorable way. Unfortunately, perfection seemed to be far in the unpredictable future, when it came to harbors.

Markot followed this repetitive working process at least twenty times, until he decided to look, with his only eye, towards the numerous lights far away in the ocean. There, about ten ships were waiting for their turn to come and go through the pleasant unloading procedure. They were clearly eager to solve their weight problem and then, light as a feather, to continue their journey in open waters towards the next load of heavy goods, waiting for them somewhere around the globe. They did not fear the challenges ahead of that they had been constructed for. Moreover, the ships had no intention to ever go down and reach the bottom of the ocean. One of them, however, was quite different. Markot believed it was second in size. It was much brighter than the rest, as it had many more lights, turned on, and it was situated much nearer to the shore. Was this a cruise ship? Yes, it was, despite the lack of sensible reason behind the fact that it was there in the first place. Who in their right mind would pay to be brought to the shores of this unattractive Northern port? Obviously, there must be plenty of enthusiasts, judging by the number of well-lit cabins. But was it not much better to cruise in the warm waters near the Equator, where one could enjoy the breathtaking views? Did it not make more sense to go on a ship, which was going to take you to all the impressive world famous destinations in attractive and exotic countries? The idea-consultant could not understand such people. But he was perfectly aware that it was impossible to understand everyone. As long as he could understand his desperate clients and offer them good ideas, nothing else mattered.

Frozen to death, Markot left all the ships, different in size, color and purpose, where they belonged, and headed towards his car, hoping that he would succeed in his searching on the following day. He was coming again after work to look for his Savior. This time, he planned to leave earlier and possibly catch on of the day workers before their shift finished.

When the idea-consultant got home, he realized that the icy cold wind outside had helped his swelling to go down and become almost half in size. The enormous ripe orange had turned into an average little tangerine, which continued to get even smaller. Markot trusted the undisputable fast action of the ice, so he put some more on the injured spot. He did not get a minute of sleep. He tried not to think about anything, but his mind just hovered from topic to topic. He was thinking about everything that had happened to him in the last ten hours of his life. About Little John and his mother, who was supposed to get a present from her stupid forgetful son after six months, likely it was not! About the Idea Factory, which he was beginning to blame for his bad behavior. Markot could not quite figure out how the idea establishment made him behaves so unprofessionally, but deep down he felt that it was its fault. He was thinking about the snowman, who turned out to be much worse than he had imagined. He was supposed to be his loyal friend, who helped him when in need and who unreservedly offered his help whenever one called him. Alas, this supposedly best friend was never actually a friend in the first place. The idea-consultant also remembered the twisted pleasant feeling he had at the beginning of the meeting, when he realized his infinite superiority over his greasy customer, who was probably suffering from a high blood pressure. Tired of this midnight chaotic thinking, an hour before dawn, Markot actually fell asleep.

In the morning, there was not a trace of his injury. His eye could see fine and the purple bruise did not seem to be a great problem. His cheekbone was not broken, either. According to the rules, Markot could still come to work, no matter if the way he looked might not be that seemly for his customers. Broken leg or an arm in plaster were never a problem. Often, some idea-consultants came to work with crutches. Only if the condition was serious enough to hinder the working process of offering ideas to the customer, the idea-consultant would be freed from work and stayed at home or in hospital, until he felt better again to welcome more desperate clients. The regulations did not allow for abusing the system with the excuse: "I'm feeling sick and I can't come to work today". Anyone, who dared lie that they could not fulfill their responsibilities, got dismissed immediately and received a hefty fine. The fine was huge even for an idea-consultant of First rank. If the culprit had not been saving for at least five years, they simply could not afford to pay the penalty. Worse, they would probably need to work double that time, but elsewhere. This meant that the entire monthly salary from the new low-paid job, after the compulsory dismissal, would have to get transferred into the bank account of the Idea Factory. The situation resembled a financial slavery, very similar to that of Little John, with the only difference that one had not let a single fish back in the water. As expected, no one had ever breached this rule, regarding made up sickness stories and injury related fibs.

Colton

Markot was about to have another "first day" at the Idea Factory. This time, the real Markot was going to confront the clients' problems, but without a protective wall or a 'snowy' support. The inexperienced idea-consultant, who was often leaning from one extreme to the other, had no idea how his new image would be received by his clients. A huge surprise awaited him.

"Hi, please, welcome! I'm so glad to meet you! It is entirely my pleasure to help you! Thank you for coming!" the annoyingly polite host had stood up to meet the customer. He had stretched his arm out in the friendliest manner. The handshake was energetic, as if them two had not seen each other for ten years. Markot had a wide grin on his face, which clearly made the client feel uncomfortable. The consultant looked quite sinister because of the combination between his bruised eye and sparkling white teeth.

"Hello." the man replied, slightly taken aback, while Markot was still shaking his hand up and down.

"I'm so glad that you're here! Please, welcome! Feel at home, this is your seat. I will do anything to help you. Are you ready to begin? We have plenty of time, so when you say, we can start. Whenever you say."

"I'm ready."

"Perfect. We shall begin, then with the first stage. I'll explain everything about what it involves and if you have any questions, please, do not hesitate to ask me. Don't be afraid, I'm here to answer all your queries. I don't want you to feel uncomfortable at any moment!"

"I won't."

"You could talk to me about the tiniest concern you might have, at any time. Don't worry!" the relaxed customer was beginning to worry about the fact that he was persistently reminded that he should not.

"I won't."

"What is your name? I'm Markot."

"Colton."

"Nice to meet you, Mr. Colton!" the idea-consultant offered his hand again, across the metal table. The second shaking of hands lasted a bit less. It was strange to shake hands with the same person twice in the space of a minute, was it not? "Right, now we've met, we can start with the first stage. You've mentioned that you are ready, but if you need more time to adapt, or if you have any questions..."

"No, I'm fine."

"Alright. We begin with the first part. You'll have to answer the question "why are you here?" and tell me the reason behind your visit. You know, what kind of problem has made you come to the Factory, but you will speak, when a minute has passed, during which we will sit quiet. And when you feel that it's time, just answer my question. I hope you've understood, but if you want to ask me anything..."

"Yes, I got it." the client confirmed snappily, so he could quickly cut the annoying idea-consultant short.

"Perfect. So now, we'll stop talking for one minute."

The time, allocated for analyzing the customer was often used by the latter to analyze the consultant himself. Folks just wondered

171

about what kind of person was going to solve their difficult problem. Colton started to examine Markot in the same way that Markot would have done it – analyzing his clothes and how he looked. Well, the idea-consultants wore plain clothes, so they did not attract any attention or distract the client. However, there were a couple of things with this consultant that did divert from the rule. Two darker stains were visible next to the small top pocket of his creased black suit jacket. Was it car oil? No, blood. Of course, the several cuts around the bruised eye must have caused this. Or whoever had hit the idea-consultant, they might have punched his nose – and drop by drop, the blood had gone straight onto the garment. No matter which theory was correct, Colton got the gist of what had happened. The client discovered yet another imperfection in Markot's look. There were no traces of blood on his shirt, but Colton could clearly see some yellow dry stains from sweat around the collar. Obviously, the young man had wanted to save on washing and chose to wear the same old clothes for several days. There was no way for Colton to know, however, that after the yesterday's unplanned adventure, Markot had gone to bed straight in his clothes, without any intention to change his shirt in the morning. It looked like that after the catharsis, he experienced because of Little John, suddenly looking smart and perfect, had become irrelevant to him. The visitor moved his eyes next onto the consultant's hair. It was very possible that Markot did not have a mirror at home, because his hair was rather squashed on the right side. He had stayed in the same position, while pressing the ice on his injury and this had resulted in not getting proper sleep, as well as ending up with the dodgy hairstyle. Despite being cut quite short, there was this lump of static hair, sticking straight up.

The client was studying his object in the same way the graduates from the Academy did, not because he knew the working techniques of these experienced professionals, but because anyone in his shoes would have done it. The first thing we see in others is their clothes, their physical features and then, after a brief exchange of a few words, we inevitably throw ourselves into judging the character. Any averagely intelligent person followed this exact formula. Who had programmed us to be so similar and at the same time – so poles apart, Colton did not know and neither did Markot. Colton finished successfully with the first part of his analysis and moved onto the idea-consultant's personality.

It was quite obvious that he was a helpful man, always ready to assist and be at the customer's service. He spoke excitedly and was rather enthusiastic about the meeting, as if the client was an important persona of a celebrity status. Markot's image of the keen good guy was emphasized by his eager body position – leaning far too much towards the client, with his elbows, rested on the metal table. By stepping into the personal space of the visitor, Markot only wanted to express his impatience to hear about the problem, which had brought the man to him. Every cell in his body was devoted to his job and every tooth on display expressed the joy of meeting his new customer. Well, it was all too good to be true. Colton had a good idea about how the consultants at the Factory were supposed to behave and he was aware of the huge discrepancy between this and Markot's demeanor. The client expected to be welcomed by a much older person, who was possibly going grey, and displaying perfection in every sense. He expected to see a man with a stone face, a deep voice and emanating a clear authority. The guest had done his research well beforehand, and all his friends and colleagues, who had been to the Factory, described the consultant's persona exactly in this way. He was also told that the idea-consultant was super intelligent, showed vast knowledge about everything, talked only the right stuff, had the right attitude, and at the end of the meeting, simply delivered the best idea with the flare and ease, he was supposed to have. Some might have exaggerated their story a bit, but all in all, they were correct. "Why is this young man behaving like a kid, then? He sounds like a hypocrite! Why does he look so fake and acts, as if being my best friend? There must be some trickery involved!" Colton was right to think like this and anyone in his place would have felt in this way. The last drop in the ocean that convinced Colton not to believe in anything Markot said to him, although he had not even explained the reason for his visit, yet, was the fact that he had a bruised eye. "An idea-consultant, who had been beaten up? He would not have got punched, if he did not do something stupid, would he? So not only he behaved like a naïve idiot, with a wide grin on his face, but also he was possibly a provocateur! He is simply

173

waiting for me to tell him why I am here and he'll start with the uncomfortable questions! He won't go far with me! Not with me!"

Unaware of the unpleasant surprise, he was about to receive, Markot got on with the analysis of his client, totally confident and relaxed that he would solve his problem, no matter how complicated it might be. Colton was dressed in plain clothes that usually middle-classed folks had. He looked normal, of an average height and weight. "Hmm, could Little John really loose weight?" Markot was not very concentrated and quickly shifted the focus from his subject onto the protagonist of the previous day and thus, he put an untimely end to his lame analysis of Colton. "What is John doing right now? He's probably there, on the docks, working away for free! He gets nothing and asks his mother for money, most likely! Well, he might be begging his friends for some cash but… but how many people would pick such an Enormous friend? Most people would feel embarrassed to be seen on the street with Little John, who happily shouts in front of the strangers around: 'Hey, my friend!' Not me, though! I won't be embarrassed! Never! Hmm, he still doesn't know how to surprise his mother and hasn't got the money to do so! What was his sleep like last night, I wonder? Surely, he must have been very upset. He feels sorry about punching me, certainly, but I deserved it. That's right. I deserved it! I'll find him. I'll find him and I'll help him. I'll find him…"

"Sorry, I didn't get this?" Colton asked because the consultant had been speaking under his breath for a while. The minute had just passed. Good job that the customer spoke first and got Markot out of his trance, otherwise he would have carried on repeating the key phrase for ages.

"A-a-ah, don't mind me. You can answer the question now. If you are not ready, I can give you more time. It's not a problem…"

"I want to go to a different room." firmly said the visitor.

"How do you mean? What different room? If you need more time to adapt to your environment and relax, please don't worry… You've got time! Some people feel nervous, when they come to us, it's normal…"

"I want to see a different consultant. I believe you won't manage. I want a different one."

174

"But, Mr. Colton, I'll do everything possible to help you. I am confident that I can. Don't worry! Let's start and you will see that this will be the case! I will really solve your problem. I can even share a little secret with you!" Markot leaned forward even more, then he put his hand next to his mouth and whispered: "What I can do for you, none of my colleagues can or will!"

As Colton did not quite understand what the consultant meant by this, he immediately decided that this guy was a proper lunatic, who most probably applied some really painful and torturous methods in his work with the clients. Right, this was another reason for making an exit as soon as possible!

"I don't think you are prepared enough. Nothing personal. I'll just see one of your colleagues…"

"But why, Mr. Colton? Please, don't! I'll do anything, anything to help you…" for the first time in the long history of the Idea Factory, an idea-consultant winged and begged at the same time. What a disgrace!

"I don't want to offend you…"

"Give me a chance!" Markot entwined his fingers in a prayer.

"I don't know, I…"

"Come on, please, I can do this, I promise!"

"I'm just saying that I don't think you can help me, I just think that…"

"I can do this. I know I can, no matter what the problem is. Please!"

"I've already decided. It will be better for me, if I see someone else. I'm sorry." the customer uttered without remorse and stood up. He did not offer his hand for goodbye, but headed straight for the door.

"You can't do this!" Markot shot at his back. He could not figure out why he did not resort to the restrictive rules, designed entirely in his favor, much earlier, instead of humiliating himself by begging Colton.

"I can't do what?" Colton sounded surprised.

"You can't see another idea-consultant."

"What do you mean? I'll pay. I'll go to a different consultant in a different room and voila! Where does it say that I can't do this?"

"You can't, because you need to go back outside to the end of the queue first. Besides, you can't pay the same amount for a consultant of Third rank. You will have to pay the fee for a colleague of the higher ranks. These are the rules."

"That's not true. You're lying!"

"I'm not here to lie to you, but to help people like you and offer the best idea that would solve your problem. Now, please, just sit down and we can…"

"Stop with your silly little games! Let me go to another room nearby, for which I shall pay and you just get on with your job. They'll send you someone else here in a minute, right?"

"You can't leave, Mr. Colton, unless you've made a decision to come here another day! Then, you'll have to queue again and pay a much higher fee than the one you paid today. I'm not telling you all this to make you feel bad. I just want you to give me a chance to do my job. Don't worry! I don't want you to worry about anything…"

"I'm not worrying about anything and stop repeating this over and over again!" the client was feeling rather vexed, but he realized that he did not have any other option, but to hang on for a bit and talk to the mad good-wisher Markot. Colton's bank account balance clearly stated that he could afford a couple of meetings with a consultant of Third rank, but none with anyone, who was positioned higher.

"Alright, I won't. Just have a seat and we'll start again, as nothing has happened. When you're ready just tell me why you've come here. Whenever you're ready!"

"Wait a second! If I can't leave the room, then, someone else can just come in here and replace you, can't they, instead of me going back to the queue again and part with some extra money? Just go out and call anyone of your colleagues!" the guest ordered, convinced that his wish was totally reasonable and could be easily fulfilled.

"This is impossible!" Markot snapped at him, but he did not miss to show his wide grin again. "It's against the rules. This is my room and no one else can work here, but me!"

"What about those behind the glass? Let one of them come here. Hey, come here, come in, come in!" Colton prompted with a clear gesture someone from the 'onlookers' to join in. The customer had learned from a "trusted source" – an acquaintance of his, who was a

176

bit of a fantasist – that there were people, behind the mirror, who were watching and who would interfere immediately if the consultant made a blunder. Well, this was the case now.

"There's no one there. No one is watching us, Mr. Colton. I will really do everything to help you. Let us begin. Come on, please!"

"There isn't anyone, you say? What if you're lying to me? How do I know that you're not lying?"

"I'm not lying and there's no one behind the glass. The conversations that take place in any of the rooms have never been supervised. Don't worry! Of course, if you have any further questions, I'll be glad to answer them straight away. But then, we'll start, won't we?"

"I'm not going to tell you anything! I don't trust you. You're blackmailing me into staying here and I just want to see someone else and you, you..."

"Mr. Colton, I can assure you that I've got the necessary skills and that I can resolve your problem. When you share it with me, you will feel so much better. Now just calm down and we'll start when you're ready. Please, come back and sit down."

"I want my money back! Give me my money! I want it back! I'll come another time and see a different consultant."

"I can't give you your money back and I must stress on the fact that no one in the Factory can do this for you. Once you've crossed the line, near the tree, all Factory rules come into effect and begin to apply to you. We don't give refunds here." the wide smile on Markot's face was making the visitor feel even more uncomfortable. Normal people did not grin happily and argue at the same time. No one would do such thing, apart from the most benevolent idea-consultant at the Factory.

"You will give it to me, then! I will get it personally from you, once I leave the premises. I'll get it from you to the last penny! From you, personally!" Mr. Colton looked rather enraged. He seriously thought of the possibility to take the law into his own hands and fight this happy-go-lucky idiot, who was strangely called an idea-consultant. The customer clenched his hands into fists and stepped forward towards the enemy.

177

"I wouldn't want to disappoint you, but this isn't possible, either. By paying the fee, you've accepted our conditions, so there's no way we could refund your payment…"

"No, no, leave the Factory out of this. I want my money back from you. I will find where you live and I'll pay you a visit one day in person. This is when you'll give me my money back!"

"You can't do this, Mr. Colton. If you try to bother a consultant after working hours, the consequences for you will be rather severe. You'll probably end up in a cell for at least a week, while sometimes…"

"Is this a threat? You feel that because you're working here, you can just threaten me? I'm not scared and as I've said, I'm going to find you and get my money back from you, personally!" the customer was waving his index finger and he really wished a bullet could shoot out from it and go straight through the head of this looser.

"Mr. Colton, let's not say things that will never happen, but talk about what has brought you here. I promise you that after I help you, you will be very pleased and there will be no regrets about the money you've spent. Are you ready to begin?"

"I'm not ready for anything! I will find you! I'm not scared of you! I will find you!" the client's face turned so red that it was clear he was seconds away from jumping and hitting Markot.

"I do not doubt that. You can even tell me when you're going to visit me, so I come out and meet you as a friend! Money, however, I cannot give you. This is against the rules. Besides, I believe that if you calm down a little and we start talking, you will see that I can be quite useful to you. Come on, Mr. Colton, for an -nth time, I'm asking you to give me a chance to help you!"

"I'm not giving you anything! I've given you enough and I simply want my money back. It's not just you, who can threaten and blackmail people. I can do that, too! Would you like the entire city to learn about the crazy idea-consultant, hmm? Do you want… what was your name? Your name I want to know! What is it?"

"Markot." the name was presented immediately, accompanied by an even wider and very inappropriate grin.

"Markot. Everyone will learn who Markot is and no one will ever come to see you here. I will tell everyone that you are no good and you can't do your job, that you are blackmailing people, instead of helping them, and yes, you're lying to them, you're lying, you…"

"This can't happen, either, because, the clients come to us on a random basis. My name is not important, Mr. Colton. You are free to do what you want when you get out of here, but please allow me now to help you. Please!"

"Oh, no, no, no! I'm not playing the game. Forget it! I'm not one of these naïve morons, who believe you. Not me!"

"Mr. Colton, do you actually realize that you are still here and you haven't left, yet? I don't want you to go and I'm not asking you to, but if you're not letting me to help you… What then? What are we going to do?"

"You will send me to see someone else or you'll give me my money back! Your choice!"

"Mr. Colton, I cannot make this choice, there are rules in the Factory…"

"I've got my own rules, too! It's not just the Factory that has got them. According to my rules, you have to give me my money back. And if you don't, someone might come and bruise your other eye, in the dark, on your way home, after work." the angry customer smiled as well, while uttering his indirect threat.

"There is no need for this. When I give you my best idea, you'll see that everything will be fine. I can assure you. We only need to begin our conversation and you will see that I will find an answer to your problem. I am asking you sincerely…"

"What? You're scared now, are you?" the client took a professional boxer stance, ready to throw a right blow. Of course, the distance between the two was still far too big.

"I'm not afraid. Actually, Mr. Colton, if I share with you what the consequences will be for you, should you hit an idea-consultant, then, maybe, you will change your mind about attacking me!"

"Hmm, I'll get behind bars for a couple of days! Big deal! I can take this, no problem!"

"I want to help you. I don't want any of my clients to end up in prison because of me. Mr. Colton, I believe I've exhausted all peaceful resources in order to set you at ease and predispose you to a friendly chat. If you don't feel like talking, I can only accept and respect your firm decision. Please, leave the room now. I wish you a

179

good fortune and I hope you find a solution to your problem. Good luck, Mr. Colton!" Markot put an end to the drama in the most theatrical and friendliest manner that he was capable of. He stood up. With an idiotic smile on his face, he made a step towards the infuriated client and offered his hand for a warm goodbye.

"Piss off!" Colton pushed his hand out of the way with a rage. It was time. The distance between them was just right. "The barrel with gun powder" was about to jump and attack Markot. The latter, however, had no intention to become the victim of assault in two consecutive days and simply called the security, following the Factory rules. The professionally trained men entered the room like a shot and before Colton had any time to realize what was happening, he found himself being carried out through one of the back exits, where he was going to be thrown like an unwanted piece of garbage. This happened to anyone, who ignored the idea-consultant - the man, who had all the powers in the interrogation room.

The new Markot, who had suddenly embraced all virtues, was waiting for his next client with a slight feeling of discomfort. Something did not add up. It seemed that his friendly attitude openly provoked Colton, instead of bringing the good in him. How was it possible that a friendly hand and a permanent smile could be interpreted as a threat and a lack of competence? The moderate amicable tone of voice got the guy infuriated, instead of predisposing him to a mutually beneficial pleasant conversation. The customer demanded to see a different consultant and go to another interrogation room. It was far too obvious that it was almost painful for him to even breathe the same air as Markot. The consultant's good intentions and overzealous desire to make friends with the client and not look on him as just another desperate guy, actually worked against Markot. This, however, was just one side of the story. It was possible that the meeting failed entirely because of the stubborn personality of Mr. Colton and Markot's benevolence could not be regarded as the main reason. Most likely, the mistrustful and wary visitor treated his own colleagues in the same awkward way. His relatives, surely, had been subjected to his frequent unreasonable and skeptical outbursts, only to end up falling out with him. If one was aware of how short-tempered Colton was, then his disagreement with the young idea-consultant was to be expected. Markot had the whole day ahead of him to make his mind up, whether his politeness was the problem or simply his customers were mentally unstable. For him the truth was clear, but he wanted to really make sure of it.

Road to Redemption

The road conditions could be considered unreservedly as being rather hostile. The abundant snowfall from the night before, along with the low temperatures, plummeting even further down, had turned the motorways in the district into something that could no longer be regarded as part of the highway system. The emergency road services had employed all their human resources and available machinery, in order to overcome the dire situation and ensure that tens of thousands of vehicles could drive normally. Nature was way more powerful. As soon as the heavy snow was removed from the road, a new portion from the skies quickly settled into the clearance. Nothing could deter Markot, however, from finding Little John and despite the fact that the consultant had to drive much more carefully than usual, he was confident in his success. He would get there, he would find him and he was going to help him. Those were the three steps he had to go through and not even a meter of snow, not the ice that was a few inches thick, nothing was going to stop him. Still thinking about his fat savior, a few kilometers away from the city, the driver had a small accident. Suddenly, his car slid and bumped into the hard shoulder. Good job, that there were not any other vehicles, dancing behind Markot, otherwise they would have piled up, crashing straight into his car. The collision got him back into the slippery reality. The consultant stayed still for about a minute and then carried back on the road to redemption. Meanwhile, the trip was long enough for him to reevaluate and think over the way he was supposed to behave with his clients.

After Colton, three clients managed to see the nice idea-consultant, before sunset. The lady sitting in the metal chair was well impressed by Markot's attention. Like any beautiful woman, full of herself, she actually liked the idea-consultant. Nice looking boy, smart, well brought up, polite and shrewd – what woman would not like the idea to be served by him? However, the idea-consultant was not there to serve his female customers, but to offer them the best idea, which was going to solve their problems. Well, it took a very long time, until the moment of truth arrived. The visitor behaved like a queen and she did not miss to share everything she felt like, no matter that it did not relate in any way to the reasons behind her visit to the Factory. She would sidetrack and rant on about some boring subjects, which did not help Markot and only took up minutes from the consultant's precious time. His delicate and timid attempts to get the lady back on track and stop her from detracting again came to no avail. She felt no discomfort to continue blabbing on about her favorite horses, about the fact that she would never try riding them, because the stallions' beautiful bodies and muscles could not be tempered by the presence of a jockey. Moreover, her own splendid figure might suffer from the waywardness of this divine wild animal. The two-legged chatterbox also shared how much she loved shopping, where she indulged in this activity, how many times a week, etc. Markot kept smiling at the lady as if inviting her to carry on with the talking all day long. Still, the idea-consultant managed somehow to read between the lines and realize what her problem was and two hours later, he delivered the idea to her. The typical marital dilemma, which involved the naughty stable-man, who she possibly liked even more than her precious horses, was a case of no complexity. The woman was fully satisfied with her idea, which would allow her to continue to enjoy secretly her favorite things in life. She left the interrogation room, leaving the nice young man to wait for his next client and giving him the chance for his ears to recover from the marathon listening, he had been subjected to.

The third and the fourth customer were very different from Colton and the blabbermouth. However, Markot did not have an easy time with them, either. They did no listen to him, as they should, and randomly interjected during the interview. They interrupted and pointed out unnecessary details to him. The customers simply did not show respect for the idea-consultant and the rank he had achieved. They also failed to follow closely the three stages, especially the first one. The minute, designated for reflection was taken by client N'3 as a good opportunity to talk about the fluctuation of the stock exchange, where customer N'4 considered that this unnecessary rule could be ignored altogether. Markot tried his best to stay polite, while the clients kept behaving as if being at home. The torture for him did not end until he saw the back of his last visitor, who left with his great idea.

Why did they do this? One smiles at you, should you not smile back? Kindness called for kindness. Well, this might be working when one was out and about on the street, at the cinema, at the restaurant, but not when one had to meet desperate people every day, who see in you their last spec of hope. The rules. Markot finally realized how important they were. It was hard without them. Rules should never be relaxed. The Factory was based on hundreds of rules, which should not be ever breached. Failing to observe them led to the chaos, where clients took liberties and the consultant's mental health simply suffered. Thanks to the rules, Markot was the one that could do anything with them, as long as it resulted in a quality idea at the end. The customers had no choice, but to listen and behave accordingly, otherwise they would lose their money and get nothing for it. So simple! The client had something to lose, whereas the consultants had their rules. Follow them and everything will be alright! They empowered Markot to put an end to his meeting with Colton and get rid of him from the start, instead of wasting his time with pitiful pleas, which were totally out of order. What about the horse-woman? If she did not want to get on track and answer directly to the questions, she should have been sent straightaway back to the stables to scratch on her pets. This was her favorite pastime she had shared. The last two smug clients could have also been sent out in the cold. They deserved it. Markot should have acted fast and harshly from the start. He should have shown who had the ultimate power in the room and whose orders had to be obeyed. In this way, he would not have had any problems with any of the four customers. Even Colton would have stayed, shared his troubles and got the idea he had come for. That was the truth, the only truth and the whole truth.

The idea-consultant was an idea-consultant, because the rules made him what he was. Markot had deserted the basic rules, so he could help his clients and show them his sincere sympathy, but this unfortunately dragged him down to the bottom, covered with "corpses" of idea-consultants. He did not feel like going there, however. The decision was clear. He had to stick his hand back in the furnace and get hold of the discarded snowman again. He had to make his skin feel the cold and become numb, if he wanted to be able to carry on with his work. Otherwise, every day the customers would simply tread all over him, while wasting his time with their nonsense. He could not work like this. Not in the Idea Factory, anyway! The soulless image that he tried to escape from after Little John's attack, had to be adopted again. However, Markot did intent to find the golden middle. He needed to discover some sort of equilibrium between applying the strict rules, which gave him the supreme powers in the interrogation room, and actually showing an open concern for those, who really deserved it. He was going to treat the good people well, as long as they stayed good throughout the meeting. In contrast, Markot would resort to the snowman's aid and to the strict rules, every time he felt people abused his benevolence. For anyone, who was unpleasant, the strategy would be – rules, rules and only rules. From the next day, his behavior was going to change and in effect, Markot was going to have his third debut at work. He was in the lead by two steps amongst his colleagues on this.

The road sign showed that there were 4km left to the harbor. Markot could not wait anymore. He felt an even greater desire, today, to help Little John than if he found him the day before. He had to do this, he just had to: to give him the money, to offer him the idea about the unforgettable birthday surprise for his mother, to give him everything and mend his mistake in this way. Well, he had to find him first, though! Markot decided that he should approach the situation, this time, like a true idea-consultant. He did not intend to roam aimlessly around the enormous harbor. The young man made a decision to check all the security checkpoints first, as advised on his previous late visit. There were eight admission points altogether. One was already checked, so he had seven left for today.

The idea-consultant was driving along the street that was parallel to the outer fence and with his head, turned to the left, he started to look for his target. Not looking at the tarmac road straight ahead nearly played a bad joke on him for a second time, but this time, it could have been a much more serious damage than the innocent bumping into the hard-shoulder. Suddenly, one total idiot, a true fan of life threatening overtakes, just came out of nowhere. He appeared from behind one of the huge trucks, which went about their business in the harbor. He managed to sneak the back end of his old banger at the last minute and saved not only himself, but also the accidental visitor Markot. This challenging incident quickly became a history and after a kilometer, the nice two-colored barrier appeared next to the little port cabin. Markot stopped to make his enquiries. One cabin, two, three, four – he managed to check half of them within an hour, but no one had ever heard about a man, called John, who was not small, but was known as Little. The planned rescue tour finally showed some good results, when Markot stopped at the next checkpoint. He felt hopeful in the same way his desperate clients felt after hearing the right idea. The man with the specs behind the glass managed to tell him something about Little Jim at last.

"A-a-ah, yes, I know him! Of course, I know him. Little Jim, he's popular around here, I know him!" Despite sounding very enthusiastic, the guard did not actually remove his eyes from the small TV screen that was sat on the second chair in his tiny work place.

"No, Sir, I'm looking for someone, called John, known as Little John, not Jim."

"Exactly, come on now, I know him!" the chatty old man stopped looking at the entertaining box this time. He was not pleased with the way Markot looked.

"Hey, you are not from the Police, are you?"

"No, Sir, I'm... I'm a lawyer."

"What do you need him for? Are you sure that you ain't a cop, hmm? I was a policeman once upon a time. Yes! I can see them coming from a mile, my colleagues." the distrustful guy squinted with his eye, as if he was trying to measure up a distant object, without the aid of any technical equipment.

"I am really a lawyer. Don't worry. John's done nothing wrong and no one's suing him or anything like this. I want to give him some money."

"Ha-ha, why don't you give some to me then? You've come to the right place. Hmm, let me ask you, now that you know the Law... How much do you think I should be getting for the extra hours, I work in the night? How much, 'cause they are playing up with my wages, I know, but..."

"I can't tell you that, because I specialize in divorce cases."

"Ah, alright, then. It's no big deal, 'cause at my age... to complain or not, it's a one way street - to the cemetery... ha-ha-ha-ha..."

"Now, can you tell me something about Little John?"

"Jim, you mean?" the guard corrected him incorrectly.

"Actually, his name is John. The boy is quite overweight and works down, where the fishing boats are."

"Yes, yes, I know him, the fat guy, but wasn't he called Jim. Do you know how many people call him Little Jim? You might have got it wrong, you know! Yes, Jim must be it."

"I don't think that there's a mistake. But if you're sure, I suppose you must be right. And do you know by any chance where I could find him? Where does he live?"

"Here, I can't help you, boy. I watch who comes in and out and just lift the barrier. I'm doing twelve-hour shifts and this is it. I don't ask them what they are up to! I don't get paid for this, you know?"

"Yes, I know that. What about his colleagues, do you know any of them? Maybe, they can point me in the right direction where to find him!"

"I'm not that close with the fishermen. Your man, what ship did you say he's working on?"

"I think he doesn't work on any ship, he just helps unloading them, when they arrive at the dock."

"A-ah, then, I maybe got it wrong. Little Jim works on the ships, him, yes, I know. Yes, I'm sure of it, but he could be helping with the unloading, too. Can you give me any other clues?"

"No, I can't think of anything else." Markot did not want to share the idiotic story with releasing the fish in the water, because he did not want people to laugh at John. He did not deserve to be laughed at.

"You know what? Why don't you go in and ask them? Down there, if you go about a kilometer, you'll see the first fishermen. Someone must know of him. Your man might be even still there, 'cause I don't think he's passed through here."

"But aren't they already finished by this time?"

"Finished? You've seen what the weather's been like today, haven't you? Some are still there, I think. Go on and you'll find who they are. I'm telling you, I'm not that close with the fishermen. But

186

watch it they don't ask you to give them a hand, 'cause the fishermen always try to make everyone get on with their job, when they feel a little tired ha-ha-ha-ha…"

Markot did not get the joke much, but this did not stop the porter to enjoy it out loud. He thanked him and headed in the right direction. This day was very cold, indeed. The boats got iced up very easily and only the morning sun saved them from going down. It could take about three days for the entire harbor to end up without its busy bees, if the sun decided to take a longer break than its usual. Markot, unlike his Mentor, was not familiar with the sea and the art of sailing. He never showed an interest and even if he had, Richardson and his watchful wife would have diverted him straight away towards the back entrance of the Idea Factory, without the right to freely choose. The idea-consultant could not estimate what a kilometer was, or its half, so he began to count his steps. He was aware that three of those made a meter, so the calculations would add up at the end. Markot was walking and counting, while not really thinking about anything else. He did not want to make a mistake. As there were not many people, who employed the full capacity of their brain and that could do more than one thing at the same time, if Markot was one of them, while striding and counting away, he would have definitely asked himself about what he would do if he saw Little Jim amongst the fishermen. Not Little John, but Little Jim – the one that the guard was talking about. Well, the consultant was going to ask him and the other exhausted men about where Little John could be. But what if they did not know and they disliked the fact that he was asking too much? Of course it could be all an honest mistake and the real Little John might appear before his eyes in his full size and kilograms, which were held in place and protected only by the enormous skin from spilling out and causing an eco catastrophe. What was he going to do then? He did not have that much money in cash and with regards to the idea about the birthday surprise, he had not actually thought of anything in particular. What he could offer him in this moment of time was a materialistic and an ideological zilch!

Markot was finally about to complete the kilometer and stop his semi-automatic step counter. The fishing section of the harbor was situated a few hundred meters away. Actually, the consultant would have found the place alright, even if he did not count his strides. The stench clearly pointed that this was the right place. The huge fishing trawlers stood prominently to the front. They could hold tons of fish in one go. Next to the big vessels were the smaller fishing boats. They looked like as if they were their offspring, which one day would grow up if they "ate" well. Who knows? It seemed that every vessel had gone back to their stands and their crew – back to their homes. The workers might have gone through one security checkpoint in the morning, but this did not mean that they passed through the same one on their way out.

The idea-consultant noticed some human activity around two medium sized fishing boats. He saw straight away that amongst the fishermen, working late, there was no one, who matched the oversized description of Little John, not even half of it. The situation was the same on the other boat, too. No one had heard about the fat guy, but interestingly, they had not heard of Little Jim, either. Markot had to come back during daylight and approach the situation differently. Possibly, it would make more sense to ask randomly passers-by on the streets of the port city than, say, come back after work on the following day. Asking in pubs, shops and restaurants could also prove more useful. The disappointed idea-consultant left behind the sleeping ships to get ready for yet another heavy struggle with the waves on the following day and headed back towards his vehicle, parked at the entrance. The old guard did not even notice him. The aging man, who loved drinking at any time of the day, had gone to a very different place in his head, after consuming a fair quantity of alcohol. A place, where he got paid as much as he wanted and where he did not have to do the long twelve-hour shifts in his tiny cabin. He would actually come to work tipsy, but still capable of "helping" people like Markot.

The visits of the last two security points did not come to any result, as the inhabitants of the cabins could not give the consultant any new piece of information. They had not heard even of Little Jim and generally, the guards were not that chatty, anyway.

On his way home, the idea-consultant thought of a daring possibility. He was aware that this would be an offense that no one ever allowed themselves to commit. A newbie of the Third rank, working at the Idea Factory would never do anything of the kind. A colleague, Second rank, who got his fat check at the end of the month without delay, would not even think about skiving for a day. It was out of question, when it came down to the highest ranks, too. Hmm, Markot could have been the first one that got the day off work and went to go about his own business! No! They would fire him immediately. No way he can "survive" this. The idea about skiving was very quickly replaced by a new one, which was much easier to follow through and had no adverse consequences for the perpetrator. Often, the idea-consultants offered ideas to their customers, which involved seeing a specialist, who dealt exactly with the type of problem they had encountered. Markot remembered what he had been taught about it at the Academy. If the client suffered from an illness, one would just tell him where to find the best doctors. That was the best one could do. If the person wanted to become a famous singer, the advice would be to find a singing coach. Should the customer feel that nature had not been generous enough in order to achieve results in sport, then, the best idea would be for the client to see a professional athlete, who had won medals, etc. So Markot had to look for someone good at finding other people, who could tell him where about Little John lived. He was just thinking over his possibilities about finding that sort of person and suddenly, the idea-consultant jumped on the brakes. This could not be! No way! Driving back on the same road that was parallel to the never-ending fence, going round the harbor, all of a sudden on the next dark bend, the headlights flashed over and lit something large that was waddling, instead of walking. The object filled up the entire pavement, which was big enough for three slim persons to fit on, and slowly transferred his weight alternately from one foot to the other. Markot turned off the engine in the middle of the road to avoid being noticed. It was obvious that Little John, if this was him, did not hear the loud squeaking of the brakes. Markot quickly realized, however, that if anyone was driving behind him, they could easily crash into his car. A second incident for the day was simply undesirable. He hastily turned the engine on again. The consultant passed by the enormous man and managed to secretly get a good look at him. Markot did not want to intrude on the stranger, but in effect, yes, the fat pedestrian was him. Yes! It was Little John! It could not be anyone else and the evidence was in his hands. That was why he walked in this way. Because he was eating. Always hungry, the fatso was stuffing his face with a triple sandwich. He did not notice the car; he did not notice anyone or anything around him. He was enchanted by this special moment, devoted to his food until the last bite went down and got lost in his stomach. Markot drove off a bit further and stopped the car in the first lay-by. He could see, in his right-side mirror, the figure of Little John approaching. Judging by the speed he was walking, Markot estimated that the "greasy ball" would reach his car within a minute, which was enough for the consultant to decide what to do. He felt rather strange. At the doorstep of the so much sought and desired redemption, he actually did not know where to start. Should he come out and kneel before his fat savior, beg him in tears for forgiveness? No, this scenario suited more some unstable persons or women, and not someone like him. Markot could avoid all the drama and just admit his mistake like a civilized citizen. He could simply offer, in a professional manner, to reimburse Little John, without putting himself in an embarrassing position. He could apologize, then drive him home and just sort things out like adults. However, one of them did not act like one and this was a big challenge, as the facts could never change. The mentally retarded idiot could easily react aggressively again. He had at least three reasons to hate Markot. Firstly, he was still offended by the derogatory words; he had to hear about his sick mother. John was deeply hurt by this and maybe a couple of days were not enough to heal the wound in his heart. Secondly, Little John might feel like attacking the consultant again, because he still did not know how to surprise his mother. The meeting with Markot ended abruptly before he actually received the valuable piece of advice. There was no way that the fatso would manage to come up with anything original, if he was left to rely on his own devices. Finally, Little John could be filled up with hatred towards the arrogant idea-consultant, for the rest of his life, because he lost his entire savings down to him. The oversized client had heard that the staff at the Idea Factory could help even if one parted with all their money – it just did not matter. The consultants knew everything and could offer a good advice about what one should do. They were always there to think of something. And what now? No idea, no money, just one big nothing!

Ten more meters and the huge always-hungry monster was about to reach the car. There was no time. Markot panicked. He had to act. He was a man of action, who was mature enough to fully accept the unexpected consequences of the meeting. The consultant decided to invite John in his car, without laughing at him or playing silly mocking games at his expense. Five, four, three, two – and Markot opened the car window to call John. He felt the icy cold air and just a second before he attracted his attention; he nervously pressed the button again to close the window. Little John was not going to fit in the car!!! Markot realized that there was a significant discrepancy between the size of the door, when fully opened, and the size of Little John. There was no way he could get in. The wobbly ravenous man kept stuffing himself with mummy's sandwich and failed to notice the parked vehicle. The idea-consultant felt angry with himself and bumped his head in the center of the steering wheel. The horn beeped, as expected, and Markot jumped. He felt a slight pain in his eye, despite that he did not hit the car horn that hard. Little John carried on walking down the pavement. He did not turn round to check where the warning sound came from. He was certain that it was not meant for him.

Sometimes, the Good Samaritan was a person of no face, or voice. He might exist to do good, but seeking no publicity, he would rather keep his name a secret. Plenty of people believed that one should not boast about how good they had been, how much they had given away and so on. Markot could become like one of those people. It was not mandatory to meet up with Little John face to face. Helping him indirectly would still redeem his wrongdoing and would give the consultant the same level of satisfaction. Markot was going to send enough money to the fatso, together with detailed instructions about how to prepare the most impressive birthday surprise for his sick mother. The consultant thought that he could also put small sums of money through their letterbox, monthly or once every few months, just so he was sure they did not go without. Markot would solve the problem incognito. Yes, this might be the better option. The mystery financial and ideological benefactor got out of his car and followed Little John from a safe distance. The "chase" was slower than he wished it was. The fat boy was done with the food and speeded up his heavy striding. However, he had to stop every two hundred meters and get some rest. He could not catch his breath and taking in the cold air made him feel pain in his struggling lungs. "Let's hope he did not live far, otherwise he might drop dead before he got home." Markot felt guilty about his macabre thoughts, although he could well turn out to be right on this. Little John managed to recover and undertook an unexpected maneuver. He had to cross the road and like a kid, who had learned his lesson too well, he looked carefully both ways several times before stepping out on the street. His sharp vision helped him clock Markot, who had got much nearer to him than before. Their eyes met for less than a second. The idea-consultant looked away, pretending he was there accidentally, which was not far from the truth. The fat moron reached the other "shore", as if nothing happened. Did he not recognize him or he did not want to recognize him? The pursuer was convinced that Little John realized within a spec of time who was following him. His eyes trembled and this would not have happened if the chaser was a complete stranger. "He doesn't want me to help him. He thinks I should not be given the chance to help him, especially after what I've said about his mother. He's probably right! But I'm so sorry, I, I…" Markot almost felt again the bitter taste of his tears. He was not going to give up, not when he was so close. The savior could not run away from him anymore and he could not hide anywhere. The idea-consultant had to bring things to some sort of closure, no matter if the fatso was going to accept the money, his idea or simply if he decided to assault him again with his huge greasy fist. Markot pulled himself together, tried to calm his heartbeat, if a double heart rate could be regarded as normal, and then, he carried on walking behind Little John. The cat-and-mouse game, where the mouse was enormous and the cat looked like it had been systematically underfed, kept on going for another half an hour or so. The mouse lived very near to his workplace, but because of the numerous breaks, he needed to make, it felt as if it was far. Home at last! Little John climbed up the three steps, leading to the porch. He turned the key to unlock and managed to sneak in sideways through the narrow door. Actually the entrance was normal in size. It was him, who was not. All the lights in the house were out, which could only mean that his sick mother was already in bed. Markot dared to stand a few meters from the door and heard how the lock clicked.

Now that he achieved what he had come for, the idea-consultant headed back towards his deserted car. Something was still eating him, however, in the way mice were eating crumbs of cookies. How could he actually offer his help to Little John? This had to be done in such a way that he managed to realize what was happening. Say, if the idea about the surprise was too complicated, the fat retard might not be able to follow it through. And what about if Markot gave him the money first? Say, if he found it on the street by chance? Well, then he might not even think about spending it on his mum's fiftieth anniversary and make that evening unforgettable. The dumb pig might not guess that the money was for that purpose and simply spend it on something else – most likely that was high in calories. Markot had to be really careful, otherwise the mysterious charitable act could turn easily into wasting everything, like losing a fat wallet, full of cash, in the ocean.

The Good Samaritans sometimes resort to known or unknown to them middlemen. They would give their instructions and the agent, hired to undertake the special mission, would go on to complete the benevolent act. Of course, the mediator would get paid a fair amount of cash for his work. Markot had to find someone he could trust, someone, who could manage, if paid, to surprise a sick woman, whose son was as heavy as a baby whale. The idea was not bad, only if the consultant did not take the apocalyptically damaging incident with Little John too personally. He simply did not want for anyone to know his innermost secret. He had to deal with everything by himself, otherwise the redemption was not going to be complete. The black limousine was waiting for him in the lay-by, the way he had left it. He got in and drove off.

People are hard beasts and survivors, as long as the situation, presented to them was challenging enough, in order to call for their full potential for self-preservation. In moments like this, they were capable of doing the impossible. Well, Markot did not need some sort of a miracle, but just needed to realistically look at what he had. The snowman was back at his disposal, so the idea-consultant decided to use him in his personal time, too. As it has been well known, personality disorder is a mental condition, which required one to take antipsychotic medication for life, usually. Markot was under no threat to be locked in a mental institution, because he was certain that he could always become his old self. There was no danger for him to get entrapped forever in the tight hold of his cold-blooded "partner".

The snowman was lying in his bed and went on working through the entire night. The dawn was breaking outside, but he felt like still being in a dead-end street. Whatever he came up with, there would be always some overwhelming encumbrances. A new idea and then nothing again! It was time for Markot to get up, tired from his lack of sleep, and get ready for work, leaving the unproductive snowman behind. And it was then, when a simple solution appeared in front of him. The idea-consultant could not quite say for sure, whether his other self had come up with the answer or it was the real him. As it happened that Little John left before the end of the third stage, then he could just come again to the Idea Factory and find out how to surprise his sick mother. The rules stated that the fatso would have to see someone more experienced from the higher ranks, because he did not have the right to go back to a consultant of the same level. The consultants of the Second rank were definitely going to help him and the money for their outrageously costly service was going to come from... The idea-consultant felt the happiness pumping through his veins. He felt pleasantly warm. He was over the moon with joy. At last, Markot had come up with the perfect solution! That evening, he was going to leave the money with a note in front of the right house in the port city next-door. There was no way that the retard would get it all wrong, because the message was going to be clear and simple. Still, one should never overrate stupid people or invest too much trust in them. One could tell them that they were alright for the sake of their self-esteem, but in reality they remained what they were – complete idiots.

The conscientious security guards made note of every visitor, so they could easily check, whether Little John had been for a second time or he had wasted the money with no intention to visit the Idea Factory ever again. Well, one should also take into consideration the fact that he might have completely and inadvertently forgotten again about his mother's birthday. This would not be the first time and besides, the special event was half a year away from that day.

Yet another new self of Markot arrived at work without a hitch, although the curved wheel fender touched the tire every time he went round a bend. He was not bothered about the damage. To him the car was simply a pile of beautifully designed sheet metal. The idea-consultant was waiting for his customer, ready to display in front of him, for the first time in practice, the combination between a firm cold peremptoriness and at the same time, a warm friendly and kind approach. Markot began to yawn, before anyone had entered the room, yet, and every next yawn was getting wider and wider. The lack of sleep and his general weariness were not going to disappear throughout the entire day. The rules allowed for any natural reactions, but it was not advisable for the idea-consultant to resort to those too many times. His heavy eyelids and the redness of his eyes only matched the repetitive movement of opening his mouth, inviting Markot to place his hands on the metal table, where he could rest deservedly his dysfunctional head, as if they were a pillow. He was so, so sleepy. He could press the red button and get half an hour rest, but this was so little that it would only irritate the bear, who was ready to hibernate until the spring. Well, at last, his professional attitude won and the first client woke him up like a cup of strong coffee. The idea-consultant felt fresh and sharp, so he went through the three stages as he should and solved the problem with very little effort. With his second visitor, Markot resorted to the "automatic gear box", occasionally pressing on the accelerator, without any intention to step on the brakes. His excellent concentration helped him follow the rules closely, which only led to another brilliant idea. Again and again, everything was going just perfect, until the end of the working day. The snowman could easily be, now, renamed as the iron man. No errors, no arguments with the customers – just a perfectly completed consultant's job! But where was the nice Markot from the previous day? He did not appear today, despite the secret promise that he would also take part if the client was a good person. Most likely Markot's sleepiness had prompted the snowman to replace his good and kind self.

The over-exhausted idea-consultant could not give up now. Not today. If he lied down wherever and in whatever uncomfortable position, he was definitely going to fall asleep until the morning. He got out a pen and a piece of paper, folded in four, and began to write something. Little John was familiar with the alphabet, so he should be able to read alright. To make it easier for him, the consultant picked simple and commonly used words. The font was also easy on the eyes. The message about how to spend the money looked like a ransom letter, but the resemblance was definitely going to stay unnoticed by the fat retard.

Often, people were better at communicating verbally their thoughts rather than putting them down on paper. Markot was one of them. It would have been much easier for him to tell the guy his instructions, instead of writing them in a letter. Despite both types of communication having the same origin, nothing came out quite as it should on the white sheet. Markot had to cross out stuff here and there, until the letter became unsuitable for the end fat user. The consultant turned the piece of paper on the other side and started all over again. He simplified the instructions by dividing them into five points and sub-points under sections 3 and 4, which were not mandatory. Then, he left the Idea Factory and went to the bank. He got out a substantial sum of money, put down the action plan neatly on a piece of white paper and headed for the third time towards the harbor town.

One of Them

It is not easy to be God. You want it so much that you are prepared to do anything to achieve your aim, but what then? When it becomes a reality and you join the team of the know-it-alls, the invincible and the perfect, then you feel that the dream suddenly turns out to be very different from what you have imagined. The Gods also commit sins, have weaknesses and generally share dozens of features with the ordinary people. What does make them Gods then? How have they managed to take on the role, when clearly it does not correspond to the way they behave, think, speak, or even the way they lived their lives? Andir was shocked. Now that he had become a full member of the untouchable elite, this really opened his eyes. It seemed that his twenty years of climbing up the career ladder was in vain. What he saw was beyond his imagination.

The Idea Factory was created, so it manufactured tons of great ideas, which could solve any problem. The professionally trained idea-consultants helped their desperate clients and did their best to come up with the best intellectual product. Every day, different people would come in the interrogation rooms, bringing their different problems and at the end of the meeting, they were supposed to receive an idea of the highest quality. Andir was aware very well of what was required from him and how he had to do his job. He followed the rules. He never made any mistakes. After all, if he was not that good, they would not have invited him, would they? But why, though, did the idea-consultants of the First rank, always tried to avoid the rules? A few of his colleagues, for instance, unashamed, lit a cigarette during his very first and official conference meeting, after he returned from the Academy. Smoking was prohibited at the Idea Factory. They were truly enjoying puffing away the unhealthy cigarettes and then, breathing out heavily the smoke. No one told them off, no one mentioned anything about this and the discussion just went on as if no rule had been just breached. Those, sitting nearest to the "smoking chimneys", had the burning smoke in their eyes and mouth, making them cough occasionally. But they did not complain, either, and kept quiet. Moreover, the smokers used the floor like an ashtray. The cigarette butt seemed to fall in the "right" place, wherever it landed. Ignorant slobs! Andir felt like banging on the table and nearly ordered his colleagues to leave the room. This was not right! This was against the rules! They should not behave like this. He did not do anything about it. And even if he could do it, there would not have been any effect. The Gods took their annual exams in front of other Gods. If he was playing up, the smokers could just turn against him and he would be out. There had never been a case, when someone from the highest rank got thrown out of the Idea Factory. Still, there was always the danger of this happening and besides, there was always a first time for everything! Andir was a perfectionist and did not want to risk his career.

The arrogant breaching of the rules did not stop there. When the meeting finished, some of the less shy Gods decided that it was appropriate to discuss out loud their more interesting customers from that day. Nightmare! This was just so, so, so outrageous! Confidentiality was of utmost priority! Recording was not allowed; no one could listen to the conversation behind the glass... Discussions about this were prohibited. And this guy was blabbing on how this "creature" came in today that looked like a woman and a man at the same time. The "thing" had fallen out with its dad, who had disowned him or her. The "creature" simply wanted an idea on how to rekindle the family relations with the father. Andir heard everything, because he was standing right next to the narrator. Everyone in the room could decipher the content of the conversation. But no, they all pretended they were deaf or something. Big deal that one of the basic rules had been breached, if not squashed, to be precise! The story got the listener truly amused. The idea-consultant, First rank, was laughing his heart out! He found everything so funny that completely forgot about the rules. He did not care. Nobody cared about anything. Clearly the conference hall, where all important decisions, related to the Idea Factory were discussed, was in effect regarded as an island: An isolated island, at the end of the world, where anything could go and where there was no rules and laws. Andir was staring at the documents that were given to him to look at for his presentation at one of the next meetings, when he heard another unseemly conversation. He heard about a female client, who had a constant desire to be in the company of men. Andir immediately stopped listening. He felt as if he was in a hospital, where everyone was sick and contagious, including the doctors and nurses, and only he was pure and clean. He left the room of sin with the feeling of never wanting to go back in there.

Andir's hospital analogy meant just one thing – this awaited him, too. He was also going to get sick. His strong immune system, protected by the rules, could resist for so long, but could never win at the end. The purest idea-consultant, who was still unaware of what was expecting him, went along to his second working meeting. The rules were yet again breached unanimously to no one's surprise. Apart of the smoking and discussing the crazy clients, there was also the drinking! One of the top cats in consultancy, totally unashamed, kept reaching for a small metal flask, tucked in his inner pocket. He would get sharp swig of the reviving liquid now and again. It was obvious that the liquid was prohibited for the under eighteens, but why did he do this so demonstratively? Could he not wait for the end of the meeting and like a proper alcoholic, just go and hide in a corner or visit the rest rooms or something? He simply did not care. Most likely all the oldies in the group had an affinity to spirits. A body search would definitely bring out more than a few little flasks.

198

Well, no one brought the issue up. Again. Everyone kept quiet and pretended that they did not notice. But they did. Everyone could notice. It was no secret. Rules were dead. The Factory was no longer what it used to be, but the worse of all was that the guardians of the Idea establishment cheated collectively.

The idea-consultant, who had joined the Kingdom of Gods last, froze. The thought that filled his head just cut him in half. What if the island was not just in this hall, but had spread into each of their interrogation rooms? They could do whatever they wanted with their clients! Why bother with the three stages, the correct posture and all the tiny details that accompanied the process of creating an idea? Why bother observing the rules in there, if they did not bother with following them here? What was the difference? There was not any!

At the end of the meeting, everyone got up to leave, but Andir. He stayed on and decided to analyze the collective behavior of his colleagues, which was so out of order. He was experienced and perceptive enough to do this. Maybe, if he found the reasons behind their attitude, then, he could offer them an idea on how they could manage to embrace the rules again. This was his vocation – to help – was it not?

Emotional?!? The idea-consultants, First rank, were possibly the biggest morons. They would not climb up to the top, otherwise, without going crazy. Professional approach was above everything and the wall then, stayed intact! But why did they behave like small children – why were they laughing, sulking, shouting? They did not apply their self-control at all! They waved their arms around and gesticulated in a way that no idea-consultant, under any circumstances should do this. No matter sitting down or standing, their bodies always did something that was not allowed or appropriate in their position. Their faces changed expressions whenever they felt like it. The dozens of tiny facial muscles worked intensively to convey the right emotion. How none of them got a stiff face to this moment was still something to be yet seen! It was clear that they did not want to hide. But did they pretend, when a desperate client sat down in front of them? How did the consultants actually do their job without following some basic rules? The clothes. The over expensive suits some of Andir's colleagues came to work in, were inconsistent with the collectively agreed plain dress code for all.

Andir had noticed this before, but did not quite feel it mattered so much at the time. Now, however, the blunders were far easier to see. One of the Gods, a total smug, was wearing some super expensive white leather shoes, which could be noticed from miles away. Every customer of his would probably adore the fashionable choice. But the rules stated that the idea-consultant had to be dressed in plain and boring clothes. Shoes were always black and the suit was also black. The shirt had to be white and the black-and-white masterpiece was complete. Another eccentric devotee of luxury items had come to work with a very golden gold wristwatch. The expensive piece of jewelry sparkled in its own right and attracted attention like a magnet. The idea-consultants were allowed to wear time-measuring devices, but they could not bring their personal items to work. Instead, they were given the same watches. Each of them followed the Factory tradition and had a plain white face and a black leather strap. Another flaw, Andir noticed in the hands of a colleague, whose name he could not quite remember. The guy was playing with praying beads. This might be having a positive effect on him, but the consultants should never play with anything and that was that. The hands rested on the thighs and until the client left the room, they could not be removed from their position. The customer could simply get distracted and begin asking questions about the item in the consultant's hands. No one benefited from this. It was just a waste of time.

If he tried really hard, Andir would have discovered plenty of faults in the way his colleagues looked. However, he decided to put on one side the exterior issues, because he was more interested in their main topic of conversation. Strangely, the arrogant Gods kept repeating the word "Money" in almost every sentence. At the actual meeting, there was not a financial issue to discuss on the agenda. But why after the end of it, everyone started talking about the Factory's budget policy with regards to their wages? It was obvious that they thought of their huge income as insufficient. They all complained about their meager monthly salary and collectively kept convincing each other of the urgent measures they should take, so that their cash flow is rapidly increased. One only had to say that they should all get more money and the others quickly agreed. Soon, someone else would go on to confirm that this was the right idea and everyone nodded affirmatively, voicing their wish: "yes, yes, yes" or "very good idea". "More money! And the sooner, the better!" Andir did not participate in this, not only because he would have been completely ignored, if he tried, but also because he believed that the top consultants were getting enough already and they had no grounds to ask for more. Such an increase was pointless. Just 5% of his salary was enough to live on, the rest he could spend as he wished. All middle-classed businessmen would have burst with envy, if they had the chance to look at the long string of numbers, his bank account displayed. There were quite a few millionaires amongst the older consultants of First rank. No doubt about it! Why did they want more? The idea-consultant did not need to buy a house or any other property. They got their apartments for free and were not allowed to move places. The car was also given for free. So the only area they could really go in and indulge in a spending spree was the wife and her expensive presents or the kids and the fees for an elite university. But even spoiling one's family for those, who were married, had its limits. Andir could not understand their lust for more money. Maybe, they wanted more money, because they simply could and in reality, they were not truly interested in the money itself.

The analysis was interrupted abruptly. Andir could not stand this anymore. He was waiting for the greedy devils to finish chatting and leave. Then, he would also get the hell out of there. He did not want to walk out of the conference hall at the same time with them, because they disgusted him. Only the idea that he could have anything to do with the depraved Gods made him feel appalled. Andir's troubled thoughts remained hidden from his so much despised colleagues. They did not even notice him. The consultants did not want to communicate with him, not because they disliked him, but because it was too soon for them. For them he was still a stranger. An intruder. They needed time to get to know him. When the last two colleagues of his left the room, Andir stood up to put his coat on. He could not wait to get out of there. Chirank, however, had other plans for him.

The small and quite revolting idea-consultant was the chairman of the conference meetings. He was responsible to read out the agenda at every work related gathering. The privilege was not down to his age or professional achievements – he was neither the oldest, nor the longest member of the elite. His voice was simply a true gift. A gift to envy, no doubt. Chirank was capable of telling any story in the most intriguing and captivating way. It did not matter if the target audience comprised children, or the tale involved horror tragedies, full of blood. His silky voice was pleasure to the ears. Moreover, the man's pronunciation, intonation and power of the voice were just perfect. Always. He paused at the right places like a professional narrator in the most natural way. He never erred, either. He could have easily become a radio host, if he did not opt to get into consultancy. He did not look great to be shown on TV for sure, though. Ugliness was of course as relative as beauty, but in Chirank's case, there was nothing relative! His wrinkled skin made him look about eighty, although he was born exactly sixty-two years ago. He had solid dark circles under his eyes, as if someone, who really hated him, had beaten him up. In effect, they had been there for a very long time. Even when he was young, he was not handsome and hardly resembled a human being. His tiny body had obviously stopped growing and developing at some point during his school years. He wobbled, because his right leg was shorter than the other more than just a few millimeters. Sometimes people would think he was about to fall on the ground and rushed to his rescue, as they did not realize at first that Chirank was disabled and this was how he actually walked. His front "rabbit" tooth was much darker and made his smile really unpleasant view. He smiled very rarely. The white hair here and there was not pretty sight, either. His invisibly thin lips and crooked nose were as ugly as his shapeless pointed ears. Chirank was aware of his looks. Every time, when he looked at himself in the mirror, he felt very displeased about the result of the love relationship between his mother and father. He got nothing good from his parents, who might have loved him tremendously, but even they could never think that their kid was the best looking, when they were still alive. Despite all this, he was a very good idea-consultant. He was diplomatic, patient, a person of great self-control – an accomplished professional. His natural gift had prompted all his clients to immediately ignore the monstrous package on the outside and they quickly shared without any qualms their difficult problem, which had made them to visit the Idea Factory. His voice brought them into a trance and they often believed that the beautiful sound came out from a beautiful person and not from what they could see in front of them. Yes, eyes could often fool us. Andir was honest in his judgment. To him, when this man spoke, he felt like a higher being was talking to him. However, when Chirank was quiet, he felt like turning round in disgust, puking his guts out.

"Andir, I want you to stay for a bit longer. We need to talk." every time he employed his verbal weapon, people got the shivers. Andir felt in the same way.

"Right, Sir. If we have to."

"I hope, this won't take too much time." the head of the meetings took his place in the center, whereas his newly accepted colleague went to his and sat down. There were seven empty chairs between them, because the rules stated that no one could take someone else's seat even if the idea-consultant was not present in the room. Andir always followed the rules closely.

"So what's the matter, Sir?"

"Andir, why did you sit there? Come and sit closer!"

"I think I better stay where I am, Sir."

"You want to talk from a distance? Come on, come closer!"

"I prefer to stay here, Sir."

"Do you want some whiskey?" the cupboard, situated next to Chirank's right side, happened to be an unsuspected mini-bar. The ugly waiter stretched a little bit and reached for a couple of glasses and a bottle that was half full. He filled them up skillfully and placed the one for Andir at an arm distance. "If he wants to drink, he has to get up and come here!" the amber bait had been set up.

"Sir, with all due respect, I think we should not do this! Drinking is banned. As it is sitting in someone else's chair. And smoking, and a lot of other things. Rules are..."

"What rules? Our rules, which we watch for at the exams, whether any of them have been breeched? Andir, don't be so naïve!"

"Sir, the rules are for all, especially for us, from the highest rank. We have to set an example and not ignore the rules."

"And who will find out? Is there anyone else in the room? I can't see anyone! Don't worry so much! All day long, we have to put up with the clients' nonsense, then at our meetings – more nonsense, so I believe that it is good to relax sometimes! Come here! You'll like it!" Chirank waved at the stubborn rules-chaser in attempt to prompt him to come closer, after which he picked his glass. He must have been thirsty, because he drank it in one go. He refilled it quickly. "Are you coming? Andir, we really need to discuss a few important issues and I don't feel like shouting across the room."

"I don't want to make you shout, Sir, but can we at least put the alcohol away?"

"Of course, we can." both glasses were dried up immediately – an act, which clearly interpreted the verb 'put away' rather interestingly. Chirank placed everything back in the cupboard and with a jolly face began to wait for Andir to finally go nearer. The Gods were equal, so he could not force him into doing anything, but let him act of his own accord. Andir's oppositional attitude was rather predictable for someone, who joined the closed society of the idea-consultants, First rank, only a week ago. Therefore, the tipsy speaker was not so bothered by this.

"Sir, I know I'm new here, but the breaching of the rules by some of the consultants, while in the conference hall, was unexpected for me. The rules must be always observed, without exception..."

"Yes, it is very obvious that you've just joined us. You sound like a consultant of the Second rank. Blinkered. Very blinkered, Andir!"

"Sir, the rules are designed to put boundaries. That is why I sound like this."

"You may not like it if we have a drink or light the odd cigarette, but we've done our job for the day. The clients are happy. Everything's good!"

"This is correct, Sir, and I do not dispute our colleagues' professionalism in the slightest, but the rules need to be observed and I don't think that..."

"Drop the rules!"

"I cannot do this, Sir, and I think that none of us should. They are the most important thing, more important than us..."

"More important than us? Than you and I? Who is responsible for the rules – us or the Factory?"

"We are, but..."

"Andir, they are our responsibility. We, the idea-consultants, First rank, decide on the future of the Idea Factory. It is all up to us."

Chirank was beginning to become a little vexed by the idealism of his handsome colleague. This was not the reason he had asked him to stay after work.

"I know that it's all up to us, Sir, but I just wanted to point out that the rules…"

"Enough about the damn rules! We have more important things to do right now."

"But, Sir, I think that…"

"I said – enough!" he snapped at Andir, but at the same time, he did not sound harsh. "Andir, before you joined us and became a full member of the First ranks, we've had four meetings with our colleagues, where we've been discussing some proposals for changes."

"What kind of changes?" Andir sounded a bit jumpy, as he believed that there was no scope for improvement at the conservative Idea Factory.

"There a two aspects that we believe need some revision. The first one concerns the number of the idea-consultants, First rank. With you, joining us, we think we got the perfect number. We think that we should not accept any more people into our society. We shall promote consultants, only in the instance of someone's demise."

"But, Sir, in this way, we are going to kill any ambition the consultants of Second rank might have. Isn't this measure quite extreme? They will never be able to get to this position!"

"That's not true, Andir. You're clearly not listening to me. They will be able one day, when one of us kicks the bucket. And by the look of it, they won't be waiting for that long. Ha-ha-ha!" his laughter was pleasantly ringing. He had about three drinks and this made him a bit soft and relaxed.

"Sir, why did you accept me, then, instead of voting it out earlier?"

"You are a different story. We delayed this for three years, so at the end, we just had to accept someone in. Your exam results are good, you don't have any 'zero' clients or incidents in your work, generally. Be happy you've joined us! You deserve it."

"I'm grateful to you, Sir, but I still believe that in this way, we do a lot of damage to the Second ranks…"

"Here we go again, Andir. You keep talking as if you're one of them and not as being one of us. You'll get used to it."

"Sir, what do the others think? Do all of our colleagues think in this way, because I don't believe that such a crucial change is…"

"It's been unanimously agreed, Andir. Richardson objected at first, but later he also agreed that it would be the best solution for the Factory."

"For the Factory." the idea-consultant, First rank, repeated, but he did not add "or for you?" Why was Richardson against the enclosed circle of the Gods? This question had one possible answer. Most likely he hoped that one day Markot would get near the top and he, then, would just send him an "invitation" to join them. The father would do everything for his adopted son. Although, he would never deserve this honor. Never! Richardson must be aware of his own son's mediocrity. Andir's interesting train of thought was interrupted by Chirank, who had not finished yet with him.

"The second proposal, I'm supposed to inform you about, is much more attractive. We've established that we could increase our salaries by forty percent. Forty percent more from the beginning of the next month and we'll be getting the bonus for a year and a half."

"Yes, Sir, I think I heard the colleagues discussing the issue…"

"They keep talking about this all the time. They are very impatient. The surplus we had initially allowed us to raise the salaries by fifty percent, but then, some unexpected expenditure to do with the Academy brought this figure down."

"Forty is aplenty, Sir. The idea-consultants, Third rank, will be very pleased about this!"

"The Third ranks? We are not giving anything to them! The increase is just for us!"

"But, Sir, if we get forty percent, this will affect the balance. There will be a huge discrepancy between us and the other ranks. It won't be fair, Sir!"

"The discrepancy exists anyway. Hierarchy means hierarchy! We must get the most!"

"I agree, Sir, but even now we get three times more than the Second ranks and approximately eighteen times more than the Third ranks. Why more?" he knew the figures, because for a long time salaries had not changed at the Factory.

"Andir, the Factory is working at a very good profit. The surplus is just waiting to be distributed as we see fit. There's no way we give it away to people, who have not deserved it. It's just not happening!"

"Sir, I'm not saying that we have to make our wages the same as the rest of the ranks, but to keep the distribution proportional. Isn't this the fairest way?"

"What's fair is what we say!"

"But, Sir, all the idea-consultants do the same thing in the same rooms and I believe that if there should be an increase, then everyone must get their cut and…"

"Don't lower us to their level, Andir! They are not like us. The youngsters of the Third ranks are light years away from what a true idea-consultant should be. We carry the entire Factory on our shoulders. When they get a 'zero' customer, where do you think he goes to?"

"I'm aware that they're not that experienced but…"

"Those from the Second ranks are not all great, either. They lack a lot of skills, so don't try to make them as if that's not the case."

"I did not mean to overrate anyone, but I think that…"

"Andir, you're thinking too much. You still need time to understand that the things that go on in this room are very different. What we want from you is to vote for the two changes at the meeting. Nothing else."

"And what if I don't support this?"

"You are not serious, are you?" Chirank felt that Andir was calling his bluff, but still, he had to ask.

"Sir, I wouldn't want to object our colleagues in any way, but I believe that if we open a new discussion, we could agree to a slightly more relaxed rule with regards to the admission of the Second ranks and decide on a fairer distribution of the surplus." common sense spoke, but the time, the place and the audience were wrong.

"There'll be no further discussion! We're not going to waste our time. The decision is made and unanimously accepted. You are only here to get informed about the vote."

"And what if I vote against?"

"We will still be able to pass the first change, but not the issue with the money, because we all have to agree on how the surplus is going to be used up."

"So I can actually stop the increase?"

"Andir, you can't stop anything. If we want, we could change at any time the way we vote on financial matters. For this, we don't need an unanimous vote, so your participation becomes pointless."

"So you are prepared to circumvent the rules? That's forbidden and you..."

"No, it's not. We'll circumvent the rules, according to the rules. The rules allow for circumvention. Andir, why do you want to oppose everyone?"

"Sir, I believe the rules are there to be followed..."

"Yes, but you sound as if you are against your colleagues. I did not expect this from you. I am really surprised. Your potential to be a great idea-consultant is unarguable. I'm looking at you and I see that your stance is perfect, you speak confidently, your reasoning is fine, you never make blunders and you follow the rules in a way that I've never done. Yes, you're good, but you have no idea what your colleagues are like. They'll just squash you, if you try to go against them. I'm just the speaker, but I know what will happen. Why are you doing this?"

"Sir, the rules are being breached and I can't just stay quiet and watch! What is the future for the Idea Factory, if we carry on like this?"

"Andir, you need more time to understand all this. See things as they really are!" the pleasant voice was supposed to have an effect on the rebellious "patient", who was so perplexed by his own unreal fantasies that he could not grasp true reality.

"But, Sir, if the rules mean nothing to you, to me – they are everything! I can't agree to all this!"

"Andir, you've climbed up high! How many years did it take you to move from Second to First rank?"

"Fifteen."

"That's quite a long time. Now you're facing different type of challenges. Only in a few months, you'll start feeling as if you've been in the First ranks for a decade."

"I doubt that, Sir! Is there anything else you need to tell me about? Can I go now?" he could not stand it anymore. He had to leave. Chirank might be a charming speaker, but he had also turned his back on the rules. The worst was that none of the Gods would ever resort to the rules again. Traitors!

"There's another very important issue, which will be part of the next meeting's agenda for the day. If you're not in a hurry, I can introduce you to the main points? You're better off staying, really!"

"I've got plenty of time, Sir." he only said this, so he did not appear disrespectful. That was why he kept addressing him with "Sir", instead of using his name.

"Andir, you have heard about the Club, haven't you?"

"What club, Sir?"

"The Club of the unhappy customers, those, who have been blacklisted."

"Yes, Sir, of course. I've heard about it."

"I don't know, the lower ranks might have called it differently, but it's all about the same people. We believe that very soon, there will be a problem. We don't have solid evidence of how and when they'll try to make huge damages to the Factory. We've only heard that the person is just waiting for a signal to go ahead and complete the task and that the target is our destruction."

"But this is impossible! Sir, the blacklisted are never admitted again in the Factory! They are banned for life!" Andir got truly scared. The thought that someone could harm the most precious thing in his life horrified him.

"Those in the list are not the real problem. But they have some followers, who don't like us very much. They have never been our clients."

"Sir, I don't understand. Even if a customer decides to do something damaging, he wouldn't be able to do a lot of harm, because it is impossible for him to bring in a weapon or try to burn the place, or something…"

"That's right, Andir. We are all well aware of that."

"Besides, the structure of the building is like that, so any damage will be rather partial. The destruction of the Factory is not possible! It's not possible, Sir!"

"Don't be so certain. If we underestimate the potential threat, we can be very unpleasantly surprised."

"Sir, if someone tried to do anything, the idea-consultants are good and fast enough to use their reflexes. When we sense an aggressive visitor, we always react in the right way." After John's life threatening attack, Andir was the most suspicious employee in the Idea Factory. He knew that if he needed, he would call the security well before his client got him entrapped.

"The whole point is that we are not talking about a client."

"How do you mean, Sir, "we're not talking about a client?""

"The threat, most likely, is coming from an idea-consultant, who is a follower and adherent."

"A consultant? One of us?" Andir felt completely shocked. Despite the years of experience and his mastered ability of self-control, the new God showed his surprise. He instinctively looked round to check if they were still alone in the room.

"Andir, I can assure you that the person we're looking for does not have an access to this room. He's from the lower ranks."

"Sir, I have no idea who gave you this piece of information, but I think that all this is absolutely impossible. We've all been through the Academy and if there was someone, who doesn't want to help people, he would get caught straight away. The Mentor would sense it first and not allow the person to get to here!"

"You're right, Andir. But this doesn't help us at all. What if the idea-consultant was recruited after leaving the Academy?"

"Do you know what rank he is from? Third? Second?"

"No, we don't know. That is why we keep our eyes open for absolutely everyone. Of course, we may be looking in the wrong direction."

"What do you mean, Sir?"

"It's possible that the information is misleading, so it distracts our attention, and in effect, no threat is coming from an idea-consultant. And while we are wondering about how to expose one of our colleagues, the real perpetrator is let to run free. Andir, we're not sure about anything and that is our biggest problem."

"Is it possible that the threat is amongst the security guards?"

"It could be anyone. We are bringing the matter up for a discussion at our next meeting and agree to the necessary measures we have to take. This time it is serious."

"We'll find him, whoever he is. I'm certain, Sir!"

"Let's hope you're right, Andir! Let's hope!" with these words the older man, who had an affinity for alcohol, put an end to their meeting. He wanted to be as optimistic as Andir, but actually had a negative premonition. The future of the Idea Factory was ominous and the end – imminent?

Andir finally left the hall. He could not wait to leave before, but now that he had heard about the threat, the consultant was impatient about the next meeting. They all had to make a pact on this most important cause – the Idea Factory, despite their differences about abiding the rules. Andir had to turn a blind eye about the smoking and the drinking and ignore the top cats' aloof attitude. Who was going to help people, if the sinister plan was put into action and the Factory was destroyed? This person had to be stopped at all cost.

◆ ◆ ◆

The idea-consultants work in the same interrogation room during their entire career. So being at the top, Andir still had to go to his old familiar room and basically, everything was just the same. If he was blindfolded and went into a different room, he would have recognized immediately that it was not "her". The air in his room and the interior were just unique and he could never get it wrong. The long lasting symbiosis between the two of them had conjured up the perfect team. His newly acquired divine status did not interfere with the way Andir did his job, based on the high standards imposed on him by the rules and himself. He could never lower those standards, because his work then would become slack. This just would not be Andir. Not him!

The clients, however, were very different. Not all, but almost. They felt at awe with the idea-consultant, because the fee, they had paid to see him was rather high. Paying that much, made one treat the person, who was going to help them, accordingly and in correspondence with their high status. The commoners bowed before the king, did they not? Therefore, when visiting God, one needs to make a double effort to follow the divine etiquette. Only one tenth of all the praises, given to the know-it-all idea-consultant of First rank, were actually deserved. Most clients did not want to flatter them, but they did. The payment was made; the door was closed, so they felt they had to do the smooth talking. They thought they were supposed to.

Andir had experience with backscratchers, but he never had them in such a great number before. A Second rank might get some fake compliments from two-three people a week, whereas now, it was the same quantity in a day. The solution to this problem was hidden again in the rules. In the small interrogation room, the power was in his hands, which meant that the customers had to take off the mask and go through what they got together to actually do. Otherwise, they were out in the cold in no time, with no money and no idea. As expected, the negative prospect, regarding the meeting prompted the unnecessary flattering words simply to cease and the clients quickly got to play the idea-consultant's game.

People often exaggerated, when describing an object, they truly admire, or if they had heard that others did. The customers believed that the First rank is really something big. They were better than them, better than their friends, better than everyone. If this was not the case, how then, the consultant ever managed to give an idea and solve the problem of someone, they had just met? Well, there was something better, then! Up there – in the head. Andir had numerous awards from his school years, and later, at the Academy, when he had to prepare himself for the unpredictable work in the Idea Factory. He was aware that he was in the top two percent amongst the world population, in terms of intelligence. And since he had become one of the Gods, the clients believed that he was extraordinarily smart. For instance, when he was still a consultant of Third rank for five years, the customers regarded him as one of them, on their level, or maybe just a step above them, if we were honest. Climbing up the career ladder changed his clients' opinion about him, too. They thought that the consultant, Second rank was so much smarter than them. But now, they really went over the top with their flattering nonsense, which they really believed. The customers were obvious hypocrites, when they were saying to him how happy they were to be served by such an amazingly experienced consultant. People were prepared to argue with Andir and tell him that he was at least five times more intelligent than them.

With some exceptions, almost everyone, who resorted to the services of "God", was simply desperate. No argument about it! Some, however, had turned their own desperation into a cult. They felt that their problem was complex and hard to solve and instead of paying much less money for a professional advice, they would decide on getting the best service by a top consultant, who could give them the right answer. Those clients just over exaggerated the severity of their situation and believed that no one else could ever get into such predicament. Their desperation grew by their own over worrying and tendency towards self-destruction. It was worse with those, who had had their problem for years. They kind of loved to feel bad and live in despair. They had the inexplicable and strange desire to feel in that way. They would finally come to the man, who was going to put an end to their misery, but at the same time, the customers did not want the story to ever finish. Good wins over evil, but is it not a bit early for victory to come? Just a handful of evil, please... It was hard after all, to get out of the habit of being under constant stress, or not being able to sleep for more than three hours in one go. Andir could not understand those people. They got the best idea, which saved them from their desperation but they still left somehow disappointed. Since he had joined the Gods, Andir had to deal with at least ten masochistically inclined customers, who had affinity towards distress and all negative emotions. The consultants of Second and Third rank were lucky enough to serve acceptably desperate clients and very rarely dealt with such fanatical people.

Andir, the God, usually met two types of clients – rich or poor. The poor believed that if they were paying the high fee to see a top consultant, then, they would be getting the best service. Despite not being able to afford it, as their monthly account balance was simply not sufficient, they just wanted the expensive service. A poor client saved for months, even years in some cases, to go and see Andir. Those people borrowed money from friends, took credits from banks, deprived their family of essential goods just so they can get the colossal sum together. So at the end of the third stage, the poor customers not only got their ready solution, but they also felt as if their dream had come true. Everyone, who was underprivileged dreamt to become rich, did they not? They wanted to live like those affluent people, who did not care what it said on the price tag, and visit the same paradise holiday places as them or eat in the same expensive restaurants. The poor felt as if they got a spec of the luxurious life, when they entered Andir's interrogation room, because they knew that it was predominantly the rich, who resorted to his service. Andir was experienced enough to excuse their behavior and he pitied them for their efforts to pretend that they were something, they were actually not, especially, doing it in completely the wrong place.

The rich never gave a thought about the poor and did not care about the fee. They praised the idea-consultant like the others, but from time to time mentioned accidentally how great they were, too. Those customers boasted, as if unintentionally, about their properties, expensive cars and piles of money, as well as about how powerful they were. Andir, however, quickly managed to put them on the right track; by making them stick to the rules, instead of showing off. Often, it appeared that they did not have any problems to solve. Most of the rich clients visited the Factory not to get an idea for their made-up simple dilemma, but just so they could later on brag that they had been there and not only that, but they had seen the best consultant. There was no two ways about it – the best or nothing – was their life motto. Yes, there were such people! It was terrible that while these clients were sitting on the unmovable metal chair, there were customers, who had real problems and they were freezing out there in the queue. The rules stated clearly, however, that everyone, including the rich pretenders, had to be treated equally. Andir did not like the wealthy snobs, but he was professional enough to swallow his qualms about this. What was required of him was to do his job, despite the exaggerated nonsense he had to hear and no matter how the clients got the fee together or how rich they were.

◆ ◆ ◆

Hours before the important meeting, Andir could not concentrate at all. He felt quite apathetic about everything. He did not put a lot of effort in really getting into the clients' problems, but he still managed to do his job alright. Fortunately, he had to deal predominantly with averagely desperate people, who came in with easy to solve problems. At the end of the day, everyone was happy.

The consultant had a few days before the discussion to work on his strategic plan. Andir decided to follow the advice of his ugly colleague, now being aware that he could not do much about the proposals for changes – the admission of the Second ranks into the First, as well as the salary increase by forty percent. Basically, he was going to vote with a "yes", along with everyone else. They all had to act and concentrate on the threat. The consultants need to really discuss the situation and look at it from every possible angle.

Andir employed his full mental capacity to think of something, but to no avail. The reality was that it was impossible for anyone to physically destroy the Idea Factory and its busy bees – the employees. There was no reason for anyone to force the idea-consultants to stop helping the ordinary desperate citizens. Let's hope that the colleagues had come up with something, otherwise there would be a very unpleasant surprise, if what Chirank said was true. No one likes nasty surprises, especially when they affect the standard of living that one had been used to.

The meeting was about to start in less than ten minutes. Andir was climbing up the stairs towards the conference hall, completely ready to share his ideas with the people in the room, he was just about to enter. He walked by the group of colleagues, who had already arrived, and sat down, in his seat to wait for the rest of the Gods to come and join them. Again, he remained unnoticed by the others. No one looked at him, because there was no reason for them to do it. No one felt like talking to him. They chatted, however, together. This time, Andir was not surprised to hear that they were talking again about money. After all, the second topic on the meeting's agenda concerned the unnecessary forty percent salary increase that was so unreasonable. He felt quite lonely and was deeply troubled by the fact that rules were constantly breached. He tried really hard not to look, where regulations kept being violated, but it wasn't easy at all. The smokers continued with their bad and unhealthy habit. They did not care that their cigarettes released a vile smoke, which poisoned the others, turning them into passive smokers. They lit the cigarettes one after another, as if their craving grew every time they had put one out. The evidence of their bad addiction was the yellowy skin on their fingers. They were digging their own graves.

This time, the metal flask stayed hidden away in the pocket of the alcoholic, who really enjoyed its contents at the last meeting. The old God's eyes had turned sparkly well before he came in the hall. He had had the opportunity to drink all day in his interrogation room? Who knows? The ten-minute break between each client gave plenty of time for indulging in a couple of double shots. The rest of the guys with an affinity to alcohol looked as if they had also got their dose. Andir had a good picture about who those people might be. He was aware about Chirank and the old guy, but there were definitely other black sheep in the flock. The man, sitting next to Andir had a visible tremor in his hands, due to the likely cold turkey, he was experiencing. Andir could feel the alcohol fumes, coming from him, although the guy was not speaking to him. He must have had at least a half a liter. Three more colleagues could easily be regarded as suspects, too. They were nervously peeking behind the ugly speaker, showing that they were very much aware of what was in the cupboard. They probably often opened it to reach for the bottle after work, when there was not a scheduled meeting at the hall. Andir, however did not have the evidence, whether all of them were part of the same cigarette-and-alcohol crowd.

The working meeting started as usual. Chirank said his introductory piece, full of clichés. His undeniable talent made everyone quiet in a very subordinate way. The idea-consultants around the oval table gaped at the man, who was the source of the voice, so pleasing to the ear. The speaker read out the first bull point on the agenda slowly, but not too slow, clearly, but in a flowing manner. The pronunciation was perfect and the words were uttered in the most attractive timbre. It was so nice that everyone felt like the mesmerizing melody should never stop. Never. Chirank reached the last punctuation sign before the second bull point and gave his colleagues the opportunity to share their thoughts before proceeding to the vote. As the major points, regarding the admission of the Second ranks into the elite were discussed at the previous meetings, now everyone had to simply put their vote into practice: raise their hand for a 'yes', or not raise it – for a 'no'. Abstention was not an option. Seconds later, when even the newcomer did not object, the change was passed and accepted.

The other important amendment to vote for was the one, everyone looked forward to, as if it was the dessert, or the cherry of the cake. Money! While the speaker was reading the proposal out, the greedy Gods got truly animated. Everyone was rubbing their hands with content, gesticulated with explicit expressions on their faces. Sleazy grins clearly showed their inner mercantile satisfaction. Some licked instinctively their lips, munched quietly on a non-existent food, swallowed noisily in expectation of the monetary grub. People behaved like this, when starving. The stomach usually rumbled in anticipation of the coming hot meal. Money – the printed valuable paper – lacked any gustatory qualities and could not satiate physical hunger. There were not any calories in the dry ink, for certain. Maybe, these people were not aware that banknotes were not edible? It was clear that the general salivating was not going to stop any sooner, even after the voting, because the third point that was to be passed, was connected to the second one. This meant that it also irritated the stomach. The financial "blood sugar" was going high to some truly critical levels. Andir was not informed about that topic, which was proposed at the last minute. Basically, the fees for one to see a consultant, First rank, were going up by twenty percent. Only in this way, the salary increase was going to be substantiated even when the surplus was no longer available to cover up the extra "investment". There was no surprise in all this! They just wanted more and more. No doubt that the top cats were going to get it their way. The status quo had to be preserved as a general unspoken priority. The newly joined God could have objected, when Chirank offered the opportunity to everyone to do so, but he did not. Andir felt he had to keep quiet, because all this was not that important.

The crucial topic to discuss had moved to forth position now. Who was the baddy and how could he get caught before it was too late? Andir raised his arm in a clear "yes". The third amendment was also passed. He just knew that his colleagues would never change. No matter what he could tell them and how well he could prove his argument about the unnecessary increase, they were not going to listen. They were all the same, like eggs in an egg box, which were selected to be of the same size, color and smell. If cracked, one would discover inside the same egg white and yolk, and nothing else. If one dared to break the calcified shell of an idea-consultant of First rank, they would find out that the Gods were identically mad. That was why, the different egg in the lot did not dare object. Andir knew he would lose.

The Idea Factory always attracted all sorts of rumors. People loved to talk about it, fantasized some stories, which were inevitably passed on to other people, who would add their own version about things. The origin of the rumors was no secret to any of the top consultants. They were aware of the threats, which were never going to cease. Moreover, the unhappy clients' club was destined to expand. About several hundred desperate customers were seen each day, so it was impossible for every one of them to leave the Factory totally satisfied. There was always at least one person, who would happily set the building alight, if they could, of course, as it was incased in metal panels. Now the threat seemed real. Andir was not aware about the worrying tip-off in detail or where it was coming from, but he was certain that it was not to be looked upon lightly, if the entire executive management of the Factory had been employed to deal with it.

Chirank presented the forth proposal in the same clear-ringing silvery voice as before. His colleagues, however, reacted differently. There was a bit of a commotion in the room. People bristled up and fidgeted in their seats. Some stood up, so they could hear better, ready to speak up and share their opinion, as soon as Chirank finished. There was an absolute silence in the hall. Before the divine voice went quiet, Chirank suggested to his colleagues to share and present their ideas. Although, all of them were equal, some were more pushy than the rest. One consultant was quick enough to get everyone's attention and proposed a seemingly effective and easy solution. Security. More security. If the number of guards was increased, this would pump up the level of security, too. Inevitably, the potential perpetrator would grow more hesitant. Even less educated people than those in the room could have easily refuted such hideous suggestion. The idea-consultants sent the idea in the recycle bin in no time. There were several reasons for that. Firstly, why need more security, when no one knew where exactly the threat was coming from? Secondly, the main suspect was an idea-consultant of the lower ranks. Everyone in the hall was aware that the consultants were never subjects to a security check. The guards could not lay a finger on them. Last, but not least, what if the possible threat was coming from one of the security people? By hiring more, the task of exposing him on time would become much harder. The reasons did not stop there, but three were enough for the opponents to put the point across.

One of the smokers opened his mouth, full of yellowy teeth, to produce, yet, another hypothetical theory. He believed that the youngsters from the Third ranks should be subjected to some severe grilling, because only a consultant, who was inexperienced, timid and have low self-esteem, could get recruited for the task. And yes, such people were amongst the lowest ranks. The grilling usually took place at the exams. If the committee consisted of four instead of three members, the mental torture could go on for hours, until the enemy spilled the beans. Half of the audience stood up against such cruelty with arguments that were difficult to swallow. The Third ranks were inexperienced. They were young and were still learning. If annihilated at the exams, they would probably never recover and never develop their potential as consultants. For some, it would be simply too much and they could later really slip up with the clients, making a blunder after blunder, until they just leave the Factory job and join the unhappy clients' club, or to be precise – its branch: the club of the unhappy former idea-consultants. There was another valid point – they were scared to even think of a way to destroy the Factory. Basically, the possible culprit was not amongst them.

The Second ranks were a different story, however. The consultant, who brought the focus onto the middle level, was not a smoker, but liked his drink, most likely. He was right. The "middles" could easily accommodate in their ranks someone smart enough, who was capable of doing the extreme. In their case, however, a grilling at the exams would simply not do the job. These consultants had passed too many annual tests successfully and it was very difficult to apply a psychological pressure on them. How could one catch them out, then? It was prohibited for anyone to follow an idea-consultant or interfere with their personal life outside the Factory. Well, the only option, then, was the lie detector and its relative efficiency. Rarely anyone resorted to using the device, which pointed what was true or false on the basis of minute changes in the physiological functions of a person. Unfortunately, a good idea-consultant could easily play the game, no problem! Their self-control had been mastered to an inhuman level and even if they failed to a couple of questions, the results of the test would simply be announced as inconclusive and would be discredited. No! A detector was out of question. What about if the very first proposal of the meeting played a role in all this? The simple idea was suggested by an innocently looking consultant, who was sitting to the right of Chirank. If the idea-consultants, Second rank, were told about the admission of new members in the elite of Gods being abolished, this might provoke them quite a bit. It was not mandatory for the top cats to make the changes known to everyone, but if they did? Yes, what if they told their inferior colleagues about never getting the chance to become one of them? What would be their reaction to the fact that the road to promotion was forever blocked? To hope to join the best only in the instance of one of the Gods dying was excruciatingly discouraging. Without a doubt, this could unlock the secretly kept discontent and turn it into hatred or even a huge desire to destroy the Factory, which could appear above the surface. Or might be not?

The influx of badly thought out ideas got exhausted in less than half an hour. The idea-consultant with the bluest eyes in the room changed the general tone of the futile discussion in a different direction. Not 'who', but 'how' should be the question! How could anyone make the Idea Factory stop being what it was? A fresh debate on the building's strengths from engineering point of view resulted in the conclusion that the solid multi-cell construction could not suffer a significant damage. Hurling dangerous objects, explosion, arson, or a power cut were possible threats, but were quickly disproved by their own nightmare, called Logic. Moreover, a serious precedent was also missing. Throwing snowballs was just a warm-up game to pass the time amongst the queuing customers, until their turn came, and could not be regarded as a real threat. The safe white stuff had never been replaced with grenades, for instance, or anything of military nature. People knew what could follow, so they never dared do anything stupid. They were afraid. Their fear was comparable to the fear of suddenly meeting a starving polar bear. Some actually would have preferred the bear than the chance to attack the Factory.

The top consultants kept accelerating towards the dead end of a one-way street, while trying to imagine how they could personally get harmed by all this. Of course, if all of them died, there would be no one left to work in the Factory and the establishment would cease to exist. How was it possible their physical being to be affected to such an extent, when they were the sole masters of their interrogation rooms; there were dozens of stocky guys outside, prepared to help and in the evenings, the consultants went back to their well protected homes? Health-wise, they had all been in pretty good condition for their age. The plague had not been around in the North for centuries and the fantasy that they could be poisoned via their food and drink was implausible.

On the road? There was the clue. All the consultants were not safe on their way to work or back, driving home. However, this idea had its obvious weaknesses, too. The heavy weather conditions limited the use of the powerful engines under the bonnets. This meant, that one could only drive slowly. And although the low speed made it possible for someone to attack them, it was not very likely that such assault would be deadly for the entire Factory staff. Moreover, the intelligence on this had revealed that the perpetrator is alone. No one had mentioned two, three or more people, let along an organized group.

The conversation was lacking any new ideas. The idea-consultants were now repeating themselves by adding some different elements to the old ideas, which were, however, even more contradictive. They seemed stuck now – a sure sign that it was time to vote. The conclusions that crystallized out of the debate were purely cosmetic and did not solve anything. The first one was for them to employ more guards. Then, the Third and Second ranks were going to be subjected to the lie detector on top of their excruciating annual exams. In addition, those guys, who had been working for less than three years at the Factory, were going to be subjected to a horrendous grilling by four, instead of three examiners. Chirank announced the beginning of the vote. He made it clear that they had to vote for all the proposals at the same time, instead of one by one. As usual, he offered the opportunity to everyone to speak up, if they had anything to add, or be silent forever. Once the proposals were passed, they could not be brought back for revision. Andir spoke. Everyone pretended not to hear him. He said something again, but was ignored. They did not hear him once more.

"One of us!" he stood up from his chair and raised his voice. This time, even if everyone had earplugs, they would have still grasped his brief suggestion.

"What?!?"

"Sir, I think that we're missing something very important here."

"What do you mean, Andir?"

"This is ridiculous. It can't be anyone of us." the old drunk first shared the general belief in their own innocence, which he thought, it was preposterous to be even doubted.

"Sir, I'm not accusing anyone in this hall. I'm only saying that..."

"You're not accusing, but you're saying. What's the difference, Andir? I announce that the vote on the measures from our last proposal can begin..."

"Mr. Chairman, allow me to speak."

"I don't think that..."

"Speak up, Andir. I'm interested now and I imagine the others are, too. So how is it possible that the enemy could be one of us? Let him speak, Chirank!" Markot's authoritative father gave the permission and his colleagues remained silent. It was rather interesting for them to find out who could be the possible culprit, when they all believed that it could not be anyone of them. The standing man, no doubt, had to point the wrong man. But who?

"Actually I..."

"Hang on, Andir. I have an offer for you."

"What offer, Mr. Richardson?'"

"If what you are going to tell us is rubbish, then, we'll add another point to vote for on the daily agenda. Do you agree?"

"What point, Sir?"

"We'll dismiss you from three consecutive meetings."

"But, Sir, according to the rules, an idea-consultant cannot be..."

"I know the rules, Andir. That's why I need your agreement on this beforehand. So, do you accept my offer?"

"I do. If I don't manage to convince you, I shall miss three of our working meetings."

"Chirank, note down our colleague's wish." the chairman added another bull point to the list and got ready to hear about who was the baddy amongst them.

"We are all ears, Andir."

"Thank you, Sir. I know it may sound as unthinkable, but I don't want to offend anyone. Please, accept my apologies, should anyone of you has felt affronted." the expressions, perched on their faces, showed that the consultants had felt hurt and a lot more. They were

222

never going to forget the insult and Andir was going to be hated until the rest of their lives.

"Dear Colleagues, today, we've discussed all possibilities about the people, who have the potential to harm the Idea Factory. It can't be the guards or the youngsters of the Third rank and those of the Second – it's just hard to believe... Then, it looks like that it's almost impossible to find out who this person can be. But we missed to look at ourselves. The top consultants are the most powerful in the Factory. We are the keepers here, the engine, which cannot stop, otherwise everything will just go to hell."

"Andir, we all agreed that it's not feasible for us to all perish at the same time and..."

"Sir, I have not said that anyone of us is going to die. We'll be fine and we'll keep coming to work and will always attend our meetings. Nothing will change, unless there is a start of a secret propaganda within. Let's imagine that one of us, say me, is a threat to the Factory! How can I harm it?"

"Are you asking or telling us? This meeting will never end like this!"

"I'm sorry for the delay, Sir. I just want to point out that now I've become much closer to the consultants of First rank, since my admission in your group, whereas before, I've never had the chance to speak to you apart of resorting to the regular small talk. I know that, according to the rules, we can never discuss work, the clients..."

"We know the rules! What are you heading at?"

"Sir, I think that now I'm free to communicate with you all, I can easily brainwash you with some subversive idea against the Factory, of course, by applying my influence on you, one by one..."

"Ha-ha-ha, Andir, don't overrate yourself so much!" naturally, it was Richardson, who expressed the general opinion with a pinch of ridicule.

"Don't forget, I'm supposed to be just an example. We all know that there are much more influential consultants amongst us, who can steadily and methodically try to change..." Andir got his own back on Richardson, although inadvertently. It was like a smack in the face of his most prominent colleague.

"Andir, you're talking complete nonsense! Can't you see that? We're not listening anymore!"

"Sir, I…"

"Chirank, let's proceed."

"But, Sir, I haven't finished and…" Andir found himself in a rather common situation. The enlightened, who was aware of a well kept secret, decided to stand up, so everyone could see him. He was trying to teach the ignorant that were around him and open their eyes. There was no point, however. None of them could see him or hear him.

"It's all over, Andir. Take your seat now. Dear colleagues, we can move on, now, and vote on the new measures." a forest of raised hands appeared as quickly as it disappeared.

"Thank you all. Now let's vote for the last proposal, according to which Andir agreed to be released from the attendance of three consecutive meetings. Please, give your vote." the decision was accepted unanimously. Even Andir voted against himself, as promised.

"Thank you again." Chirank did not announce the end of the meeting, but everyone got the message. Their wives and children were awaiting them in their cozy warm homes. The new measures were going into effect on the following day, whereas for Andir – in seven days, when the next meeting was taking place.

The consultants did not want to hear him out and there was nothing strange about this. But the problem was different. They simply did not want to believe him. They did not even imagine that the insurgent, recruited by the Club, could be one of them. The most influential consultants, who were kind of accused indirectly, included Chirank, Richardson and the old drunk. The first one was the chairman of the meetings and apart of owning an amazing voice, he was popular for his manipulative skills. The second consultant was a star, like the Sun, and most of colleagues gravitated in his orbit, mainly because he could boast with some positive qualities. Andir could bet on the fact that the others would always find it hard to reject Richardson's magnetism or that they would ever express their own opinion, which had not been influenced by anything else. The drunk was the one of the most honorable consultants that everyone showed him his total respect. He had a great influence, too.

Any ideas on the future of the Factory, suggested by the three of them, together or individually, could easily infiltrate people's heads. So hypothetically, they could all effortlessly jeopardize the safety of the Idea Factory, if one assumed that they had bad ideas about it. Andir had not yet pondered about what the possible danger could be. Actually, he had no intention to accuse anyone in particular by name, but felt that it was necessary to broaden their horizons by offering them a scope for thought. One idea could be followed by a dozen of new helpful ideas.

His courage to speak up his opinion proved to be a silly move. He did not have to do this, while in the conference hall. Andir learned this the hard way. In the months to follow, the Gods formed a pact against him, designed to squash him in the same way they breached the rules.

When his punishment expired and he went to the next meeting, all his colleagues continued to ignore him. They were not kids, so they could not be that crossed with him, surely. However, he realized soon enough that nothing could ever be the same, when the last point of the meeting was read out by Chirank. The idea-consultants decided that from then on, Andir's vote would not be counted for, even when significant decisions had to be made. This was against the rules, but the rules also stated that they could be altered at any time without a full majority. The ugly speaker of the meeting explained the motives behind the idea that the voice of one of the Gods had to be eliminated: "provocative behavior in breach of the rules"; "expressing outrageous suggestions, which were damaging to the reputation of all consultants of First rank"; "passive participation in the meetings"; "clear belligerence during the meetings that could cause a conflict situation"... The ten sins that Andir had apparently committed brought him on his knees. Well, at the end Chirank mentioned something about restoring Andir's full rights, should he show an improvement that was noted by all his colleagues, but this was more or less said as a joke. No one there truly believed that God Andir would ever regain his position. The worst of all was that he had to attend the meetings, although this was thoroughly pointless. They wanted him to be present and watch him suffer. He should never forget how he got into this situation.

225

Andir continued to present his clients with good ideas. He did not encounter not one problem that was difficult to solve, in his interrogation room. The 'zero' clients, who were being sent to him by the lower ranks, did not prove to be a hard job for him, either. Life, as being in service to people for so much money, was nice. Another meeting was about to start. No one talked to him, or even noticed him. The mean old men really had some fun with him, by asking him about his opinion on some issues and then quickly interrupted him, as if to show that they did not care what he thought. The fact that no one took notice of his vote, did not stop him to exercise it at every opportunity. If he dared to abstain from raising his hand for a "yes", everyone would attack him, like street dogs, to try to find out why he was objecting their decision. They would throw numerous questions at him, but when he attempted to answer, someone inevitably got up to point out that it was irrelevant what Andir thought or did not think. The consultant was not stupid, so the third time that this happened, he simply stopped taking notice of their nasty tricks. Meeting after meeting, he had to endure their mocking, which by the way got less and less effective. Still, he felt even more isolated by the group. Andir got used to the thick cigarette smoke that always filled up the hall, their full glasses, he got used to everything. They had won.

He wondered, if they would accept him back, in the case he displayed an attitude that suited them all. If he played the game of the three most influential consultants, then they might feel sorry for him and show him their mercy. Then, they would probably reinstall what they had deprived him from. No. Not Andir, not him! He had achieved his dream to become one of them, but now, he had a new dream. He decided to never get to resemble any of the Gods. He was not like them. His mission was far too simple – to help his desperate clients.

The Club of the Unhappy-s

In reality, they did not have a special place to attend their secret meetings. They operated without having an organization and very few of them actually knew each other. The only common thing between them was their disappointment of the Idea Factory. They hated it; they loathed the pristine idea-consultants and everything, connected to this damn place!

The customers, who did not have any real problems, were only a few, but they deserved to be sent to a mental institution, without exception or recommendation by a doctor. Their world was very different from the one we know. The consultants usually recognized very quickly their maniacal behavior, when trying to describe the misadventures, which had brought them to the Factory. These crazy people would keep coming and rant on about their false reality in the most lengthiest and made up details. They would bring inanimate objects to life, accusing them for wanting to kill them, while the mad people were asleep. These customers assigned supernatural and paranormal abilities to their relatives and friends, like magic. The examples could just go on. The consultants were aware of the exaggerated mad attitude of the clients, so they tried to be quite gentle with them, otherwise the loonies could join the Club of the unhappy customers in no time. They applied the procedures, learnt at the Academy, and just gave them the best idea, avoiding any discrimination. Of course, the idea was usually as unrealistic as the actual problem. After the job was done, the consultants just hoped that the next visitor would be sane. Sometimes, these crazy customers could not swallow the idea, as they thought it was not the right one. It would not help them and that was it. The clients would start swearing at the consultants and insult them with all sorts of unseemly words that came to their minds. The more aggressive of them did not even wait, but attacked the consultant, who would get rescued quickly by the security guards. Those customers were immediately blacklisted from ever coming to the Idea Factory.

Another sub-division of the Club comprised normal people, who lived in reality. They were rational and with a good sense of judgment: normal clients, who had normal problems. When they sat on the metal chair, they simply behaved. Like any guest, they did not want to leave a bad impression in the presence of their intellectually superior host. The three stages would pass, so that the moment of truth came – the moment, when the problem embraced the idea, which was the true cure for it. The dilemma was quickly deleted in the client's mind. Well, when the visitor did not like the idea, then what? The rational, far from crazy customer, would then make a scandal, shouting and threatening away the poor consultant, who had actually done his job perfectly fine, but the visitor could not grasp the solution. It was simply alien to him, even though it sounded effective. He did not want it. The customer would reject the idea, leave the room in a strop or got thrown out by the security, only to become the next member of the Club. There were more to come, normal or crazy, there would be always someone, who left the Factory, full of discontent.

The idea-consultants were so much filtered through the Academy, before reaching their jobs at the Factory. There was never a guarantee who would fail now and again, despite the thorough selection process that the new recruits had to go through. There was no way that the Mentor and the lecturers could know, if some of the candidates were actually no good for the job, despite that they had seemed suitable at first. When the idea-consultants became part of the system and got their own interrogation room, some of them slightly changed. They got too big for their shoes and behaved aloof with the customers. Third ranks they were, but really full of themselves. The high salary gave them the chance to get quite busy and outgoing after work. Temptations of all sorts were right behind the corner, although the consultant's job was to resist them. Whenever caught of misdemeanor, at the annual exams, the culprits had to walk out of the job at once. Often, the young infringers would fight over the "unfair" decision, arguing that there was not enough evidence. This was actually in most cases true, but the experienced committee of the three Gods always sensed, when the rules had been badly breached, and showed no mercy in their decision. Sometimes, the top cats made an error and dismissed innocent consultants. Still, whenever they uttered: "Get out of here!" there was no return. Joining again the jobseekers' reality, the former consultants quickly realized what they had lost. No other job was going to pay even half of what they had been getting at the Factory. These people were prepared to do anything, if only they could go back and sit on the uncomfortable metal chair, so they could meet yet another desperate client. Instead, however, they joined the Club of the unhappy-s and stayed there. For how long? – Each of them decided for themselves.

Some were there for several months, others – for years. There also were those, who never left the Club.

The security guards comprised the last element that was directly related to the Factory, which became part of the Club. The Idea Factory was rather generous to these guys, so no one was really happy to leave this cushy number. The guards always did their job properly and never got in the way of the consultants. They never entered the interrogation rooms for no reason, nor did they hide behind the big glass. The security was comprised of highly professional men, who were almost perfect and showed no reason for getting dismissed. The idea-consultants of First rank were responsible for employing the guards, so they were the ones, deciding how many they needed, what their duties were and where exactly they should stand on the premises. Well, there was no one to supervise the guards because all the consultants worked in their rooms. There was a way, of course, to find out, whether there had ever been a breach of security. At the annual tests, when the lower ranks endured their grilling, the guards were also invited in the room, one by one, for a friendly chat. The security never knew that they had been tested along with the others. The Gods would ask the guards some general security questions, but at the same time, they always managed to glean some alternative information from these boys. Who had got late for their shift? How many of the colleagues went to a birthday party and arrived hung-over at work on the following day? This would have been equal to a bad physical shape, which meant that the security had been jeopardized, if there was a problem. So those, who had fun at the party, became jobseekers on the following day. The guards' employment contract was full of clauses, which offered a wide scope for interpretation. Basically, the dismissal was always right and within the Law. The Gods were not that stupid, nevertheless, and never sacked skilled workers just because they went a party in their free time. The nucleus, providing the Factory security stayed on and only the insignificant branches got cut off irrevocably.

The imaginary hall that would have accommodated the Club of the unhappy people was only half full, if one only counted in the clients and the ex-employees of the Factory. The other half comprised the indirect victims of the humanitarian activity of this unusual establishment.

To be precise, this included the closest people of the unhappy customer. The problem grows by the day and if you don't find a solution, soon it will just explode. You ask your wife for advice, but she can't help you. She supports you in the struggle; she is right behind you and does her duty, wishing your luck to find the answer. You simply become even more stressed, because the problem is getting serious. You feel insignificant, incapable; you can't believe that this is happening to you. Your closest relatives happen to hear about the problem, too. Parents, brothers, sisters, cousins, people that you are sharing the same blood with, but you may have never met before and their names are unfamiliar to you. Despair is your guide, however. But they all can't help you with their versatile attempts to offer you some advice. Then, all of sudden, SHE appears. The Idea Factory perched on the little hill. She knows everything. Well, not the actual building, but the idea-consultants that work there. The man focuses on this only chance. Money gets collected somehow. You've got it at last. You feel its weight very well, in your inner pocket. If you get shot right in this spot, the banknotes will definitely stop the bullet. Money is what you need to get your life back on track. Your wife gets up with you in the middle of the night to make you something to eat. She kisses you goodbye and wishes you luck. Hopefully, you won't be waiting long out in the cold and you will manage to get in today. The woman is waiting for her man to come back smiling, feeling again the happiness, he has lost recently. She does not expect a bad result. She has heard that some people come out unhappy, but those, pleased with the outcome are much more in number. It will be alright. They will tell him how to solve his problem.

Time drags. Lunchtime has passed and he's still not back, yet. Maybe, there's been a problem at the queue? Well, jumping the queue, or pushing your way in is forbidden, so... He'll get in later. There are still a few hours left until sunset. Oh, he's back. She can hear his steps out on the porch. At last! The loyal wife, who has been waiting impatiently, welcomes a man, who is in very low spirits. He's not smiling, and he should, shouldn't he...? He probably couldn't reach the gate... Never mind! He'll get in tomorrow, unless… She can't believe it! The thick idea-consultant has offered a stupid idea. This is not a solution, but how…?

The desperate clients, who left the Factory with an ineffective idea, simply appeared at the starting point. The problem remained as big as before, staring at them with a grumpy face. It got the upper hand on them. From that day onwards, this family was never the same again. It was irrelevant, whether it was the man or the woman, who had joined the Club, the other half got affected, as well. The couple would quarrel a lot; there would be the arguments and the tears. The domestic physical and psychological violence would become a reality. There was actually death, in some cases. Relatives got killed by the unhappy customer, not just the wife. Sometimes, the clients would attempt suicide, despite not having the right to take away something that was a gift. A meter of sturdy rope was enough to do the job. A fatal ending was a perfect solution to the problem. But again the family would also suffer along with the poor guy. The nearest and dearest usually suffered the most and hated the Factory more than the actual person. This was the perfect prerequisite for them to join the Club.

Your friends are like a family to you, sometimes. You can share a lot with them that you wouldn't do – with your relatives. You just want to protect them from the trouble. You can do this by yourself. Still, you trust your friends of so many years unreservedly. The big fat problem suddenly appears. It is so powerful that you fall in despair within days. You ring your pals to ask for their help. They respond immediately, no matter what the time of the day it is. But they can't help you. They don't have the right idea. Theirs are good, but not good enough. You don't actually remember who's told you about the Factory. Sounds great. The Idea Factory is a place, where people hire an idea-consultant, who conjures up an idea for their problem. They can lend you money, too. Sometimes they come with you, to see you off. This can be lucky. The intelligent employee has done his job, but something still feels wrong. The solution is not quite what the client has expected to hear. It's hard to do and it could well not work. He is not pleased. At the starting point again. This is when the friends come to support him. They want to lift him on his feet, but to no avail. He blames them for suggesting to him to visit the Factory. And for what? For nothing! And what about the piles of cash that he left in there? Real friends would never do this. Alienation was the next step. He did not want to see them and just avoided them. He would walk through different streets, where he would not bump into them. He did not pick up the phone. He was hiding. The former friends got their membership card, as soon as they felt they should blame the Idea Factory about everything. SHE took him away from them. Welcome to the Club.

Your colleagues at work may not be your best friends. But if you spend more time with them than with your wife, family and friends, then it will not be so unusual if you share with your most trusted colleagues the problem, which has appeared on the horizon. You can assume that they will try to help you, well, not the jealous colleagues, of course. Why not? One of them had been in the Idea Factory and everything was fine, the idea was more than fine, too. You ask yourself about why you haven't thought of this much earlier. Considering your colleague's positive experience, you decide to follow into his footsteps and visit the place. It's not far. You just need to get a day off work and join the queue. "Hmm, where has all this snow come from? If it keeps snowing like this, by the end of the day, it will get higher than me. Well, I'll be in by then." You sense that the solution is close, standing there, a few meters away from the gate. Half an hour later, the idea-consultant, sitting like a statue, spits out the answer. But his answer seems to fit a different question. Maybe, he hasn't quite grasped what my point is? He is saying that he got me perfectly, but why then...? The client leaves the Factory unhappy and he knows who to blame for it. The colleague, of course. He told him to go there and get a nice working idea. Liar. Surely, he has been hoping to get promoted, whereas I'm stuck where I am, because of my problem. He'll be my boss soon. What about the rest of them? Good colleagues, I wish! When I told them about the Factory, they all agreed that this is what I should do. Maybe, they've ganged up on me! I'm not going to talk to them anymore. Everyone can mind their own business. The liar – I'll break his nose, even if I get the sack for it. This will work fine, actually. No one wants to be surrounded by betrayers at work!

There were plenty of story lines to entwine and they were so individual for every unhappy customer. The clients, however, were connected by one common thing – their relatives, friends and colleagues joined the Club out of hatred. Some of them felt this hatred stronger than the actual victim. Solidarity of hate? Contagious evil!

There were people in the Club, who were not clients, nor were they relatives or friends of a discontented customer. The last two groups hated the Factory, because they were treated differently by it. The Factory did not want them. The doors of the interrogation rooms were forever closed for these individuals. This was not fair. Why were they subjected to such obvious discrimination?

Women had deserved this treatment, because of what they were – women. Anyone, who one day could become a mother, could not become an idea-consultant, according to the rules. The restrictions meant that women could not become guards, cleaners or anything else. No women at the Idea Factory or at the Academy.

A reason behind this rule can be found, long back in the history of the establishment. The founder of the Factory had no problems with women. He had a great relationship with his own wife and had a perfect family of four. His mother had made him what he was. He was grateful to her and loved her very much. Why, then, he did not accept women in the Factory? The following theoretical assumptions were hard to prove.

One can achieve intellectual heights only if he feels comfortable in his own skin. He is concentrated, doesn't think of anything else and he doesn't distract himself. The three stages pass and his efforts are rewarded. The great idea is ready. The client is happy. If women are added to the equation, things will drastically change. The guards are going to talk about the pretty female idea-consultant in the room at the end of the corridor. It's not just her. There are a couple more that are quite fit. They are attractive enough, displaying their natural charm. Well, if the guards could only be allowed to chat them up, if they wanted... But if they are thinking about the girls, then, they won't be thinking about their work! The colleagues, the idea-consultants, are not blind, either. The lonely idea-consultant, who is restricted by the rules, had to be made of steel not to notice the gorgeous female colleague. He is a gentleman and cannot just ignore her, when he bumps into her at work, pretending not to see her. He would put a wide smile on his face and turn round to have a good look at her bum. The salacious employee would not be devoted enough to what he is being paid for. The women, of course, will do the same – look at the stock. Surrounded by handsome, smart and financially stable men, they could see their potential partners in them. Good choice for every woman, who is striving to find security, which the idea-consultant could easily provide for her. Yes, but the rules say "No". They can't talk, touch, flirt? Then what? They will start seeing each other secretly; enjoy the clandestine relationship, until the inevitable dismissal follows. The Factory will not be able to rely on perfect idea-consultants anymore. The sensitive dribblers will be out on the street in no time.

Another reason for banning women from working at the Idea Factory was the potential problems that could occur from the way the clients would treat them. Firstly, it is much easier to trust a man than someone in a skirt. To win the customer's trust is of great priority. Women will take twice as much time to do this, which means inefficiency. The working process will become clumsy. Women will actually try much harder, following the rules in attempt to come up with the best idea. They will want to show that they are not any less or worse than men. Sometimes, there will be better female idea-consultants than their male colleagues. But what would happen if a single male customer came in the interrogation room? He would get his imagination going and fantasize about the attractive woman in a sexual context. "Hmm, the table looks comfortable..." And if the female consultant's breasts are bigger than normal, who knows? The buttons of her shirt are about to pop. The female clients would begrudge the fact that Nature had been so generous to the woman opposite them. The unattractive female visitor would be full of envy, which would hinder her ability to explain freely the nature of her problem. She would probably spare some important details and subvert the consultant's job in this way. There would be no winners in this situation. Women would be basically in the way of everything and everyone and the work was going to suffer. Hiring some ugly hags was not a solution. The initiator behind the ban had outlined the basic issues, related to this. Of course, one could think of more reasons, which supported the motto "Women should never work at the Idea Factory".

Sensible theories like this were not embraced, however, by the women and their numerous organizations. They believed that there were not any jobs out there, which were designed just for men. We were all equal, despite our physical differences. Women promised that they would never breach the rules and that they would do their duties like every other idea-consultant. They were going to do the impossible to be accepted in the group. They were prepared to stay longer at the Academy, and take harder exams and basically put up with possibly a harsher approach, if they had to. These gentle creatures never stopped dreaming about their wish to come true. They loved being considered as independent and strong. Despite all their efforts to change the current situation, the Gods would have never included the issue of admitting women-employees in the Factory even for a debate, on their meeting daily agenda. Never! The stubbornness of the idea-consultants, First rank, had created some proud members of the Club out of all these feminist women.

The Idea Factory was one and only. There was not any such establishment anywhere else in the world. There had been several attempts of other countries to copy the model, but it didn't work. So the state, which could boast with its unique Factory, accepted plenty of foreigners in peril. They also came to benefit from the service of the idea-consultants and get an idea. The foreign nationals knew that this was the right place. The rules allowed people with different passports, than the locals, to join the queue. If they were not pushing, waited patiently for their turn to come and parted with their money, then they deserved to enter any of the interrogation rooms, where the wise consultant was there for them. The only condition was that these clients had to speak the local language. Well, soon a problem appeared. Suddenly, there was a wave of foreign candidates. The building was save, elevated on the hill, but the influx could drown many of the locals in the queue. "How is it possible someone from the other side of the world to come here and have the same rights as me? In my own country?" The local citizens' discontent resulted in issuing new quotas for outsiders. In effect, the aim was to avoid any international scandal, which would involve the Factory. Good job that there would always be local potential customers for centuries to come; otherwise the market would have remained open for foreigners. The quota went down to a hundred per month, then fifty, until the Gods turned the "tap" off completely a few years ago. No more foreign nationals, unless they could afford to pay for the elite service of consultants of the highest rank. Greedy bastards. The unlucky population of the neighboring countries suffered the most and hated the most. They were only a few hours away from reaching the solution to their problem, but they were not going to be let in. Those, living further away, also hated the Factory, but maybe, not as much. The Club was growing, and growing... and although, some victims had long forgiven the Idea Factory for what it had done to them, the tendency seemed to stay strong. Actually, none of the Club members could really destroy the Factory or even harm it. The idea-consultants had simply taken the rumors about the threat far too seriously than they should have.

The Redemption

The car started to make squeaking sounds. Markot had heard the muffled and sporadic noises of disagreement since the morning, on his way to work, as if the vehicle was unhappy to be driven in such bad condition. Now the rattling sound, coming from the front, on the right, showed that soon one of the wheels could pop. It had to be fixed. Markot was not very good with cars, but he was aware that things did not look OK. A three-wheeler was not good to him. He nearly got to Little John's house so he was praying that the car did not give up on him only a few streets away from his target destination. If the worse came, he would walk the rest. There was no going back now. No way. It was interesting, however, how he was going to get back, when his mission was over. He would think of something. The young consultant quite liked the idea of hitch hiking through the night. He had never hitched before, if he did not count the one time he got in a car with his real mother, only because the driver felt like having some company. The guy did not even realize that the woman was about to leave her kid in an orphanage. Markot did not remember much of this journey, because he was very tired and just wanted to sleep at the time. The consultant, Third rank, had enough money to pay for a taxi, but he hoped it would not come to this.

Markot was about to enter the stage of the redemption plan, which was going to be called in a rather banal way: "the handing of

236

the money and the instructions", when he realized that there was no need for him to be in such a hurry. Anyone, who could walk, was capable of delivering the fat envelope and the note – from a two-year old toddler to some arthritic eighty-years old person. Alright, the idea-consultant was going to complete the task, but the problem could occur after that. The mother of the hippopotamus was a gravely sick woman, but she might be able to get up and open the door, only to find the envelope that was meant for someone else. What would she think, while she was reading the note? What about the money? She might panic or think it was stolen and then, quickly inform the police like any good citizen would do. It was doubtful that she had ever seen such a great sum in cash, so this could be a cause for a significant shock. Even death. Markot could kill her in this way. He should not allow such course of events. One should not hurt anyone, while they were trying to sincerely help somebody from the bottom of their heart. This saying was not thought up by the idea-consultant, but it was full of wisdom that suited the occasion.

Our fat main protagonist's mother was ill, which meant she might be immobile, lying in her bed. But the passers-by, walking near her house, were most likely fit to enjoy using their legs alright. Although it was quite late and dark, someone could have spotted the white object on the floor near her front door. They only had to turn round and notice the contrasting white item on the dark ground. Someone curious, who had a fine understanding of appropriating something that was not theirs – "no one has picked it, so this means that they don't need it, then" – could have just go for it and bang, a windfall! A guest, coming for a visit, could also discover it. It could be a neighbor, who had decided to see her old friend or a doctor, doing a home visit, after work, because the old lady had phoned during the day with a complaint. The possibilities for interference were endless. Markot's task had to be postponed. Say, in crime films, the cops watched the gangsters and their house for months, so they could collect as much information as possible, before the attack. He was going to do exactly this, too. He decided to watch the house for a few consecutive evenings. In this way, he would be certain that Little John came back from work at approximately the same time and make sure that no one else picked up what was meant to be for him.

Day one. The black car and its only driver-passenger were located straight opposite the house. Markot had parked quite near, but this was fine for an expert in the spying like him. He could not switch on the air-con, because the engine was off. The cold sneaked slowly through the well-insulated windows. The consultant had embraced himself to slow down the heat, escaping his body. He rubbed his back in the seat every now and again, knowing that friction creates heat. An hour passed, but John was nowhere to be seen. He should be here soon. Visibility was good, Markot did not feel sleepy, so he should be able to notice him. The house was dark. There was no light in any of the rooms. The idea-consultant pictured the layout of the house. At least a couple of the rooms must be at the back and the lady could be sitting there.

The fat guy appeared, from the same direction. The second and third day were identical to the first one. Markot would stop at the same place and wait until the huge walking bodily mass came back home to his mother. After the fourth night of surveillance, the rookie detective finally managed to make his conclusions from the gathered information and decide on some practical methods of action that he could apply. His fears that some late guest could jeopardize his intentions proved to be rather groundless. No one popped by, no one knocked on the door, nor did anyone press the broken doorbell. The passers-by did not even look at the plain house. There was simply nothing to look at. There was more good news. Little John was as punctual as a clock that might run behind by just ten minutes. He would waddle slowly up the steps to the porch, so he did not get tired. He would, then, take a few deep breaths and unlock the front door. Every day was the same. Perfect! Markot could not wait to come again tomorrow and complete his plan.

The idea-consultants were given cars to go to work. They could use this vehicle in their free time, as well. In the case of a car accident, they got a replacement straight away, if the old car was no good anymore. Markot wanted to be certain that today was free of any blunders. He was feeling great, so his car should be in good shape, too. The idea-consultant picked up the keys for one of the spare company vehicles. He briefly informed about his incident on the slippery road, when he crashed into the hard shoulder. Light accidents like this happened all the time.

He arrived. The entry hall on the first floor was well lit. Maybe, John had come back from work earlier? Markot hoped that everything would be over this evening and although it did not matter if it was any other day, he just wanted to get it done and over with. If John was as punctual as every other day, then he would be here in an hour and find the money and the note, which were going to bring Markot the ultimate redemption. The last step of the plan was easy to do. The Good Samaritan watches carefully for the appearance of the always hungry monster. Then, he gets out of his car before John comes near the house. The consultant runs to the spot, noted with the imaginary "X", drops the parcel and quickly returns to his vehicle. By this time, Little John should have another twenty meters to walk, until he reaches the corner, behind which his target is located. The most important of all for Markot, was judging well his time. He relied on his physical fitness and speed that were going to help him complete the job unnoticed. Well, even if the fatso walked faster that day, managed to go round the corner earlier than expected and saw the stranger running down from the porch, for Markot, this would not be a problem, because he could collect his car later.

The envelope and the note were placed on the passenger seat, where the navigator of any mad rally driver would be usually sitting. Markot did not want to hold them, because his palms were sweating and the paper would have creased straight away. He promised to himself to look carefully both ways before he crossed the road. It would have been quite ironic to be hit by a car in this moment. He was running late. Little John was nowhere to be seen. The weather conditions were pretty much the same as the day before and the one before that. Then, why was he late? He had probably stopped to get a sandwich or four, more like it. It was time for the snowman to take over, because the nice Markot was getting a little vexed. He froze his emotions by placing the cold mask on his face and felt as concentrated as when a client presented a very hard to solve problem in the interrogation room.

There were hardly any people on the street. Folks were long back home, enjoying their dinner with their families. A group of at least three people passed very close by, to the right side of the car and blocked the streetlight for a moment. Markot turned round to see the cause of the eclipse. He could not believe his eyes, when he saw that the group was actually made out of Little John. He stood in front of the car, hesitantly looking both ways. The big fat man did not notice the familiar face that was staring from behind the front window. John crossed the street and simply went home. The idea-consultant realized what had just happened so unexpectedly, when the fatso opened his front door. Too late.

Markot had fallen in the trap of his own limited expectations. Every experienced spy, every policeman on watch, observing the gangsters' nest, knew that despite how predictable could be the behavior of the subject; one could never rely only on this. Law enforcement guys would have watched the house from every angle to make sure that they did not get into the same predicament as Markot did. They had to surprise and not let be surprised. Well, tomorrow was another day. Markot drove off very disappointed. The time, he needed to get home was enough for him to wholeheartedly promise to the well familiar face, looking at him from the rear-vision mirror, that the plan would be completed successfully within the next 24 hours. "You can do it, Markot, you can do it!"

The desperate clients were always interesting. Some were not, but sometimes this made them even more interesting than those that were. Markot, however, did not take notice of who was or was not interesting. For him, it was important to create the best ideas for people, by applying the skills of both – the snowman and the Good Samaritan.

The man, who contributed to the consultant's plan, was quite ordinary in his appearance or basically, not that interesting. The problem that had brought him to the Idea Factory was connected to his wife, with whom he was about to celebrate their wedding anniversary – ten years of marriage. Markot had customers like him and he knew very well what to do. However, the client's wife was a little different from the rest. When the guy was talking about her, he did not mention her name. As if she was going to reprimand him, if he revealed what her parents had called her. The second stage of the meeting resembled a quiz – the game host asked the questions and the guest replied to everything at length. "What does your wife do for a living?" "Nothing." <Nothing> was the correct answer, but it did not bring any points. The client explained that his wife was on mother's leave and simply took care of their little daughter. How cute! Then, the visitor was asked about her hobbies. It was a logical question, because some great presents could be related to one's favorite hobby. Well, she did not have any. This was not good. Markot carried on asking, but the terrible answers he got, did not help him in any way. He got the following image about the woman: she was rather antisocial, had a mania about cleanness, and was obsessed with bringing up her daughter in the best possible way. The idea of both of them going on holiday abroad, just the two of them, without the kid, was rejected immediately. She was not going to leave her baby behind, until it was time for her to go to university. Jewelry, flowers, a surprise party and all the rest of traditional presents were suggested by Markot in the hope that he would get it right for the madam, somehow. Her beloved husband kept declining every idea, because of either some inconsistency with her personality or a kind of physical intolerance that she had. She did not wear any jewelry, she was allergic to flowers, she did not eat sweets, because she thought she was fat and she actually was. She hated parties. Any occasions that brought people together to eat and drink –totally revolted her. Well, it was time to move on to the third stage, otherwise the very first client for the day was going to stay at least until noon.

Often, the customer himself came up with the right solution for his problem. It was not rare, when the person was inches away from the answer, waiting outside the Factory. He only needed someone to give him a little clue, as if to offer him a tiny push in the right direction. The idea-consultant simply unleashed what had been already there in the client's "locked" mind – the answer to the most important question. Markot was about to present his rather silly idea, when the visitor came up with the right solution. Why did he not ask his wife what she would like, after all these years, when he always got confronted with a similar dilemma before the fateful date? He had never asked her directly before. He wanted to surprise her and surprises were usually kept a secret from the person, they were meant to be for. Or maybe not? He took her to an expensive restaurant for their first wedding anniversary. Everything felt by the book: the atmosphere was amazing, the bill could have caused a heart attack to some and the menu could simply put France to shame. She, however, was sick. Her runny nose and high temperature ruined the event. Well, bad luck and nothing could be done. The following year, they went to an isolated lodge in the mountain. A romantic candle-lit dinner at the backdrop of the roaring fire. The logs crackled. What an idyll! The special evening went perfect, but on the next morning, the skiing skills of the pretentious lady totally failed her. She broke her leg and from then on, hated all types of winter sports, as well as the retard, who had taken her there. The third attempt for a celebration was successful as much as no one got hurt. They stayed in and her husband gave her a double present – electrical gadgets, which immediately enhanced the kitchen and also, a very overpriced vacuum cleaner. She liked those. They had dinner in the living room, dressed overly smart. Afterwards, they watched together like a real family, an interesting film on TV. How boring and on such a memorable day that was stuck in their minds forever. Yes, it was so boring that his wife did not ever miss to remind him of this day, every time it was convenient or not so convenient in the future. Nine consecutive times something always was not quite right. Failures followed one after another. Enough with the mistakes. "I shall ask her and I'll do everything she wants. There is no way that she will be left unhappy this time. There are no two ways about it!" Markot had no choice, but to agree with the suggestion. To look as if he had contributed to the idea, as well, he proposed that it was best if the lady went and got whatever she wanted herself. Of course, if it was required, her husband could accompany her. He was always there for her, until death parted them – her, who never knew what she wanted, and him, the unlucky and guilty of all sins.

Poor woman! It was probably not that easy for her, raising this enormous child. No argument about this – he had always been overweight. Trying to feed him, getting the right size clothes for him, dealing with his learning disability problems – it was a nightmare, indeed. Markot could not say for sure whether the lady found it hard or not, but he was now happy to know that there was a way he could find redemption for his mistakes. The new plan that he got the idea for from the "happily" married customer from this morning, did not involve Little John. The consultant decided not to give any money directly to the fatso. He came for an idea about how to surprise his mother for her birthday and this was exactly what Markot was going to do. He was going to surprise directly the mother. The idea-consultant was prepared to make any wish of hers come true, no matter how much it would cost him. As long as it was possible to fulfill, she could consider it done. He was emanating euphoria, sitting behind the wheel and driving along the black tarmac roads, covered with thin ice. The harbor town had no objections against the frequent visits of the idea-consultant, despite the fact that these were not necessary. After all, the birthday event was not until 5 months and 28 days after. Markot had forgotten obviously. Never mind. He went there again and parked outside the house. He wanted to look at it for a bit. It calmed him down.

Static electricity was usually quite weak and could not harm even young kids. Markot reached for the money envelope, so he could put it away in the glove compartment, but the natural electric shock objected. He removed his hand so fast that he banged his elbow on the side shoulder of the seat. Maybe, this was a sign for him not to leave the place before completing his mission. The idea-consultants could not allow themselves to be superstitious or believe in some nonsense. At work, the rules were quite clear: one could not discuss "improvable supernatural phenomena". The consultants knew everything, but they were also aware that there were things that they could not know everything about. Markot acted impulsively, when he picked up the money and went to pay up for his redemption.

He pressed the doorbell, which did not produce the expected alarming sound. The consultant held the button for a bit longer. His thumb was hurting from bending it so hard, while pressing on the signaling device. He could have almost broken it, if he applied more force to it. Nothing again. Dead silence. It's broken. Maybe there was no one in the house? But he knew that this was not true. Markot had to act fast, because the greasy ball was coming home in half an hour. His fist knocked on the door not too loudly. After all, he was not trying to break in. Nothing again. He knocked a few more times, each knock – creating a louder noise. No light appeared in the entry hall, nor did any steps could be heard from the inside. The electric hit he got a minute ago meant nothing. Obviously, inexplicable signs of fate did not exist.

Markot was just about ready to get back in his car, when the door opened. Little John's sick mother appeared at the doorframe and looked around grumpily to check if the neighbor's naughty kids dared to disturb her at this time of the day. She was holding tight onto her walking stick, prepared to use it if she needed to punish the little rascals, should they come close enough. When she heard the noise at the door, she was on the upper floor. That was why it took such a long time to get down the steps.

The "rascal" quickly ran back towards her, without looking both ways, when he crossed the road. Good job that some invisible force had stopped the traffic at this precise moment. Despite the heights of science these days, time dilation was only possible under certain conditions or if one took some pills, of a specific color and taste, which might slow down fictitiously the seconds, the minutes, etc. The idea-consultant stood rather closely in front of the woman, after he got the last few meters by making three lion-size strides. He stepped back a few inches. Within a second, he was going to introduce himself and have a little chat with the lady. One second. Despite Markot not having a whole minute at his disposal, he managed to make a brief analysis of the little mastodon's mother. Poor. The house was in an alright neighborhood, but it did not look very well maintained. Markot, however, made his conclusions about the poverty of the family, because of the woman's appearance. Her dressing gown was so worn out and faded, made by patched together small rhomboids. Those had been different in color, once upon a time, but now, the whole garment was one-colored. The sleeves, at the elbows, were also patched with some darker pieces of cloth. At the front, three of the discolored tetragons had visible burnt holes, maybe, from a cigarette. The clothing was not good even for a rag. She could have found it on the rubbish tip. The slippers, she was wearing, only confirmed the fact that the last improvement of her wardrobe must have happened well before the birth of the fattiest baby in the world. The footwear had large holes and if it was not for her woolen socks, all her toes would have been out in the open. In the same way the clients got analyzed, Markot continued to examine her physical features. She looked tired, stooping slightly, with skin that was wrinkled and thin. The lady seemed much older than her age. She was not even fifty years old, yet. Unfortunately, the illness, which Markot had no way to find the name of, unless he peeked into her medical dossier, was slowly pushing her towards the once nice and green meadow at the end of town, which now was covered with crosses and marble headstones. Her pale face looked as if it did not receive enough blood by that miser, called heart.

The conclusion of the analysis was pretty obvious - this lady had a crying need for money, happiness and surprises. The consultant grasped all this within just a second. Wow! So sometimes, the brain could put even the fastest computer to shame, that was for sure!

"Hi! My name is Markot and I've come to present you with the prize you've won in our game. Congratulations! You're the winner!"

"Did you bang on my door?"

"Yes, Madam. I am sorry, but your doorbell's not working, so I had to knock and..."

"What's this game?" the young 'old' lady, who stood a whole meter and a half above the ground, asked suspiciously.

"The City Council awards one of its best local citizens for the last year by entering the names of all the residents, who have not broken the law, in a special draw. You have won!" the idea-consultant could have come up with something much better, but considering the speed of events, this explanation would do the job just fine.

"What's the prize?"

"There's a big cash sum of money in this envelope. Here you are!"

"Thank you." the winner hesitantly took her prize. She did not look to check the content of the envelope, because she believed that the boy was exaggerating. He spoke like all these TV hosts, who tried to make you participate in their game by phone and then they dish out some ludicrously small sums of money. The ill disabled woman looked cold and it was obvious that she wanted to go inside pretty soon. She got her parcel alright, so why stand out, freezing in the cold for any longer? Markot, however, did not intend to let her go just yet.

"I do apologize for keeping you out. Just one question! I'm instructed to ask the winner about the prize. What are you going to do with the money?"

"I don't know, yet."

"After all, you don't know how much it is. It's quite a lot, actually. I can assure you. Why don't you open the envelope and see for yourself and then you can answer my question?"

"I'll open it later." she squeezed her walking stick even tighter and thought: "This guy clearly doesn't know what the sum is and now he's dying to find out. Look at him, his eyes will pop out of their orbits, he's so keen that he'll burst with rage, if he doesn't see what's inside! Dirty jealous bastard!"

"You better do it now, so we can be sure that you've got the correct amount!"

"Later!"

"Madam, I think you better open it now!"

"Why?"

"Because if there's been some misunderstanding or an error, I have to inform about it and we'll set things right. It's for your own good."

"Yes, there must be some mistake, here! Are you sure that this is the right envelope for me?" despite that she looked inside quite discretely, so that the grinning, but envious "postman" could not see anything, she managed to guess roughly how much the money was, even without wearing her glasses.

"I am absolutely, sure."

"There are two wads of... but this is..."

"Yes, this is correct. Everything is fine, then. Now, can you answer my question, please? I'm sorry, but my boss wants my report on this later."

"I don't know, this is... this is, it's so much money and..."

"Have you got a dream that you've always wanted to come true? Maybe, you'd like to go away, on some exotic holiday?

"I don't know, we don't go anywhere. I'm sick and I don't..."

"Well, I hope, then, that the money will help towards a better medical care and that you'll get well soon. You could buy something for your home or..."

"I'll give it to my son." there was no doubt that Little John's mother, who was beyond moved in this second, was going to do exactly that. But why would a retarded fatso need so much money? He would invest it in food, most likely. If he lived forever, he could probably eat up the entire globe in about two billion years, (plus-minus a few million).

"But what about you? What will you buy for yourself? What do you need the most?"

"Nothing. I'll give it to John. He had some problems at work, down on the docks. He's a little special." she did not call him stupid, but what mother would? "And it's just happened that he owes a lot of money that he needs to return. At last, my boy can have a clean start."

"Yes, this sounds great! But still, isn't there a chance that you will leave a little something for yourself?"

"No. I don't want my son to be in debt."

"You are right. No one does. Thank you for your cooperation. I wish you and your son good luck. And who knows, you may win again! Have a nice evening!"

It was not until now that Markot realized what the best surprise would be for Little John's mother. He would have never come up with this idea, if he did not talk to her first. The best birthday surprise that her son could give her had nothing to do with her. She did not want anything for herself. Her mother's instinct prompted her to want the best for her son in the same way other women felt about their young, but normal kids. She wanted him to be alright. She could be happy only if he was happy. The best present for her would be if her son paid his debt to the owner of the little fishes, which ended up back in the ocean. Another one could be if her pig of a son found a new and better-paid job, where he felt fulfilled. His mother, then, would be ecstatic and she would definitely forget, even for a short while, about all her pains and aches, which had tortured her day and night, all these years.

The idea-consultant felt light as a feather. His steps were springy and his car seemed easier to drive, as if it had become lighter, too. The feeling of redemption was indescribable and priceless. He could not compare it to anything he had experienced. The best of all was that the consultant knew how to make the sick woman happy for her birthday. He was going to make another payment, which would lead to the ultimate redemption. It would probably be another windfall, placed in a white fat envelope. The money, no doubt, was going to make life easier for the lady and her fat son, who would be free of any debts by then. Well, it was impossible to win twice the same annual prize in a space of six months, but Markot would think of yet another prize draw that her son had entered unknowingly. The idea-consultant was going to give her the money that her son had won, on her actual birthday, just before Little John came back from work. The unpredictable fatso was not supposed to see him, otherwise he could react in a way that spoiled the whole idea. Markot believed he could make the biggest surprise that could ever exist just happen, by completing the final stage. The Idea Factory and its numerous unimaginative busy bees could only dream on about ever coming up with an idea, which caused such never-ending happiness that, he was about to make.

Markot came back to work, purified and cured, and without the heavy psychological burden. He carried on with his duties like a fast pendulum, which could never cease moving and find the right stop. The idea-consultant, Third rank, would meet his clients in the interrogation room, hear them out and then, simply give them an idea. One day, he was the snowman – cold, harsh, perfect in his work and treating his hopeless customers as if they were inanimate objects. As long as he offered a quality piece of advice at the end of the third stage, it meant that he had provided a professional service. On the following day, however, he had a tremendous feeling of guilt and did his best to compensate for his aloofness from the previous day. The fatso had hit him for that exact reason, did he not? Markot could not afford and allow a similar situation to occur ever again. Another payback for a new redemption was not going to break the bank, but why should he really repeat the same mistake? Inferior species never did this. So he would try to be friendly and smiley with the clients, where in return, they wasted his time, like the stablewoman, by talking nonsense and breaching the rules. His kindness meant that he, too, did not follow closely the regulations, which in effect was bringing him to the bottom of this profession. He had already been there, so this was simply not the right way. On the third day, the in-between Markot would arrive at work, who was half made from snow and the other half – from flesh and blood. However, sometimes his moderate type of behavior prevented him from coping with some truly difficult clients. So the qualities of the cold-blooded and those of the warm-blooded just did not mix well, which resulted in his inability to do his job. Often, the two personalities fought against each other, forgetting that it was the problem of the person on the opposite chair that it was important, not their private battle. The consultant continued to alternate his three personas and their variations, while at work, until the big day arrived, when he had to offer the next portion of happiness to Little John and his troubled mother. He left the money and everything was just perfect. The following day was when it would be the end for him. It was the annual exam, when all the unforgivable mistakes were going to come to light and he was going to lose his job. So what? He had learned the truth, at least. He was certain he had.

The Truth?

There were not any strict rules with regards to the election of the examining committee. The Factory allowed the Gods to group in threes as they wished and see fit. During the last few years, when the promotion of consultants into the highest ranks had stopped for an indefinite period, the members of the groups hardly ever swapped places. However, Andir, who had no rights, changed the current situation. He had to be accepted in the committee, because the rules stated that every God had to participate directly in the unpleasant process of the annual examinations. It was decided that the easiest way to include Andir in all this was if he confronted the newly accepted colleagues of Third rank, who had to face a group of four nasty examiners. At the last meeting, the renegade was attached to Richardson's team, which included also one of the mild alcoholics and the heavy smoker, who had the horrendous habit of chucking his cigarette buts under the chair, as if this was totally acceptable. At first, there was a debate about which group Andir should join. The Gods' arrogant faces showed only contempt. No one wanted him and they did not even try to hide it. Andir decided that he should save them from their troubles by voting for his exclusion from the membership of any of the committees. He would simply meet his clients and earn money for his colleagues' fat salaries, instead of making them vexed with his presence. After all, he could never speak up, as he was just formally present amongst them. Still, he did not share his idea, because he was sure about what they were going to do – everything that was opposite of what he wanted. Markot's father only took him under his wing, because he could not stand the whole issue that dragged on. The other two members did not say anything, but it was clear that they did not want him, either.

The resentful old men were getting excited about the annual tests, because they broke the monotony of the mundane working days. Every day was just the same as the day before. Distressed customers shared their challenging problems, then, the three stages passed, an idea was offered and voila! Next one! At sunset, the consultants would go up to the meeting hall for yet another of their working discussions. Whatever they had to debate over, they did as quickly as possible. The Gods just could not wait to indulge in enjoying the forbidden fruits. The smokers filled up the "baskets" with their cigarettes and the killing smoke and the drunkards carried around bottles and glasses, filled to the top with alcohol drinks. Together, like a large sinful family, they all discussed the funniest snippets of the conversations with customers, which were supposed to be confidential. The idea-consultants just really liked to laugh at the crazy clients and felt no shame, guilt or remorse about it. As usual, they did not care about the rules. Although, the meetings were not set to take place every day, it did not stop the Gods to go to the conference hall and do the same sins again and again. The exams were the thing that even for a short while broke the routine. The senior consultants expected the freshmen to get into the cage, so they could tear them apart, gnaw at them and spit the remnants out. After this procedure of bloodsucking fresh energy, the oldies felt rejuvenated, livelier and more divine than ever. The less Factory experience the victim had, the stronger the concentration of the elixir of youth was for the old men. The newcomers amongst the Third ranks were the most wanted. Those, who had never actually been before the committee, usually won the gold medal in the "gastronomical" test. All Gods wished they had such "dish" on their table. However, the youngsters had to be equally shared at the end, if arguments were to be avoided. No one in the committees liked dealing with the Second ranks at their tests. The taste of their meat, which was tough and chewy, was far too familiar. Well, now and again, one could encounter a sample amongst them that was worthy to the Gods' fine and sensitive digestive system.

Andir did not like eating meat. He got his proteins usually from milk and eggs. He would eat a medium stake just once a week. He was never bothered by the annual exams and never thought of himself as being a victim. Even when he was a case of offering the highest nutritious value at his first ever exam, he did not encounter any difficulties with the committee. They tried to make him feel like an idiot, but he kept his cool and did not allow to be broken, despite them relying on exactly that. They hoped that the young idea-consultant would slip at the unprovoked attacks and confess something. There were plenty of manipulative techniques, which could come at hand, when one was trying to make the victim reevaluate their way of thinking and speak. Those consultants, who were of a sound character, who were well prepared and followed closely the rules, could feel at ease about the whole testing procedure. They could not be affected by this type of provocations. Andir was quite understanding about the way the three Gods tried to ridicule him. It wasn't pleasant, for sure, but, after all, it was their responsibility to find out who had breached the rules and who did not deserve to have their own interrogation room anymore.

Once, the consultant climbed one step up the ladder, the tests changed. The pressure was well familiar as much as the phrases that were so well learned by heart. One could feel safe about keeping their job, as long as he did not feel emotionally damaged by the customers he had to see throughout the year. Andir had been tested by different committees, comprised by his present colleagues. The rules did not allow for anyone to share what went on between them and the members of the committee, so Andir never looked back. He was far too loyal and truly respected the Factory rules.

The idea-consultants of the lower ranks were aware that the new list had been published. They could check who and when had to appear in the conference hall. The candidates for "slaughter" were not listed in an alphabetical order, nor did their working experience was reflected in the array. Chirank was responsible for creating the list, but he put it up together, indiscriminately selecting the consultants and placing them with random committees as if the final result did not matter to anyone. But it did. Richardson, for instance, wanted Markot to be attached to his team at all costs. Since father and son became colleagues, they had spoken on the phone just once. He worried that the young man might start talking about his work, or the customers. If he slipped and said the wrong thing, he could lose

251

the job of his life. How many people had got the sack for even less of a breach of the rules? His poor mum had the chance to hear his voice over the phone once every week, but she, too, did not dare to hold him on the line for more than a minute. She cared if he was eating well and whether he slept through the night alright. She was so worried that twenty years of her life, devoted to her non-biological son and his quest of becoming an idea-consultant, could go down the drain. She would wish him 'Good night' and then cry her heart out in fear for him. Recently, she felt tearful during the day, as well, because she worried about the forthcoming exams. Despite her unreserved trust in Markot's abilities, she knew him best. His waywardness, when he was young, could be explained with age, but now, if he let himself to show such a weakness, he would lose his dream job.

"Accidentally" the chairman placed Markot's name on the appropriate list. Richardson felt calm, knowing that the worrying test was taking place before his eyes. If the young one began to slip in the wrong direction, his proud father would quickly intervene and prevent his son from being potentially dismissed. The other two Gods and Andir were going to keep quiet for sure.

Markot entered with a wide grin on his face. He did not seem bothered about showing strong emotions, which was against the rules. He knew. They did not. He sat down and rested his back on the chair. The idea-consultant placed his hands on the table, although they were not supposed to be there. At least he was dressed accordingly. His matching black shoes also looked in place. The whitish line on them, caused by the snow, was so unnoticeable that did not provoke the interest of the four-member committee that was staring at him.

His demeanor was unoriginal. He did not look round like people would normally do, when they got in the conference hall for the first time. He recognized his father, as well as his Mentor. Markot smiled at the other two unfamiliar to him people. One could see the guilt on his face from the start, but why was he so happy, then?

"Name?" the father asked his own son. Unnecessary question, but rules were rules.

"Markot, Sir."

"Rank?"

252

"Third, Sir."

"Working experience?"

"One year, Sir."

"Today, you need to prove before the revered committee that you haven't breached the rules. As it's your first time here, in front of the committee, I'll explain to you the basics of the way this exam will take place." Richardson paused for a moment in the hope that Markot would read it as a broad hint that he should wipe the forbidden expression off his face before the important part of the conversation had actually started. Nothing. The smile remained where it was. His lips curled even more, as if to express the accumulating joy and happiness. "We'll be asking you questions, which you must answer. We decide, when the answer is satisfactory and when it's not, before we move on to the next one. You cannot lie. If we catch you lying, it will result in immediate dismissal. We want details. You cannot speak in general terms, nor can you answer vaguely and partially. You cannot disagree or argue with us. You cannot…"

"Sir, and what can I do?" Markot interjected still smiling. Never before a "baby-in-arms" from the Third ranks had been so arrogantly cocky. Usually, everyone was about to fill the nappy in awe with the committee.

"A-ah! I've not finished yet!" daddy raised his voice slightly in an authoritative way, as if to tell his naughty son off. The silent members of the committee looked at each other. They could not believe their ears. How dare the boy speak like this! Andir, too, did not understand what was happening. His intuition told him that Markot was in deep trouble, so deep that there was no coming back. But why did this situation make him so happy? "You cannot interrupt the members of the committee. You cannot hide any information, related to a possible breach of conduct, which has been set out in the Factory regulation code. You cannot underrate any of your mistakes that have jeopardized these rules. You cannot leave the room until we tell you to do so. You cannot…"

"Sir, and what can I do?" daddy's boy asked again, pleased with himself. This just could not be true! He must have lost his mind! This was the reason why Richardson was there. Markot was heading

253

towards his downfall and needed to be lifted up immediately before it was too late. Strict measures had to taken at once.

"Markot, shut your damn mouth! Don't open it unless I say so. Is that clear?"

"Yes, Sir."

"You cannot…"

"Sir, are we going to reach the part that I can actually have the right to say something soon?"

"Shut up! Shut up! Don't open your mouth! I'm telling you that you can't open your mouth!" the father hissed threateningly like a headmaster, who was telling his last graders off before leaving school only to become criminals and recidivists.

The smoker was dying to light a cigarette a minute ago. Suddenly his nicotine craving was wiped out at the sight of the evolving family drama. The show had begun and he was sitting in the front row. The alcoholic had already drunk a few hundred milliliters of firewater before coming into the room, but even he got affected by what was happening - he sobered up completely. The fourth examiner, who had been deprived of any rights, tried to analyze his student. Andir was looking for some behavioral clues, which could help him find out the reason behind the young man's outrageous attitude. He did not manage to get any answers. Markot looked like the same mediocre idea-consultant that he saw at their last meeting in the Academy. Only the inexplicable sincere smile on his face was a new feature today.

"That's better." Richardson said, when he saw that the person, who he loved as if he was his own flesh and blood, accepted the fact that he should not speak. The mini storm was under control. Daddy calmed down and carried on. But why was Markot still grinning like a retard? "You cannot offend or insult any of the committee members. You cannot twist your answers to suit you in a way that this could conceal any blunders that you might have made. You have one chance to admit your sins and that is now! Before we start with the questions, you must tell us if you have acted against the regulations in some unpredictable situation in the past year. If you confess, we'll take into consideration your honesty and decide what kind of punishment you deserve." no one ever confessed, when given the chance, because this would have resulted in the inevitable dismissal. It was better that they tried to hide the truth to the end until the truth came out or if at all, under the pressure of the experienced consultants, First rank.

"I can speak now, Sir, is that it?"

"Yes, but if you have nothing to confess, we can begin with the questions. I shall start first, unless…"

"No, Dad, you're wrong. I have something to say. I've got plenty to talk about with you, Andir and them."

"Markot, I've told you to stop it! This is not a game. You can't call me this. You must not call any of us by their name. We address the higher ranks by…"

"I know how, Sir." the naughty little kid playfully stressed on the three-letter noble title.

"You can't interrupt me! If you don't stop this, very soon you're going to lose your job, boy. Get back to your senses! Have you lost your mind?" Richardson was on the edge. He had never lost his self-control before like this for his entire career. Things were getting personal now and he did not see it coming, for sure. His adopted son had lost his senses and his professional fate was now in Richardson's bony hands.

"Don't worry, Dad. I'm about to lose it anyway."

"Dear colleagues, please, don't mind him. We'll take a break now. Five minutes."

"I don't need a break."

"The pressure seems to be getting at him. Ten minutes, actually. He's never been before an examination committee and…"

"I want to speak, Dad!"

"Markot!" Richardson looked at his son in the sternest way he could possibly look. "Not a word now! We're taking a break."

"I'm staying here, Dad. You've just said yourself that if I've breached the rules, now it's the time for me to let you know."

"I don't think we need to take a break, either." Andir interjected, standing between father and son. He wanted to hear the confession, his student was about to own up to, and just did not care what the all powerful Richardson thought about it. Interesting! The divine, but feeble-bodied daddy was suddenly beginning to look pathetic. Very pathetic. His halo was just about flickering and for his piercing blue eyes – they now looked rather ordinary and unimpressive.

"Andir, don't even think about this!"

"Sir, by sticking with the rules, you just gave the…"

"Don't talk to me about rules! I am the rules!" the raging father banged on the solid wooden table with his fist. "You'll do what I say. We're taking a ten-minute break. You'll leave me alone with Markot and then, we'll proceed. We'll start all over again and everything will be alright!"

"No, Dad. There's no point. I've decided."

"Markot, you've not decided anything! You're confused. You're rushing things and you're just being silly! After the break, we can…"

"Dad, stop! Don't you hear me?"

"Son, don't do this! Don't!" the God was moved. We all know that when God allows his feelings to get to him, seas on Earth turn stormy, capable of sinking fleets, until the emotional tempest abates.

"I'm sorry, Dad. I'm not going to be an idea-consultant from tomorrow."

"Don't talk nonsense! If you don't stop this at once, I will not be able to help you and…"

"I don't need help, but you! Allow me to speak, Dad!"

"I can't, Markot!" the influential father resorted to the best rescue solution. He stood up slowly and walked towards the exit, looking away from the child, he had taken care of for so many years. Before he pressed on the door handle, he turned round to remind the others that he expected from them to do the same. "Colleagues, follow me. We are not going to test this rebellious young man today. The schedule has changed." The smoker and the alcoholic responded to the request and left their seats in solidarity. Andir remained seated. "You, too."

"I'm sorry, Sir, but I think I'll stay."

"No, Andir, you're not! Leave the hall!" this order was inconsistent with the precious Factory rules.

"You can't tell me what to do. I'm staying. According to the rules, if a member of the committee cannot fulfill his duties or he can't stay until the hearing is over, he has the right to leave. The other members, however, can stay and finalize what's been already started. It's too late now to cancel the meeting."

"Andir!" Richardson called out his name so loud that his colleagues almost jumped in fear. They had never heard him shouting like this. The raging father did not expect such a display of disobedience. The disappointment from Markot's immature behavior turned into incontrollable wrath towards Andir.

"So you'll stand up against me? Are you sure about this?" the spectators jumped again from the noise of the loud questions.

"Sir, I'm not doing anything that is against the rules! The rules, which you constantly breach. If Markot wants to speak, then, he can, to me!"

"I've always known that you're quite brave, Andir!"

"This is not bravery, I just conscientiously apply the…"

"Even then…" the senior equal interjected again, getting fed up with listening about the rules. "When I called you to inform you about your promotion, there was something about you. I sensed it. There was hesitance and doubt. You had done something, then, in breach of your favorite rules? And I caught you."

"Sir, you could not catch me on the tests."

"Ha-ha-ha, I got you! Our strict follower of the rules has just given himself away. You did not deny it straight away, which only means that you've lied to the committee at your last exam." Richardson looked wickedly happy, when he walked by the curved table and stood a meter away from his stubborn colleague. His canine teeth were visible to their base. He could just punch Andir in the face, creating an orange of a bulge and then stick his teeth in the consultant's neck.

"I've done nothing, Sir. I simply passed my test." it was too late for excuses. It was enough to be suspected even in the most innocent little lie, no matter how long ago it had been uttered.

"You're right, Andir, but it doesn't matter in the slightest. Your turn will come, too, once we get over and done with the lower ranks. We will crucify you, for sure. Believe me, it will be very easy, now the three of us have heard what you've just said. You've signed your release form. Right, dear colleagues? You've heard every word of his?"

"Yes, Ritchie, yes, we've heard everything." Cowards! They were going to be his servants forever.

"Get off your ass and leave! As I told you, Markot's exam has been postponed."

"I'm not doing it, Sir. Rules are rules, whether you like it or not."

"Hey, Andir!" the defender of his only child shouted and leaned forward, as if he wanted his bad breath to be felt by the renegade, so that he realized his superiority and gave up before it was too late. "You're going to lose your job! I'm warning you! After your exam, I'm going to personally propose that we vote for your dismissal."

"You cannot, Sir. You can't prove anything. I've never breached any rules."

"So what? You think that this can stop me? When these two and I tell the others that you've confessed, everyone will believe us. Three witnesses are enough. We have a great imagination, don't worry!" a wide grin was stuck on his face, in a similar way like Markot. The difference between the two was that the emotions behind were completely the opposite.

"But you'll be lying, then, I've said nothing and I've not violated any of the…"

"O-o-oh! Poor, Andir, you got scared or something? Don't you remember what you've said at the meeting, when we were looking for the destroyer? Do you remember?"

Andir actually felt quite apprehensive. It looked like they were going to eliminate him in the same way he had suggested at the meeting, when he got stripped from all his rights. The ever so powerful God – Markot's daddy – was going to falsely imply that Andir had admitted about committing some terrible offence. The kind support of the smoker and the drunkard had been secured, too. The two slaves would confirm even the most unbelievable story as soon as Ritchie asked them to. The rest of the Gods, his colleagues, were going to be fooled, no doubt about it. Afterwards, it was just the vote to get over and done with, and the most disliked God was going to be removed. The end. This would be the end for Andir, the idea-consultant, First rank. The man, who had gone to the top, after twenty years of service, helping thousands of desperate clients, was going to end up on the street. Crushed, betrayed, deceived and discarded. Andir looked down, when he imagined what Richardson was capable of doing to him. He was about to comply with the order of leaving the hall. The consultant looked at Markot, who seemed still rather cheerful, as if to apologize to him for not staying with him until the end and for breaking the rules. The young guy smiled at him. He looked overly happy. But why? Andir was dying to find out about what had changed his student so much. What did make him want to leave the prestigious job behind, the big salary and the chance to help people in trouble? Could curiosity kill the fear? Andir, personally, could not remember if the two states had ever been in an open duel before.

"I'm staying! I'm not leaving until I get to hear Markot out. These are the rules."

"You'll be sorry! You'll be gravely sorry!" Richardson's nostrils flared like that of a raging bull. The blue crystals turned red. Was he going to hit Andir? Instead, he turned round and together with his silent and well behaved protégés, left the room. It was irrelevant what his son was about to share with his Mentor, because this was not going to change the setting up of a new date and time for his exam. This time, Markot would be standing before the committee as the very promising idea-consultant, Third rank. Daddy just needed two or three days, when he could brainwash nicely his adopted son and nail into his head the idea, which was gone a little rusty, that to be an idea-consultant was the greatest profession in the world. For Richardson, who was now fuming, this was just a temporary state, like having the flu, which soon would simply pass. The kid was going to quickly realize that great and generous life chances should be strongly embraced and should never be left to slip away.

"Thank you for staying, Sir. My father..."

"I did not stay for you, but for the rules! Richardson had no right to cancel the exam. The three of them should have stayed."

"Sir, I don't want to frighten you, but my father will do everything in his power to eliminate you. He is very strong headed and never gives up."

"I'm not afraid of your father. I'm not afraid of anyone." Andir did not sound convincing, because since it was just the two of them, left in the hall, he was beginning to feel the growing fear, turning into panic. He got the shivers. He was about to lose his job for real. He had achieved everything in his career. He made his dream come true and now, he messed everything up. He did not feel right amongst the corrupt Gods, but for him what had always mattered was the customers. If the Factory got rid of him, the poor clients would not have the chance to rely on his professional services anymore. Whether the self-sacrifice was worth it, he was about to find out from the young offender, sitting opposite him. "We'll carry on with the exam. Do you have any questions, regarding the rules that idea-consultant, First rank – Richardson just explained to you?"

"No, Sir."

"What have you done, Markot? What's made you come here today, smiling like an idiot, knowing that you'll get the sack? I want to hear all the details!"

"I've had this client, Sir. He's very fat. It was half a year ago. I insulted his mother, when he had actually come to ask for an idea about what surprise to give her on her birthday. He hit me, Sir. I don't really remember how it happened, Sir, but I woke up on the floor."

"Is that it? Markot, you can't give up, only because a client has attacked you! It just happens sometimes. You've had quite a shock and…"

"No, Sir. It's not like that. The man, who hit me, actually helped me to realize things. I know now what the Idea Factory really is, what kind of people our clients and us, the consultants, actually are. It's all clear to me now."

"You've been taught about this at the Academy, Markot. They call it posttraumatic stress. You have looked at you job from a different angle, after your experience of violence and…"

"This is correct, Sir, but…"

"Wait a minute!" Andir stopped him there, because he realized the vast space of time that had passed since the day of the assault and today's exam. "You mentioned something like half a year… Couldn't you overcome the incident by finding a reasonable explanation all this time?"

"Sir, you don't understand. It was my fault. I was guilty and I deserved it. So he hit me."

"Markot, you've taken things too personal. You've made a mistake. I have to admit that the wall sometimes cracks, unable to withstand the pressure. Some clients are…"

"You're wrong, Sir! My wall was solid. At the time, I was the snowman that you taught me to be. I was hard, confident, showing no weakness. But this behavior only made me inhuman. I've realized that by following the rules, we treat our customers as if they are not people. We can't show our emotions, we can't shake hands… We have no rights to do anything apart of offering them an idea…"

"Markot, you…"

"Hear me out, Sir!" the idea-consultant, Third rank was really getting into it and did not want to be interrupted. Although he was not in a position to give out orders, the Mentor complied with his wish. "We get to see our customers – the first, the second, the third, till sunset. Then, we go home only to come back on the next day and meet more clients. We want to help these people and give them the best idea, but this is impossible. I've thought a lot about this and always come to the same conclusion that it's impossible."

"What's impossible, Markot? People come and leave with their idea. I can't see anything impossible here. You're young and if you come across a more complicated case, you can always send on the customer to us. There are some strange people out there, but we can…"

"No, Sir, I'm not talking about the 'zero' clients, but about those that one cannot offer an idea to. There just isn't one for them. Their problem is unsolvable. And we're simply lying to these people, Sir. We look them in the eye, behave as if we're great and lie to them. At the end of the third stage, we just come up with some nonsense, only because we have to tell them something. Because we know everything. People get fooled by our know-it-all and 'can-it-all' attitude. They think that we're superior to them, but we're simply lying to them!"

"This is a gross exaggeration, Markot. We're not lying to them. To those, who present a problem that cannot be solved, we offer a kind of good piece of advice rather than a direct answer to their question."

"An absolute lie, Sir!"

"Markot, after all, you're now talking about a tiny section of our distressed visitors. Let's not forget that the rest of them, the most actually, come to us with easy to solve problems and we really help them. That's what's valuable about being an idea-consultant. Our calling to be…"

"You're wrong, Sir! Do you know what happens after you've given the perfect idea to the client? What does happen after that?"

"Eh, Markot, we don't…"

"I know. The guy, who hit me, did not get his idea, because the incident took place during the second stage. But later, I found him, Sir. It was on the following day, after I finished work. I wanted to mend my mistake and help him and his sick mother."

"But this is prohibited, the rules..." Andir was getting banal with his rules. Like father, like son – Markot was not in the mood to listen about them and interrupted the lecture about how the entire society of idea-consultants was suppose to stick to the millions of regulations.

"I found their house. I only had to knock on the door, apologize to the boy for insulting his mother and give him the idea. But it didn't work out this way. It's not that simple, once you're outside the Factory. The roads are slippery and icy, so you need to drive carefully. The interrogation room doesn't let the blistering cold wind in. We sit all day in these prison cells, where we feel great and invincible against the cold winter outside. It's cozy in here and people stand in the queue outside, freezing. The security doesn't let anyone touch us. They get paid to take care of our safety, I can't blame them. We are like in a state of solitary confinement, Sir. We are cowards, who don't dare show our faces out of the Factory. Sir, I just want to point out that we, the idea-consultants, don't actually do anything here, but just have our heads buried in the sand. Our pointless work is incomplete, because we don't take any responsibility for our ideas. We offer the next one, without caring whether it will work or not. Once the customer has left, we don't actually know whether we've succeeded to solve his problem or we've failed. That's why we never fail and we never turn a customer away. It's because there's no way that we could find out about our failure. Instead, we carry on with banging out more ideas, but we aren't interested if they have worked, when put into practice. Sir, the only way to find out if we've done a good job is to check and follow what happens after. If we don't do this, but just sit and wait for the next visitor, well, then, it means that we're doing nothing. Nothing!" Markot's ardent tone of voice was typical for every revolutionary, who was trying to change the world for the better.

The rebel continued his tirade even more passionately:

"Here, I discovered another drawback. Sir, I've realized that we will still be in the wrong, if we follow through each case and see how every client's doing after the idea's been offered to them. We are in the wrong from the very start, trying to conjure up the answer to their problem. The whole process is wrong, because we are too careful to protect ourselves. We always try to make sure that the other people's problems don't affect us in any way. We see the visitor, he or she tells us in brief what the problem is and hurray, the idea is ready. The wall always stands between us. In this way, though, we can't ever get to the bottom of things. Unless we get rid of the wall and try to put ourselves into the client's shoes, so we can really feel the problem, even a tiny part of it, otherwise, our ideas will be worth nothing. No wall, no snowman or any other safety measures, this is what I mean! And, Sir, we can get it wrong again. Wrong, yes, once again!" it was hard to follow Markot's train of thought, maybe, because it was his first time that he shared his ideas about the Factory or because he was getting too fanatical in his speech. Andir was watching him with an interest that he never had the chance to display in public. Still, he could not quite understand a few things.

"How do you mean?" the more experienced consultant asked in surprise. He was feeling now like the student.

"We can produce a better idea for our clients if we get rid of the wall and feel their problem as if it's ours. I'm sure of it. But the basic mistake remains. We're wrong, Sir, for sitting around here, instead of going to the people and work amongst them, where they actually encounter their problems. We need to be close to them, so we can get to know the core of their problems. We shouldn't sit and wait for them to come to us and tell us about their dilemmas. We need to get to know the other participants – their families and friends. We should meet everyone, who is connected to the problem. Only in this way, we can collect enough information. Then, we need to help them, Sir. We need to employ fully our mental capacity and come up with something that is really good and worthwhile. Something that will work. Then, we need to follow up how it has been applied. Only in this way, we'll be actually useful to people. And the most important of all, Sir, is not to be afraid of failure. Letdowns are part of life, too, and we can't escape them, because they are inevitable, Sir. It seems that failures don't exist only in this place, only we never fail and only here, people get unrealistic ideas. The Idea Factory?!" the young man puffed out with an expression of ridicule on his face. "A better name for it would have been the Illusion Factory."

Markot, painfully right about everything, stopped his tirade that could have brought him a first prize. The ball, now, was in the Mentor's court, but it looked like that he was not keen on having it. Andir was trying to grasp what he had just heard. Was this possible? The inexperienced consultant of Third rank managed to crush the perfectly working system of the Idea Factory!

"And what about the people, Sir?" the youngster took another deep breath and continued with putting the puzzle together in the same eager way as before. "They just sit and wait for the ready meal. We tell them that we know everything and they believe us. The Factory knows everything and it can do everything for them. The idea-consultants can do everything. People find it easier to give up and come to us. We offer the simple solution to them. Just pay up and the job's done. Sir, we contribute to making folks helpless. We kill their innate ability to fight off their setbacks in life until they overcome the challenges they have encountered. Their "immune system" just gives up at the end, because we know everything. Almost all of my customers in the past year gave up. They did not want to suffer and live up through their victory over the problem. They did not want to shed inconsolably tears day and night. They did not want to sweat over their dilemmas. People avoided losing a drop of their blood over this, even if it meant that they would get a fast, free of charge answer to the problem. People preferred to lie down on the floor and wait for their problems to pass over them like a steamroller, and just before the heavy machine was about to squash them, they quickly got up and ran to us for help. Why don't they fight? I've asked myself numerous times! I've asked myself after work, or while waiting for my next client, or while driving on the way to work. Why isn't this man trying to solve his problem on his own, but instead, he's sitting and waiting for my help? He's waiting for me to tell him. I know, Sir, that this may sound a bit extreme, but we make people, who trust us, ill. We make them feel inadequate. The others, who have not given up and have fought to the full, but failed, come to us to get a non-existing hope, a dead hope! Those customers have not accepted the defeat, because we – the smart liars of the Factory, perched on the white hill, tell them that this is not the

264

end. That there's a way, but actually, there isn't. We extend pointlessly their agony. The unsolvable problem has won. They just have to accept this and carry on with their lives."

"Markot, I... I just don't know what to say..."

"Sir, I understand that my confession sounds shocking to you. I'm aware that if my father's stayed, he would have gone mad. But this is the truth. My truth about the Factory, the idea-consultants and about everything that goes on in the interrogation rooms. I've been so happy, Sir, since I got to the truth, I can't even describe it."

"I can see that, Markot. Do you have anything else to add?"

"Yes, Sir, I do. I'd like to share with you that I've realized something and as much as I find it hard to admit it, I feel I need to. The Idea Factory will always exist. It is perfect. The way the customers come in and get seen in the interrogation rooms, without being watched from behind the enormous and unnecessary mirror. Third parties don't observe or listen to the conversations. There are no witnesses. Everything is ideal. The system works like a well-maintained machine, which will never fail. I've always wondered about whether it has a weak spot, not because I wish to cause damage or anything, but for the sake of it. There isn't one, Sir. I couldn't find any weaknesses in the system. The customers can't do anything to it and they'll never dare to, anyway. They are afraid, for sure! They're panicking, once they go through the gate. The Factory throws a spell on them and suppresses their thoughts. They suddenly begin to look like well-behaved pets. We have so few instances of clients attacking us that this can be only regarded as a proof of their enormous fear. I won't be surprised if the customers get their composure back, once they leave the premises. They probably feel braver, then, and start talking about stuff that they couldn't share, when on the inside. But this is no threat to anyone. It's nothing, really! Just nonsense. Even I, now talking against the Factory, aware that I'm about to lose my job from tomorrow, I don't affect in any way the process of its normal operation. And that is, when considering that I'm an idea-consultant, not some nobody. You and the rest of the colleagues from all ranks will continue to work tomorrow as normal, following the rules. When you are no longer here, there'll be others to step in. People, who want to do this job, will always join the Academy. They'll do their best, in order to get to their own interrogation room. They do it, because they want a prestigious job and money, but at what price? They don't know! The rules make us become inanimate talking statues. It's just too late, when one realizes what this is all about. The wages are in the bank and there is no turning back. The idea-consultants, Sir, don't want to wake up to the truth and simply give up. The rules put limits in front of us and we stop talking normally amongst ourselves. We never treat the people, we meet, like friends and we should! We always have to keep quiet about our job. This is such a clever way to make us well behaved and we never want to leave. The Factory becomes untouchable, because we never discuss anything about it with no one. Comments about it are banned, so we cannot listen to other people's opinion about it. We'd rather change the subject quickly, in fear of getting caught at the exams, because we've accidentally slipped. Sir, have you ever imagined what could happen if Factory employees get allowed to talk freely to anyone they wish? Staff would have come up with dozens of reasons about why they dislike their workplace. I'm positive that this is actually the case now, but these colleagues cannot admit their qualms to no one. The system's won, yet again. I'll be the first ever idea-consultant, who's leaving the job of his own accord. I know that the committee would have denounced me anyway, even if I did not confess anything. Despite this, I'm leaving because I want to. This is my free choice and not a result of breaching the rules. And, Sir, the reason that the Factory will exist forever is not down to us or the colleagues, joining the system, when we are no longer here. The building itself and the idea-consultants are not the main players. It's them. It's the desperate clients, waiting in the queue for their turn to come at last. The Factory is working, because the surge of customers will never stop. The assembly line will never cease to work, as long as we exploit the weak-willed and irresolute folks, or those, who may be strong, but are too lazy to get their hands dirty. I'm talking about everyone, who is willing to stand in front of the marked tree early in the morning, no matter what their reason is to come here. Next, please…" the rebel went quiet all of a sudden. This was the beautiful ending of the young man's denouncing speech. He had nothing else to say.

"What are you going to do from now on, Markot?"

"I'll fight, Sir! I'll confront every obstacle I come across or stands in my way. If I get the chance to help someone, I'll do it, according to my principles and not using those of the Factory. Even if I don't succeed, at least I know that I've tried and I've done my best."

"You'll need to find another job."

"Yes, Sir. I've been thinking to get something at the docks in the neighboring town. The people, who helped me find out the truth, live there. Besides, I've always dreamt about going at sea. I hope they take me. I'm not sure, but I have this feeling that I'll like it."

"And your father? What are you going to tell him?"

"The same as I've just told you, Sir. If he loves me, he'll understand. I think, he's always known that my place is not here, but he's been scared to admit it. He believed in me much more than I believed in myself. He'll overcome all this. And you, Sir? What are you going to do, if they fire you?"

"I don't know, Markot! I hope it doesn't come to this. I want to help the desperate clients as I've done so far. I abide the rules and I don't intend to breach any of them in the future." A lie! What a big fat lie! It was greasier than Little John! In this very moment, Andir wanted more than anything, to get out of the Illusion Factory, described to him by Markot, and never come back. What he had just learned from the young man was that in twenty years of good service, he might have not helped a single person, because a follow-up control had never been applied, once the idea was offered to the customer. Or, he might have helped all of them? There was not a way that Andir could ever know. Markot was right about everything. About everything, indeed. The thought about the unknown failures, he might have had, weighed the most and made the Mentor come to his final decision. He was also going to look for another job from tomorrow. The former sailor could follow into his student's steps and go on a ship again. Who knows? One day, they both might find themselves, working together, but this time – in the middle of the ocean!

The meeting ended with a friendly, yet, forbidden, handshake. An exam this was not. Markot left the hall, on his way to happiness, full of dreams that he had never thought he could have before, because they breached the rules. Andir went back home. It was the last time he drove on the road, he took daily for the past twenty years. He did not go to work on the next day. So what? The immortal Idea Factory was going to find him a replacement, someone, who would continue with the pointless consulting activity.

www.ingramcontent.com/pod-product-compliance
Lightning Source LLC
Chambersburg PA
CBHW021230250626
47155CB00008B/2943

* 9 7 8 0 9 9 3 6 1 8 2 2 2 *